HELEN
BIANCHIN
Greek's Pride

HELEN BIANCHIN

COLLECTION

February 2016

March 2016

April 2016

May 2016

June 2016

July 2016

HELEN
BIANCHIN
Greek's Pride

MILLS & BOON

First Published in Great Britain 2016
By Mills & Boon, an imprint of HarperCollins*Publishers*
1 London Bridge Street, London, SE1 9GF

GREEK'S PRIDE © 2016 Harlequin Books S.A.

The Stefanos Marriage © 1990 Helen Bianchin
A Passionate Surrender © 2002 Helen Bianchin
The Greek Bridegroom © 2002 Helen Bianchin

ISBN: 978-0-263-92149-6

09-0516

Printed and bound in Spain
by CPI, Barcelona

THE STEFANOS MARRIAGE
HELEN BIANCHIN

Helen Bianchin was born in New Zealand and travelled to Australia before marrying her Italian-born husband. After three years they moved, returned to New Zealand with their daughter, had two sons and then resettled in Australia.

Encouraged by friends to recount anecdotes of her years as a tobacco sharefarmer's wife living in an Italian community, Helen began setting words on paper and her first novel was published in 1975.

Currently Helen resides in Queensland, the three children now married with children of their own. An animal lover, Helen says her two beautiful Birman cats regard her study as much theirs as hers, choosing to leap onto her desk every afternoon to sit upright between the computer monitor and keyboard as a reminder they need to be fed...like right now!

CHAPTER ONE

THE TRAFFIC WAS unusually heavy as Alyse eased her stylish Honda hatchback on to the Stirling highway. From this distance the many tall buildings etched against the city skyline appeared wreathed in a shimmering haze, and the sun's piercing rays reflected against the sapphire depths of the Swan River as she followed its gentle curve into the heart of Perth.

Parking took an age, and she uttered a silent prayer in celestial thanks that she wasn't a regular city commuter as she competed with the early-morning populace striding the pavements to their individual places of work.

A telephone call from her solicitor late the previous afternoon requesting her presence in his office as soon as possible was perplexing, to say the least, and a slight frown creased her brow as she entered the modern edifice of gleaming black marble and non-reflecting tinted glass that housed his professional suite.

Gaining the foyer, Alyse stepped briskly towards a cluster of people waiting for any one of three lifts to transport them to their designated floor. As she drew close her attention was caught by a tall, dark-suited man standing slightly apart from the rest, and her eyes lingered with brief curiosity.

Broad-chiselled facial bone-structure in profile provided an excellent foil for the patrician slope of his nose and rugged sculptured jaw. Well-groomed thick dark hair was professionally shaped and worn fractionally longer than the current trend.

In his mid-thirties, she judged, aware there was something about his stance that portrayed an animalistic sense of power—a physical magnetism that was riveting.

As if he sensed her scrutiny, he turned slightly, and she was shaken by the intensity of piercing eyes that were neither blue nor grey but a curious mixture of both.

Suddenly she became supremely conscious of her projected image, aware that the fashionably tailored black suit worn with a demurely styled white silk blouse lent a professional air to her petite frame and shoulder-length strawberry-blonde hair, which, combined with delicate-boned features, reflected poise and dignity.

It took every ounce of control not to blink or lower her eyes beneath his slow analytical appraisal, and for some inexplicable reason she felt each separate nerve-ending tense as a primitive emotion stirred deep within her, alien and unguarded.

For a few timeless seconds her eyes seemed locked with his, and she could have sworn the quickening beat of her heart must sound loud enough for anyone standing close by to hear. A reaction, she decided shakily, that was related to nothing more than recognition of a devastatingly sexual alchemy.

No *one* man deserved to have such power at his command. Yet there was a lurking cynicism, a slight wariness apparent beneath the sophisticated veneer, almost as if he expected her to instigate an attempt at conversation, initiating a subtle invitation—to God knew what? Her *bed*?

Innate pride tinged with defiance lent her eyes a fiery sparkle and provided an infinitesimal tilt to her chin as she checked the hands of the clock positioned high on the marble-slabbed wall.

Two lifts reached the ground floor simultaneously, and she stood back, opting to enter the one closest her, aware too late that the man seemed intent on following in her wake.

The lift filled rapidly, and she determinedly fixed her attention on the instrument panel, all too aware of the man standing within touching distance. Despite her four-inch stiletto heels he towered head and shoulders above her, and this close she could sense the slight aroma of his cologne.

It was crazy to feel so positively *stifled*, yet she was supremely conscious of every single breath, every pulsebeat. It wasn't a sensation she enjoyed, and she was intensely relieved when the lift slid to a halt at her chosen floor.

Alyse's gratitude at being freed from his unsettling presence was short-lived when she discovered that he too had vacated the lift and was seemingly intent on entering the same suite of offices.

Moving towards Reception, she gave her name and that of the legal partner with whom she had an appointment, then selected a nearby chair. Reaching for a magazine, she flipped idly through the glossy pages with pretended interest, increasingly aware of the man standing negligently at ease on the edge of her peripheral vision.

With a hand thrust into the trouser pocket of his

impeccably tailored suit he looked every inch the powerful potentate, portraying a dramatic mesh of blatant
masculinity and elemental ruthlessness. Someone it
would be infinitely wiser to have as a friend than an
enemy, Alyse perceived wryly.

Something about him bothered her—an intrinsic familiarity she was unable to pinpoint. She knew they
had never met, for he wasn't a man you would forget
in a hurry!

'Miss Anderson? If you'd care to follow me, Mr
Mannering will see you now.'

Alyse followed the elegantly attired secretary down
a wide, spacious corridor into a modern office offering a magnificent view of the city. Acknowledging the
solicitor's greeting, she selected one of three armchairs
opposite his desk and graciously sank into its leather-
cushioned depth.

'There seems to be some urgency in your need to
see me,' she declared, taking time to cross one slim
nylon-clad leg over the other as she looked askance at
the faintly harassed-looking man viewing her with a
degree of thoughtful speculation.

'Indeed. A most unexpected development,' Hugh
Mannering conceded as he reached for a manilla folder
and riffled through its contents. 'These papers were delivered by courier yesterday afternoon, and followed an
hour later by a telephone call from the man who instigated their dispatch.'

A slight frown momentarily creased her brow. 'I
thought Antonia's estate was quite straightforward.'

'Her estate—yes. Custody of your sister's son, however, is not.'

Alyse felt something squeeze painfully in the region of her heart. 'What do you mean?'

He bent his head, and his spectacles slid fractionally down his nose, allowing him the opportunity to view her over the top of the frame. 'I have copies of legal documentation by a delegate of the Stefanos family laying claim to Georg—' he paused to consult the name outlined within the documented text '—Georgiou. Infant son of Georgiou Stavro Stefanos, born to Antonia Grace Anderson at a disclosed maternity hospital in suburban Perth just over two months ago.'

Alyse paled with shock, her eyes large liquid pools mirroring disbelief as she looked at the solicitor with mounting horror. 'They can't do that!' she protested in a voice that betrayed shaky incredulity.

The man opposite appeared nonplussed. 'Antonia died intestate, without written authority delegating legal responsibility for her son. As her only surviving relative, you naturally assumed the role of surrogate mother and guardian.' He paused to clear his throat. 'However, technically, the child is an orphan, and a decision would, in the normal course of events, be made by the Department of Family Services as to the manner in which the child is to be cared for, having regard to all relevant circumstances with the welfare of the child as the paramount consideration. An application to adopt the child can be lodged with the Department by any interested party.' He paused to spare her a compassionate glance. 'A matter I had every intention of bringing to your attention.'

'Are you trying to say that my sister's lover's family have as much right to adopt her son as I do?' Alyse demanded in a fervent need to reduce reiterated legalese to its simplest form.

The solicitor's expression mirrored his spoken response. 'Yes.'

'But that's impossible! The clear facts of Georgiou's chosen dissociation from Antonia's letters would be a mark against him in any court of law.'

Tears welled unbidden as Alyse thought of her sister. Six years Alyse's junior, Antonia had been so carefree, so *young.* Too young at nineteen to suffer the consequences of a brief holiday romance abroad. Yet suffer she did, discovering within weeks of her return from an idyllic cruise of the Greek Islands that her capricious behaviour had resulted in pregnancy.

A letter dispatched at once to an address in Athens brought no response, nor, several weeks later, with the aid of a translator, did attempted telephone contact, for all that could be determined was that the number they sought was ex-directory and therefore unobtainable.

Truly a love-child, little Georgiou had survived by his mother's refusal to consider abortion, and he'd entered the world after a long struggle that had had the medics in attendance opting for surgical intervention via emergency Caesarian section. Fate, however, had delivered an incredibly cruel blow when complications which had plagued Antonia since giving birth had brought on a sudden collapse, followed within days by her tragic death.

Shattered beyond belief, Alyse had stoically attended to all the relevant arrangements, and employed a manageress for her childrenswear boutique during those first terrible weeks until she could arrange for a reliable babysitter.

Now, she had organised a satisfactory routine whereby a babysitter came in each morning, and the boutique was managed during the afternoon hours, thus ensuring that Alyse could spend as much time as possible with a young baby whose imposing Christian name had long since been affectionately shortened to Georg.

'I can understand your concern, Alyse. Mr Stefanos has offered to explain, personally, the reasons supporting his claim.'

Undisguised surprise widened her eyes, followed immediately by a degree of incredible anger. 'He's actually *dared* to come here in person, after all this time?'

Hugh Mannering regarded her carefully for several seconds, then offered slowly, 'It's in your own interest to at least listen to what he has to say.'

The solicitor depressed a button on the intercom console and issued his secretary with appropriate instructions.

Within a matter of seconds the door opened, and the tall compelling-looking man who had succeeded in shattering Alyse's composure only half an hour earlier entered the room.

She felt her stomach lurch, then contract in inexplicable apprehension. Who *was* he? She had seen sufficient of Antonia's holiday snapshots to be certain that the reflection depicted on celluloid and *this* man were not one and the same.

Hugh Mannering made the introduction with polite civility. 'Alyse Anderson—Aleksi Stefanos.'

'Miss Anderson.' The acknowledgment was voiced in a deep, faintly accented drawl, and an icy chill feathered across the surface of her skin. His eyes swept her features in raking appraisal, then locked with her startled gaze for a brief second before he directed his attention to the man opposite.

'I presume you have informed Miss Anderson of the relevant details?'

'Perhaps Mr Stefanos,' Alyse stressed carefully as he folded his lengthy frame into an adjacent chair, 'would care to reveal precisely his connection with the father of my sister's child?'

There could be no doubt she intended war, and it irked her incredibly that he was amused beneath the thin veneer of politeness evident.

'Forgive me, Miss Anderson.' He inclined his head cynically. 'I am Georgiou's elder brother—stepbrother, to be exact.'

'One presumes Georg,' she paused, deliberately refusing to give the name its correct pronunciation, 'dispatched you as his emissary?'

The pale eyes hardened until they resembled obsidian grey shards. 'Georgiou is dead. A horrific car accident last year left him a paraplegic, and complications took their final toll little more than a month ago.'

Alyse's mind reeled at the implication of a bizarre coincidence as Aleksi Stefanos went on to reveal in a voice devoid of any emotion,

'My family had no knowledge of your sister's existence, let alone her predicament, until several carefully concealed letters were discovered a week after Georgiou's death. Time was needed to verify certain facts before suitable arrangements could be made.'

'What arrangements?'

'The child will, of course, be brought up a Stefanos.'

Alyse's eyes blazed with brilliant fire. 'He most certainly will not!'

'You contest my right to do so?'

'*Your* right?' she retorted deliberately.

'Indeed. As he is the first male Stefanos grandchild, there can be no question of his rightful heritage.'

'Georg's birth is registered as Georgiou *Anderson*, Mr Stefanos. And as Antonia's closest relative *I* have accepted sole responsibility for her son.'

He appeared to be visibly unmoved, and her chin lifted fractionally as she held his glittering gaze.

'Verification of blood groupings has established beyond doubt that my brother is the father of your sister's child,' he revealed with chilling cynicism.

Alyse felt the rush of anger as it consumed her slim frame. How dared he even *suggest* otherwise! 'What did you imagine Antonia had in mind when she dispatched those letters begging for help, Mr Stefanos?' she managed in icy rage. 'Blackmail?'

'The thought did occur.'

'Why,' she breathed with barely controlled fury, 'you insulting, arrogant—'

'Please continue,' he invited as she faltered to a speechless halt.

'Bastard!' she threw with disdain, and glimpsed an inflexible hardness in the depths of his eyes. 'Antonia had no need of *money*—your brother's, or that of his family. As Mr Mannering will confirm, both my sister and I benefited financially when our parents died some years ago—sufficient to ensure we could afford a comfortable lifestyle without the need to supplement it in any way other than with a weekly wage. On leaving school, Antonia joined me in business.' She had never felt so positively *enraged* in her life. 'Your brother, Mr Stefanos,' she stressed, 'proposed *marriage* during their

shared holiday, and promised to send for Antonia within
a week of his return to Athens for the express purpose
of meeting his family and announcing their engagement.' Her eyes clouded with pain as she vividly recalled the effect Georgiou's subsequent rejection had
had on her sister.

'Georgiou's accident occurred the day after his return,' Aleksi Stefanos told her. 'He lay in hospital unconscious for weeks, and afterwards it was some time
before he became fully aware of the extent of his injuries. By then it was doubtful if he could foresee a future
for himself in the role of husband.'

'He could have written!' Alyse exclaimed in impassioned condemnation. 'His silence caused Antonia
months of untold anguish. And you underestimate my
sister, Mr Stefanos,' she continued bleakly, 'if you think
she would have rejected Georgiou simply because of his
injuries. She loved him.'

'And *love*, in your opinion, conquers all?'

Her eyes gleamed with hidden anger, sheer prisms
of deep blue sapphire. 'Antonia deserved the chance to
prove it,' she said with quiet vehemence. Her chin lifted,
tilting at a proud angle.

His raking scrutiny was daunting, but she refused to
break his gaze. 'And you, Miss Anderson?' he queried
with deceptive softness. 'Would *you* have given a man
such unswerving loyalty?'

Alyse didn't deign to answer, and the silence inside
the room was such that it was almost possible to hear
the sound of human breathing.

'Perhaps an attempt could be made to resolve the situation?' Alyse heard the mild intervention and turned
slowly towards the bespectacled man seated behind his

desk. For a while she had forgotten his existence, and she watched as his glance shifted from her to the hateful Aleksi Stefanos. 'I know I can speak for Alyse in saying that she intends lodging an adoption application immediately.'

'Legally, as a single woman, Miss Anderson lacks sufficient standing to supersede my right to my brother's child,' Aleksi Stefanos declared with dangerous silkiness.

'Only if you're married,' Alyse insisted, directing the solicitor a brief enquiring glance and feeling triumphant on receiving his nod in silent acquiescence. 'Are you married, Mr Stefanos?'

'No,' he answered with smooth detachment. 'Something I intend remedying without delay.'

'Really? You're *engaged* to be married?' She couldn't remember being so positively *bitchy*!

'My intended marital status is unimportant, Miss Anderson, and none of your business.'

'Oh, but it is, Mr Stefanos,' she insisted sweetly. 'You see, if *marriage* is a prerequisite in my battle to adopt Georg, then I too shall fight you in the marriage stakes by taking a husband as soon as possible.' She turned towards the solicitor. 'Would that strengthen my case?'

Hugh Mannering looked distinctly uncomfortable. 'I should warn you against the folly of marrying in haste, simply for the sole purpose of providing your nephew with a surrogate father. Mr Stefanos would undoubtedly contest the validity of your motive.'

'As I would contest *his* motive,' she insisted fiercely, 'if he were to marry immediately.'

'I'm almost inclined to venture that it's unfortunate you could not marry each other,' Mr Mannering opined, 'thus providing the child with a stable relationship, instead of engaging in lengthy proceedings with the Government's Family Services Department to determine *who* should succeed as legal adoptive parent.'

Alyse looked at him as if he had suddenly gone mad. 'You can't possibly be serious?'

The solicitor effected an imperceptible shrug. 'A marriage of convenience isn't an uncommon occurrence.'

'Maybe not,' she responded with undue asperity. 'But I doubt if Mr Stefanos would be prepared to compromise in such a manner.'

'Why so sure, Miss Anderson?' The drawled query grated her raw nerves like steel razing through silk.

'Oh, really,' Alyse dismissed, 'such a solution is the height of foolishness, and totally out of the question.'

'Indeed?' His smile made her feel like a dove about to be caught up in the deadly claws of a marauding hawk. 'I consider it has a degree of merit.'

'While *I* can't think of anything worse than being imprisoned in marriage with a man like you!'

If he could have shaken her within an inch of her life, he would have done so. It was there in his eyes, the curious stillness of his features, and she controlled the desire to shiver, choosing instead to clasp her hands together in an instinctive protective gesture.

Against *what*? a tiny voice taunted. He couldn't possibly pose a threat, for heaven's sake!

'There's nothing further to be gained by continuing with this conversation.' With graceful fluidity she rose to her feet. 'Good afternoon, Mr Mannering,' she said with distinct politeness before spearing her adversary with a dark, venomous glance. '*Goodbye*, Mr Stefanos.'

Uncaring of the solicitor's attempt to defuse the situation, she walked to the door, opened it, then quietly closed it behind her before making her way to the outer office.

It wasn't until she was in her car and intent on negotiating busy traffic that reaction began to set in.

Damn. *Damn* Aleksi Stefanos! Her hands clenched on the wheel until the knuckles showed white, and she was so consumed with silent rage that it was nothing short of a miracle that she reached the boutique without suffering a minor accident.

CHAPTER TWO

THE REMAINDER OF the morning flew by as Alyse conferred with the boutique's manageress, Miriam Stanford, checked stock and tended to customers. It was almost midday before she was able to leave, and she felt immensely relieved to reach the comfortable sanctuary of her home.

As soon as the babysitter left, Alyse put a load of laundry into the washing machine, completed a few household chores, and was ready for Georg at the sound of his first wakening cry.

After changing him, she gave him his bottle, then made everything ready for his afternoon walk—an outing he appeared to adore, for he offered a contented smile as she placed him in the pram and secured the patterned quilt.

The air was fresh and cool, the winter sun fingering the spreading branches of trees lining the wide suburban street, and Alyse walked briskly, her eyes bright with love as she watched every gesture, every fleeting expression on her young nephew's face. He was so active, so alive for his tender age, and growing visibly with every passing day.

A slight frown furrowed her brow, and her features

assumed a serious bleakness as she mentally reviewed the morning's consultation in Hugh Mannering's office. Was there really any possibility that she might fail in a bid to adopt Georg? *Could* the hateful Aleksi Stefanos's adoption application succeed? It was clear she must phone the solicitor as soon as possible.

On returning home Alyse gave Georg his bath, laughing ruefully as she finally managed to get his wriggling slippery body washed and dry, then dusted with talc and dressed in clean clothes. She gave him his bottle and settled him into his cot.

Now for the call to Hugh Mannering.

'Can I lose Georg?' Alyse queried with stark disregard for the conversational niceties.

'Any permanent resolution will take considerable time,' the solicitor stressed carefully. 'Technically, the Family Services Department investigates each applicant's capability to adequately care for the child, and ultimately a decision is made.'

'Off the record,' she persisted, 'who has the best chance?'

'It's impossible to ignore facts, Alyse. I've studied indisputable records documenting Aleksi Stefanos's financial status, and the man has an impressive list of assets.'

A chill finger slithered the length of her spine, and she suppressed the desire to shiver. 'Assets which far outstrip mine, I imagine?'

'My dear, you are fortunate to enjoy financial security of a kind that would be the envy of most young women your age. However, it is only a small percentage in comparison.'

'Damn him!' The oath fell from her lips in husky condemnation.

'The child's welfare is of prime importance,' the solicitor reminded her quietly. 'I'll have the application ready for your signature tomorrow.'

The inclination to have a snack instead of preparing herself a meal was all too tempting, and Alyse settled for an omelette with an accompanying salad, then followed it with fresh fruit.

She should make an effort to do some sewing—at least attempt to hand-finish a number of tiny smocked dresses which had been delivered to the house by one of her outworkers this morning. Certainly the boutique could do with the extra supplies.

The dishes done and the washing folded, Alyse collected a bundle of garments from its enveloping plastic and settled herself comfortably in the lounge with her sewing basket. Working diligently, she applied neat stitches with precise care, clipped thread, then deftly rethreaded the needle and began on the next garment.

Damn! The soft curse disrupted the stillness of the room. The third in an hour, and no less vicious simply because it was quietly voiced.

Alyse looked at the tiny prick of blood the latest needle stab had wrought, and raised her eyes heavenward in mute supplication.

Just this one garment, and she'd pack it all away for the evening, she pleaded in a silent deal with her favourite saint. Although it would prove less vexing if she cast aside hand-finishing for the evening and relaxed in front of the television with a reviving cup of coffee. Yet tonight she needed to immerse herself to-

HELEN BIANCHIN   23

tally in her work in an attempt to alleviate the build-up
of nervous tension.

Specialising in exquisitely embroidered babywear
sold under her own label, *Alyse*, she had by dint of hard
work, she reflected, changed a successful hobby into a
thriving business. Now there was a boutique in a modern upmarket shopping centre catering for babies and
young children's clothes featuring her own exclusive
label among several imported lines.

Five minutes later Alyse breathed a sigh of relief as
the tiny garment was completed. Stretching her arms
high, she flexed her shoulders in a bid to ease the knot
of muscular tension.

Georg's wakening cry sounded loud in the stillness
of the house, and she quickly heated his bottle, fed him,
then settled him down for the night.

In the hallway she momentarily caught sight of
her mirrored reflection, and paused, aware that it was
hardly surprising that the combination of grief and lack
of appetite had reduced her petite form to positive slen-
derness. There were dark smudges beneath solemn blue
eyes, and the angles of her facial bone-structure appeared delicate and more clearly defined.

Minutes later she sank into a chair in the lounge
nursing a mug of hot coffee, longing not for the first
time for someone in whom she could confide.

If her parents were still alive, it might be different,
she brooded, but both had died within months of each
other only a year after she had finished school, and she
had been too busy establishing a niche in the workforce
as well as guiding Antonia through a vulnerable puberty
to enjoy too close an empathy with friends.

The sudden peal of the doorbell shattered the qui-

etness of the room, and she hurried quickly to answer
it, vaguely apprehensive yet partly curious as to who
could possibly be calling at this time of the evening.

Checking that the safety chain was in place, she queried cautiously, 'Who is it?'

'Aleksi Stefanos.'

Stefanos. The name seemed etched in her brain with
the clarity of diamond-engraved marble, and she closed
her eyes in a purely reflex action as undisguised anger
replaced initial shock.

'How did you get my address?' she wanted to know.

'The telephone directory.' His voice held an infinite
degree of cynicism.

'How *dare* you come here?' Alyse demanded, trying
her best to ignore the prickle of fear steadily creating
havoc with her nervous system.

'Surely eight-thirty isn't unacceptably late?' his
drawling voice enquired through the thick wood-
panelled door, and she drew in a deep angry breath,
then released it slowly.

'I have absolutely nothing to say to you.'

'May I remind you that I have every right to visit
my nephew?'

For some inexplicable reason his dry mocking tones
sent an icy chill feathering the length of her spine.
Damn him! Who did he think he was, for heaven's sake?

'Georg is asleep, Mr Stefanos.'

Her curt dismissing revelation was greeted with om-
inous silence, and she unconsciously held her breath,
willing him to go away.

'Asleep or awake, Miss Anderson, it makes little difference.'

Alyse closed her eyes and released her breath in one

drawn-out sigh of frustration. Without doubt, Aleksi Stefanos possessed sufficient steel-willed determination to be incredibly persistent. If she refused to let him see Georg tonight, he'd insist on a suitable time tomorrow. Either way, he would eventually succeed in his objective.

Without releasing the safety chain, she opened the door a fraction, noticing idly that he had exchanged his formal suit for light grey trousers and a sweater in fine dark wool. Even from within the protection of her home, he presented a disturbing factor she could only view with disfavour.

'Will you give me your word that you won't try to abduct Georg?' she asked him.

His eyes flared, then became hard and implacable, his facial muscles reassembling over sculptured bone to present a mask of silent anger.

'It isn't in my interests to resort to abduction,' he warned inflexibly. 'Perhaps you should be reminded that your failure to co-operate will be taken into consideration and assuredly used against you.'

The temptation to tell him precisely what he could do with his legal advisers was almost impossible to ignore, but common sense reared its logical head just in time, and Alyse released the safety chain, then stood back to permit him entry.

'Thank you.'

His cynicism was not lost on her, and it took considerable effort to remain civil. 'Georg's room is at the rear of the house.'

Without even glancing at him, she led the way, aware that he followed close behind her. She didn't consciously hurry, but her footsteps were quick, and consequently she felt slightly breathless when she reached the end of the hallway.

Carefully she opened the door, swinging it wide so the shaft of light illuminated the room. Large and airy, it had been converted to a nursery months before Georg's birth, the fresh white paint with its water-colour murals on each wall the perfect foil for various items of nursery furniture, and a number of colourful mobiles hung suspended from the ceiling.

Fiercely protective, Alyse glanced towards the man opposite for any sign that he might disturb her charge, and saw there was no visible change in his expression.

What had she expected? A softening of that hard exterior? Instead there was a curious bleakness, a sense of purpose that Alyse found distinctly chilling.

Almost as if Georg sensed he was the object of a silent battle, he stirred, moving his arms as he wriggled on to his back, his tiny legs kicking at the blanket until, with a faint murmur, he settled again.

Alyse wanted to cry out that Georg was *hers*, and nothing, *no one*, was going to take him away from her.

Perhaps some of her resolve showed in her expressive features, for she glimpsed a muscle tighten at the edge of Aleksi Stefanos's powerful jaw an instant before he moved back from the cot, and she followed him from the room, carefully closing the door behind her.

It appeared he was in no hurry to leave, for he entered the lounge without asking, and stood, a hand thrust into each trouser pocket.

'Perhaps we could talk?' he suggested, subjecting her to an analytical scrutiny which in no way enhanced her temper.

'I was under the impression we covered just about everything this morning.'

Chillingly bleak eyes riveted hers, trapping her in his gaze, and Alyse was prompted to comment, 'It's a pity Georgiou himself didn't accord his son's existence such reverent importance.'

'There were, I think you will have to agree, extenuating circumstances.'

'If he really did *love* my sister,' she stressed, 'he would have seen to it that someone—even *you*—answered any one of her letters. He had a responsibility which was ignored, no matter how bravely he grappled with his own disabilities.'

His gaze didn't waver. 'I imagine he was tortured by the thought of Antonia bearing a child he would never see.'

'The only bonus to come out of the entire débâcle is Georg.'

He looked at her hard and long before he finally spoke. 'You must understand, he cannot be raised other than as a Stefanos.'

Alyse saw the grim resolve apparent, and suddenly felt afraid. 'Why?' she queried baldly. 'A man without a wife could only offer the services of a nanny, which, even if it were a full-time live-in employment, can't compare with my love and attention.'

His shoulders shifted imperceptibly, almost as if he were reassembling a troublesome burden, and his features assumed an inscrutability she had no hope of penetrating.

'You too employ the part-time services of a nanny in the guise of babysitter. Is this not so?' An eyebrow slanted in silent query. 'By your own admission, you operate a successful business. With each subsequent month, my nephew will become more active, sleep less, and demand more attention. While you delegate, in part, your business duties, you will also be delegating the amount of time you can spend with Georg. I fail to see a significant difference between your brand of caring and mine.'

'On that presumption you imagine I'll concede defeat?' Alyse queried angrily.

'I would be prepared to settle an extremely large sum in your bank account for the privilege.'

She shook her head, unable to comprehend what she was hearing. 'Bribery, Mr Stefanos? No amount of money would persuade me to part with Antonia's son.' She cast him a look of such disdainful dislike, a lesser man would have withered beneath it. 'Now, will you please leave?'

'I haven't finished what I came to say.'

He must have a skin thicker than a rhinoceros! Alyse could feel the anger emanate through the pores of her skin until her whole body was consumed with it. 'If you don't leave *immediately*, I'll call the police!'

'Go ahead,' he directed with pitiless disregard.

'This is my home, dammit!' Alyse reiterated heatedly.

His eyes were dark and infinitely dangerous. 'You walked out on a legal consultation this morning, and now you refuse to discuss Georg's welfare.' It was his turn to subject her to a raking scrutiny, his smile wholly cynical as he glimpsed the tide of colour wash over her cheeks. 'I imagine the police will be sympathetic.'

'They'll also throw you out!'

'They'll suggest I leave,' he corrected. 'And conduct

any further discussion with you via a legal representative.' He paused, and his eyes were hard and obdurate, reflecting inflexible masculine strength of will. 'My stepbrother's child has a legal right to his stake in the Stefanos heritage. It is what Georgiou would have wanted; what my father wants. If Antonia were still alive,' he paused deliberately, 'I believe *she* would have wanted her son to be acknowledged by her lover's family, and to receive the financial benefits and recognition that are his due.'

Alyse's eyes sharpened as their depths became clearly defined. 'I intend having you and your *family* fully investigated.'

As a possible threat, it failed dismally, for he merely acknowledged her words with a cynical smile.

'Allow me to give you the relevant information ahead of official confirmation.'

Beneath the edge of mockery was a degree of inimical anger that feathered fear down the length of her spine and raised all her fine body hairs in protective self-defence.

'My father and stepmother reside in Athens. *I*, however, left my native Greece at the relatively young age of twenty to settle in Australia. Initially Sydney—working as a builder's labourer seven days a week, contractual obligations and weather permitting. After three years I moved to the Gold Coast, where I bought land and built houses before venturing into building construction. The ensuing thirteen years have escalated my company to a prestigious position within the building industry. Without doubt,' he continued drily, 'I possess sufficient independent wealth to garner instant approval with the

Family Services Department, and there are no mythical skeletons in any one of my closets.'

'Hardly a complete résumé, Mr Stefanos,' Alyse discounted scathingly.

'How far back into the past do you wish to delve? Does the fact that my mother was Polish, hence my unusual Christian name, condemn me? That she died when I was very young? Is that sufficient, Miss Anderson?' One eyebrow slanted above dark eyes heavily opaque with the rigors of memory. 'Perhaps you'd like to hear that a sweet, gentle Englishwoman eased my father's pain, married him and bore a male child without displacing my position as the eldest Stefanos son or alienating my father's affection for me in any way. She became the mother I'd never known, and we keep in constant touch, exchanging visits at least once each year.'

'And now that Georgiou is dead, they want to play an integral part in Georg's life.' Alyse uttered the words in a curiously flat voice, and was unprepared for the whip-hard anger in *his*.

'Are you so impossibly selfish that you fail to understand what Georg's existence means to them?' he demanded.

'I know what it means to *me*,' she cried out, sorely tried. 'If Antonia hadn't written to Georgiou, if—'

'Don't colour facts with unfounded prejudice,' Aleksi Stefanos cut in harshly. 'The letters exist as irrefutable proof. *I* intend assuming the role of Georg's father,' he pursued, his voice assuming a deadly softness. 'Don't doubt it for a minute.'

'Whereas I insist on the role of *mother*!' she blazed.

'You're not prepared to compromise in any way?'

'*Compromise?* Are *you* prepared to compromise?

Why should it be *me* who has to forgo the opportunity of happiness in a marriage of my choice?'

His eyes narrowed fractionally. 'Is there a contender waiting in the wings, Miss Anderson? Someone sufficiently foolish to think he can conquer your fiery spirit and win?'

'What makes you think *you* could?'

His eyes gleamed with latent humour, then dropped lazily to trace the full curve of her lips before slipping down to the swell of her breasts, assessing each feature with such diabolical ease that she found it impossible to still the faint flush of pink that coloured her cheeks.

'I possess sufficient experience with women to know you'd resent any form of male domination, yet conversely refuse to condone a spineless wimp who gave way to your every demand.' Alyse stood speechless as his gaze wandered back to meet hers and hold it with indolent amusement. A sensation not unlike excitement uncoiled deep within her, and spread throughout her body with the speed of liquid fire, turning all the highly sensitised nerve-endings into a state of sensual awareness so intense it made her feel exhilaratingly *alive*, yet at the same time terribly afraid.

'The man in my life most certainly won't be you, Mr Stefanos!' she snapped.

'One of the country's best legal brains has given me his assurance that my adoption application will succeed,' he revealed. 'This morning's consultation in Hugh Mannering's office was arranged because I felt honour-bound to personally present facts regarding my stepbrother's accident and subsequent death. As to Georg's future...' he paused significantly '...the only way you can have any part in it will be to opt for marriage—to me.'

'You alternately threaten, employ a form of emotional blackmail, attempt to buy me off, then offer a marriage convenient only to *you*?' The slow-boiling anger which had simmered long beneath the surface of her control finally bubbled over. 'Go to *hell*, Mr Stefanos!'

The atmosphere in the lounge was so highly charged, Alyse almost expected it to explode into combustible flame.

He looked at her for what seemed an age, then his voice sounded cold—as icy as an Arctic gale. 'Think carefully before you burn any figurative bridges,' he warned silkily.

Alyse glared at him balefully, hating him, abhorring what he represented. 'Get out of my house. *Now!*' Taut, incredibly angry words that bordered close on the edge of rage as she moved swiftly from the room.

In the foyer she reached for the catch securing the front door, then gasped out loud as Aleksi Stefanos caught hold of her shoulders and turned her towards him with galling ease.

One glance at those compelling features was sufficient to determine his intention, and she struggled fruitlessly against his sheer strength.

'The temptation to teach you the lesson I consider you deserve is almost irresistible,' he drawled.

His anger was clearly evident, and, hopelessly helpless, Alyse clenched her jaw tight as his head lowered in an attempt to avoid his mouth, only to cry out as he caught the soft inner tissue with his teeth, and she had no defence against the plundering force of a kiss so intense that the muscles of her throat, her jaw, screamed in silent agony as he completed a ravaging possession that violated her very soul.

Just as suddenly as it had begun, it was over, and she sank back against the wall, her eyes stricken with silent hatred.

At that precise moment a loud wailing cry erupted from the bedroom, and Alyse turned blindly towards the nursery. Crossing to Georg's cot, she leant forward and lifted his tiny body into her arms. He smelled of soap and talc, and his baby cheek was satin-smooth against her own as she cradled him close.

His cries subsided into muffled hiccups, bringing stupid tears to her own eyes, and she blinked rapidly to still their flow, aware within seconds that her efforts were in vain as they spilled and began trickling ignominiously down each cheek.

This morning life had been so simple. Yet within twelve hours Aleksi Stefanos had managed to turn it upside down.

She turned as the subject of her most dire thoughts followed her into the nursery.

'You bastard!' she berated him in a painful whisper. 'Have you no scruples?'

'None whatsoever where Georg is concerned,' Aleksi Stefanos drawled dispassionately.

'What you're suggesting amounts to emotional blackmail, damn you!' Her voice emerged as a vengeful undertone, and Georg gave a slight whimpering cry, then settled as she gently rocked his small body in her arms.

'What I'm suggesting,' Aleksi Stefanos declared hardily, 'is parents, a home, and a stable existence for Georg.'

'Where's the stability in two people who don't even *like* each other?' Damn him—who did he think he was, for heaven's sake?

An icy shiver shook her slim frame in the knowledge that he knew precisely who he was and the extent of his own power.

'The alternatives are specific,' he continued as if she hadn't spoken, 'the choice entirely your own. You have until tomorrow evening to give me your answer.'

She was dimly aware that he moved past her to open the door, and it was that final, almost silent click as he closed it behind him that made her frighteningly aware of his control.

CHAPTER THREE

ALYSE STOOD WHERE she was for what seemed an age before settling Georg into his cot, then she moved slowly to the front of the house, secured the lock and made for her own room, where she undressed and slid wearily into bed.

Damn. *Damn* him, she cursed vengefully. Aleksi Stefanos had no right to place her in such an invidious position. For the first time she felt consumed with doubt, apprehensive to such a degree that it was impossible to relax.

Images flooded her mind, each one more painful than the last, and she closed her eyes tightly against the bitter knowledge that adoption was absolute, so *final*.

If Aleksi Stefanos was successful with his application, he would remove Georg several thousand kilometres away to the opposite side of the continent. To see him at all, she would have to rely on Aleksi Stefanos's generosity, and it would be difficult with her business interests, to be able to arrange a trip to Queensland's Gold Coast more than once a year.

The mere thought brought tears to her eyes, and she cursed afresh. At least divorced parents got to *share* custody of their children.

However, to become divorced, one first had to marry, Alyse mused in contemplative speculation. Maybe... No, it wasn't possible. Or was it? How long would the marriage have to last? A year? Surely no longer than two, she decided, her mind racing.

If she did opt for marriage, she could have a contract drawn up giving Miriam a percentage of the profits, thus providing an incentive ensuring that the boutique continued to trade at a premium. As far as the house was concerned, she could lease it out. Her car would have to be sold, but that wouldn't matter, for she could easily buy another on her return.

A calculating gleam darkened her blue eyes, and a tiny smile curved her generous mouth.

When Aleksi Stefanos contacted her tomorrow, he would discover that she was surprisingly amenable. It was infinitely worth a year or two out of her life if it meant she got to keep Georg.

For the first time in the six weeks since Antonia's funeral, Alyse slept without a care to disturb her subconscious, and woke refreshed, eager to start the new day.

With so much to attend to, she drew up a list, and simply crossed every item off as she dealt with it.

A call to Hugh Mannering determined that marriage to Aleksi Stefanos would reduce the adoption proceedings to a mere formality, and he expressed delight that she was taking such a sensible step.

Alyse responded with a tongue-in-cheek agreement, and chose not to alarm her legal adviser by revealing the true extent of her plans.

Miriam was delighted to be promoted, and proved

more than willing to assume management of the boutique for as long as necessary.

By late afternoon Alyse was able to relax, sure that everything was in place.

A light evening meal of cold chicken and salad provided an easy alternative to cooking, and she followed it with fresh fruit.

The telephone rang twice between seven and eight o'clock, and neither call was from Aleksi Stefanos.

A cloud of doubt dulled her eyes as she pondered the irony of him not ringing at all, only to start visibly when the insistent burr of the phone sounded shortly before nine.

It had to be him, and she let it peal five times in a fit of sheer perversity before picking up the receiver.

'Alyse?' His slightly accented drawl was unmistakable, his use of her Christian name an impossible liberty, she decided as she attempted to still a sense of foreboding. 'Have you reached a decision?'

He certainly didn't believe in wasting words! A tinge of anger heightened her mood. Careful, a tiny voice cautioned. You don't want to blow it. 'Yes.'

There was silence for a few seconds as he waited for her to continue, and when she didn't he queried with ill-concealed mockery, 'Must I draw it from you like blood from a stone?'

If it wasn't for Georg she'd slam down the receiver without the slightest compunction. 'I've considered your proposition,' she said tightly, 'and I've decided to accept.' There, she'd actually said it.

'My parents arrive from Athens at the beginning of next week,' Aleksi Stefanos told her without preamble, and she would have given anything to ruffle that imperturbable composure. 'They're naturally eager to see Georg, and there's no reason why you both shouldn't fly back to Queensland with me on Friday.'

'I can't possibly be ready by then,' Alyse protested, visibly shaken at the way he was assuming control.

'Professional packers will ensure that everything in the house is satisfactorily dealt with,' he said matter-of-factly. 'Whatever you need can be air-freighted to the Coast, and the rest put into storage. The house can be put into the hands of a competent letting agent, and managerial control arranged at the boutique. I suggest you instruct Hugh Mannering to draw up a power of attorney and liaise with him. All it takes is a few phone calls. To satisfy the Family Services Department, it would be advisable if a civil marriage ceremony is held here in Perth—Thursday, if it can be arranged. Relevant documentation regarding Georg's adoption can then be signed ready for lodgement, leaving us free of any added complications in removing him from the State.'

'Dear heaven,' Alyse breathed unsteadily, 'you don't believe in wasting time!'

'I'll give you a contact number where I can be reached,' he continued as if she hadn't spoken, relaying a set of digits she had to ask him to repeat as she quickly wrote them down. 'Any questions?'

'At least *ten*,' she declared with unaccustomed sarcasm.

'They can wait until dinner tomorrow evening.'

'With everything I have to do, I won't have *time* for dinner!'

'I'll collect you at six.'

There was a click as he replaced the receiver, and Alyse felt like screaming in vexation. What had she expected—small talk? *Revenge*, she decided, would be very sweet!

Removing the receiver, she placed a call to Miriam Stanford and asked if the manageress could work the entire day tomorrow, informed her briefly of her intended plans and promised she would be in at some stage during the afternoon.

Alyse slept badly, and rose just after dawn determined to complete a host of household chores, allowing herself no respite as she conducted a thorough spring-clean of the large old home, stoically forcing herself to sort through Antonia's possessions—something she'd continually put off until now.

It was incredibly sad, for there were so many things to remind her of the happy young girl Antonia had been, the affection and laughter they had shared. Impossible to really believe she was no longer alive, when celluloid prints and vivid memories provided such a painful reminder.

Despite her resolve to push Aleksi Stefanos to the edge of her mind, it was impossible not to feel mildly apprehensive as she settled Georg with the babysitter before retiring to the bathroom to shower, then dress for the evening ahead.

Selecting an elegant slim-fitting off-the-shoulder gown in deep sapphire blue, she teamed it with black stiletto-heeled shoes, tended to her make-up with painstaking care, then brushed her shoulder-length strawberry-blonde hair into its customary smooth bell before adding a generous touch of Van Cleef & Arpels' *Gem* to several pulsebeats. Her only added jewellery was a diamond pendant, matching earstuds and bracelet.

At five minutes to six she checked last-minute details

with the babysitter, brushed a fleeting kiss to Georg's forehead, then moved towards the lounge, aware of a gnawing nervousness in the pit of her stomach with every step she took.

Now that she was faced with seeing him again, she began to wonder if she was slightly mad to toy with a man of Aleksi Stefanos's calibre. He undoubtedly ate little girls for breakfast, and although she was no naïve nineteen-year-old, her experience with men had been pitifully limited to platonic friendships that had affection as their base rather than any degree of passion. It hardly equipped her to act a required part.

Yet act she must—at least until she had his wedding ring on her finger. Afterwards she could set the rules by which the marriage would continue, and for how long.

Punctuality was obviously one of his more admirable traits, for just as she reached the foyer there was the soft sound of car tyres on the gravel drive followed almost immediately by the muted clunk of a car door closing.

At once she was conscious of an elevated nervous tension, and it took every ounce of courage to move forward and open the door.

Standing in its aperture, Aleksi Stefanos looked the epitome of male sophistication attired in a formal dark suit. Exuding more than his fair share of dynamic masculinity, he had an element of tensile steel beneath the polite veneer, a formidableness and sense of purpose that was daunting.

'Alyse.' There was an edge of mockery apparent, and she met his gaze with fearless disregard, blindly ignoring the increased tempo of her heartbeat.

Just a glance at the sensual curve of his mouth was enough to remember how it felt to be positively *absorbed* by the man, for no one in their wildest imagination could term what he had subjected her to as merely a *kiss*.

Conscious of his narrowed gaze, Alyse stood aside to allow him entry, acknowledging politely, 'Mr Stefanos.'

'Surely you can force yourself to say Aleksi?' he chastised with ill-concealed mockery.

Alyse choked back a swift refusal. Steady, she cautioned—anger will get you precisely nowhere. Opting for the line of least resistance, she ventured evenly, 'If you insist.' Remembering her manners, she indicated the lounge. 'Please come in. Would you care for a drink?'

'Unless you'd prefer one, I suggest we leave,' he countered smoothly. 'I've booked a table for six-thirty.'

Without a further word she preceded him to the car, allowing him to reach forward and open the door, and she slid into the passenger seat, aware of his close proximity seconds later as he slipped in behind the wheel and set the large vehicle in motion.

'Where are we dining?' As a conversational gambit, it was sadly lacking in originality, but anything was better than silence, Alyse decided wildly as they joined the flow of traffic leading into the city.

'My hotel.'

She turned towards him in thinly veiled astonishment. 'I could have met you there.'

'Thus preserving feminine independence?' Aleksi mocked as he spared her a quick assessing appraisal before returning his attention to the computer-controlled intersection.

'I'll take a cab home.'

One eyebrow quirked in visible amusement as the

lights changed, and he eased the car forward. 'Impossible,' he declared smoothly, and she felt like hitting him for appearing so damnably implacable.

'Would it dent your chauvinistic male ego?' she queried sweetly, and heard his soft laughter.

'Not in the least. However, as my fiancée and soon-to-be wife, you can't be permitted.'

She closed her eyes, then slowly opened them seconds later. It was the only defence she had in masking the incredible fury she harboured against him.

As if he sensed her inner battle, he slid a tape into the cassette-deck, and she leaned back against the headrest, her eyes fixed on the tall city buildings and the wide sweep of river.

Alyse was familiar with the hotel, if not the restaurant, and when they were seated she permitted Aleksi to fill an elegant flute with Dom Perignon, sipping the superb champagne in the hope that it might afford her a measure of courage to face the evening ahead.

Aleksi conferred with the waiter over the menu, asking her what she wanted before placing their order, then he leaned well back in his chair and subjected her to a veiled scrutiny.

'Aren't you in the least curious to learn what arrangements I've made?'

She lifted her glass and took a generous swallow before replacing it on the table. 'I have no doubt you'll reveal them soon enough.' Tiny aerated bubbles of alcohol set up a tingling warmth inside her stomach and began transporting them through every vein in her body.

'We have an eleven o'clock appointment with the register office on Thursday, followed by a consultation with Hugh Mannering at two, and at three we're due to present ourselves at the Family Services Department. On Friday we catch the late morning flight en route to the Coast,' he informed her cynically.

The enormity of what she was about to undertake seemed to assume gigantic proportions, and she suffered his raking scrutiny with unblinking solemnity.

'This is no time for second thoughts,' Aleksi stated in a voice that was silky-smooth and infinitely dangerous. 'The reason for a marriage between us is obvious,' he declared hardily, 'and will be accepted as such.'

'Am I supposed to get down on my knees and kiss your feet in sheer gratitude for the privilege?' Her voice dripped ice, and she saw his blue-grey eyes assume a chilling ruthlessness.

'Careful,' he warned dangerously. 'I insist we present a veneer of politeness in the company of others.' He directed her a swift calculated appraisal that sent shivers of fear scudding the length of her spine. 'In private you can fight me as much as you like.'

'In private,' she conceded with ill-concealed fury, 'I shall probably render you grievous bodily harm!'

'Don't expect me not to retaliate,' he drawled.

'Do that, and I'll have you up for assault!'

His eyes narrowed and assumed the hue of a dark storm-tossed sea. 'I wasn't aware I alluded to physical abuse.'

Her eyes widened into huge pools of incredulity as comprehension dawned, and she fought valiantly against an all-encompassing anger. 'Abuse is still an ugly word, whether it be mental or physical,' she said tightly.

'Then perhaps you would be advised to keep a rein on your temper.'

'I must have been mad to agree to *any* alliance with you!' she declared bitterly, sure she'd become a victim of temporary insanity.

'Georg is the crux,' Aleksi remarked cynically, and she cried out in vengeful disavowal,

'I don't have much choice, damn you!'

'I offered you the opportunity of assuming the role of Georg's mother.'

'The only problem is that *you* form part of the package!'

'Oh, it mightn't be too bad.' His smile was totally lacking in humour. 'I live in a beautiful home—a showcase to display my expertise within the building industry. I enjoy the company of a close circle of friends, and frequently entertain. The Gold Coast is far from dull. I'm sure you'll manage to amuse yourself.'

'When do you intend informing your parents of our impending marriage?' asked Alyse.

'I already have,' he drawled with hateful cynicism. 'They're delighted that we've chosen such a sensible solution.'

'Are your parents visiting for very long?'

'Question-and-answer time, Alyse? Or simply sheer curiosity?'

An angry flush crept over her cheeks, and her eyes sparked with brilliant blue fire. 'I imagined it was a legitimate query.' If they'd been alone, she would have thrown the contents of her glass in his face. 'Perhaps I should opt for silence.'

'Apparent subservience?' he queried sardonically. 'Somehow I can't perceive you acquiring that particular mantle.'

'No,' Alyse agreed coolly out of deference to the

waiter, who deftly removed their plates and busied himself serving the main course.

The grilled fish with hollandaise sauce and accompanying assortment of vegetables was assembled with artistic flair and infinitely tempting to the most discerning palate. Yet she was so incredibly angry she was hard pressed to do the course the justice it deserved. Afterwards she declined dessert and the cheeseboard, and simply opted for coffee, noting with silent rage that Aleksi Stefanos's appetite appeared totally unaffected.

'Perhaps you could bring yourself to tell me what progress *you* have made?' he suggested.

Alyse met his gaze with fearless disregard. 'Everything is taken care of—the boutique, leasing the house. All that remains for me to do is *pack*.'

'And shop for a wedding dress,' he added with hateful ease, one eyebrow slanting with a degree of mocking humour, and a diabolical imp prompted her to query,

'Traditional white?' Her own eyebrow matched his in a deliberate arch.

'Do you have any objection?'

You're darned right I have! she felt like screaming. 'Surely a civil ceremony doesn't warrant such extravagance?'

'Humour me.'

'The hell I will! A classic-designed suit is adequate.' She paused, her eyes wide and startlingly direct. 'In black, or red. Something that makes a definite statement.'

He leaned further back in his chair, his posture portraying indolent ease. Yet there was a degree of tightly coiled strength apparent, and a prickle of apprehension feathered the surface of her skin.

'Flamboyant reluctance?' Aleksi queried with deceptive mildness. 'You choose to be recorded for posterity in a manner that will doubtless raise questions from our son, ten—fifteen years from now?'

Her lips parted to say that ten years down the track she would no longer be his wife. In fact, the requisite two would be two too many! Except that no sound escaped as she snapped her mouth firmly closed. 'I'll agree to a cream linen suit, matching accessories and a floral bouquet,' she told him.

'Adequate,' he drawled. 'But not precisely what I had in mind.'

'Well, isn't that just too damned bad?' Alyse snapped with scant attempt at politeness. 'Perhaps you've decided to compound the farce with formal tails and an elegant striped silk cravat?'

'Are you usually so quarrelsome, or is your behaviour merely an attempt to oppose me?'

Her eyes flashed pure crystalline sapphire. 'Oh, both. I'm no timid little dove.'

A lazy smile broadened the generous curve of his mouth. 'Even the wildest bird can be trained to enjoy captivity.'

A surge of anger rose to the surface, bringing a tinge of pink to her cheeks and sharpening her features. 'That's precisely the type of sexist remark I'd expect you to make!' She looked at him with increasing hostility. 'If you've finished your coffee, I'd like to leave.'

'So early, Alyse?' he mocked as he signalled the waiter to bring their bill. 'You've no desire to go on to a nightclub?'

'What would be the point? We're at daggers drawn now!' She tempered the remark with a totally false smile that almost felled the waiter, but didn't fool Aleksi in the slightest.

'We'll doubtless shatter every romantic illusion your babysitter possesses if I return you before the witching hour of midnight,' he remarked.

'As there's nothing in the least romantic about our alliance, it hardly matters, does it?' She stood to her feet and preceded him from the restaurant, uncaring that he followed close behind.

In the car she sat in silence, conscious of the faint swish of tyres on the wet bitumen. There was movement everywhere, people walking, colourful flashes of neon as the large vehicle purred through the city streets, and she became fascinated by the reflection caught in the still waters of the Swan River as they headed west towards Peppermint Grove.

'I'll arrange for a chauffeured limousine to collect you at ten-thirty on Thursday morning,' Aleksi declared as he brought the car to a halt in her driveway. 'You have the phone number of my hotel if you need to contact me.'

Polite, distant, and totally businesslike. It was almost as if he was deliberately playing an extremely shrewd game with every single manoeuvre carefully planned, Alyse brooded, aware of a chill shiver that owed nothing to the cool midwinter temperature.

'I doubt if there'll be the necessity,' she declared as she reached for the door-clasp, only to catch her breath in startled surprise as he slid out from behind the wheel and walked round to open her door.

Moving swiftly from the passenger seat, she stood still, unsure of his intention, her movements momentarily suspended as she prepared for a rapid flight into the safety of the house. If he *dared* to kiss her, she'd hit him!

His faint mocking smile was almost her undoing, and she drew a deep steadying breath before issuing a stilted, 'Goodnight.'

Without so much as a backward glance she walked to the front door, put her key in the lock, then closed the door carefully behind her.

Inside was warmth and light, the endearing familiarity of a home where there were no shadows, no insecurity.

Summoning a smile as she moved into the lounge, she checked with the babysitter and paid her before looking in on Georg, then she simply locked up and prepared for bed.

CHAPTER FOUR

THE CIVIL CEREMONY was incredibly brief, and only the fleeting appearance of Hugh Mannering provided a familiar face as Alyse affixed 'Stefanos' after 'Alyse' on the marriage certificate.

There were photographs, several of them taken by a professional, followed by lunch in the elegant dining-room of an inner city hotel.

Their appearance attracted circumspect interest. Her pencil-slim skirt with a long-line jacket in pale cream linen and matching accessories portrayed designer elegance, while Aleksi's impeccably tailored silver-grey suit merely accentuated his magnetic masculine appeal. Together, they scarcely presented the image of loving newlyweds, and she wondered a trifle wryly if they looked married.

Food was the last thing on her mind, and she ate mechanically, totally unappreciative of the superb seafood starter or the equally splendid lobster thermidor that followed. Even the champagne, Dom Perignon, suffered the sacrilege of being sipped seemingly without taste, and she declined both dessert and the cheeseboard in favour of strong aromatic black coffee.

Conversation between them verged on the banal, and

Alyse heaved a mental sigh of relief when Aleksi indicated that they should leave if they were to keep their appointment with Hugh Mannering and the Department of Social Services.

'We'll take a taxi,' he said as they stepped out on to the pavement.

Within minutes he managed to hail one, and Alyse sat in silence, her gaze caught by the twin fitted rings adorning her left hand. The prismatic facets of a large solitaire diamond sparked blue and green fire in a brilliant burst from reflected sunlight, providing a perfect setting for its matching diamond-set wedding-ring.

'They suit you.'

Alyse glanced towards the owner of that drawling voice, and met his gaze without any difficulty at all. 'A simple gold band would have been sufficient,' she acknowledged with utter seriousness.

'No, it wouldn't.' There was an edge of mockery apparent, and she summoned up a dazzling smile.

'I forgot the *image* factor.'

He deigned not to comment, and it was something of a relief when the taxi cruised to a halt outside the building housing the solicitor's offices.

Fifty minutes later they summoned yet another taxi and instructed the driver to take them to the Family Services Department.

Bureaucratic red tape had a tendency to be time-consuming, with appointments rarely running to schedule, and today appeared no different. Consequently it was late afternoon before they emerged into the cool winter sunlight.

'A celebratory drink?'

There was a wealth of satisfaction in knowing that

the initial legalities surrounding Georg's pending adoption were now officially in place, and Alyse found herself tilting her head as she met Aleksi's penetrating gaze. Quite without reason she found herself feeling slightly breathless, and desperately in need of a few hours away from his disturbing presence.

'There are still quite a few things I have to do.' Nothing of drastic importance, but he didn't need to know that. 'Could we combine it with dinner?'

'I'll organise yours and Georg's combined luggage and have it sent to the hotel. I'm sure the babysitter won't object to a change of venue.'

Her eyes widened in surprise, then long lashes swept down to form a protective veil. 'Is that really necessary?' she managed with remarkable steadiness, and detected cynicism in his drawling response.

'For the purpose of convention, we'll begin our marriage together by sharing the same roof. It's the hotel, or your home. Choose.'

'Just as long as you understand it won't involve the same bed.'

'Did I suggest that it would?'

Alyse closed her eyes, then slowly opened them again. Careful, a tiny voice cautioned. 'In comparison, I'm sure your luggage is far less substantial than Georg's and mine combined,' she declared in stilted tones, and watched as he hailed a taxi and instructed the driver to take them to his hotel.

His suite was situated on the twelfth floor and offered a magnificent view of the river. Alyse crossed the deep-piled carpet to stand at the window, all too aware of the intimacy projected by the opulently spreaded king-size bed.

'Help yourself to a drink,' Aleksi directed. 'The bar-fridge is fully stocked, and there's tea and coffee.' With-out waiting for her reply, he moved towards the bedside phone and lifted the receiver, stating his intention to check out.

Anything remotely alcoholic would go straight to her head. 'I'd prefer coffee,' she said as he replaced the receiver, and good manners were responsible for her asking, 'Will you have some?'

When it was made, she sipped the instant brew appre-ciatively while Aleksi emptied contents of drawers and wardrobe into a masculine-styled bag. It was a chore he executed with the deft ease of long practice, and when it was completed he drained his coffee in a few mea-sured swallows.

'Shall we leave?'

Alyse stood to her feet at once and preceded him from the suite, aware of an increasing sense of trepi-dation as she walked at his side.

It couldn't be fear, she analysed as they rode the lift down to the ground floor, for she wasn't afraid of him. Yet in some strange way he presented a threat, for she was aware of an elemental quality apparent, a primeval recognition that raised all her fine body hairs in pro-tective self-defence.

It was after five when they reached suburban Pepper-mint Grove, and Alyse was grateful for the babysitter's presence as she effected the necessary introductions before escorting Aleksi to one of the spare bedrooms.

'You can leave your bag here. I'll make up the bed later.'

She felt awkward and ill at ease, and her chin tilted

slightly as she met his mocking gaze. Damn you, she longed to scream at him. I *hate* you!

'I'll check on Georg.' Without another word she turned and left the room, telling herself she didn't care whether he followed her or not.

Georg was fast asleep, and Alyse moved silently towards her own bedroom, where she quickly shed her shoes, then exchanged her suit for a towelling robe.

Despite the babysitter's being hired until late evening, Alyse wanted to bath and feed Georg herself before settling him down for the night. It was a ritual she adored, and tonight it held special meaning, for only due legal process separated Georg from being officially hers.

Almost on cue she heard his first wakening cry, and she reached him within seconds, loving the way his tears ceased the moment she picked him up.

Bathing and feeding took almost an hour, and Alyse was supremely conscious of Aleksi's presence during the latter thirty minutes.

'May I?'

With extreme care she placed Georg into the crook of Aleksi's arm, watching every movement with the eagle eye of a mother-hen.

'I won't drop him,' Aleksi drawled with hateful cynicism, and her eyes darkened to a deep cerulean blue.

'I never imagined you would,' she snapped, aware that the babysitter was in the kitchen preparing her own dinner and therefore happily in ignorance of their barbed exchange.

Alyse willed Georg to cry, thus signalling his displeasure at being placed in a stranger's care, but he failed to comply and merely lay still, his bright eyes wide and dark. One could be forgiven for imagining he was fascinated, and perhaps he was, she decided uncharitably, for there had to be an awareness of change from her own scent and body-softness in comparison with his uncle's muscularly hard male-contoured frame.

Aleksi's expression was inscrutably intent, and she watched as he placed a forefinger into Georg's baby palm, detecting a momentary flaring of triumph as tiny fingers closed around it.

'He's a beautiful child,' she said quietly, and suffered Aleksi's swift scrutiny.

'He's my brother's son.' He paused slightly, then added with soft emphasis, '*Our* son.'

For some reason a chill shiver feathered its way down her spine. His words sounded irrevocable, almost as if he was issuing a silent warning. Yet he could have no inkling of her intention to instigate a divorce and gain custody of Georg—could he?

Stop it, she bade silently. You're merely being fanciful.

'He really should go down for the night.' She purposely shifted her gaze to Georg, who in total contrariness looked as if he had every intention of remaining wide awake.

'Why don't you go and change?' Aleksi suggested. 'The babysitter can settle him into his cot, and you can check him before we leave.'

A slight frown momentarily furrowed Alyse's brow.

'Dinner,' he elaborated.

The thought of suffering through another meal in his sole company was the last thing she wanted, but the alternative of staying in was even worse. 'I'm not very hungry, and I still have to pack.' It was a token protest at best, and he knew it.

'We won't be late.'

Dammit, what she'd give to ruffle that implacable composure! A sobering thought occurred that she *had*, and the result wasn't something she'd willingly choose to repeat.

'In that case, I'll go and get ready.'

'Unequivocal compliance, Alyse?'

'Conditional accedence,' she corrected, and leaning forward she brushed her lips to Georg's forehead. 'Goodnight, darling,' she bade softly. 'Sleep well.'

The gesture brought her far too close to Aleksi, and she straightened at once, moving away without so much as a backward glance as she left the room.

Selecting something suitable to wear took scant minutes, and she chose to freshen her make-up, merely adding a light dusting of powder and reapplying lipstick before running a brush through her hair.

Slipping into shoes, she collected a clutch-purse, then took one quick glance at her mirrored reflection, uncaring that the tailored black dress and red jacket provided a striking foil for her attractive features and pale shining hair.

As she emerged from her room she almost collided with Aleksi, and she bore his scrutiny with equanimity.

'Georg is already fast asleep,' he enlightened her quietly as he walked at her side to the lounge.

'Aleksi has written down the name and telephone number of the restaurant in case of any emergency,' the babysitter revealed, her eyes sparkling as they moved from one to the other, and Alyse could have sworn there was a degree of wistful envy in the young girl's expression. 'Please enjoy yourselves, and stay as long as you want. I don't mind.'

One glance at Aleksi Stefanos had been sufficient for the romantic eighteen-year-old to weave an impossible imaginary fantasy that bore no similarity whatsoever to reality!

Alyse could only proffer a sweet smile and utter her thanks, although inwardly she felt like screaming in vexation.

'Save it until we're in the car,' murmured Aleksi as he stood aside for her to precede him from the house, and she turned towards him with the smile still firmly pinned in place.

'Thus preserving the required image, I suppose?'

His gaze was full of mockery. 'Of course.'

Her expression registered an entire gamut of emotions, and she struggled to contain them as she slid into the passenger seat. 'Oh, go to hell!'

'I would advise putting a curb on your tongue.' His voice was dangerously soft, and in the dim interior of the car it was impossible to determine his expression. Not that she cared, she assured herself. He could bring down the wrath of a veritable Nemesis on her head, and it wouldn't matter at all.

The restaurant Aleksi had chosen was intimate, and offered superb cuisine. As a perfect complement, he ordered a bottle of Cristal, and proposed a solemn toast to their future together.

It wasn't something Alyse coveted, and she merely sipped the excellent champagne and forked morsels of food into her mouth with seemingly mechanical regularity.

Consequently it was a relief when coffee was served,

and she breathed a silent sigh as Aleksi summoned the waiter for their bill.

In the car she sat in silence, grateful that he made no attempt at idle conversation, and the moment they arrived home she moved indoors with indecent haste, paid the babysitter and presented her with a parting gift, forcing a smile as the girl gave her an impulsive hug and bestowed her best wishes on them both.

'I'll make up your bed,' Alyse declared minutes after Anna's departure, 'then finish packing.'

'If you retrieve the necessary bed-linen, I'm sure I can manage,' Aleksi drawled, and she retaliated with deliberate sarcasm,

'A domesticated husband—how nice! Can you cook too?'

'Adequately. I also iron.'

'It almost seems too much!'

'Me, or my—abilities?' Aleksi's emphasis was deliberate, and she directed him an arctic glare.

'As I haven't experienced any of your abilities, I'm hardly in a position to comment.'

'Is that an invitation?'

His sarcasm was the living end. 'You know damn well it's not!' She moved quickly past him into the hallway and flung open the linen closet. 'You should have stayed at the hotel,' she declared, and was utterly incensed when she glimpsed his silent humour.

'Alone?' Aleksi mocked.

Alyse closed her eyes, then opened them again in a gesture of pure exasperation. 'Take a clean towel with you if you want to shower. Goodnight,' she added pointedly. Without a further word she walked towards her bedroom, then went in and closed the door behind her.

If he dared to follow her, she'd do him a mortal injury, she determined vengefully as she set about filling a suitcase with the remainder of her clothes. When the chore was completed she looked in on Georg, then crept back to her room, undressed, and slipped into bed.

She was so tired she should have fallen asleep within minutes, except there were fragmented images torturing her subconscious mind, the most vivid of which was the compelling form of Aleksi Stefanos. He appeared as a dark, threatening force: compelling, and infinitely powerful.

She had married in haste, out of love and loyalty to her sister and baby Georg. Would she repent at leisure, transported several thousand kilometres to the opposite side of the continent, where Aleksi Stefanos was in command?

Alyse found it impossible not to feel apprehensive as she boarded the large Boeing jet the following morning, and as each aeronautical mile brought them steadily closer to their destination the anxiety intensified.

A stopover in Melbourne and change in aircraft was instrumental in the final leg of their flight, and Alyse followed Aleksi into the arrival lounge at Coolangatta, aware that Georg, who had travelled surprisingly well, was now wide awake and would soon require the bottle the airline stewardess had kindly heated prior to disembarking.

Aleksi gave every appearance of being a doting uncle—*father*, she corrected silently, incredibly aware that he exuded dynamic masculinity attired in dark casual-style trousers, pale shirt and impeccably designed jacket that served to emphasise his breadth of shoulder—and she mentally squared her own, tilting her chin fractionally as he moved forward to lift various items of their luggage from the carousel and load them on to a trolley.

'I arranged to have my car brought to the airport,' he told her as Georg broke into a fractious wail. 'Wait here while I collect it from the car park.'

Alyse nodded in silent acquiescence, her entire attention caught up by the baby in the carrycot, whose tiny legs began to kick in vigorous rejection of what she suspected was a freshly soiled nappy.

By the time Aleksi returned Georg was crying lustily, and she opted to care for the baby's needs while Aleksi dealt with the luggage.

'Forceful young fellow,' Aleksi drawled minutes later as he eased the large BMW away from the terminal.

'Who's obviously intent on continuing in the same domineering vein as his forefathers,' Alyse offered sweetly as she gave Georg his bottle.

'Of whom you know very little,' reproved Aleksi, shooting her a quick mocking glance via the rear-view mirror, and she was quick with a loaded response.

'Oh, I wouldn't say that. I'm learning more each day.' She deliberately focused her attention on Georg, pacing the baby's attempt to drain the contents of his bottle in record speed, then when he had finished she burped him and laid him down in the carrycot, watching anxiously until he lapsed into a fitful doze.

Alyse pretended an interest in the darkened scenery beyond the windscreen, viewing the clearly lit highway and abundance of neon signs with apparent absorption.

'Is this your first visit to the Gold Coast?' he asked.

She turned towards him, glimpsing strength of purpose in features made all the more arresting by reflected headlights in the dim interior of the car.

'My parents brought Antonia and me here for a holiday about ten years ago,' she revealed.

The tiny lines fanning out from his eyes became more pronounced and his mouth widened into a slight smile. 'You'll notice a lot of changes.'

'For the better, I hope?'

'That would depend on whether you prefer the relaxed, casual holiday atmosphere the locals enjoyed all year round with only the inconvenience of visiting tourists during peak season, or the bustling commercial centre Surfers' Paradise has now become.'

'I guess one has to admit it's progress,' Alyse opined as the luxurious vehicle purred swiftly north along the double-lane highway.

'There's been a massive injection of Japanese-controlled funds into the area—hotels, resorts, golf courses,' Aleksi told her. 'The flow-on has resulted in a building boom: houses, shopping centres, high-rise developments, offices.'

'As a builder, you must be very pleased with the increased business.' It was a non-committal comment, and not meant to be judgemental. However, it earned her a quick piercing glance before the road reclaimed his attention.

'The Coast has a long history of boom-and-bust cycles in building and real estate. Only the foolish choose to disregard facts and fail to plan ahead.'

No one in their right mind could call Aleksi Stefanos a fool, Alyse thought wryly. Remembering the force of his kiss, the steel-like strength of his arms as they had held her immobile, provided a vivid reminder of what manner of man she intended playing against. Yet it was a game she must win.

As the BMW pulled into the outer lane and sped swiftly past a line of slower-moving vehicles with ease, Alyse could only wonder at its horsepower capacity. There were outlines of densely covered hills reaching into the distance as Aleksi veered inland from the coastal highway.

'Sovereign Islands comprises a number of bridge-linked residentially developed islands situated to the east of Paradise Point, less than an hour's drive from the airport,' he told her. 'It's a prestigious security-guarded estate, and accessible by road from the mainland via a private bridge. Every home site has deep-water anchorage.'

'A gilded prison for the fabulously wealthy, with a luxury vessel moored at the bottom of every garden?'

'The residents prefer to call it civilised protection, and are prepared to pay for the privilege.'

'Suitably cushioned from the harsh realities of life.' Alyse couldn't believe she was resorting to sarcasm. It simply wasn't her style. Yet for some unknown reason the man behind the wheel generated the most adverse feelings in her, making her want to lash out against him in every possible way.

He didn't bother to reply, and she sat in silence, aware of an increasing anxiety as the car sped steadily north. Her home in Perth seemed a million kilometres away; the relative ease of life as she'd known it equally distant.

Her marriage was one of necessity, and merely mutually convenient. So why was she as wound up as a tightly coiled spring?

'We're almost there,' Aleksi declared drily, and Alyse spared her surroundings a swift encompassing glance, noting the numerous brightly lit architect-designed homes and established well-kept grounds.

Aleksi had said his home was a showcase, and she silently agreed as he turned the car on to a tiled driveway fronting a magnificent double-storeyed residence that seemed far too large for one man alone.

Pale granite walls were reflected by the car's powerful headlights, their lines imposing and classically defined. At a touch of the remote control module the wide garage doors tilted upwards, and Aleksi brought the BMW to a smooth halt alongside a Patrol four-wheel-drive vehicle.

Minutes later Alyse followed him into a large entrance foyer featuring a vaulted ceiling of tinted glass. A magnificent chandelier hung suspended from its centre, lending spaciousness and an abundance of light reflected by off-white walls and deep-piled cream-textured carpet. The central focus was a wide double staircase leading to the upper floor.

Wide glass-panelled doors stood open revealing an enormous lounge furnished with delicately carved antique furniture, and there were several carefully placed oil paintings gracing the walls, providing essential colour.

'I suggest you settle Georg,' said Aleksi as he brought in the luggage. His expression was a inscrutable mask as he chose a passageway to his left, and Alyse had little option but to follow in his wake.

'The master suite has an adjoining sitting-room overlooking the canal—' with a wide sweep of his arm he indicated a door immediately opposite '—an en suite bathroom, and, to the left, a changing-room with two separate walk-in wardrobes.'

The décor had an elegance that was restful and visually pleasant, utilising a skilful mix of pale green and a soft shade of peach as a complement to the overall cream.

'There's the requisite nursery furniture in the sitting-room,' he continued, moving forward. 'And a spare bed which you can use until—'

'Until—*what*?' Alyse's eyes blazed blue fire in an unspoken challenge.

'You're ready to share mine,' he drawled with imperturbable calm.

She was so incredibly furious that she almost shook with anger, and she failed to feel Georg stir in her arms, nor did she register his slight whimper in sleepy protest. 'That will be *never*!'

Dark eyebrows slanted above eyes that held hers in deliberate mocking appraisal. 'My dear Alyse,' chided Aleksi with chilling softness, 'surely you expect the marriage to be consummated?'

Her eyes widened with angry incredulity. 'In a house this large, there have to be other adequate bedrooms from which I can choose.'

'Several,' Aleksi agreed. 'However, this is where you'll stay.'

Her chin tilted in a gesture of indignant mutiny. 'The hell I will!'

'Eventually you must fall asleep.' He gave a careless shrug as he indicated the large bed. 'When you do, I'll simply transfer you here.'

'You unspeakable fiend!' she lashed out. 'I won't let you do that.'

'How do you propose to stop me?'

His expression was resolute, and only an innocent would fail to detect tensile steel beneath the silky smoothness of his voice.

Alyse's heart lurched painfully, then skipped a beat. Only a wide aperture separated the sitting-room from the bedroom, with no door whatsoever to afford her any privacy.

'You're an unfeeling, insensitive—' She faltered to a furious halt, momentarily lost for adequate words in verbal description. '*Brute!*'

Something flickered in the depths of his eyes, then it was successfully masked. 'I suggest you settle Georg before he becomes confused and bewildered by the degree of anger you're projecting.' He turned towards the bedroom door. 'I'll be in the kitchen, making coffee.'

Alyse wanted to throw something at his departing back, and the only thing that stopped her was the fact that she held Georg in her arms.

Experiencing momentary defeat, she turned towards the sitting-room, seeing at a glance that it was sufficiently large to hold a pair of single chairs and a sofa, as well as a bed and nursery furniture.

Placing the baby down into the cot, she gently covered him, lingering long enough to see that he was asleep before moving back into the bedroom.

Defiance emanated from every pore in her body as she retrieved her nightwear from her bag. A shower would surely ease some of her tension, she decided as she made her way into the luxuriously fitted bathroom. Afterwards she'd beard Aleksi in the kitchen and reaffirm her determination for entirely separate sleeping quarters for herself and Georg.

It was heaven to stand beneath the jet of pulsating hot water, and she took her time before using one of several large fluffy bathtowels to dry the excess moisture from her body. Her toilette completed, she slipped on a nightgown and added a matching robe.

There were bottles to sterilise and formula to make up in case Georg should wake through the night, and, collecting the necessary carry-bag, she went in search of the kitchen.

She found it off a passageway on the opposite side of the lounge, and she studiously ignored the tall dark-haired man in the process of pouring black aromatic coffee from a percolator into one of two cups set out on the servery.

Luxuriously spacious, the kitchen was a delight featuring the latest in electronic equipment, and in normal circumstances she would have expressed pleasure in its design.

'I'm sure you'll find whatever you need in the cupboards,' Aleksi drawled as he added sugar and a splash of whisky.

'Thank you.' Her words were stilted and barely polite as she set about her task.

'A married couple come in daily to maintain the house and grounds,' he informed her matter-of-factly. 'And a catering firm is hired whenever I entertain.'

'With such splendid organisation, you hardly need a wife,' she retorted, impossibly angry with him—and herself, for imagining he might permit a celibate co-habitation.

'Don't sulk, Alyse,' he derided drily, and she rounded on him with ill-concealed fury.

'I am not *sulking*! I'm simply too damned angry to

be bothered conducting any sort of civilised conversation with you!' With tense movements she put the newly made formula in the refrigerator.

'The bedroom arrangement stays,' Aleksi declared with hard inflexibility, and her eyes became brilliant blue pools as she stood looking at him, refusing to be intimidated by his powerful height and sheer indomitable strength.

'All hell will freeze over before I'll willingly share any bed you happen to occupy!'

A faint smile tugged the edges of his mouth, and the expression in his eyes was wholly cynical. 'Why not have some coffee?' he queried mildly, and Alyse was so incensed by his imperturbable calm that she refused just for the sheer hell of opposing him.

'I'd prefer water.'

He shrugged and drained the contents of his cup. 'I'll be out most of tomorrow, checking progress on a number of sites, consulting with project managers. I've written down the name and phone number of a highly reputable babysitter in case you need to go out, and I'll leave a set of keys for the house and the car, together with some money in case there's anything you need.'

'I have money of my own,' she declared fiercely, and saw one eyebrow lift in silent quizzical query.

'Call it a housekeeping allowance,' Aleksi insisted as he leaned against the servery. 'And don't argue,' he warned with dangerous softness.

Without a further word she turned and filled a glass with chilled water, then drank it. With head held high she crossed the kitchen, her expression one of icy aloofness. 'I'm going to bed.' It was after eleven, and she was weary almost beyond belief.

'I'll show you how to operate the security system,' he insisted, straightening to his full height.

Five minutes later she entered the master suite, aware that he followed in her wake. Her back was rigid with silent anger as she made her way through to the sitting-room, and once there she flung off her robe, slid into bed, closed her eyes and determinedly shut out the muted sound of the shower operating in the en suite bathroom.

Much to her annoyance she remained awake long after the adjoining bedroom light was extinguished, and lay staring into the darkness, incredibly aware of Aleksi's proximity.

She hated him, she denounced in angry silence. *Hated* him. Why, he had to be the most damnable man she'd ever had the misfortune to meet. Indomitable, inflexible, *impossible*!

She must have slept, for she came sharply awake feeling totally disorientated and unsure of her whereabouts for a brief few seconds before memory surfaced, and she lay still, willing conscious recognition for the sound which had alerted her subconscious mind.

Georg? Perhaps he was unsettled after the long flight and restless in new surroundings.

Slipping cautiously out of bed, she trod silently across the room to the cot, her eyes adjusting to the reflection of the low-burning nightlight as she anxiously inspected his still form.

Wide eyes stared at her with unblinking solemnity, and Alyse shook her head in smiling admonition. With practised ease she changed his nappy, then covered him, only to hear him emit a whimpering cry.

Within seconds it became an unrelenting wail, and,

quickly flinging on a wrap, she picked him up, mur-
muring softly as she cradled him.

'Problems?'

Alyse turned in startled surprise at the sound of
Aleksi's voice so close behind her. 'He's only very recently started missing a late-night feed,' she told him
quietly. 'I think the flight may have unsettled him.'

'Give him to me while you heat his bottle.'

'I can easily take him into the kitchen, then you won't
be disturbed.'

'Go and do it, Alyse,' drawled Aleksi, calmly lifting
Georg from out of her arms.

Her chin tilted fractionally as she met his unequivocal gaze, then just as she was about to argue the baby
began to cry in earnest and, defeated, she stepped past
Aleksi and made her way from the bedroom, fumbling
occasionally as she searched for elusive light switches.

The tap emitted hot water at a single touch. *Boil-
ing* hot, she discovered, biting her lips hard against a
shocked curse as she withdrew her scalded hand. Ignoring the stinging pain, she warmed a bottle of prepared
formula, then hurried back to the bedroom.

Aleksi was sitting on the edge of the bed cradling the
tiny infant, and Alyse experienced a shaft of elemental
jealousy at his complete absorption.

She wanted to snatch Georg out of his arms and retreat from the implied intimacy of the lamplit room
with its large bed and the dynamic man who seemed
to dominate it without any effort at all.

'I'll take him now,' she declared firmly, and her hand
brushed his as she retrieved the baby, sending an electric charge through her veins.

Sheer dislike, she dismissed as she tended to Georg's

needs, and on the edge of sleep she took heart in the fact that she would have most of the day to herself. A prospect she found infinitely pleasing, for without Aleksi's disturbing presence she could explore the house at will, even swim in the pool while Georg slept. And attempt to come to terms with a lifestyle and a husband she neither needed nor coveted.

CHAPTER FIVE

ALYSE ENTERTAINED NO qualms whatsoever as she followed Georg's pre-dawn routine. If Aleksi insisted that she and Georg occupy the master suite, then he could darned well suffer the consequences of sleep interrupted by a baby's internal feeding clock, she determined as she settled Georg after his bottle. Gathering up jeans, a warm long-sleeved sweater and fresh underwear, she crossed to the en suite bathroom and took a leisurely shower.

When she re-entered the bedroom Aleksi was in the process of sliding out of bed, and she hastily averted her eyes from an expanse of muscular flesh barely protected from total nudity by a swirl of bedlinen.

'Good morning.'

His drawled amusement put her on an immediate defensive, and her eyes lit with ill-disguised antagonism as she uttered a perfunctory acknowledgment on her way to the sitting-room.

Damn him! she cursed as she quickly straightened her bed, tugging sheets with more than necessary force. He possessed an ability to raise her hackles to such a degree that she was in danger of completely losing her temper at the mere sight of him!

Aleksi was already in the kitchen when she entered it some five minutes later, and she cast his tall rangy jeans-clad, black-sweatered frame the briefest of glances as she took a cup and filled it with freshly brewed coffee, blithely ignoring the fact that he was in the process of breaking eggs into a pan.

'Breakfast?'

She met his dark gaze with equanimity. 'It's barely six. I'll get something later.'

A newspaper lay folded on the servery and she idly scanned the headlines as she sipped the contents of her cup.

'There's an electronic device connected to the intercom system that can be activated to ensure that Georg is heard from any room in the house,' Aleksi told her.

'You were very confident of succeeding, weren't you?' Alyse couldn't help saying bitterly. 'The abundance of nursery furniture, toys—everything organised before you left for Perth.'

He skilfully transferred the contents from the pan on to a plate, collected toast and coffee and took a seat at the breakfast table.

His silence angered her immeasurably, and some devilish imp urged her along a path to conflagration. 'No comment?' she demanded.

He looked up, and she nearly died at the ruthless intensity of his gaze. 'Why indulge in senseless fantasy?'

'Don't you mean fallacy? Somehow it seems more appropriate.'

'Are you usually this argumentative so early in the morning? Or is it simply an attempt to test the extent of my temper?'

There could be no doubt he possessed one, and she

cursed herself for a fool for daring to probe the limit of his control. Yet beneath that innate recognition was a determined refusal to be intimidated in any way.

'Do you have a problem with women who dare to question your opinion?' she countered, permitting one eyebrow to lift in a delicate arch. 'Doubtless all your female *friends*,' she paused with faint emphasis, 'agree with everything you say to a point of being sickeningly obsequious. Whereas I couldn't give a damn.'

'That's a sweeping generalisation, when you know nothing about any of my friends.'

'Oh, I'm sure there's any number of gorgeous socialites willing to give their all at the merest indication of your interest,' she derided. 'I wonder how they'll accept the news that you've suddenly plunged into matrimony and legally adopted a son?'

Aleksi subjected her to a long level glance. 'I owe no one an explanation for any decision I choose to make.' He picked up his cup and drained the last of his coffee. 'The keys to the BMW are on the pedestal table beside my bed.' He rose from the table with catlike grace. 'Enjoy your day.'

'Thank you,' Alyse responded with ill-concealed mockery, watching as he crossed the kitchen before disappearing down the hallway.

She heard the slight snap of a door closing, followed by the muted sound of an engine being fired and a vehicle reversing, then silence.

Suddenly the whole day lay ahead of her, and with at least three hours before Georg was due to waken again, she hurriedly finished her coffee and made her way towards the foyer.

Mounting the staircase, she slowly explored the four

bedrooms and adjoining bathrooms, plus a guest suite, all beautifully furnished and displaying impeccable taste.

Returning downstairs, she wandered at will through the lounge, formal dining-room, guest powder-room, and utilities, and merely stood at the door leading into an imposing study, noting the large executive desk, computer equipment, leather chairs and an impressive collection of filing cabinets. There were also several design awards in frames on the wall, witness to Aleksi's success.

From there she moved towards the kitchen, discovering another flight of stairs leading from an informal family room down to a third level comprising a large informal lounge, billiard-room, gymnasium, and sauna. Wide glass sliding doors from the lounge and billiard-room led out on to a large patio and free-form swimming-pool.

The colour-scheme utilised throughout the entire home was a combination of cream and varying shades of pale green and peach, presenting a visually pleasing effect that highlighted modern architecture without providing stereotyped sterility.

A thorough inspection of the pantry, refrigerator and freezer revealed that there was no need to replenish anything for several days, and a small sigh of relief escaped her lips as she emptied cereal and milk into a bowl and sat down at the breakfast table with the daily newspaper.

Afterwards there was time to tidy the dishes before Georg was due to waken, and with determined resolve she moved through the master suite to the sitting-room and quietly retrieved her bags. She was damned if she'd calmly accept Aleksi's dictum and share the same suite of rooms!

It was relatively simple to transfer everything upstairs, although as the day progressed a tiny seed of anxiety began to niggle at her subconscious.

Dismissing it, she set about preparing an evening meal of chunky minestrone, followed by chicken Kiev and an assortment of vegetables, with brandied pears for dessert.

It was almost six when Alyse heard Aleksi return, and her stomach began a series of nervous somersaults as he came into the kitchen, which was totally ridiculous, she derided silently.

'I hardly expected such wifely solicitude,' he drawled, viewing her slight frown of concentration with amusement.

Alyse glanced up from stirring the minestrone and felt her senses quicken. He looked strong and vital, and far too disturbingly male for any woman's peace of mind.

Her eyes flashed him a glance of deep sapphire-blue before she returned her attention to the saucepan. 'Is there any reason why I shouldn't prepare a meal?'

'Of course not,' Aleksi returned smoothly as he leaned against the edge of the servery.

She could sense the mockery in his voice, and hated him for it. 'Stop treating me like a naïve nineteen-year-old!' she flung with a degree of acerbity.

'How would you have me treat you, Alyse?'

'With some respect for my feelings,' she returned fiercely.

'Perhaps you'd care to elaborate?'

It was pointless evading the issue, and besides, it

was only a matter of time before he'd discover Georg's absence from the nursery.

She drew a deep breath, then released it slowly. 'I've moved my belongings into an upstairs bedroom.'

The eyes that lanced hers were dark and unfathomable.

'I suggest you move them back down again,' he drawled with dangerous silkiness.

'*No.* I refuse to allow you to play cat to my mouse by dictating my sleeping arrangements.'

'Is that what I'm doing?'

Oh, she could *hit* him! 'Yes! I won't be coerced to conform by a display of sheer male dominance.'

'My dear Alyse, you sound almost afraid. Are you?'

Now she was really angry, and sheer bravado forced her to counter, 'Do I look afraid?'

'Perhaps you should be. I don't suffer fools gladly.'

'What's that supposed to mean?'

At that precise moment a loud wail emitted through the monitor, and Alyse threw Aleksi a totally exasperated look.

'It's time for his bottle.'

'I'll fetch him while you heat it.'

Momentarily defeated, she retrieved a fresh bottle from the refrigerator and filled a container with hot water.

Aleksi was a natural, she conceded several minutes later as he caught up the bottle, took a nearby chair and calmly proceeded to feed Georg.

'He should be changed first,' Alyse protested, meeting those dark challenging eyes, and heard him respond with quiet mockery,

'I already have.'

There was little she could do except give a seemingly careless shrug and return her attention to a variety of saucepans on the stove, although it rankled that
he should display such an adeptness when she had so
readily cast him into an entirely different mould.

Alyse settled Georg in his cot while Aleksi had a
shower, and it was almost seven when they sat down
to dinner.

'This is good,' he remarked.

Alyse inclined her head in silent acknowledgment.
'What would you have done if I hadn't prepared a meal?'

His gaze was startlingly direct. 'Organised a babysitter, and frequented a restaurant.'

'I mightn't have wanted to go.'

'Perversity, Alyse, simply for the hell of it?'

She couldn't remember arguing with anyone, not
even Antonia at her most difficult. Yet something kept
prompting her towards a confrontation with Aleksi at
every turn, and deep within some devilish imp danced
in sheer delight at the danger of it all.

'No comment?' he queried.

She met his gaze with equanimity. 'I have a feeling
that anything I say will be used against me.'

'Perhaps we should opt for a partial truce?'

She was powerless to prevent the wry smile that
tugged at the edges of her mouth. 'Would it last?'

'Probably not,' Aleksi agreed with a degree of cynicism. 'However, I'd prefer that we at least project an
outward display of civility in the company of my parents.'

'Why? They know the reason for our marriage, and
are aware it isn't an alliance made in heaven.' Alyse
sipped from a glass of superb white wine. 'If you

expect me to indulge in calculated displays of affection, forget it.'

He spooned the last of his minestrone, then waited for her to finish.

'I'd prefer to help myself,' Alyse said at once, knowing he'd serve her a far too generous portion. She wasn't very hungry, and merely selected a few vegetables, then toyed with dessert.

'There are numerous friends and business associates who will be anxious to meet you, and a party next Saturday evening will provide an excellent opportunity.' He leaned back in his chair and surveyed her with a veiled scrutiny. 'I'll organise the caterers.'

She got to her feet and began stacking plates, unable to prevent a flaring of resentment as he lent his assistance.

'I can manage,' she said stiffly, hating his close proximity within the large kitchen.

'I'll rinse, you can load the dishwasher,' Aleksi told her, and she gritted her teeth in the knowledge that his actions were deliberate.

'You now have a wife to take care of all this,' Alyse voiced sweetly. 'Why not relax in the lounge with an after-dinner port, or retire to your study?'

'So you can pretend I don't exist?'

Oh, he was too clever by far! '*Yes*, damn you.'

Dark eyes gleamed with ill-concealed humour. 'No one would guess a firebrand exists beneath that cool façade,' he mused cynically, causing her resentment to flare.

'I didn't possess a temper until you forced your way into my life!'

'*Forced*, Alyse?' he queried with soft emphasis. 'I've never had to coerce a woman into anything.'

His implication was intentional, and Alyse quite suddenly had had enough. Placing the plate she held carefully on to the bench, she turned and made to move past him.

'Since you obviously believe in equality, *you* finish the dishes. I'm going for a walk.'

'In the dark, and alone?'

Her eyes flared with brilliant blue fire. 'I need some fresh air, but most of all, I need a temporary escape from *you*!'

'No, Alyse.' His voice sounded like silk being razed by tensile steel, and she reacted without thought, hardly aware of her hand swinging in a swift arc until it connected with a resounding slap on the side of his jaw.

For a wild moment she thought he meant to strike her back, and she cried out as he caught hold of her hands and drew her inextricably close. Any attempt to struggle was defeated the instant it began, and after several futile minutes she simply stood in defiant silence.

Her pulse tripped its beat and measurably quickened at the degree of icy anger apparent. He possessed sufficient strength to break her wrists, and she flinched as he tightened his grasp. 'You're hurting me!'

'If you continue this kind of foolish behaviour, believe me, you *will* get hurt.'

His threat wasn't an idle one, yet she stood defiant beneath his compelling gaze. 'That's precisely the type of chauvinistic threat I'd expect you to make!'

With slow deliberation he released her wrists and slid his hands up to her shoulders, impelling her forward, then his mouth was on hers, hard and possessively demanding.

Alyse clenched her teeth against his intended invasion, and a silent scream rose and died in her throat beneath the relentless determined pressure. She began to struggle, flailing her fists against his arms, his ribs—anywhere she could connect in an effort to break free.

She gave a muffled moan of entreaty as he effortlessly caught hold of her hands and held them together behind her back—an action that brought her even closer against his hard masculine frame, and there was nothing she could do to prevent the hand that slid to her breast.

A soundless gasp escaped her lips as she felt his fingers slip the buttons on her blouse, then slide beneath the silk of her bra. She wanted to scream in outrage as his mouth forced open her own, and his tongue became a pillaging, destructive force that had her silently begging him to stop.

When he finally released her, she swayed and almost fell, and a husky oath burned her ears in explicit, softly explosive force.

Her lips felt numb and swollen, and she unconsciously began a tentative seeking exploration with the tip of her tongue, discovering ravaged tissues that had been heartlessly ground against her teeth.

Firm fingers lifted her chin, and her lashes swiftly lowered in automatic self-defence against the hurt and humiliation she knew to be evident in their depths.

Standing quite still, she bore his silent scrutiny until every nerve stretched to its furthest limitation.

'Let me go. Please.' She had to get away from him before the ache behind her eyes manifested itself in silent futile tears.

Without a word he released her, watching as she slowly turned and walked from the room.

The temptation to run was paramount, except where could she run to that he wouldn't follow? A hollow laugh choked in her throat as she ascended the stairs. Escape, even temporary, afforded her a necessary respite, and uncaring of Aleksi's objection to her move upstairs, she crept into Georg's room and silently undressed.

It wasn't fair—*nothing* was fair, she decided as she lay quietly in bed. Sleep was never more distant, and despite her resolve it was impossible not to dwell on the fact that the day after tomorrow Aleksi's parents would arrive. An event she wasn't sure whether to view with relief or despair.

A silent scream rose to the surface as she heard an imperceptible click, followed by the inward swing of the bedroom door. Anger replaced fright as she saw Aleksi's tall frame outlined against the aperture, and she unconsciously drew the covers more firmly about her shoulders.

She watched in horrified fascination as he crossed to the cot and carefully transferred Georg on to the bed beside her.

'What do you think you're doing?' she vented in a sibilant whisper.

'I imagine it's perfectly clear,' he drawled as he effortlessly picked up the cot and carried it from the room.

Within minutes he was back, and she stared in disbelief as he scooped the baby into his arms. At the door he turned slightly to face her.

'You can walk, or be carried,' he said quietly. 'The choice is yours.'

Then he was gone, and Alyse was left seething with helpless anger. *Choice?* What choice did she have, for heaven's sake! Yet she was damned if she'd meekly follow him downstairs and slip into bed, defeated.

With each passing second she was aware of her own foolishness; to thwart him was the height of folly, and would doubtless bring retribution of a kind she would be infinitely wise to avoid. Except that wisdom, at this precise moment, was not high on her list.

Fool, an inner voice cautioned. *Fool.* Haven't you suffered enough punishment already, without wilfully setting yourself up for more?

Even as she considered capitulation, Aleksi re-entered the room, and she held his narrowed gaze with undisguised defiance as he moved to the side of the bed.

Without a word he wrenched the covers from her grasp, then leant forward and lifted her into his arms.

Alyse struggled, hating the ease with which he held her. 'Put me down, you fiend!'

'I can only wonder when you'll learn that to oppose me is a totally useless exercise,' he said cynically, catching one flailing fist and restraining it with galling ease.

'If you're hoping for meek subservience, it will never happen!' Dear lord, he was strong; any movement she made was immediately rendered ineffectual.

'You'd have to be incredibly naïve not to realise there's a certain danger in continually offering resistance,' he drawled, and she momentarily froze as fear licked her veins.

'Sex, simply for the sake of it?' she queried, meeting his gaze with considerable bravery. 'How long did you allow me, Aleksi—two, three nights?'

She could feel his anger unfurl, emanating as finely

tuned tension over which she had little indication of his measure of control. Her eyes blazed a brilliant clear blue, not crystalline sapphire but holding the coolness of lapis lazuli.

'Well, get it over and done with, damn you! Although I doubt if you'll gain much satisfaction from copulating with an uninterested block of ice!'

His eyes seemed incredibly dark, and his mouth assumed a cruelty that made her want to retract every foolish word. In seeming slow motion he released her down on to the floor in front of him, and she stood mesmerised as he subjected her to a slow, raking appraisal.

Her nightgown was satin-finished silk edged with lace and provided adequate cover, but beneath his studied gaze she felt positively naked. A delicate pink tinged her cheeks as his eyes lingered on the gentle swell of her breasts, then slid low to the shadowed cleft between her thighs before slowly returning to the soft curves beneath the revealing neckline.

Against her will, a curious warmth began somewhere in the centre of her being and slowly spread until it encompassed her entire body.

Reaching out, he brushed gentle fingers against her cheek, then let them drift to trace the contours of her mouth before slipping to the edge of her neck, where he trailed the delicate pulsing cord to examine with tactile sensuality the soft hollows beneath her throat.

Her eyes widened, but her gaze didn't falter as his hand slid to the soft curve of her breast and slowly outlined its shape between thumb and forefinger. When he reached the sensitive peak it was all she could do not to gasp out loud, and she suppressed a tiny shiver as he rendered a similar exploration to its twin.

Slowly and with infinite care, he slid his hand to the shoestring straps and slipped first one, then the other from her shoulders.

For what seemed an age he just looked at her, and she stood mesmerised, unable to gain anything from his expression. Then he lowered his head down to hers, and she tensed as his mouth took possession of her own.

Except that the hard, relentless pressure never eventuated, and in its place was a soft open-mouthed kiss that was nothing less than a deliberate seduction of the senses.

His tongue began a subtle exploration, seeking out all the vulnerable ridges, the tender, sensitive indentations, before beginning a delicate tracery of the tissues inside her cheek.

He seemed to fill her mouth, coaxing something from her she felt afraid to give, and she released a silent groan of relief as his lips left hers to settle in one of the vulnerable hollows at the base of her throat.

Then she gave an audible gasp as she felt his lips slide down to her breast, and the gasp became a cry of outrage as he took the peak into his mouth and savoured it gently, letting his teeth graze the sensitised nub until she almost screamed against the myriad sensations he was able to evoke.

Oh, dear lord, what had she invited? To remain quiescent was madness, yet to twist out of his grasp would only prove that she was vulnerable to his potent brand of sensual sexuality.

Just when she thought she could stand it no longer, Aleksi shifted his attention to its twin, and she arched her neck, her whole body stretching like a finely tuned bow in the hands of a master virtuoso.

It wasn't until she felt his hand on her stomach that she realised her nightgown had slithered to a silken heap at her feet, and a despairing moan escaped her throat.

At that moment his head shifted, and his mouth resumed a provocative possession that took hold of her inhibitions and tossed them high, bringing a response that left her weak-willed and malleable.

Then it was over, and she could only look at him in helpless fascination as he slowly pushed her to arm's length.

His lips assumed a mocking curve as he taunted with dangerous softness. '*Ice*, Alyse?'

The sound of his voice acted like a cascade of chilled water, and her own eyes widened into deep blue pools, mirroring shame and humiliation. She crossed her arms in defence of her lack of attire, hating the warmth that coloured her cheeks, and there was nothing she could do to prevent the shiver that feathered its way across the surface of her skin.

Without a word he bent to retrieve her nightgown from the floor, slipped it over her head, then slid an arm beneath her knees.

She wanted to protest, except that there was a painful lump in her throat defying speech, and the will to fight had temporarily fled as each descending step down the elegant staircase brought her closer—*to what*? Sexual possession?

In the centre of the master bedroom he released her, setting her on her feet, and she stood hesitant, poised for flight like a frightened gazelle.

'Go to bed.'

Alyse reared her head in startled surprise, and her eyes felt huge in a face she knew to be waxen-pale.

'Yours,' Aleksi added with soft cynicism. 'Before I change my mind and put you in mine.'

Her lips parted, then slowly closed again. There wasn't a thing she could say that wouldn't compound the situation, so she didn't even try, choosing instead to walk away from him with as much dignity as she could muster.

Sleep proved an elusive entity, and she lay awake pondering whether his actions were motivated by cruelty or kindness. Somehow she couldn't imagine it to be the latter.

CHAPTER SIX

ALYSE CHOSE TO stay at home with Georg when Aleksi drove to collect his parents from Brisbane airport on the pretext that it would give them time alone together in which to talk. It would also give her the opportunity to prepare dinner.

As their expected arrival drew closer, Alyse became consumed with nerves, and even careful scrutiny of a family photograph did little to ease her apprehension.

Alexandros Stefanos was an older, more distinguished replica of his indomitable son, although less forbidding, and Rachel looked serene and dignified. Both were smiling, and Alyse wondered if they would regard her kindly.

She fervently hoped so, for she was infinitely more in need of an ally than an enemy.

After initial indecision over what to wear, Alyse selected a stylishly cut leather skirt and teamed it with a knitted jumper patterned in varying shades of soft blue and lilac.

It was late afternoon when the BMW pulled into the garage, and her stomach tightened into a painful knot at the sound of the door into the hall opening, followed by two deep voices mingling with a light feminine laugh.

Drawing in a deep breath, she released it slowly and made her way towards the foyer, where an attractive mature woman stood poised, looking every bit as apprehensive as Alyse felt.

Even as Alyse came to a hesitant halt, the older woman's mouth parted in a tentative smile, and her eyes filled with reflected warmth.

'Alyse,' she greeted quietly. 'How very nice to meet you.'

'Mrs Stefanos,' Alyse returned, unsure precisely how she should address her mother-in-law. The circumstances were unusual, to say the least!

'Oh, *Rachel*, please,' Aleksi's stepmother said at once, reaching forward to catch hold of both Alyse's hands. 'And Alexandros,' she added, shifting slightly to one side to allow her husband the opportunity to move forward.

It was going to be all right, Alyse decided as she submitted to Alexandros Stefanos's firm handshake. Perhaps some of her relief showed, for Aleksi spared her a reassuring smile that held surprising warmth.

'I'll take your luggage upstairs to the guest suite, then we'll have a drink,' he said.

'I'll give you a hand,' Alexandros indicated in a deeply accented voice, and Alyse turned towards Rachel.

'Come and sit down. Georg is due to wake soon.'

The older woman's eyes misted. 'Oh, my dear, you can't begin to know how much I want to see him!'

'He's beautiful,' Alyse accorded simply as she sank into a sofa close to the one Rachel had chosen.

'You love him very much.' It was a statement of fact, and Alyse's gaze was clear and unblinking.

'Enough not to be able to give him up. For Antonia's sake, as well as my own,' she added quietly.

An expression very much like sympathy softened Aleksi's stepmother's features—that, and a certain understanding. 'Aleksi is very much Alexandros's son,' she offered gently. 'Yet beneath the surface lies a wealth of caring. I know he'll be a dedicated father, and,' she paused, then added hesitantly, 'a protective husband.'

But I don't want a husband, Alyse felt like crying out in anguished rejection of the man who had placed a wedding band on her finger only days before. And if I did, I certainly wouldn't have chosen your diabolical stepson!

The sound of male voices and muted laughter reached their ears, and Alyse turned towards the men as they came into the lounge.

'A drink is called for,' declared Aleksi, moving across to the bar. 'Alexandros? Rachel?'

Somehow she had imagined an adherence to formality, and Aleksi's easy use of his parents' Christian names came as a surprise.

'Some of your Queensland beer,' Alexandros requested, taking a seat beside his wife. 'It's refreshingly light.'

'I'll have mineral water,' Rachel acknowledged with a faint smile. 'Anything stronger will put me to sleep.'

'Alyse?'

'Mineral water,' she told him, then turned to Rachel. 'Unless you'd prefer tea or coffee?'

'My dear, no,' the older woman refused gently. 'Something cold will be fine.'

Georg woke a few minutes later, his lusty wail

sounding loud through the intercom system, and Alyse dispensed with her glass and hurriedly rose to her feet.

'I'll change him, then bring him out.' She met Rachel's anxious smile. 'Unless you'd like to come with me?'

'I'd love to,' the older woman said at once, and together they crossed the lounge to the hall.

By the time they reached the master bedroom Georg was in full cry, his small face red and angry.

'Oh, you little darling!' Rachel murmured softly as his cries subsided into a watery smile the instant he sighted them.

'He's very shrewd,' Alyse accorded, her movements deft as she removed his decidedly damp nappy and exchanged it for a dry one. 'There, sweetheart,' she crooned, nuzzling his baby cheek, 'all ready for your bottle.'

His feet kicked in silent acknowledgment, and Rachel gave a delighted laugh.

'Georgiou used to do that too.'

Alyse felt a pang of regret for the older woman's sorrow. 'Would you care to take him? I thought you might like to give him his bottle in the lounge.'

Rachel's eyes shimmered with unshed tears. 'Thank you.'

It was heart-wrenching to see the effect Georg had on his grandparents, and Alyse had to blink quickly more than once to dispel the suspicious dampness that momentarily blurred her vision.

An hour later the baby was resettled in his cot for the night, and Rachel retired upstairs to freshen up while Alyse put the finishing touches to dinner.

After much deliberation, she had elected to serve

a chicken consommé, followed by roast chicken with a variety of vegetables, and settled on fresh fruit for dessert. Unsure of Alexandros's palate, she'd added a cheese platter decorated with stuffed olives and grapes.

The meal was a definite success, and with most of her nervousness gone Alyse was able to relax.

'Tomorrow you must rest,' Aleksi told his parents as they sipped coffee in the lounge. 'In the afternoon I'll drive you into town and settle you both into the apartment, then in the evening we'll dine out together.'

Startled, Alyse felt her eyes widen in surprise, and Rachel quickly intervened in explanation.

'Aleksi owns an apartment in the heart of Surfers Paradise. Alexandros and I will stay there until we leave for Sydney to visit with my sister, after which we'll return and spend the remainder of our holiday on the Coast.'

Her expression softened as Alyse was about to demur.

'*Yes*, my dear. We value our independence and respect yours. The circumstances regarding your marriage are unusual,' Rachel added gently. 'You and Aleksi need time together alone.'

Alyse wanted to protest that the marriage was only one of convenience, and would remain so for as long as it took for her to escape to Perth with Georg. Except that she wouldn't consider voicing the words.

'And now,' Rachel declared, standing to her feet, 'if you don't mind, we'll retire.' Her smile wavered slightly as it moved from her husband to her stepson. 'It's been a long trip, and I'm really very tired.'

Alyse rose at once. 'Of course.' Her heart softened at the older woman's obvious weariness. 'There's everything you need in your suite.'

'Thank you, my dear.'

It seemed good manners to walk at Aleksi's side as his parents made their way into the foyer, and it wasn't until Rachel and Alexandros were safely upstairs that she turned back towards the lounge.

'I'll make some more coffee,' Aleksi said smoothly. 'I have a few hours' work ahead of me in the study.'

'There's plenty left in the percolator,' Alyse said with a slight shrug. 'It will take a minute to reheat. I'll bring it in, if you like.'

With a curt nod he turned towards the study, and it was only a matter of minutes before she entered that masculine sanctum and set a cup of steaming aromatic brew on his desk.

He was seated, leaning well back into a comfortable leather executive chair, and he regarded her with eyes that were direct and faintly probing.

'What do you think of my parents?'

'I hardly know them,' she said stiffly, longing to escape. In the company of Rachel and Alexandros she had been able to tolerate his company without too much difficulty, but now they were alone she was acutely aware of a growing tension.

'You like Rachel.' It was a statement, rather than a query, which she didn't bother to deny. 'And my father?'

'He seems kind,' she offered politely, and saw his mouth curve to form a cynical smile.

'Far kinder than his son?'

Her polite façade snapped. 'Yes. *You* seem to delight in being an uncivilised tyrant!'

An eyebrow rose in sardonic query. 'Whatever will you come up with next?'

Her eyes flashed a brilliant blue. 'Oh, I'm sure I'll think of something!'

The creases at the corners of his eyes deepened. 'I have no doubt you will.'

The temptation to pick something up from his desk and throw it at him was almost irresistible, and her hands clenched at her sides in silent restraint as she turned towards the door.

'Goodnight, Alyse.'

His drawled, faintly mocking tones followed her into the hall, and she muttered dire threats beneath her breath all the way into the kitchen.

An hour later she lay silently seething in bed, plotting his figurative downfall in so many numerous ways that it carried her to the edge of sleep and beyond.

It was almost midday when Rachel and Alexandros came downstairs, coinciding with Aleksi's arrival home, and after a relaxing meal Rachel eagerly saw to her grandson's needs, gave him his bottle, then settled him down for the afternoon.

Over coffee there was an opportunity for Alyse to become better acquainted with Aleksi's stepmother, and it was relatively simple to fill in details of Antonia's life, although she was aware of Aleksi's seemingly detached regard throughout a number of amusing anecdotes.

'I have some photographs,' Alyse told her. 'Most of them are in albums which are somewhere in transit between here and Perth, but I brought a few snaps with me that you might like to see.'

They were pictures of Antonia laughing, beautiful and lissom with flowing blonde hair and a stunning smile.

'What about you, Alyse?' Aleksi asked quietly. 'Were all the snaps taken only of Antonia?'

'No. No, of course not,' she answered quickly. 'There didn't seem much point in bringing the others with me.'

His gaze was startlingly direct. 'Why not?' Humour tugged the edges of his mouth. 'I would have enjoyed seeing you as a child.'

'Perhaps I should insist that you drag out shots depicting your pubescent youth,' Alyse said sweetly, and heard Alexandros's deep laugh.

'He was all bones, so tall, and very intense. An exceptional student.'

'Yes, I'm sure he was,' Alyse agreed with a faint smile.

'At nineteen he filled out,' Rachel informed her, shooting Aleksi a faintly wicked grin, 'developing splendid muscles, a deep voice, and a certain attraction for the opposite sex. Girls utilised every excuse under the sun to practise their own blossoming feminine wiles on him.'

'With great success, I'm sure,' Alyse remarked drily, and heard his husky laugh.

'I managed to keep one step ahead of each of them.'

'Shattering dreams and breaking hearts, no doubt?' The words were lightly voiced and faintly bantering, but his eyes stilled for a second, then assumed a brooding mockery.

'What about your dreams, Alyse?' he countered, silently forcing her to hold his gaze.

She swallowed the lump that had somehow risen in her throat, aware that their amusing conversational gambit had undergone a subtle change. 'I was no different from other teenage girls,' she said quietly. 'Except that my vision was centred on a successful career.'

'In which young men didn't feature at all?'

How could she say that Antonia was a carefree spirit who unwittingly attracted men without the slightest effort, while Alyse was merely the older sister, a shadowy blueprint content to shoulder responsibility? Yet there had never been any feelings of resentment or jealousy, simply an acceptance of individual personalities.

'I enjoyed a social life,' she defended. 'Tennis, squash, sailing at weekends, and there was the cinema, theatre, dancing.' Her chin lifted fractionally as she summoned a brilliant smile. 'Now I have a wealthy husband who owns a beautiful home, and an adored adopted son.' Her eyes glittered, sheer sapphire. 'Most women would rate that as being the culmination of all their dreams.'

Aleksi's soft laugh was almost her undoing, and it was only his parents' presence that prevented her from launching into a lashing castigation.

'Shall I make afternoon tea?' It was amazing that her voice sounded so calm, and she deliberately schooled her expression into a polite mask as she rose to her feet.

In the kitchen she filled the percolator with water, selected a fresh filter, spooned in ground coffee and set it on the element. Her hands seemed to move of their own accord, opening cupboards, setting cups on to saucers, extracting sugar, milk and cream, then setting a cake she'd made that morning on to a plate ready to take into the lounge.

When the coffee was ready, she put everything on to a mobile trolley and wheeled it into the lounge, dispensing everything with an outward serenity that would, had she been an actress, have earned plaudits from her peers.

Conversation, as if by tacit agreement, touched on a variety of subjects but centred on none, and it was almost four o'clock when Aleksi rose to his feet with the expressed intention of driving Rachel and Alexandros into town.

'I'm looking forward to this evening, my dear,' Rachel declared as she slid into the rear seat of the car, and Alyse gave her a smile that was genuinely warm.

'So am I,' she assured her, then stood back as Aleksi reversed the BMW down the driveway.

Indoors, she quickly restored the lounge to order and then dispensed cups and saucers into the dishwasher before crossing to the bedroom for a quick shower. Georg would wake in an hour, and she'd prefer to settle him down for the night rather than leave him to the baby-sitter.

Selecting something suitable to wear was relatively simple, and she chose an elegant two-piece suit in brilliant red silk, opted against wearing a blouse, and decided on high-heeled black suede shoes and matching clutch-purse. Make-up was understated, with skilful attention to her eyes, then she blowdried her hair and slipped on a silk robe, confident that within five minutes of settling Georg she could be ready.

The sound of the front door closing alerted her attention, and seconds later Aleksi entered the room.

'The babysitter will be here at six,' he told her as he shed his jacket and tossed it on to the bed. 'We'll collect my parents at six-thirty, and our table is booked for an hour later.'

Alyse merely nodded as his fingers slid to the buttons on his shirt, and he paused, his eyes narrowing on her averted gaze.

'Is there some problem with that?'

'None at all,' she said stiffly.

'Don't indulge in a fit of the sulks,' Aleksi cautioned, and she rounded on him at once with all the pent-up fury she'd harboured over the past hour.

'I am not sulking!' she snapped angrily. 'I just don't care to be figuratively dissected, piece by piece, in the presence of your parents, simply as a means of amusement!'

One eyebrow arched, and his mouth assumed its customary cynicism. 'What, precisely, are you referring to?'

'I didn't sit at home while Antonia went out and had all the fun,' she told him, holding his gaze without any difficulty at all.

'But you assumed responsibility for her welfare, did you not?' Aleksi queried with deceptive mildness. 'And, as the eldest, shouldered burdens which had your parents been alive would have given you more freedom?'

'If you're suggesting I assumed the role of surrogate parent, you couldn't be more wrong!'

He stood regarding her in silence for what seemed an age. 'Then tell me what you did out of work hours, aside from keep house?'

Her eyes became stormy. 'I don't owe you any explanations.'

'Then why become defensive when I suggested you took the elder sister role so seriously?'

'Because you implied a denial of any social existence, which isn't true.'

'So you went out on dates, enjoyed the company of men?'

The desire to shock was paramount. 'Yes,' she said shortly, knowing it to be an extension of the truth. Her chin tilted slightly, and her eyes assumed a dangerous sparkle. 'What comes next, Aleksi? Do we each conduct a head-count of previous sexual partners?'

'Have there been so many?'

'I don't consider it bears any relevance to our relationship,' she said steadily, and saw his eyes narrow.

'Do you doubt my ability to please you?'

The conversation had shifted on to dangerous ground, and Alyse felt her stomach nerves tighten at the thought of that strong body bent over her own in pursuit of sexual pleasure.

'Are you suggesting we indulge in sex simply for the sake of it in a mutual claim for conjugal rights?'

His eyes gleamed with sardonic humour. 'My dear Alyse, do you perceive sex merely as a duty?' He lifted a hand and cupped her jaw, letting his thumb brush her cheek. 'Either your experience is limited or your lovers have been selfishly insensitive.'

It was impossible to still the faint rush of colour to her cheeks, and her eyes silently warred with his as she sought to control her temper.

Slowly he lowered his head, and she stood in mesmerised fascination as his lips caressed her temple, then slid down to trace the outline of her mouth in a gentle exploration that was incredibly evocative.

A faint quiver of apprehension ran through her body, and her mouth trembled as his tongue probed its soft contours, then slid between her lips to wreak sweet havoc with the sensitised tissues.

It would be so easy to melt into his arms and deepen the kiss. For a few timeless seconds Alyse ignored the spasms of alarm racing to her brain in warning of the only possible conclusion such an action would have.

A soft hiccuping cry emerged from the adjoining sitting-room, and within seconds Georg was in full swing, demanding sustenance in no uncertain terms.

'Pity,' murmured Aleksi as he released her, and her eyes widened, then clouded with sudden realisation as she turned quickly away from him.

Crossing into the sitting-room, she picked Georg up from his cot and changed him, then made her way to the kitchen where she heated his bottle and fed him.

He sucked hungrily, and she slowed him down, talking gently as she always did, sure that he was able to understand simply by the tone of her voice that he was very much loved. He seemed to grow with each passing day, and her heart filled with pride as she leant forward to brush her lips against his tiny forehead.

He was worth everything, *anything* she had to endure as Aleksi Stefanos's wife. A truly beautiful child who deserved to be cherished, she decided wistfully as she settled him almost an hour later.

Swiftly discarding her robe, she quickly donned the silk evening suit and slipped her feet into the elegant high-heeled suede shoes. A brisk brush brought her hair into smooth order, and she sprayed a generous quantity of her favourite perfume to several pulsebeats before standing back to survey the result in the full-length mirror.

Muted chimes sounded through the intercom, and Aleksi emerged from his dressing-room.

'That will be Melanie. She's a dedicated law student, the eldest of five, and extremely capable. I'll let her in.'

The breath caught in Alyse's throat at the sight of him, and she rapidly schooled her expression as she took in his immaculate dark suit, thin-striped shirt and impeccably knotted tie.

Any feelings of unease at leaving Georg with a total stranger were dispelled within minutes of meeting the girl Aleksi introduced as the daughter of one of his associates.

'I've written down the phone number of the restaurant,' he told her, handing over a slip of paper. 'And the apartment, in case we stop for coffee when we drop off my parents. We'll be home around midnight. If it's going to be any later, I'll ring.'

'Georg is already asleep,' Alyse added. 'I doubt if he'll wake, but if he does it's probably because he needs changing. If he won't settle, give him a bottle. He's just started sleeping through the night, except for the occasional evening. If you'll come with me, I'll show you where everything is.'

Fifteen minutes later she was seated in the luxurious BMW as it purred along the ocean-front road that led into the heart of Surfers Paradise.

'Where are we dining?' she asked.

'The Sheraton-Mirage; it's located on the Spit.'

'Where anyone important is *seen*, no doubt.' She hadn't meant to sound cynical, and she suffered his swift analytical glance as a consequence.

'Rachel fell in love with the resort complex when she

and my father were here last year. It's at her request that we're dining there tonight.'

She should apologise, she knew, but the words refused to emerge, and she sat in silence until the car pulled to a halt at the entrance to a prestigious multi-storey apartment block overlooking the ocean.

At attendant slid in behind the wheel as Alyse followed Aleksi into the elegant foyer, and seconds later a lift transported them swiftly to an upper floor.

The apartment was much larger than she had expected, with magnificent views through floor-to-ceiling plate glass of the north and southern coastline. Pinpricks of light sparkled from a multitude of high-rise towers lining the coastal tourist strip, and beneath the velvet evening skyline the scene resembled a magical fairy-land that stretched as far as the eye could see.

'You look stunning, my dear,' Rachel complimented Alyse quietly.

'Yes, doesn't she?'

Alyse heard Aleksi's faintly mocking drawl, and opted to ignore it. 'Thank you.'

'Would you prefer to have a drink here, or wait until we're at the complex?'

'The complex, I think,' Rachel concurred. 'I'm sure Alyse will be as enchanted with it as I am.'

A correct deduction, Alyse decided on entering the wide lobby with its deep-piled blue carpets, cream marble tiles and exotic antiques. The central waterfall was spectacular, as was the tiled lagoon with its island bar.

'We must come out during the day,' Rachel declared with a smile. 'The marina shopping complex directly across the road is delightful. We could explore it together, and share a coffee and chat.'

'My wife adores to shop,' Alexandros informed Alyse with a deep drawl not unlike that of his son.

They took a seat in the lounge-bar and Alyse declined anything alcoholic, aware of Aleksi's faintly hooded appraisal as she voiced her preference for an order identical to his stepmother's request for mineral water spiked with fresh orange juice.

'My dear, don't feel you must abstain simply because I choose to do so.'

'I don't drink,' she revealed quietly. 'Except for champagne on special occasions.'

'Dom Perignon?' queried Rachel with hopeful conspiracy, and Alyse smiled in silent acquiescence.

'In that case, we'll indulge you both at dinner,' said Aleksi, giving the waiter their order, then he sat well back in his chair, looking infinitely relaxed and at ease.

Alyse would have given anything to be rid of the nervous tension that steadily created painful cramps in her stomach. It was madness to feel so intensely vulnerable; insane, to be so frighteningly aware of the man seated within touching distance.

The image of his kiss, so warm and infinitely evocative, rose up to taunt her, and she had to summon all her reserves of willpower to present a smiling, seemingly relaxed façade.

No matter what private aspirations Rachel and Alexandros held for their son's marriage, it was apparent that the union afforded them tremendous pleasure. Equally obvious was an approval of their daughter-in-law, and Alyse experienced a feeling of deep regret— not only for Antonia's loss, but for her own. If she could have selected ideal parents-in-law, it would be difficult to choose a nicer couple than Aleksi's father and stepmother.

Such introspection was dangerous, and it was a relief when they entered the restaurant and were shown to their table.

CHAPTER SEVEN

THE SETTING WAS superb, the food a gourmet's delight, presented with flair and artistry. Except that Alyse's appetite seemed to be non-existent as she selected cream of mushroom soup, then followed it with crumbed prawn cutlets.

After sipping half a flute of champagne she felt more at ease, but she was supremely conscious of Aleksi's solicitous attention, the accidental brush of his fingers against her own, and the acute sensation that he was instigating a deliberate seduction.

Consequently it was a relief when Alexandros asked if she'd care to join him on the dance floor.

Alyse spared Rachel an enquiring smile. 'Do you mind?'

'Of course not, my dear.' Rachel's features assumed a faintly mischievous expression. 'Aleksi and I will join you.'

Alexandros, as Aleksi's father insisted she call him, was every bit as commanding as his indomitable son, Alyse decided as she rose graciously from the table and allowed him to lead her on to the restaurant's small dance floor. There was the same vital, almost electric energy apparent, an awareness of male sensuality that had little to do with chronological age. Alexandros Stefanos was charming: polite, deferential, and genuine. The sort of man a woman could entrust with her life.

'You're light on your feet, like a feather,' he complimented her. 'So graceful.'

'You're an accomplished partner,' she returned with a faint smile.

'And you're very kind.'

Am I? she thought silently. I'm not at all kindly disposed towards your son. Out loud, she said, 'I hope you and Rachel are enjoying your holiday.'

'My dear, how can I explain the joy among the grief in discovering that Georgiou had fathered a son? He's very much loved, that child, his existence so precious to us all.'

Alyse couldn't think of a single thing to say, and she circled the floor in silence, hardly aware of the music or their fellow dancers on the floor.

'Shall we change partners?' a deep voice drawled from close by, and she missed her step, distinctly ill at ease that she was about to be relinquished into the waiting arms of her husband.

Aleksi's hold was far from conventional, and she wanted to scream with vexation.

'Must you?' she hissed, totally enraged at the proprietorial possessiveness of his grasp. She was all too aware of a subjugation so infinite, it was impossible not to feel afraid.

'Dance with my wife?'

His resort to mockery was deliberate, and momentarily defeated in the knowledge that self-assertion would only cause a scene, Alyse tilted her head and gave him a brilliant smile.

'This is *dancing*, Aleksi? You can't begin to know how much I'd like to slap your face!'

One eyebrow slanted in cynical amusement. 'Good heavens, whatever will you do when we make love? Kill me?'

'I'll have a darned good try!'

His eyes darkened with ill-concealed humour. 'Yes, I do believe you will.'

There was no doubt he'd enjoy the fight, and its aftermath, while instinctive self-preservation warned that if she dared submit she would never be the same again.

The music playing was one of those incredibly poignant songs that stirred at the heartstrings, with lyrics of such depth that just hearing them almost brought tears to her eyes.

You're mad, she told herself shakily. You hate him, remember? The strain of the past few days; meeting Georg's grandparents. It was all too much.

A slight shiver feathered its way across the surface of her skin. Any kind of emotional involvement was a luxury she couldn't afford if she were to instigate a divorce and return to Perth with Georg.

'I'd like to go back to our table.' The words came out as a slightly desperate plea, and she strained away from him in her anxiety to escape the intimacy of his hold.

'The band will take a break soon. Besides, my parents are still dancing. We should return together, don't you think?' His voice sounded mild close to her ear, and she felt his breath stir at her temple, teasing a few tendrils of hair.

'I have the beginnings of a headache,' she improvised, and felt immeasurably relieved as he led her to the edge of the dance floor, his gaze sharp and far too discerning for her peace of mind.

'Fact, or fiction?'

Her eyes blazed a brilliant blue. 'Does it really matter?' Angry beyond belief, she turned and moved quickly away from him.

On reaching the brightly lit powder-room she crossed to an empty space in front of the long mirror and pretended interest in her features.

She was far too pale, she decided in analytical appraisal, and her eyes bore a vaguely haunted look, reflecting an inner tension that was akin to a vulnerable animal confronted by a hunting predator.

A tiny bubble of derisive laughter rose and died in her throat at her illogical parallel. Dear lord, she'd have to get a hold on herself. Imaginative flights of fancy were of no help whatsoever in her resolve against Aleksi Stefanos.

The invention of a headache wasn't entirely an untruth, for a persistent niggle began to manifest itself behind one eye, and she attributed its cause directly to her husband.

Aware that her escape could only be a temporary respite, she resolutely withdrew a lipstick from her evening purse and tidied her hair to its smooth bell-like style before returning to their table.

'My dear, are you all right?' Rachel asked the moment Alyse was seated, and she countered the force of three pairs of apparently concerned eyes with a reassuring smile.

'Yes, thank you.'

'You're very pale. Are you sure?'

Obviously she wasn't succeeding very well in the

acting stakes! 'Georg still wakes through the night,' she explained lightly, 'and is often difficult to settle.'

'Georgiou was the same at a similar age—an angel by day, yet restless at night.' Rachel offered a conciliatory smile. 'It will soon pass.'

'Meanwhile it's proving quite disruptive to our sleep,' drawled Aleksi, shooting Alyse a particularly intimate glance.

Damn him, had he no shame? she fumed, forced into silence out of deference to his parents' presence.

'Tell me about the party you've both planned,' Rachel began, in what Alyse decided was a sympathetic attempt to change the subject.

'A delayed wedding reception,' Aleksi elaborated with bland disregard for her barely contained surprise. 'Providing an opportunity for family and friends to share the celebration of our marriage.'

Alyse felt her stomach execute a few painful somersaults. How dared he propose something so ludicrous? It was only compounding a mockery, and she wanted no part in it.

'What a wonderful idea!' his stepmother enthused, while Alyse sought to dampen an increasing sense of anger for what remained of the evening.

In the car she sat tensely on edge as Aleksi brought the luxurious vehicle to a smooth halt in the wide bricked apron at the entrance to the tall apartment block.

'Will you join us for coffee?' asked Rachel, and Alyse held her breath as Aleksi issued a reluctant refusal.

'It's quite late, and we're both anxious to get home.' His smile appeared genuinely warm. 'The babysitter is extremely capable, but it's the first time we've left Georg in her care.'

That was true enough, although it was unlikely that there had been any problems, and Alyse managed to smile as they bade each other goodnight, issuing a spontaneous invitation for the older woman to join her the next day.

However, the instant the car cleared the driveway Alyse burst into angry pent-up speech.

'You are impossible!'

'Why, specifically?' Aleksi countered cynically, and she was so incensed that if he hadn't been driving she would have hit him.

Spreading one hand, she ticked off each consecutive grudge. 'Deliberately implying that we share the same bed. And when you announced a party, I hardly imagined you'd expect me to give a repeat performance as a blushing bride.'

'My dear Alyse, do you still blush?'

She cast him a furious glare. 'I used the term in a purely figurative sense.'

'Of course.'

'Oh, don't be so damned *patronising*!'

'If you want to fight, at least wait until we reach home,' he cautioned cynically, and, momentarily defeated, Alyse turned her attention to the passing scenery beyond the windscreen.

The sky was an inky black as it merged with the shallow waters of the inner harbour, providing a startling background for brightly lit venues along the famed tourist strip. Outlines were crisp and sharp, and a pinprick sprinkling of stars lent promise of another day of sunshine in a sub-tropical winterless climate.

Aleksi chose the waterfront road, and Alyse wondered darkly if he was deliberately giving her temper an opportunity to cool.

Georg hadn't even murmured, Melanie reported, accepting the notes Aleksi placed in her hand before departing with a friendly smile.

'I'll check Georg,' said Alyse hastily.

'An excuse to escape, Alyse?'

'No, damn you!'

His eyes gleamed with latent mockery. 'I'll make coffee. Liqueur and cream?'

Resentment flared as she turned to face him. 'I'm going to bed—I've done my duty for the evening. Goodnight.'

There was a palpable pause. 'You consider an evening spent with Rachel and my father a duty?'

Alyse closed her eyes, then opened them again. 'They're both utterly charming. Their son, however, is not.'

'Indeed?' His voice sounded like velvet-encased steel. 'Perhaps you would care to clarify that?'

'You act as if I'm your wife!'

One eyebrow rose in cynical query. 'My dear Alyse, I have in my possession a marriage certificate stating clearly that you are.'

'You know very well what I mean!'

'Does it bother you that I accord you a measure of husbandly affection?'

'Courteous attention I can accept,' she acknowledged angrily. 'But intimate contact is totally unnecessary.'

His smile was peculiarly lacking in humour. 'I haven't even begun with intimacy.'

Her hand flew in an upward arc, only to be caught in a bonecrushing grip that left her gasping with pain.

'So eager to hit out, Alyse? Aren't you in the least concerned what form of punishment I might care to mete out?' he asked deliberately, pulling her inextricably close.

'Do you specialise in wife-beating, Aleksi?' she countered in defiance, and suffered momentary qualms at the anger beneath the surface of his control.

'I prefer something infinitely more subtle,' he drawled, and she retaliated without thought.

'I hardly dare ask!'

'Sheer bravado, or naïveté?'

'Oh, *both*,' she acknowledged, then gave a startled gasp as he slid an arm beneath her knees and lifted her into his arms. 'What do you think you're doing?'

The look he cast her cut right through to her soul. 'Taking you to bed. Mine,' he elaborated with icy intent.

Her eyes dilated with shock. 'Don't! Please,' she added as a genuine plea to his sensitivity, rather than as an afterthought.

'You sound almost afraid,' he derided silkily.

Afraid I'll never be the same again, Alyse qualified silently, hating the exigent sexual chemistry that drew her towards him like a moth to flame.

'I hate you!' she flung desperately as he carried her through the lounge, and she was absolutely incensed at the speculative amusement apparent in the depths of his eyes.

In the bedroom he let her slide to her feet, and she was powerless to do anything other than stand perfectly still beneath his dark penetrating gaze.

'You react like an agitated kitten, all bristling fur and

unsheathed claws.' His smile was infinitely sensual, his eyes dark and slumbrous as he took her chin between thumb and forefinger to tilt it unmercifully high. 'It will be worth the scratches you'll undoubtedly inflict, just to hear you purr.'

'Egotist,' she accorded shakily. 'What makes you think I will?'

He didn't deign to answer, and there was nothing she could do to avoid his mouth as it took possession of hers in a deliberately sensual onslaught that plundered the very depths of her soul.

With shocking ease he dispensed with her clothes, then his own, and she gave an agonised gasp as he reached for the thin scrap of lace-edged satin covering her breasts.

'Aleksi—'

'Don't?' he taunted softly, releasing the clasp and letting the bra fall to the carpet.

It was impossible to come to terms with a mixture of elation and fear, so she didn't even try, aware even as she voiced the protest that there could be no turning back. 'You can't mean to do this,' she said in agonised despair.

His hands cupped the creamy fullness of her breasts with tactile expertise, and the breath locked in her throat when his head descended and his mouth closed over one vulnerable peak. Sensation spiralled from the central core of her being, radiating through her body until she was consumed by an emotion so fiery, so damnably erotic, that it was all she could do not to beg him to assuage the hunger within.

His tasting took on a new dimension as he began to

suckle, using his teeth with such infinite delicacy that it frequently trod a fine edge between pleasure and pain.

Just when she thought she could bear it no more, he relinquished his possession and crossed to render a similar onslaught to its twin.

Unbidden, her fingers sought the thickness of his hair, raking its well-groomed length in barely controlled agitation that didn't cease when he shifted his attention to her mouth and began subjecting that sensitive cavern to a seeking exploration that gradually became an imitation of the sexual act itself.

Alyse was floating high on a cloud of sensuality so evocative that it was all she could do not to beg him to ease the ache that centred between her thighs, and, as if he was aware of her need, his hand slid down to gently probe the sweet moistness dewing there.

Like a finely tuned instrument her body leapt in response, and she became mindless, an insignificant craft caught in a swirling vortex beyond which she had no control.

It wasn't until she felt the soft mattress beneath her back that realisation forced its way through the mists of desire, and she could only stare, her eyes wide with slumbrous warmth, as Aleksi discarded his shirt, then his trousers and finally the dark hipster briefs that shielded his masculinity.

There was a potent beauty in his lean well-muscled frame, a virility that sent the blood coursing through her veins in fearful anticipation, and she unconsciously raised her gaze to his, silently pleading as he joined her on the bed.

Her lips parted tremulously as his eyes conducted a lingering appraisal of their softly swollen contours, before slipping down to the rose-tipped breasts that burgeoned beneath his gaze as if in silent recognition of his touch.

Her limbs seemed consumed by languorous inertia, and she made no protest as he began a light, trailing exploration of her waist, the soft indentation of her navel, then moved to the pale hair curling softly between her thighs.

A sharp intake of breath changed to shocked disbelief as his lips followed the path of his hand in a brazen degree of intimacy she found impossible to condone.

Liquid fire coursed through her body, arousing each separate sensory nerve-end until she moaned an entreaty for him to desist. Except that nothing she said made any difference, and in a desperate attempt to put an end to the havoc he was creating she sank her fingers into his hair and tugged—*hard*.

It had not the slightest effect, and her limbs threshed in violent rejection until he caught hold of her hands and pinned them to her sides, effectively using his elbows to still the wild movements of her legs.

For what seemed an age she lay helpless beneath his deliberate invasion, hating him with a fervour that was totally unmatched, until, shifting his body weight, he effected a deep penetrating thrust that brought an involuntary gasp from her lips as delicate tissues stretched, then filled with stinging pain.

She was so caught up with it she didn't register the brief explicit curse that husked from Aleksi's throat, and she tossed her head from side to side to escape his mouth before it settled over hers, gentle, coaxing, and inflexibly possessive as she strove to free herself.

Without thought she balled her hands into fists and

hit out at him, striking anywhere she could, then she became impossibly angry when it had no effect whatsoever.

The only weapons she had left were her teeth and her nails, and she used both, shamelessly biting his tongue, at the same time raking her nails down his ribcage, achieving some satisfaction from his harsh intake of breath.

'Witch,' he growled, lifting his mouth fractionally, and she cried out in agonised rejection.

'*Bastard!* I hate you, *hate* you, do you understand?'

His hands caught hers in a punishing grip and held them immobile above her head, and she began to struggle in earnest, fear lending her unknown strength as she fought to be free of him.

'Stop it, little fool,' he chastised, holding her with ease. 'You're only making it worse for yourself.'

Angry dark blue eyes speared his as she vented furiously, 'Get away from me, damn you!'

'Not yet.'

'Haven't you done enough?' It was a tortured accusation dredged up from the depths of her soul, and yet it failed to have the desired effect. 'Aleksi!' She would have begged if she had to, and it didn't help that he knew.

'Be still, little wildcat,' he soothed, easily holding both her hands with one of his as he gently pushed stray tendrils of hair back behind her ear. Then his mouth brushed her temple, pressed each eyelid closed in turn, before trailing down to the edge of her lips. With a touch as light as a butterfly's wing he teased their curved outline before slipping to the hollow at the base of her neck.

'Please don't.'

'What a contrary plea!' he murmured against her

throat, and she could sense the smile in his voice. 'Just relax, and trust me.'

'Why should I?' she cried in an impassioned entreaty, only wanting to be free of him.

'The hurting is over, I promise.'

'Then why won't you leave me alone?' Her eyes seared his, then became trapped beneath the latent sensuality, the sheer animal magnetism he exuded, and almost in primeval recognition an answering chord struck deep within, quivering into hesitant life.

'This is why,' husked Aleksi, covering her mouth gently with his own as he began to move, slowly at first, creating a throbbing ache that swelled until she became caught up in the deep rhythmic pattern of his possession.

Impossibly sensuous, he played her with the skilled mastery of a virtuoso, bringing forth without any difficulty at all the soft startled cries of her pleasure, and the hands that had raked his flesh now cajoled in silent supplication as she accepted everything he chose to give.

The climax, when it came, was unexpected and tumultuous, an entire gamut of emotions so exquisite it defied description in that first initial experience, and afterwards she was too spent to attempt an accurate analysis.

With a return to normality came a degree of self-loathing, and the re-emergence of hatred for the man who had instigated her emotional catalyst. She became aware of her own body, the soft bruising inside and out, and the increasing need to escape, albeit temporarily, from the large bed and the indomitable man who occupied it.

'Where do you think you're going?'

It was difficult to stand naked before his gaze, although innate dignity lifted her head to a proud angle as she turned at the sound of that quiet drawling voice.

'To have a bath,' she responded evenly, and saw his eyes narrow fractionally before she moved towards the en suite bathroom.

Once inside, she closed the door, then pressed the plug into position in the large spa-bath and released water from the taps.

Within minutes steam clouded the room, and she added plenty of bath-oil to the cascading water before stepping into its warm depth.

Aleksi walked into the room as Alyse was about to reach for a sponge, and she was so incensed at his intrusion she threw the sponge without thought, watching as it connected with his chest.

His soft husky laughter as he calmly stepped into the bath to sit facing her was the last straw, and she flew at him in a rage, flailing her fists against his shoulders, his arms, anywhere she could connect, until he caught hold of her wrists with a steel-like grip.

'Enough, Alyse.' His voice was hard and inflexible, and she looked at him with stormy eyes, ready to do further battle given the slightest opportunity.

'Can't you see I want to be alone?' It was a cry from the heart, and to her horror she felt her lower lip tremble with damnable reaction. She was physically and emotionally spent, and there was the very real threat of tears as she determined not to let him see the extent of her fragility.

Eyes that were dark and impossibly slumbrous held her own captive in mesmerised fascination, and helpless frustration welled up inside her as her chin tilted at an angry angle. 'Must you look at me like that?'

'We just made love,' he drawled with latent humour. 'How would you have me look at you?'

'I hated it!' Alyse flung incautiously.

One eyebrow rose with sardonic cynicism. 'You hated the fact that it was *I* who awakened you to the power of your own sensuality.' His lips moved to form a twisted smile. 'And you hate yourself for achieving sexual pleasure with someone you profess to dislike.'

The truth of his words was something she refused to concede. 'You behaved like a barbaric—*animal*!'

'Who took his own pleasure without any concern for yours?' he demanded with undisguised mockery.

Colour stained her cheeks, and her lashes fluttered down to form a protective veil against his discerning scrutiny. 'I'll never forgive you,' she declared with quiet vehemence. *'Never.'*

'Spoken like an innocent,' Aleksi declared with sardonic amusement, and her eyes flew open to reveal shards of brilliant sapphire.

'Not any more, thanks to you!'

Lifting a hand, he brushed his fingers along the edge of her jaw. 'I'm almost inclined to query why.'

Alyse reared back from that light teasing touch as if it was flame, wanting to scream and rage against his deliberate seduction, the sheer force of his sensual expertise. Except she was damned if she'd give him the satisfaction. Instead, she said bitterly, 'I would have preferred a less brutal initiation.'

'Yet after the pain came pleasure, did it not?'

Her eyes glittered in angry rejection. 'Never having experienced anything to compare it with, I can't comment.'

His soft husky laughter was almost her undoing, and she stood to her feet, reached for a towel, then stepped quickly out of the bath, uncaring that he followed her actions.

It was then she saw the long scratches scoring his ribcage, and she turned away, feeling sickened that she could have inflicted such physical injury.

In the bedroom she collected her nightgown and donned it, then turned hesitantly as Aleksi entered the room.

'You'll sleep here with me, Alyse. And don't argue,' he added with quiet emphasis as her lips parted to form a protest.

Before she had the opportunity to move more than a few steps towards the sitting-room he had reached her side, and her struggles were ineffectual as he calmly lifted her into his arms and carried her to the large bed.

'I don't want to sleep with you,' she said fiercely, pushing against him as he slid in between the covers.

'Maybe not,' he drawled, settling her easily into the curve of his body. 'But I insist you do.'

'You damned dictatorial tyrant!'

'My dear Alyse, I can think of a far more pleasurable way to deploy your energy than by merely wasting it in fighting me.'

She froze at his unmistakable implication. 'I won't be used and abused whenever you—'

'Feel the urge?' he completed sardonically. 'I have a twelve-hour day ahead of me, and right now all I have in mind is a few hours' sleep. Unless you have other ideas, which I'll gladly oblige, I suggest you simply relax.'

'Oh, go to hell!' she was stung into retorting as he reached out and switched off the bedside lamp.

Seconds later Alyse was aware of his warm breath against her temple, and she lay perfectly still, willing the nervous tautness in her body to ease, then slowly her eyelids flickered down as sheer exhaustion gradually took its toll and sleep provided blissful oblivion.

CHAPTER EIGHT

THE ENSUING FEW days provided an opportunity for Alyse to become better acquainted with Rachel, for each morning Aleksi's stepmother arrived in time to help with Georg's bath, then they would each take it in turns to feed him his bottle before settling him back into his cot.

There was time for a leisurely morning tea and a chat before eating a light midday lunch, after which Georg was fed, resettled, and placed into Melanie's care for the afternoon while they explored one of the many shopping complexes scattered along the Gold Coast's tourist strip.

Alexandros joined his son in a daily round of building site inspections, meetings and consultations, from which they returned together each evening.

Dinner was inevitably an informal meal, with both women sharing the preparation, and Alyse felt faintly envious of the friendship Aleksi shared with his parents. It was genuine and uncontrived, and while part of her enjoyed sharing their company, another constantly warned against forming too close an attachment for two people who, after her intended separation and divorce from Aleksi, would no longer find it possible to regard her with any affection. Somehow such a thought caused her immeasurable pain.

The nights were something else, for in Aleksi's arms she became increasingly uninhibited, to such an extent that she began to hate her own traitorous body almost as much as she assured herself that she hated *him*.

Arrangements for the party Aleksi insisted they host to celebrate their marriage proved remarkably simple, with a series of telephone calls to a variety of guests, and the hiring of a reputable catering firm.

All that remained for Alyse to do was to arrange for Melanie to babysit, and select something suitable to wear.

While the former was remarkably simple, choosing a dress took considerable time and care, although Rachel's wholehearted approval proved invaluable, and the silk and lace ensemble in deep cream highlighted the texture of her skin and the brilliant sapphire-blue of her eyes. The bodice was demure with elbow-length sleeves, with a fitted waist that accentuated her small waist, and the skirt fell in graceful folds to a fashionable length.

The guests were due to begin arriving at eight, and Alyse settled Georg upstairs just after six, then she hastily showered, taking extreme care with her hair and make-up.

Nerves were hell and damnation, she decided silently, cursing softly at the unsteadiness of her hand, and she cleansed her eyelids and started all over again.

She wished fervently that the evening were over and done with. Aleksi's friends would be super-critical of his new wife, and she had little doubt she would be dissected piece by piece from the top of her head to the tips of her elegant designer shoes.

An hour later she stood back from the mirror and viewed her overall appearance with a tiny frown.

'Problems?'

She turned at once at the sound of that deep drawling voice, noting that Aleksi displayed an inherent sophistication attired in a dark suit, white shirt and sombre tie, and she envied him the air of relaxed calm he was able to exude without any seeming effort at all.

Her eyes clouded with anxiety. 'What do you think?'

He took his time answering, and she suffered his slow appraisal with increasing apprehension.

'Beautiful,' he told her, lifting a hand to tilt her chin fractionally. His smile held a mesmerising quality, and she ran the tip of her tongue along the edge of her lower lip in a gesture of nervousness. 'I'm almost sorry I have to share you with a room full of people.' His eyes gleamed darkly. 'An intimate evening *à deux* would be more appropriate.'

Her lashes swept up in a deliberate attempt at guile. 'And waste this dress? It cost a fortune.'

His mouth curved with humour. 'I'm impressed, believe me.' Releasing her chin, he caught hold of her hand. 'Melanie is already upstairs with Georg and an enviable collection of law books. Rachel and Alexandros have arrived. The caterers have everything under control, and there's time for a quiet drink before the first of our guests are due to arrive.'

Alyse wondered if it was too late to opt out, and some of her indecision must have been apparent in her expression, for he bent forward and brushed his lips against her temple.

'It's no big deal, Alyse. In any case, I'll be here.'

'Maybe that's what I'm afraid of,' she said with

undue solemnity, and saw his smile widen with sardonic cynicism.

'Ah, this is the Alyse I know best.'

Suddenly flip, she responded, 'I wasn't aware there was more than one of me.'

His husky laughter brought a soft tinge of colour to her cheeks, and she made no demure as he led the way out into the lounge.

Everything appeared superb, Alyse decided a few hours later as she drifted politely from one group of guests to another. Background music filtered through a sophisticated electronic system, and hired staff circulated among the guests with professional ease, proffering trays of tastefully prepared morsels of food. Champagne flowed from a seemingly inexhaustible supply, and she had been introduced to so many people it was impossible to remember more than a few of their names. Beautiful, elegantly attired women, who seemed discreetly intent on discovering the latest in social gossip, while the man stood in segregated groups talking business—primarily their own as related to the state of the country's current economy.

'Darling, you really *must* come along,' a gorgeous blonde insisted, and Alyse brought her attention back to the small group of women who had commandeered her attention. 'It's a worthwhile charity. The models are superb and the clothes will be absolutely stunning.' Perfect white teeth gleamed between equally perfectly painted red lips, and the smile portrayed practised sincerity. 'Annabel will be there, Chrissie, Kate, and Marta. You'll sit with us, of course.'

'Can I let you know?' Alyse managed politely, and saw the ice-blue eyes narrow fractionally.

'Of course. Aleksi has my number.'

Within seconds she was alone again, but not for long.

'Do you need rescuing?'

A warm smile curved the edges of her mouth at the welcome intrusion of her mother-in-law. 'How did you guess?'

'Everything is going beautifully, my dear,' Rachel complimented. 'You're doing very well,' she added gently, and Alyse sobered slightly, although her smile didn't falter for a second.

'I'm the cynosure of all eyes. Circumspectly assessed, analysed, and neatly categorised—rather like a prize piece of merchandise. Will I pass muster, do you think?'

'With flying colours,' Rachel told her, and Alyse could have genuinely hugged her.

'Ah, an ally,' she breathed gratefully. 'It seems I should join numerous committees, play the requisite twice weekly game of tennis, frequent daily aerobic workouts, attend weekly classes in exotic flower arrangement, and become part of a circle who gather for social luncheons.' A wicked gleam lit her expressive eyes. 'What hours left free in the day are advisably spent visiting a beauty salon, shopping, or, importantly, organising the next luncheon, dinner party, or simply the informal get-together for Sunday brunch.'

'You don't aspire to joining the society treadmill?'

'Not to any great extent.' Her shoulders lifted slightly in an elegant shrug. 'A few luncheons might be fun. A stunning blonde whose name escapes me issued an invitation to a fashion parade held at Sanctuary Cove on Tuesday. Perhaps we could go together?'

'Lovely,' the older woman enthused. 'It will give

Alexandros an opportunity to spend a day on the golf course.'

Alyse let her gaze wander round the large room, noting idly that the various guests gave every appearance of enjoying themselves. Although who wouldn't, she thought wryly, when provided with fine food and wine, and glittering company? The women dripped diamonds, and several wore mink, elegantly styled jackets slung with apparent carelessness over slim designer-clad shoulders.

'Do you know many of the people here?' she queried tentatively.

'Most of the men are business associates, with their various wives or girlfriends,' Rachel revealed with a sympathetic smile. 'The glamorous blonde who last engaged you in conversation is Serita Hubbard—her husband is a very successful property speculator. The brunette talking to Serita is Kate, the daughter of one of Aleksi's best friends—that's Paul, her father, deep in conversation with Aleksi and Alexandros.' Rachel paused, tactfully drawing Alyse's attention to a stunning couple on the far side of the room. 'Dominic Rochas, and his sister Solange. Together they represent a highly reputable firm of interior designers.'

Tall, slim and beautifully dressed, they could easily have passed as models for an exclusive fashion house, Alyse decided without envy. Somehow they didn't seem real, and instead were merely players portraying an expected part on the stage of life.

'Given time, I'm sure I'll get to know them all,' she ventured quietly.

'Aleksi and Georg are very fortunate to have you,' Rachel complimented softly.

With a hand that shook slightly Alyse picked up her glass and savoured its contents in the hope that the excellent champagne would calm her nerves. It was all too apparent that Rachel held fond hopes for the apparent affection between her stepson and his new bride to blossom and eventually bloom into love.

Something that Aleksi seemed to deliberately foster by ensuring his glance lingered a few seconds too long, augmenting it with the touch of his hand on her arm, at her waist, not to mention the lazy indulgence he accorded her on numerous occasions in the presence of his parents.

'Put several business friends together in the same room,' a familiar voice drawled at her elbow, 'and inevitably the conversation drifts away from social pleasantries.'

Talk of the devil! Alyse turned her head slowly towards Aleksi and gave him a brilliant smile. 'I hardly noticed your absence.'

'I think that could be termed an indirect admonition,' Alexandros declared with humour as he directed his wife a musing glance. 'Yes?'

'Alyse and I have been enjoying each other's company,' Rachel acknowledged with considerable diplomacy.

'Aleksi *darling*!' an incredibly warm voice gushed with the barest hint of an accent. 'We're impossibly late, but Tony got held up in Brisbane, and we simply *flew* down. Say you forgive us?'

Alyse sensed the effervescent laughter threatening to burst out from the large-framed woman whose entire bearing could only be described as *majestic*. A dark purple silk trouser-suit with voluminous matching knee-length jacket, long trailing scarves and an abundance of jewellery completed an ensemble that on anyone else would have looked ludicrous.

'Siobhan!' Aleksi's smile was genuinely warm as he accepted her embrace. 'Tony. Allow me to introduce my wife, Alyse.'

Alyse immediately became the focus of two pairs of eyes, one set of which was femininely shrewd yet totally lacking in calculation.

'She looks perfect, darling,' Siobhan pronounced softly, and Alyse had the uncanny feeling she had been subjected to some kind of test and had unwittingly passed. 'Is she?'

Aleksi's eyes gleamed with silent humour. 'Incredibly so.'

'Siobhan, you're outrageous,' her husband drawled in resignation. 'I imagine the poor girl is almost witless with nerves.'

Wonderfully warm dark eyes gleamed as they held hers. 'Are you?' asked Siobhan.

'Like a lamb in a den of lions,' Alyse admitted with a wry smile.

Mellifluous laughter flowed richly from Siobhan's throat. 'Several of the female gender present undoubtedly are, my dear. Especially where your gorgeous hunk of a husband is concerned.'

'I suppose there must be a certain fascination for his dark brooding charm,' Alyse considered with a devilish gleam, and Siobhan grinned, totally unabashed.

'He's a sexy beast, darling. To some, it's almost a fatal attraction.'

Alyse merely smiled, and Siobhan said softly, 'How delightful—you're shy!'

'A fascinating quality,' Aleksi agreed, taking hold of Alyse's hand and threading his fingers through her own.

She tried to tug her hand away, and felt his fingers tighten in silent warning. 'Perhaps we could get together for dinner soon? Now, if you'll excuse us, we really must circulate. Enjoy yourselves,' he bade genially.

It was impossible to protest, and Alyse allowed Aleksi to lead her from one group to another in the large room, pausing for five minutes, sometimes ten, as they engaged in conversation. Georg's existence had precipitated a marriage that had aroused speculative conjecture, and by the time they had come full circle her facial muscles felt tight from maintaining a constant smile, and her nerves were raw beneath an abundance of thinly veiled curiosity.

'Another drink?' asked Aleksi.

Dared she? Somehow it seemed essential to appear to be in total command, and she had merely picked a few morsels from each course during dinner and barely nibbled from the abundance of food constantly offered by hired staff throughout the evening. 'I'd love some coffee.'

An eyebrow slanted in quizzical query. 'I can't tempt you with champagne-spiked orange juice?' His gaze was direct and vaguely analytical, and Alyse was unable to suppress the faint quickening of her pulse.

He had the strangest effect on her equilibrium, making her aware of a primitive alchemy, a dramatic pull of the senses almost beyond her comprehension, for it didn't seem possible to be able to physically enjoy sex with someone she actively disliked. Hated, she amended, unwilling to accord him much favour. Yet he projected an enviable aura of power, a distinctive mesh of male charisma and sensuality that alerted the interest of women—a primeval recognition that made her feel uncommonly resentful.

'I'd prefer coffee,' she responded with forced lightness, and he laughed, a deep, husky sound that sent shivers scudding down the length of her spine.

'The need for a clear head?' His teeth gleamed white for an instant, then became hidden beneath the curve of his mouth.

'Yes,' she admitted without prevarication.

'Stay here, and I'll fetch some.'

'I'd rather come with you.'

He examined her features, assessing the bright eyes and pale cheeks with daunting scrutiny. 'No one here would dare harm so much as a hair on your beautiful head,' he alluded cynically.

'Forgive me if I don't believe you.' She hadn't meant to sound bitter, but the implication was there, and she felt immeasurably angry—with herself, for allowing him to catch a glimpse of her vulnerability.

Without a further word he led her towards a table where an attractively attired waitress was dispensing tea and coffee, and within seconds he had placed a cup between her nerveless fingers, watching as she sipped the hot aromatic brew appreciatively while her eyes skimmed the room.

'When you've finished, we'll dance,' he told her.

Alyse brought her gaze back to the indomitable man at her side. 'You've succeeded admirably at playing the perfect husband all evening. Dancing cheek-to-cheek might be overdoing it, don't you think?'

His eyes were dark and unfathomable. 'Inconceivable, of course, that I might want to?'

She suddenly felt as if she'd skated on to very thin ice, and she resorted to restrained anger in defence. 'I'm damned if I'll act out a charade!'

'Are you so sure it will be?'

This was an infinitely dangerous game, and she wasn't at all sure she wanted to play. Yet in a room full of people, what else could she do but comply?

Her eyes glittered as he removed the empty cup from her hand and put it down on the nearby table, and her smile was deliberately winsome as he drew her out on to the terrace and into his arms.

There were strategically placed lights casting a muted glow over landscaped gardens, and the air was fresh and cool.

'You have a large number of friends,' Alyse remarked in a desperate bid to break the silence.

'Business associates, acquaintances with whom I maintain social contact,' Aleksi corrected wryly.

She tilted her head slightly. 'How cynical!'

'You think so?'

He was amused, damn him! *'Yes.'*

'Careful, little cat,' he cautioned softly, controlling with ease her effort to put some distance between them. 'Your claws are showing.'

'If they are, it's because I detest what you're doing.'

'Dancing with my wife?'

'Oh, stop being so damned—*impossible*! You know very well what I mean.'

'This party was arranged specifically to give a number of important people the opportunity to meet you. The reason for our marriage is none of their business.'

'There are several women present who appear to think it is!'

'Their problem, not mine.' He sounded so clinical, so damned—detached, that she felt sickened.

'Let me go. I want to check on Georg.'

'Melanie is ensconced upstairs doing precisely that,' drawled Aleksi, refusing to relinquish his hold. 'In a minute we'll go back inside and mingle with our guests.'

'I hate you!'

'At least it's a healthy emotion.'

It didn't *feel* healthy! In fact, it razed her nerves and turned her into a seething ball of fury.

For what remained of the evening Alyse displayed the expected role of hostess with charm and dignity, so much so that she surely deserved a medal for perseverance, she decided as she stood at her husband's side and said goodbye to the last remaining clutch of guests.

Only when the tail-lights of the final car disappeared from sight and Aleksi had firmly closed the front door did she allow the mask to slip.

'I'll pay the babysitter, and activate Georg's electronic monitor,' Aleksi determined. 'There's no point in disturbing him simply to move him downstairs.'

The fact that he was right didn't preclude her need to oppose him, and she opened her mouth, only to close it again beneath the force of his forefinger.

'Don't argue.'

She drew back her head as if touched by flame, and her eyes flashed with anger. 'I'll do as I damn well please!'

His expression assumed a musing indolence. 'Go to bed.'

She was so angry, it almost consumed her. 'And wait dutifully for you to join me?'

Without a word he turned and made for the stairs, and she watched his ascent with impotent rage.

Damned if she'd obey and retire meekly to the bedroom! Although at several minutes past two in the morning it hardly made sense to think of anything else. And perversity, simply for the sheer hell of it, was infinitely unwise.

Except she didn't feel like taking a sensible course, and without pausing to give her actions further thought she crossed the lounge and made her way downstairs.

The caterers had been extremely efficient, for apart from a few glasses there was little evidence that a party had taken place.

A quick vacuum of the carpets and the room would be restored to its usual immaculate state, she decided, and, uncaring of the late hour, she retrieved the necessary cleaner and set it in motion.

She had almost finished when the motor came to a sudden stop, and she turned to see Aleksi standing a few feet distant with the disconnected cord held in his hand.

'This can surely wait?' His voice was deceptively mild, and didn't fool her in the slightest.

'It will only take another minute, then it's done.'

'In the morning, Alyse.'

'I'd prefer to do it now.' It was as if she was on a rollercoaster to self-destruction, able to see her ultimate destination yet powerless to stop.

'Obstinacy simply for the sheer hell of it is foolish, don't you think?' Aleksi queried, depressing the automatic cord rewind button, and Alyse glared at him balefully.

'Aren't you being equally stubborn?' she returned at once.

He spared the elegant gold watch at his wrist a cursory glance. 'Two-thirty in the morning isn't conducive to a definitive discussion.'

'So once again I must play the part of a subjugated wife!'

His eyes narrowed, assuming a daunting hardness that was at variance with the softness of his voice. 'Perhaps you'd care to clarify that remark?'

Alyse stood defiant. 'I don't like being continually dictated to,' she told him angrily. 'And I especially don't like being taken for granted.' She lifted a hand, then let it fall down to her side. 'I feel like a child, forced to conform. And I'm not,' she insisted, helpless in the face of her own anger.

'Aren't you?' Aleksi brushed his fingers across her heated cheeks. 'Most women would exult in my wealth and scheme to acquire all life's so-called luxuries.'

'Are you condemning me as a child because I'm unwilling to play the vamp in bed?'

'What a delightfully evocative phrase!'

'I hate you, do you understand? *Hate* you,' she said fiercely, then gave a startled cry as he calmly took hold of her arms and lifted her over his shoulder. 'What do you think you're doing?'

He turned and began walking towards the stairs. 'I would have thought it was obvious.'

'Put me down, damn you!' There was a terrible sense of indignity at being carried in such a manner, and she hit out at him, clenching her hands into fists as she railed them against his back. 'Bastard!' she accused as he reached the ground floor and crossed the lounge. *'Barbarian!'*

On entering their bedroom he pulled her down to

stand facing him, and she looked at him through a mist of anger.

'This seems to be the only level on which we effectively communicate.' His eyes were hard and inflexible.

'Speak for yourself!' she flung incautiously.

His eyes lanced hers, their expression dark and forbidding. 'I'm tempted to make you beg for my possession.'

'What's stopping you?'

'Little fool,' Aleksi condemned with dangerous silkiness. 'Aren't you in the least afraid of my temper?'

'What would you do? Beat me?'

'Maybe I should, simply to teach you the lesson you deserve.'

'And what about the lesson I consider *you* deserve?' cried Alyse, tried almost beyond endurance. 'For forcing me into marriage, your bed...' She faltered to a shaky halt, hating him more than she thought it was possible to hate anyone.

'Your love for Antonia and Georg surpassed any minor considerations.'

'*Minor!*' An entire flood of words threatened to spill from her, except that his mouth covered hers with brutal possession, effectively stilling the flow.

'You don't hate me as much as you pretend,' Aleksi drawled as he lifted his head, and she flung heatedly,

'There's no pretence whatsoever in the way I feel about you!'

Placing a thumb and forefinger beneath her chin, he lifted it so that she had no option but to look at him.

'Perhaps you should query whether a proportion of anger doesn't originate with yourself for enjoying something you insist is merely physical lust,' he alluded silkily.

Did he know how impossible it was for her to come to terms with her own traitorous body? Even now, part of her wanted to melt into his arms, while another part urged her to pull away. It was crazy to feel like this, to be prey to a gamut of emotions so complex that understanding why seemed beyond comprehension.

'I don't enjoy it!' To admit, even to herself, that she did, was something she refused to concede.

'No?'

Aleksi sounded indolently amused, and she flinched away from the brush of his fingers as he trailed them along the edge of her jaw, then traced the throbbing cord at her neck before exploring the hollows at the base of her throat.

'Such a sweet mouth,' he mocked gently, lowering his own to within inches of her softly curved lips. 'And so very kissable.'

The breath seemed to catch in her throat. 'Stop it.' Her eyes clung to his, bright, angry, yet intensely vulnerable. 'Please.'

'Why?' Aleksi murmured as he touched the tip of his tongue against the sensual centre of her lower lip, then began to edge gently inwards in an evocative discovery of the sensitive moist tissues.

'Aleksi.' His name whispered from her lips with something akin to despair. 'No!'

A hand slid beneath her hair, cupping her nape, while the other slipped to her lower back, urging her close, and his mouth continued its light tasting; teasing, deliberately withholding the promise of passion until his touch became an exquisite torture.

She ached for him to deepen the kiss, and she gave a faint sigh as his mouth hardened in irrefutable possession, wiping out every vestige of conscious thought. A deep flame flared into pulsating life beneath his sensual mastery, and each separate nerve-end tingled alive with unbridled ardency as she gave the response he sought.

His clothes, hers, were a dispensable barrier, and she made no protest as he set about freeing them both of any material restriction.

Her body arched of its own accord as his mouth trailed her collarbone and began a downward movement to her breast, silently inviting the wicked ecstasy of his erotic touch, and she cried out as he caressed the delicate swelling bud, luxuriating in the waves of sensation pulsing through her body.

A faint cry of protest silvered the night air as he shifted slightly, then she gave a husky purr of pleasure as he trailed the valley to render a similar supplication to its aching twin.

With consummate skill his fingers traced an evocative path over her silky skin, playing each sensitive pleasure-spot to fever-pitch until she was filled with a deep, aching need that only physical release could assuage.

Alyse barely registered the silken sheets beneath her back, yet the relief she craved was withheld as his mouth feathered the path of his hand in a sensual tasting that was impossibly erotic, making the blood sing through her veins like wildfire until her very soul seemed *his*, and she began to plead, tiny guttural sounds that her conscious mind registered but refused to accept as remotely *hers*.

Hardly aware of her actions, she reached for his head,

her fingers curling into the thickness of his hair as she attempted to divert his attention, wanting, *needing* to feel his mouth on hers in hard, hungry passion.

Like something wild and untamed, her body began to thresh beneath his in blatant invitation until at last he plunged deep into the silken core, creating a pulsating rhythmic pattern that took her to the heights and beyond in an explosion of sensual ecstasy that was undeniably his pleasure as well as her own.

For a long time afterwards she seemed encased in a hazy rosy glow, and as she drifted slowly back to reality she became aware of the featherlight touch of his fingers as they traced the moist contours of her body.

She didn't feel capable of moving, and a tiny bubble of laughter died in her throat scarcely before it began.

'What do you find so amusing?'

Alyse turned her head slowly to meet the deep slumbering passion still lurking in those gleaming eyes so close to her own. 'I think you'd better stop. There's a young baby upstairs who'll soon wake for his early morning bottle.'

Aleksi's lips curved warmly as he lifted a hand to her hair and tucked a few collective tendrils back behind her ear. 'I'll feed him, then come back to bed.'

She tried to inject a degree of condemnation into her voice, and failed miserably. 'You're insatiable!'

His lips touched her shoulder, then slid to the curve of her neck in an evocative caress. 'So, my sweet, are you.'

Remembering just how she had reacted in his arms brought a tide of telltale colour to her cheeks, and her eyes clouded with shame.

'Don't,' he bade softly, 'be embarrassed at losing yourself so completely in the sexual act.'

'I might have been faking,' she said unsteadily, and almost died at the degree of lazy humour evident in the gleaming eyes so close to her own.

'Liar,' he drawled. 'Your delight was totally spontaneous.'

'And you're the expert.' She hadn't meant to sound bitter, but it tinged her voice none the less, and her lashes descended to form a protective veil against his compelling scrutiny.

'Sufficiently experienced to give consideration to your pleasure as well as my own.'

'For that I should be grateful?'

'I would advise you against provoking me to demonstrate the difference.'

A faint chill feathered across the surface of her skin, and she shivered. 'I'm going to have a shower.'

She half expected him to stop her, and when he didn't she felt vaguely resentful, electing to take over-long beneath the warm jet of water and even longer attending to her toilette.

Emerging into the bedroom, she slipped carefully into bed and lay still, only to realise within seconds that Aleksi was already asleep, his breathing steady and uncontrived.

For several long minutes she studied his features, aware that even in repose there was an inherent strength apparent, a force that was slightly daunting. Relaxed, his mouth assumed a firm curve, and she experienced the almost irresistible desire to touch it with her own.

Are you *mad*? an inner voice taunted.

With a hand that shook slightly Alyse reached out

and snapped off the bedside lamp, then laid her head
on the pillow, allowing innate weariness to transport
her into a deep, dreamless sleep.

CHAPTER NINE

SUNDAY SHOWED PROMISE of becoming one of those beautiful sunny days south-east Queensland was renowned for producing in the midst of a tropical winter. A slight breeze barely stirred the air, and the sea was a clear translucent blue with scarcely a ripple to disturb its surface.

'The weather is too good not to take the boat out,' Aleksi declared as Alyse entered the kitchen after bathing and feeding Georg. She smelled of baby talc, and her eyes were still soft with the sheer delight of his existence.

Crossing to the pantry, she extracted muesli, retrieved milk from the fridge, then poured generous portions of both into a bowl and carried it to the table.

'I'm sure Rachel and Alexandros will enjoy a day out on the Bay,' she said with studied politeness, and incurred Aleksi's sharp scrutiny.

'There can be no doubt you will come too.'

She forced herself to look at him carefully, noting the almost indecently broad shoulders, the firm sculptured features that portrayed inherent strength of will. He had finished his breakfast, and was seated opposite, a half-finished cup of coffee within easy reach.

'I'm not sure it's fair to expect Melanie to come at such short notice, especially on a Sunday, and particularly when she babysat Georg last night.' Her gaze was remarkably level as she held his dark, faintly brooding gaze. 'Besides, I don't think Georg should be left too often in a babysitter's care. Young children need constancy in their lives, not a succession of minders their parents install merely as a delegation of responsibility to ensure the pursuit of their social existence.'

One eyebrow rose to form a cynical arch. 'My dear Alyse, I totally agree. However, Georg is so young, his major concern is being kept clean and dry, with sustenance available whenever he needs it. I doubt if being left in Melanie's care will damage his psyche. Besides, we'll be back before five.'

Her eyes grew stormy. 'Are you always so damnably persistent?'

'My parents like you,' drawled Aleksi. 'And I'm prepared to do anything that's in my power to please them during the length of their stay.'

'With that in mind,' she began heatedly, 'I would have thought they'd both want to spend as much time with their grandson as possible. Not socialise, or sail the high seas.'

He was silent for a few long minutes, then he said silkily. 'During the past year they've seen their son horrifically injured, and suffered the despair of knowing his life-span was severely limited. As soon as his condition stabilised, Rachel and Alexandros turned their home into a veritable clinic, hiring a team of highly qualified medical staff to care for Georgiou. They gave up everything to spend time with him, taking alternate shifts along with the staff so that either one was always at his side.' He paused, and his voice hardened slightly. 'Now they need to relax and begin to enjoy life again. If that entails socialising and sailing, then so be it.' His eyes assumed an inexorable bleakness. 'Have I made myself clear?'

Alyse pushed her bowl aside, her appetite gone. 'Painfully so.'

'Eat your breakfast.'

'I no longer feel hungry.'

'Maybe my absence will help it return,' Aleksi said drily as he rose to his feet. 'I'll be in the study, making a few calls.'

Within two hours they were on board a large luxuriously-fitted cruiser that lay moored to a jetty on the canal at the bottom of Aleksi's garden.

Alyse had elected to wear tailored white cotton trousers with a yellow sweater. Rachel was similarly attired, and both men wore jeans and casual dark sweaters.

'This is heaven!' Rachel breathed, turning towards her stepson.

Alyse almost gasped out loud at the warmth of his smile as it rested on Rachel's features.

'We'll berth at Sanctuary Cove for lunch. Afterwards, you and Alyse can wander among the boutiques while Alexandros and I sit lazily in the sun enjoying a beer.'

'You're spoiling her,' Alexandros chided his son in a teasing accented drawl, and Rachel laughed.

'All women adore being spoiled by men, don't they, Alyse?'

She was doomed no matter what she said, and, summoning a brilliant smile, she ventured sweetly. 'Definitely.'

Aleksi shot his father a mocking glance. 'I have a feeling the Cove could prove an expensive stopover.'

After a superb seafood lunch the two women strolled at will, visiting several exclusive shops where they purchased a variety of casual resort-styled ensembles, and Alyse fell in love with a pair of imported shoes which she recklessly added to a collection of brightly designed plastic carrier-bags already in her possession.

'What did I tell you?' drawled Aleksi with amusement as Alyse and Rachel joined them in the Yacht Club's lounge.

'Alyse had bought the most gorgeous outfit,' Rachel enthused, taking hold of her husband's outstretched hand, and her sparkling smile softened as he lifted it to his lips in a gesture that made Alyse's heart execute an unaccustomed flip in silent acknowledgment of the love these two people shared. 'I've persuaded her to wear it to the fashion parade Serita Hubbard invited us to attend at the Cove on Tuesday.'

The cruiser traversed the Bay to reach Sovereign Islands just before five, and after relieving Melanie Alyse checked on Georg to find him stirring and almost ready for his bottle.

'Let me,' Rachel offered at his first wakening cry. 'I'm sure you'll want to shower and change.'

'Thanks,' Alyse acquiesced in gratitude. 'I won't be long.'

When she returned, Aleksi and Alexandros were in the kitchen, and Georg was seated on Rachel's knee, his eyes moving from one to the other, his tiny fists beating the air in undisguised delight.

'See?' beamed Alexandros with Greek pride. 'He is strong, this little one. Look at those legs, those hands!

He will grow tall.' He shot his son a laughing glance. 'A good protector for his sisters, an example for his brothers. Yes?'

It was difficult for Alyse to keep her smile in place, but she managed it—just. Part of her wanted to cry out that brothers or sisters for Georgiou's son didn't form part of her plan. Yet she could hardly blame Alexandros for assuming his son's marriage would include other children in years to come.

And what of Aleksi? Was he content with a marriage of expediency which provided a woman in his bed and a mother for his children? Or would he eventually become bored and seek sexual gratification elsewhere?

Far better that she steel her heart against any emotional involvement. Two years wasn't a lifetime, and afterwards she could rebuild her future. A future for herself, for Georg.

Dinner was an impromptu meal of grilled steak and an assortment of salads, with fresh fruit, and followed by a leisurely coffee in the lounge.

Rachel and Alexandros took their leave at nine, declaring a need for an early night, and Alyse felt strangely tired herself from the combination of sea air and warm winter sunshine.

'I'll tidy the kitchen,' she declared as Aleksi closed the front door and set the security system.

'We'll do it together.'

She was already walking ahead of him. 'I can manage.' For some reason his presence swamped her, and she wanted to be alone.

There were only a few cups and saucers, glasses the men had used for a liqueur, and she quickly rinsed and stacked them in the dishwasher, all too aware of Aleksi's presence.

'All finished,' she announced, and made to step past him.

'I've opened a separate bank account with a balance sufficient to meet whatever cash you need,' he told her. 'The details are in the escritoire in your sitting-room, as well as a supplementary card accessing my charge account.'

Alyse felt a surge of resentment, and forced herself to take a deep calming breath. 'I'd prefer to use my own money, and I already have a charge account.'

His gaze focused on her features, noting the faint wariness in the set of her mouth, the proud tilt of her chin, and the determination apparent in those beautiful blue eyes. 'Why be so fiercely independent? It's surely a husband's right to support his wife?'

'The housekeeping, and anything Georg needs,' she agreed. 'But I'll pay for my own clothes.'

'And if I insist?'

'You can insist as much as you like,' she retaliated. 'I won't be cowed into submissive obedience simply out of deference to a marriage certificate.'

Aleksi's eyes hardened fractionally, and his mouth curved to form a mocking smile. 'An enlightened feminist?'

Now she was really angry! 'If you wanted a decorative doll whose sole pleasure was to acquire jewellery and designer clothes at your expense, then you made a mistake in choosing me!'

'I don't think so,' he drawled.

'You *enjoy* our parody of a marriage?' she demanded, and was incensed to hear his husky laughter.

Lifting a hand, he slid it beneath the curtain of her hair, threading his fingers to tug gently at its length, tilting her head.

'I enjoy *you*,' Aleksi accorded silkily. 'The way you continually oppose me, simply for the sheer hell of it.'

Alyse forced herself to hold his gaze, although she was unable to prevent the slight trembling movement of her lips, and she glimpsed the faint flaring evident in the depths of his eyes.

'Be warned, it's a fight you may not win.'

She wanted to lash out and hit him, and only the chill sense of purpose apparent in those dark features stopped her. 'Do you imagine I'll be swayed into becoming emotionally involved simply because you can—' She faltered, momentarily lost for words in the heat of her anger.

'Turn you on?'

'Oh!' she raged, gasping out loud as he drew her close against him, and her struggles were in vain as his head lowered to hers. His lips were firm and warm, caressing with evocative slowness, and she wanted to cry out against his flagrant seduction. It would be so easy to close her eyes and allow herself to be swept away by the magic of his lovemaking. Against her will, the blood began to sing in her veins and her bones turned to liquid as sheer sensation overtook sanity. She became lost, adrift without sense of direction until anger at her own treacherous emotions rose to the surface, and she forcibly broke free from his devastating mouth.

'Let me go, damn you,' she said shakily, straining against the strength of his arms, and her eyes were clouded with an inner struggle she had no intention of confessing—even to herself.

Aleksi held her effortlessly, his expression an inscrutable mask, and it seemed an age before he spoke.

'Go to bed. I have to go over some plans due to be submitted at a meeting tomorrow morning.'

Without a word she turned and moved away from him, her breathing becoming more ragged with every single step, and by the time she reached the bedroom she felt as if she'd run a mile.

Perversity demanded that she sleep in the adjoining sitting-room, but at the last moment common sense prevailed.

What was the point? she decided wearily as she slid in between the sheets on her side of the large bed. Aleksi would undoubtedly remove her, and she was too tired tonight to fight.

An hour later she was still awake, a victim of her own vivid imagination, and it seemed an age before she heard the soft almost imperceptible sound of his entry into the bedroom. In the reflected illumination of Georg's night-light she watched through lowered lashes as he discarded his clothes, and she unconsciously held her breath as he slid into bed. Minutes later she heard his breathing slow and assume a deep steady rhythm.

He had fallen asleep! For some unknown reason that angered her unbearably, and she cursed her own feminine contrariness for the slow-burning ache that gradually consumed her body until she was aflame with the need for physical assuagement.

Alyse glanced around the high-domed marquee with seeming interest. There were more than a hundred women present, each so elegantly attired she could only

conclude that their main purpose was to catch the pho-
tographer's eye and thereby make the society pages.

Her vivid peacock-green silk suit teamed with black
accessories was an attractive foil for Rachel's ensemble
in cream and gold.

Champagne flowed, pressed eagerly upon them by
handsome formally suited young men.

'Have they been hired by an agency especially for
the occasion, do you think?' Alyse queried quietly of
Rachel.

'Definitely. They're too much in awe of the cream
of society's glitterati.'

'And hopeful of making a conquest?'

Rachel cast her a faintly wicked smile. 'Don't look
round, but you've definitely caught one young man's
eye.'

Alyse gave a negligent shrug in silent uninterest, and
sipped at her champagne. 'Tell me about Greece. Do
you like living there?'

Rachel's expression softened. 'We have several
homes in various parts of the world. Some are splendid, but the one I love best is situated in the bay of a
small island off the main coast. It's a fairy-tale—no
cars, just peace and solitude with the only means of
entry via boat or helicopter. It was there that Alexandros and Aleksi taught Georgiou to sail.'

Alyse sensed the older woman's sadness, and touched
her hand in a gesture of silent sympathy.

'It's all right, my dear. As one gets older, one re-
alises there is only *now*. Memories can't be changed,
and I count myself fortunate that mine are many and
such happy ones. Our two sons were a constant delight,
although Georgiou was the frivolous one, coveting the

thrill of the moment behind the wheel of a high-powered motorboat or car. I lived in constant fear of the day he might make a misjudgment.'

Alyse had to ask. 'And Aleksi?'

'He was more serious, and despite the difference in age and character he and Georgiou were very close. During those awful months after the accident, he flew back and forth to Athens countless times, and when he wasn't there he rang every second day.'

'Alyse! How wonderful of you to bring Rachel, darling,' a husky feminine voice enthused, and she turned her head to see Serita Hubbard in a vivid white ensemble that undoubtedly bore a Diane Fries label.

'Serita,' she returned politely.

'I've arranged for us to be seated together at lunch. If we do become separated during the fashion parade, just meet me in front of the marquee afterwards.' Serita's smile flashed friendly warmth. 'Must dash, there's a slight muddle with tickets supposed to be handed out by one of the committee members. She thought I'd collected them, and I was under the impression that *she* had. I need to show my list to the organiser. There are quite a few people here you've met, and Solange said she'd probably be running late. Do mingle, won't you?'

It was a brilliantly orchestrated parade, quite the best Alyse had attended, for the models were top-class professionals and the clothes not only superb, but many were available from the Cove boutiques.

'See anything you particularly like?' Rachel asked, then laughed as she glimpsed the appreciative gleam in her daughter-in-law's eyes.

'An hour with our marked catalogues after lunch?' Alyse suggested.

'Definitely,' Rachel agreed. 'And talking of lunch, we'd better head for the marquee entrance.'

The restaurant chosen for the venue was cantilevered out over the water, with splendid views of the harbour-front villas and a flotilla of luxury craft moored at an adjacent marina.

Solange was seated opposite, beside Serita, Marta, Chrissie, Kate and Annabel, and Alyse felt as if she was facing an inquisition committee.

The same impeccably suited young men who had so earnestly served champagne before the parade also waited on tables, and Alyse found it amusing to be the recipient of one particular man's attentive solicitude.

'Darling, you do seem to have made a hit,' Solange declared artlessly. 'Are you going to slip him your phone number?'

Without faltering, Alyse responded with an absence of guile. 'With a young baby to care for, I haven't the time or the inclination to foster the attention of a toy-boy.' She offered a brilliant smile. 'Besides, I doubt if Aleksi would be amused.'

Solange's eyes narrowed slightly. 'A little jealousy stimulates a marriage, surely?'

Oh, heavens, she was beginning to feel like a butterfly pinned to the wall, with numerous pairs of interested eyes waiting to see if she'd squirm! 'Do you think so?' she queried, then gave a light faintly husky laugh. 'Aleksi would probably beat me.'

Serita smiled in silent amusement, while Solange merely fixed Alyse with an unblinking glare. 'Dominic insists we host a dinner party on Saturday evening,' she drawled. 'I'll ring Aleksi with the details.' Her gaze rested on Rachel. 'You must come too, of course.'

'We leave for Sydney tomorrow to spend time with my sister, so we won't be here, I'm afraid,' Rachel declined graciously, and Solange gave a slight negligent shrug.

It was after two when Alyse and Rachel managed to slip away, and within an hour and a half they were heading towards Sovereign Islands with a few selected purchases reposing on the rear seat of the car.

Alyse had planned an informal dinner at home for Rachel and Alexandros's last evening on the Coast, and there was a certain sense of sadness apparent when it came time for them to leave, for she would miss Rachel's company.

'A week isn't long,' the older woman assured her as she gave her an affectionate hug. 'And I'll phone frequently to check on my grandson.'

'I shall probably have to restrain her from making at least three calls a day,' Alexandros declared with amusement as he slid into the rear seat of the car.

Alyse moved quickly indoors as soon as the BMW drew out of sight. The house seemed to envelop her, so large and strangely silent, and she was unable to suppress a feeling of acute vulnerability.

Georg was sleeping peacefully, and she quickly showered before slipping into bed, where she lay wide-eyed and reflective as a dozen conflicting thoughts vied for supremacy in a brain too emotionally fraught to make sense of any one of them.

When she heard Aleksi return she closed her eyes in the pretence of sleep, aware of a deep ache in the region of her heart. It would have been wonderful to seek the comfort of his arms, to have them enfold her close, and simply hold her. A few tender kisses, the soothing touch of his hands, so that she felt secure in the knowledge that she was infinitely cherished.

Except that such an image belonged in the realm of fantasy, and she gave up waiting for him to join her in bed as the minutes dragged on. The only feasible explanation seemed to be a wealth of paperwork awaiting him in the study, and when she woke the following morning it was to discover he was already up and dressed.

In a way Alyse found it a relief to spend the following few days quietly at home. There were letters to write, and she rang Miriam Stanford at the Perth boutique to learn that everything was progressing extremely smoothly—almost as if she had hardly been missed, Alyse thought wryly.

During the afternoon she prepared their evening meal, taking infinite care with a carefully selected menu. Aleksi invariably arrived home just before five, and after a quick shower he would insist on changing and feeding Georg.

'He needs to recognise a male figure in his young life,' Aleksi had said the day after Rachel and Alexandros departed for Sydney. 'Besides, this is the only time I have to give to him five nights out of seven.'

It left Alyse free to set the table and make a last-minute check on dinner. Just watching the tiny baby in Aleksi's arms wrenched her emotions, for she could imagine Aleksi being an integral part of Georg's existence, playing ball, teaching him to swim, simply being there throughout his formative adolescent years. Each time the pull at her heartstrings became a little more painful, and she was gripped with a terrifying fear that although removing Georg to Perth was right for her, it wouldn't necessarily be right for Georg.

Conversation over dinner was restricted to their individual daily activities, polite divertissements that lasted until dessert had been consumed, then Aleksi would invariably disappear into the study and not emerge until long after she had gone to bed.

The possibility that his actions might be deliberate angered her unbearably, and she found herself consciously plotting a subtle revenge.

The occasion of Solange and Dominic Rochas' dinner party seemed ideal, and on Friday morning Alyse rang Melanie and arranged for her to babysit Georg while she went shopping for something suitable to wear.

The desire to stun was uppermost, and she found exactly what she wanted in an exclusive boutique. In black, its bodice was strapless, exquisitely boned and patterned in black sequins, with a slim-fitting knee-length skirt that hugged her slender hips. A long floating silk scarf draped at her neck to flow down her back completed the outfit, and, ignoring the outrageously expensive price-tag, she simply charged it. Shoes came next, and she chose a perfume to match her new image.

As Saturday progressed it was impossible to quell her reservations, and after feeding and settling Georg into his cot she quickly showered, then settled down in front of the mirror with a variety of cosmetics.

It seemed to take an age to achieve the desired effect, but eventually she stood back, satisfied with the result. Her hair was brushed into its customary smooth bell-shape, and in a moment of indecision she caught its length and twisted it high into a knot on top of her head.

Yes? No? *'Damn,'* she muttered softly, beginning to view the evening ahead with a certain degree of dread.

Solange was someone with whom she doubted it was

possible ever to share an empathy. Even on so short an acquaintance, it was impossible not to be aware that the interior decorator lusted after Aleksi, and the mere fact that Alyse was Aleksi's wife stacked the odds heavily against her from the start.

Her dynamic husband had a lot to answer for, she decided as she crossed to the large mirrored closet and slid back the door. Although to be fair, he couldn't help his dark good looks, nor his sexual appeal, for both were an inherent quality, and, while some men might deliberately exploit such assets, honesty forced her to concede that Aleksi did not.

A tiny frown of doubt momentarily creased her forehead as she extracted *the* dress from its hanger. Although it had been selected to shock, she suddenly developed reservations as to its suitability. Remembering precisely why she had purchased it deepened her frown, and her eyes clouded with indecision. What had seemed an excellent means of revenge at the time no longer held much appeal, and she was about to slip it back on to the hanger when she heard Aleksi move into the dressing-room.

'What time have you organised for Melanie to arrive?'

'Seven,' she answered, turning slightly towards him, watching as he discarded the towel knotted low at his hips, then he stepped into dark briefs and reached for a snowy white shirt.

His physique was splendid, emanating innate power and strength, and Alyse was unable to prevent the surge of sheer sexual pleasure at the sight of him.

Impossibly cross with herself, she slid down the zip fastener and stepped into the gown. Her fingers automatically slid the zip into place, then smoothed its sleek lines over her hips before settling on the gentle swell of her breasts, which were exposed to a greater degree than she remembered when originally trying on the gown.

'Did you select that with the intention of raising every red-blooded man's blood pressure at the party tonight, or simply mine?' Aleksi drawled from behind, and she slowly turned to face him.

'Why would I deliberately want to raise yours?' she queried sweetly.

'The result is stunning, but I may not be able to stand guard at your side every minute during the evening to fend off the attention you'll undoubtedly receive,' he warned with an edge of mockery, and her eyes acquired a fiery sparkle.

'Really? Are you suggesting I should change?' There was anger just beneath the surface, and a crazy desire to oppose him.

His expression darkened fractionally. 'Yes.'

'And if I choose not to?'

'The only choice you have, Alyse, is to remove the dress yourself or have me do it for you.' His voice was hard and inflexible, and her chin lifted in angry rejection, her eyes becoming stormy pools mirroring incredulous rage.

'Why, you chauvinistic domineering *pig*,' she reiterated heatedly. 'How dare you?'

'Oh, I *dare*,' he drawled silkily, and a shiver slithered the length of her spine at his determined resolve.

'It's the latest fashion and cost a small fortune,' she flung angrily. 'And besides, I won't have you dictate what I can and can't wear!'

He reached out a hand and caught hold of her chin

between thumb and forefinger, tightening his grasp when she moved to wrench it away. 'Stop arguing simply for the sake of it.'

'I'm *not*!' She was so incredibly furious, it was all she could do not to hit him.

'Surely you know me well enough by now to understand that you can't win,' he cautioned with deadly softness.

'You mean you won't allow me to!'

He was silent for a few seemingly long seconds, and she held his gaze fearlessly.

'A woman who deliberately flaunts her body indulges in subtle advertising of a kind which promises to deliver. Wear the dress when we're dining alone, and I'll be suitably appreciative.'

'Oh, for heavens's sake! I don't believe any of this!'

'Believe,' he said hardily. 'Now, change.'

'No.'

'Defiance, Alyse, simply for the sake of it? Aren't you being rather foolish?'

'If you derive a sadistic thrill from forcibly removing a woman's clothes, then go ahead and do it.'

His eyes assumed a chilling intensity, and she was suddenly filled with foreboding. Without a word his hands closed over her shoulders, propelling her forward, and her chin tilted in silent rebellion as he lowered his head.

His mouth took possession of hers, forcing her lips apart in a demanding assault that showed little mercy and she held back a silent groan of despair as he deliberately began a wreaking devastation.

When he relinquished his hold, her jaw ached, even

her neck, and her eyes were bright with a mixture of anger and unshed tears.

His eyes bore an inscrutability she was unable to penetrate, and her mouth trembled slightly.

'Change, Alyse,' he directed inflexibly. 'Or I'll do it for you.'

She looked at him with scathing enmity. 'And if I refuse, you'll undoubtedly admininster some other form of diabolical punishment.'

'Take care,' he warned. 'My temper is on a tight rein as it is.'

'So I must conform, at whatever cost? That's almost akin to barbarism!'

An eyebrow lifted in sardonic cynicism. 'So far I've treated you with kid gloves.'

A disbelieving laugh emerged from her throat. 'You have to be joking!'

'Only an innocent would fail to appreciate the slow hand of a considerate lover intent on giving as much pleasure as he intends to take.' His expression became dark and forbidding. 'Continue opposing me, and I'll demonstrate the difference.'

Alyse looked at him with unblinking solemnity, frighteningly aware of his strength and sense of purpose. To continue waging this particular war was madness, yet some alien stubborn streak refused to allow her to capitulate.

'Don't threaten me,' she warned.

'Is that what you imagine I'm doing?' His voice held a hateful drawling quality that sent shivers of fear scudding down her spine.

'What other word would you choose?'

'Take off the dress, Alyse,' he warned softly, 'or I won't answer for the consequences.'

It was as if her limbs were frozen and entirely separate from the dictates of her brain, for she stood perfectly still, her eyes wide and unblinking as he swore softly beneath his breath.

Then she cried out as his fingers reached for the zip fastener and slid it down. Seconds later the exotic creation fell to her feet to lie in a heap of silk and heavy satin. All that remained between her and total nudity was a wisp of silky bikini briefs, and her hands rose in spontaneous reaction to cover her breasts.

With deliberate slowness Aleksi slid down the zip of his trousers, and it was only as he began to remove them that she became galvanised into action.

Except that it was far too late, and she struggled helplessly against him, hating the strength of the hands that moulded her slim curves against the hard muscular contours of his body. Her briefs were dispensed seconds after his own, and there was nothing she could do to avoid the relentless pressure of his mouth. He lifted her up against him, parting her thighs so they straddled his hips, and without any preliminaries he plunged deep inside, his powerful thrust stretching silken tissues to their furthest limitation.

Relinquishing her mouth, he lowered his head to her breast, and she cried out as he took possession of one roseate peak, savouring it with flagrant hunger before rendering several bites to the soft underside of the swollen peak.

Alyse balled her hands into fists and beat them against his shoulders then gave a startled cry of disbelief as his hands shifted down to grip her bottom, lifting her slightly as he plunged even deeper.

Then he stilled, and she felt him swell even further inside her, while the hand at her back slid to clasp her nape, urging her head back as he forced her to meet his gaze.

She wanted to vilify him for an act of savagery, yet among the outrage had been a degree of primitive enjoyment, and she hated herself almost as much as she hated him for it.

He knew; she glimpsed the knowledge in the depth of his eyes, and hated him even more for the faint mocking smile that curved his lips.

Hands that had been hard gentled as they cradled her, and he buried his mouth against the hollows at the base of her throat, teasing the rapidly beating pulse there with his tongue, then, just as she thought he was about to release her, he began a slow circling movement with his hips, taking her with him until, almost as a silent act of atonement, pleasure overtook discomfort and her senses became caught up with his, spiralling towards a mutual climax that made her cling to him in unashamed abandon.

Afterwards she showered, then dressed in a vivid emerald-green ruched satin gown with a demure neckline and fitted lines that accentuated her petite figure.

Keeping her make-up to an understated minimum, she accented her eyes and outlined her mouth in soft pink before checking on Georg.

Melanie had arrived and was comfortably settled in the lounge when Alyse emerged several minutes later, and she greeted the girl pleasantly, then accepted Aleksi's light clasp on her elbow as they took their leave and made their way to the garage.

'I rang Solange and told her not to hold dinner as we'd been unavoidably detained,' Aleksi told her as the BMW cleared the driveway. 'I've made a reservation at the Club's restaurant. We'll eat there.'

Alyse took a deep breath, then released it slowly. 'I'm not hungry.'

'You'll eat something, even if it's only *soupe du jour*,' he declared with unruffled ease.

The fact that she did owed nothing to his insistence, and seated opposite him in the well-patronised room she did justice to soup, declined a main course in favour of a second starter of sautéed prawns, refused sweets and settled for a Jamaican coffee.

It was almost ten when the BMW passed security and slid into a reserved car space in the spacious grounds adjoining a prestigious block of apartments housing Solange and Dominic Rochas' penthouse apartment, and Alyse stood in meditative silence as they rode the private lift to the uppermost floor.

CHAPTER TEN

'ALEKSI!' SOLANGE PURRED, immediately embracing him in a manner that slipped over the edge from affection and bordered on blatant intimacy. She stepped back, her eyes shifting with glittering condescension to the woman at his side. 'Alyse.' She tucked a hand into the curve at Aleksi's elbow and drew him forward.

'Solange,' Alyse murmured in polite acknowledgment. 'How lovely to see you.'

Liar, a silent voice taunted. She felt about as well equipped to parry a verbal cut and thrust with the glamorous and very definitely bitchy Solange Rochas as flying over the moon! 'Charming' was the key-word, and she'd act her socks off—subtly, of course, with the innocuous innocence of an ingénue.

'Everyone is here,' Solange declared huskily. 'I was so disappointed you couldn't make dinner.'

'We were delayed,' drawled Aleksi, and Alyse merely proffered a sweet smile when Solange cast her a brief interrogatory glance.

Aleksi had sought to teach her a lesson, and it didn't bear thinking about the resultant passion that flared between them in the aftermath of anger.

'Unfortunately,' Alyse added with sweet regret, and

almost died as Aleksi caught hold of her hand and lifted it to his lips, deliberately kissing each finger in turn.

His eyes blazed with indefinable emotion for a brief few seconds, then became dark and faintly hooded as he threaded his fingers through her own and kept them there.

Liquid fire coursed through her veins, activating each separate nerve-ending as it centred deep within the vulnerable core of her femininity, and she ached, aware of bruised tissues still sensitive from his wounding invasion.

Almost as if he was aware of her thoughts his thumb brushed back and forth across the throbbing veins at her wrist, and her pulse leapt in recognition of his touch. If she hadn't retained such a vivid memory of his wrath, she could almost imagine the gesture was meant as a silent token of—what? Apology? Remorse?

'I'm sure you had a very good reason, darling,' Solange declared, her eyes narrowing with speculative interest as she drew them into the lounge. 'I'll get you a drink, then there's something we must discuss.' She gave a brittle laugh, then offered in throwaway explanation to Alyse, 'Business, I'm afraid.' Then she turned away, effectively shutting Alyse out. 'The Holmes residence. You absolutely *must* dissuade Anthea against the shade of pink she insists on having as the main theme. It really won't do at all.'

Alyse moved slightly, watching with detached fascination as Aleksi's mouth curved into a wry smile.

'If you're unable to exercise your professional influence, Solange, then you may have to accept that it's Anthea's house and she's paying the bills.'

'But it's *my* reputation.'

'Then relinquish the commission.'

The woman's eyes glittered as she made a moue of distaste. 'The problem with the nouveaux riches, darling,' she conceded, with a careless shrug, 'is their gauche taste.'

'Why not show her a visual example of one of your previous commissions?' ventured Alyse, thereby forcing Solange's attention. 'Magazine layouts and countless sample swatches can be confusing.'

Solange looked as if she had just been confronted with an unwanted dissident. 'Something that would be an impossible intrusion on a former client's privacy,' she dismissed with patronising hauteur.

'If I were really delighted with the décor of my home, I'd be only too pleased to share it,' Alyse qualified quietly.

At that precise moment Dominic came forward to greet them, and his deep smile was infinitely mocking.

'Ah, there you are,' he greeted, flicking his sister a brief questioning glance before acknowledging Aleksi, then his gaze settled on Alyse with musing indulgence. 'You look gorgeous, as always. What can I get you to drink?'

'Mineral water will be fine,' Alyse requested without guile, while Aleksi opted for soda with a splash of whisky.

Her glass was icy, its rim sugar-frosted, and she sipped the contents, silently applauding the dash of lime juice and twist of lemon.

'Aleksi,' a soft breathy voice intruded, and Alyse turned slightly and failed to recognise the owner of that husky feminine sound. The slight pause was deliberate, as was her deliberately sexy pout. 'Didn't the babysitter arrive on time?'

Alyse shifted slightly and summoned a brilliant smile. 'Aleksi is to blame. He didn't approve of what I'd chosen to wear, and...' She trailed to a halt, made an expressive shrug, then directed the man at her side a wicked smile. 'One thing led to another.'

The stunning brunette's scarlet-painted mouth parted slightly, then tightened into a thin, uncompromising line.

'How refreshingly honest, darling,' drawled Dominic, and his eyes gleamed devilishly. 'I presume it was worth missing dinner?'

'Really, Dominic,' Solange derided in a voice dripping with vitriol, 'must you be so crude?'

'My husband can be—' Alyse paused, deliberately effecting a carefully orchestrated smile, 'very persuasive.' There, let them make of it what they chose, and be damned! She was heartily sickened by the various snide comments, the none too subtle innuendo designed to shock or at least unsettle her. Timidity had no place in her demeanour if she were to succeed within Aleksi's sophisticated circle, and it would seem her only strength lay in presenting an imperturbable if faintly humorous exterior.

Aleksi's eyes narrowed faintly, but she really didn't care any more.

'I'm sure Dominic won't mind keeping me amused for a while if Solange would prefer you to confer with Anthea,' she said sweetly, and glimpsed Solange's smile of triumph.

'I'll speak to Anthea later,' Aleksi determined mildly, although there was nothing remotely mild about the warning pressure of the hand clasping her own. 'Shall we mingle?' he queried pleasantly. 'We can't monopolise our hosts' attention.'

Solange's expression clearly revealed that he, at least, could monopolise her attention any time he chose, and Alyse had little choice but to drift at Aleksi's side as he drew her among the glittering guests.

The penthouse apartment provided a brilliant advertisement for Solange and Dominic's interior decorating expertise. Perfection personified, Alyse thought, with the smallest detail adhered to from the exquisite floral arrangements to the attire of the hired staff. Even the music had been deliberately selected to blend with conversation rather than provide a cacophonous intrusion.

'Aren't you being a little careless?' Aleksi queried with deceptive calm as they paused near the edge of the room, and Alyse idly twirled the contents of her glass.

'Another guessing game, Aleksi?' she countered, deliberately meeting his gaze.

'I find it particularly unamusing to have my wife offer provocative comments to a known society playboy.'

'Dominic?' Her eyes widened measurably, then became startlingly direct. 'Really? When almost every woman in the room homes in on your presence like a prize bitch in heat?'

'Aren't you being overly dramatic?'

'No,' she said simply, and had to force herself to stand perfectly still as he lifted a hand and brushed his fingers across her cheek.

'Does it bother you?'

Yes, she wanted to cry out. It bothers me like hell. Yet if she acknowledged how she felt it would amount to an admission of sorts, and she wasn't ready to accord him any advantage. Instead, she held his gaze and returned evenly, 'Why should it?'

Something flared in his eyes, an infinitesimal flame that was quickly masked. 'We can always leave.'

Her surprise was undisguised. 'We've only just arrived.'

'Do you want to stay?'

What a loaded question! Whichever way she answered would be equally damning and, although she didn't particularly want to remain, she wasn't ready to go home.

'Aleksi! I'm so glad you're here.'

The intrusion was welcome, and Alyse glanced with interest towards the petite blonde hovering nearby as Aleksi effected an introduction.

'Anthea Holmes, my wife Alyse.'

'How nice to meet you,' she acknowledged with gracious charm before turning towards Aleksi. 'I'm almost at my wits' end!' Her pretty hazel eyes darkened with anxiety. 'The house is superb, but I can't help wondering when I'll be able to move in.'

'Solange mentioned a conflict of interest over the colour scheme,' Aleksi acknowledged. 'What seems to be the problem?'

'A shade of pink,' Anthea said at once. 'I originally chose an extremely delicate salmon shade to blend with cream, and utilising various apricot tones as the main theme. Solange insists on shell-pink to blend with mushroom and various tones of amethyst.' She turned towards Alyse. 'What do you think?'

Oh lord, Alyse groaned inwardly. Why drag me into it? 'I wouldn't presume to infringe on Solange's territory,' she ventured diplomatically. 'But surely it's a personal choice?' Solange was bound to feel insulted if she discovered Anthea had solicited another opinion, especially *hers*, and, while the woman could never be her friend, she didn't particularly want her as an enemy.

'I'd appreciate your viewpoint.'

'Whose viewpoint, darling?'

Alyse almost groaned aloud, and was somewhat startled to see that Anthea was not in the least perturbed that Solange had overheard part of their conversation.

'I've invited Alyse to see the house.'

It was clearly evident that the cat had been well and truly placed among the pigeons, for Solange cast her a sharp narrowed glance. 'Well, of course, if you value the opinion of an unqualified outsider over and above my own...' She let her voice trail to a deliberate halt.

'Alyse is naturally interested in my work,' Aleksi inserted smoothly. 'Aware, also, that I consider my individual clients' wishes are paramount.' His dark eyes encompassed Solange's features in silent warning before switching to Anthea. 'I'll ring my painting contractor tomorrow, then confirm with you and have him meet us at the house.'

Anthea's relief was instantly evident. 'Thank you.' She touched Alyse's hand. 'I'll be mailing invitations to a housewarming party just as soon as I've settled in. You will both come, won't you?'

'We'd be delighted,' Aleksi responded warmly, and Anthea looked quite overcome.

'Another conquest, darling?' Solange asked archly the instant Anthea had melted into the crowd.

'Anthea is a very pleasant woman,' he acknowledged

coolly. 'And a valued client of mine.' But not necessarily of yours.

The words remained unspoken, yet Alyse was supremely conscious of the veiled threat. Aware also that Solange sensed his displeasure, for her features underwent a startling transformation.

'A figurative rap across the knuckles, Aleksi?' Solange queried provocatively. 'Dear little Anthea can have her salmon pink and cream with apricot, if that's what she wants. Why, when she has such rigid ideas, she should consult with an interior designer is beyond me.' Her exquisitely manicured hands fluttered through the air. 'One mustn't forget the newly rich consider it quite the thing to gather opinions without the slightest intention of applying one of them.'

'Perhaps because they prefer to impose something of their own personality,' said Alyse, and drew a raised eyebrow in response.

'Really, darling,' Solange gave a faint shudder, 'I hope this doesn't mean you intend making too many changes in Aleksi's home. It's total perfection just as it is.'

'An incredible compliment,' a drawling voice intervened, 'considering you had no part in it.'

'Dominic. Eavesdropping again?'

Alyse's glass was whisked out of her hand before she had an opportunity to protest, and she made no demur when Dominic took hold of her elbow.

'Come and let me show you the view from the window,' Dominic insisted. 'It's really spectacular.'

It was; beyond the wide expanse of plate-glass tiny pinpricks of light outlined countless high-rise buildings along the foreshore curving in an arc towards the ocean.

The sky was a crisp cool indigo, meeting and merging on the horizon with a moon-dappled darkened sea.

'It's beautiful,' Alyse said softly, caught up in the thrall of man-made monoliths of concrete steel and glass blending with the stark simplicity of nature.

'I can pay you the same compliment.'

She stood quite still at the degree of warmth in his voice. 'I shall accept that in the context in which it should be given,' she said lightly, and heard his purring laugh.

'I'm shattered,' he remarked musingly. 'I imagined you to be an innocent in paradise.'

'Innocence belongs to the very young.'

'Cynicism too,' he mocked. 'From one whose air of fragility is positively intriguing. A mystery woman-child with clear eyes and a beautiful smile. I hope Aleksi appreciates you.'

Of its own accord her smile deepened, and she laughed, a light bubbly sound filled with genuine amusement.

'No comment?'

'May I choose not to?' Alyse countered, and her eyes flew wide as he took hold of her hand.

'Old-fashioned values?'

'I consider a respect for one's privacy is merely good manners,' she corrected solemnly, and saw his eyes lose their customary jaded expression in favour of what appeared to be genuine warmth.

'What a pity Aleksi saw you first.'

Even if he hadn't, she couldn't imagine herself being smitten by Dominic's superficial charm. Whereas Aleksi possessed depth and strength of character, the man at her side bore a shallow brittleness that was undoubtedly motivated by self-obsession.

She turned slightly, unconsciously seeking a familiar dark head across the crowded room, and her eyes widened as they encountered Aleksi's riveting gaze. He was engaged in conversation with a group of men she had met but vaguely remembered, and it was almost as if he knew she had conducted a mental comparison, for she saw one eyebrow lift in silent query.

For one crazy moment she felt as if everything faded away and there was no one else in the room. It was totally mad, but she wanted to be with him. Not only by his side, but in his arms, held close, and loved with such incredible tenderness that she would probably cry from the sheer joy of it.

Her eyes widened and assumed an ethereal mistiness for an incredibly brief second, then she offered a slightly shaky smile and turned back towards Dominic, feeling completely disorientated as she launched into a conversational discourse that was unrelated to anything of particular interest.

It must have made sense, she thought vaguely, for Dominic responded with a flow of words she barely registered, let alone absorbed, and she gave a mental shake as if to clear her head.

What on earth was the matter with her?

'Dominic—you won't mind if I rescue my wife?'

Alyse heard Aleksi's deep drawling voice an instant before his arm curved round her waist, and she felt all her fine body hairs lift up in silent recognition of his presence.

'I assure you she isn't in the slightest danger.'

Never from Dominic. Aleksi, however, was an entirely different matter!

'Shall we leave?' Aleksi queried, bending his head down to hers, and she shrugged.

'If you like.'

'It's barely midnight!' protested Dominic, and Aleksi responded smoothly,

'We said before we left that we wouldn't be late.'

'But surely you can ring the babysitter?'

'I think not.'

In the car Alyse sat in silence, grateful for the light music emitting from stereo speakers, and she simply let her head fall back against the seat's headrest as the BMW purred through the darkened streets.

On reaching home Melanie reported that Georg hadn't even stirred, and Alyse checked his sleeping form while Aleksi saw the young girl into her car and then locked up.

Slipping out of her shoes, Alyse stepped through to the en suite bathroom and set about removing her make-up. Her features looked pale, and her eyes seemed much too large, she decided broodingly. Even her mouth bore a faintly bruised fullness, and she ran the tip of her tongue along the edge of her lower lip in unconscious exploration before lifting the brush to her hair.

She had only just begun when Aleksi entered the bathroom, and her hand faltered slightly as he moved close and took the brush from her nerveless fingers.

She knew she should protest, but no words left her lips, and she stood still beneath his touch, held as if enmeshed in some elusive sensual spell.

The temptation to close her eyes was irresistible, and

when the brush strokes ceased she let her lashes flicker up as she met his gaze via mirrored reflection.

His hands moved to the zip fastening of her dress, and she made no effort to prevent its slithering folds slipping down to the floor, nor the thin scrap of satin and lace of her bra as he released the clasp.

Fingers traced the length of her spine, then spanned her waist before slipping up to cup her breasts. His breath fanned her nape, and she let her head fall forward in silent invitation, unable to suppress a shiver of sheer reaction as his lips sought a vulnerable pulsebeat and savoured it until tiny shockwaves of pleasure spiralled from deep within her central core.

It was almost as if he wanted her to see the effect of his touch on her body, and she moved back against him, arching slightly as his fingers teased the soft fullness of her breasts, then shaped them as the peaks tautened and became engorged with anticipatory pleasure. With detached fascination she glimpsed the soft smudges where hours earlier his mouth had wrought havoc as he had sought to punish, and her eyes clouded in remembered pain.

Hands slid to her shoulders and turned her round to face him, and she was powerless against the caressing softness of his lips as they brushed each bruise in turn before trailing up to settle on her trembling mouth.

His touch was an evocative supplication, teasing, tasting, *loving* in a manner that made her want to cry, and when he slid an arm beneath her knees and lifted her into his arms she could only bury her face against the hollow of his neck.

In bed she closed her eyes, grateful for the darkness as he led her with infinite slowness towards the sweet oblivion of sexual fulfilment, and she clung to him unashamedly, adrift in a sea of her own emotions.

A week ago, even yesterday, she had been so positive her planned escape to Perth was what she desperately wanted. Now, the thought of walking away from Aleksi caused doubt and indecision, and for the first time she was filled with despair.

If she stayed, it would have to be for all the right reasons, and she doubted if love formed any part of his rationale. The most she could hope for would be an affectionate loyalty, a bond founded by Georg's existence. Somehow it wasn't enough.

For what seemed like an hour Alyse lay awake staring at the shadowed ceiling, a hundred differing emotions clouding her mind in kaleidoscopic confusion.

Nothing was the same; *nothing*, Alyse decided sadly as she slid carefully out of bed, each movement in seeming slow motion so as not to disturb the man sleeping silently at her side.

How could she leave? Yet how could she stay? a tiny voice taunted as she crossed to the sitting-room and paused in front of Georg's cot. He was so dear, *everything*, she decided fiercely, unable to prevent her eyes misting with unshed tears.

Moonlight streamed through the opaque curtains, creating an area of shade and silvery light, while long shadowy fingers magnified everything beyond. The balustrading surrounding the pool resembled a grotesque caricature of angles that were unrelated to its original structure, and the pool itself appeared a deep, dark void.

Like her heart. Dear lord in heaven, was it too much

to expect happiness? Was she being a fool to even hope it could be achieved?

She had no idea how long she stood there, and it was acute sensory perception rather than an actual sound that alerted her to Aleksi's presence.

'What are you doing here?' His voice was deep and husky, and she was unable to prevent the shiver that shook her slim frame.

Hands caught her shoulders in a light clasp, then slid down her arms, slipping beneath her elbows to curve round her waist as he pulled her gently back against him.

'You'll catch a chill,' he chided softly, burying his lips against the vulnerable hollow at the edge of her neck.

I am cold, so cold there should be ice instead of blood in my veins. As long as I live, I'll never be warm again.

'Come back to bed.'

No! a silent voice screamed out in silent agony. That was her downfall, the place where she fought countless battles and inevitably lost. Her eyes began to ache with barely suppressed tears, and her vision shimmered as two huge crystalline drops hovered, momentarily dammed by protective lower lashes.

'Alyse?'

Hands gently turned her towards him, and she was powerless to evade the strong fingers that took hold of her chin and tilted it upwards.

The movement released her tears, and there was nothing she could do to prevent their slow trickling descent.

It was impossible that they might escape his attention; too much to hope for that he might choose not to comment on their existence.

She looked at him, her head caught at a proud angle, its planes sharply defined, yet his profile was indistinct viewed through a watery mist that failed to dissipate no matter how often she blinked.

I'm caught in a trap, she thought, feeling incredibly sad. Bound within a silken web whose strands hold me prisoner as surely as if they were comprised of tensile steel.

'Tears?'

Amusement was sadly lacking, and in its place was a depth she was almost afraid to analyse.

A finger traced one rivulet, then followed the path of its twin. 'Why?'

For all the dreams, the love I have to give; hope, eternity.

'Alyse?'

His voice was as soft as velvet, his breath warm as it fanned her cheek, and she closed her eyes against the featherlight touch of his lips at her temples, on her eyelids, then finally her mouth.

It was seduction at its most dangerous, and she almost succumbed as he lifted her into his arms and carried her back into the bedroom. The only thing that stopped her was the degree of treachery involved; sexual pleasure without emotional commitment was no longer enough, and she couldn't pretend any more.

Gently he let her slide down to her feet.

'Suppose you tell me what's bothering you?'

Where could she begin? By saying she'd fallen in love with him? A slight tremor shook her thinly clad form at the thought of his cynicism on learning that she had joined a number of women who had fallen prey to his fatal brand of sexual sensuality.

'I'm almost afraid to insist.' There was an indefinable quality in his voice, a rawness that sent her lashes sweeping upward in swift disbelief.

Alyse was aware of him watching every visible flicker of emotion, and she forced herself to breathe steadily to deploy the deep thudding beat of her heart.

'Please,' Aleksi demanded gently, letting his hands slide up to cup her face.

Something she dared not begin to believe might be hope stirred deep within. 'I don't think I can.'

His lips touched hers with the lightness of a butterfly's wing. 'Try.'

Dared she? No matter how she voiced it, the words would sound calculatingly cold, and afterwards there could be no retraction, only expiation when mere explanation might not be enough.

'Georg deserves to have you as his father,' she faltered at last, unsure whether she had the courage to continue, and something she could have sworn was pain darkened his eyes.

There was a strained silence, then Aleksi drawled with dangerous silkiness, 'You don't consider Georg deserves to have you as his mother?'

Alyse felt as if she was treading on eggshells, yet now she'd started there was nothing else for her but to go on. 'I love him,' she burst out. 'How can you doubt that?'

'Your love for *him* isn't in question.'

The breath caught in her throat, then escaped in a ragged expulsion as her features paled, and she actually swayed, fearing she might fall. Somehow the thought that Aleksi might know the extent of her emotions made her feel physically ill. She had to get away from him, if only temporarily. 'Please—let me go,' she begged.

'Never.'

There was an inflexibility apparent that made her feel terribly afraid.

'I think you'll reconsider when you realise the only reason I entered into marriage was the prospect of obtaining a divorce and legal custody of Georg,' she began shakily, glimpsing a muscle tense along the edge of his jaw as she fought for the strength to continue. 'Almost right from the beginning I plotted the ultimate revenge,' she continued unsteadily, struggling to find the right words, aware that now she'd started, she couldn't stop. 'Two years, that's all I figured it would take before I could return with Georg to Perth.'

His silence was enervating, and after what seemed an interminable length of time she willed him to say something—anything.

'And now?'

'What would you have me say?' she queried in anguish.

'Try—honesty.'

She was weeping inside, drenched by her own silent tears. 'So you can have *your* revenge, Aleksi?'

'Is that what you think?'

'Oh, why do you have to answer every question with another?' she beseeched, sorely tried.

'Because I want it all.'

It was too soon to bare her soul. Much too soon. Love was supposed to happen gradually, not all at once. How was it possible to know if it *was* love in only a matter of weeks?

'I *can't*,' she denied in a tortured whisper.

Aleksi was silent for so long she felt almost afraid, then when he spoke his voice was edged with quiet determination.

'As soon as Rachel and Alexandros return to the Coast, we'll fly to Athens.'

A startled gasp left her lips, and he pressed a finger against them to still the words in protest.

'My parents will delight in having Georg to themselves for a while.'

'Do you always arrange things on the spur of the moment?' she questioned weakly, unable to argue.

'Are you saying you don't want to go?'

She stood hesitantly unsure for a few timeless seconds. 'No,' she whispered at last, aware with frightening certainty that her fate had been irreversibly sealed.

CHAPTER ELEVEN

THE DAYS THAT followed assumed a dreamlike quality. There was a gentleness apparent, a sense of almost secret anticipation that was fuelled by the touch of the hand, the exquisiteness of their lovemaking.

They accepted few invitations, although when they did venture out Alyse was conscious of the overt, barely concealed glances, the thinly disguised speculative gossip as Aleksi rarely let her out of his sight. At home she took delight in arranging gourmet dinners, with candlelight and wine, loving the long, leisurely conversation shared as they talked about anything and everything.

Two days after Rachel and Alexandros arrived back from Sydney Alyse and Aleksi flew out to Athens, spending two days in that ancient city before chartering a helicopter to a small remote island set like a shimmering jewel in the midst of a translucent emerald sea.

There were grapevines, orange trees, olive groves, a few goats, a dog, all lovingly tended by an elderly couple who greeted Aleksi fondly before boarding the waiting helicopter that would take them to visit relatives on another island.

'It's beautiful,' Alyse breathed as Aleksi led her towards an old, concrete-plastered, whitewashed house set on high ground.

Built around an inner courtyard, the rooms were large and airy and filled with antique furniture. Rich Persian rugs covered highly polished floors, and there were several soft-cushioned sofas in the lounge.

'As a child, I spent most of my holidays here,' Aleksi revealed.

'Did you ever return to the island after you emigrated to Australia?' Alyse asked, wandering around the large lounge at will, pausing slightly now and then to study one of the several framed family photographs resting atop items of furniture.

'Several times.'

She turned to look at him, seeing the inherent strength apparent, the sheer physical attraction, and a shadow fleetingly darkened her eyes at the number of women who had surely formed part of his life.

'To join Rachel and Alexandros, and Georgiou,' he added softly. 'This island has always been a family retreat.'

She summoned a bright smile that hid a slight degree of pain. 'It's so warm. Shall we swim before dinner?'

He was silent for a brief second, then he crossed to where she stood and caught hold of her hand. 'Why not?'

The water was crystal-clear and deliciously cool. Alyse challenged Aleksi to a race across the width of the tiny bay, and he merely gave a tigerish laugh as he deliberately let her win. In retaliation she scooped up handfuls of water and threw them at his chest, then shrieked when he pulled her into his arms.

For a moment she struggled, caught up in a playful game, then she slowly stilled, her expression hesitantly serious.

There were so many things she wanted to say, words she needed to hear, yet she was strangely afraid to begin.

A faint edge of tension was evident beneath the surface of Aleksi's control, and she looked at him in silence, her eyes wide and unblinking.

Remembering his lovemaking, the tenderness, the passion... She was tired of fighting, and stubborn pride no longer seemed to matter any more.

'Please help me,' she implored in a husky whisper.

He lifted a hand to her lips and traced a finger across the generous lower curve. 'Why not start at the beginning?'

Her mouth quivered uncontrollably, and she hesitated, unsure now that she had instigated the moment of truth if she possessed the courage to continue. It would be terrible if he was merely amused by a confession of her emotions. Impossible, if he didn't return them to quite the same degree.

'You were everything I disliked in a man,' she ventured unsteadily, her eyes silently beseeching him to understand. 'Overbearing, demanding, and far too self-assured. I told myself I hated you, and at first I did. Then I began to hate myself for being caught up in the maelstrom of physical sensation you were able to arouse.' She drew a deep breath and released it shakily. 'I didn't want to *feel* like that, and I had to fight very hard not to fall in love with you.' A soft, tremulous smile parted her lips. 'It wasn't a very successful battle, for I lost miserably.'

The tension left him in one long shuddering sigh as he gathered her close, then his mouth possessed hers, gently and with such an incredibly sweet hunger she thought she might actually die from sheer sensation, and when at last he lifted his head she could only stand in silent bemusement.

'Repeat those last few words again,' he commanded quietly.

Her beautiful blue eyes misted, and her lips trembled fractionally as she whispered, 'I love you.'

'I had begun to despair that you'd ever admit it,' Aleksi said huskily as he bent low to bestow a lingering kiss to her mouth, then he caught her close, holding her as if he never intended to let her go.

'Can't you feel what you do to me?' His smile held a certain wryness he made no attempt to hide. 'I travelled to Perth with one plan firmly in mind,' he revealed slowly. 'To get Georg at whatever cost. Yet there you were; so fiercely protective of the baby I'd vowed to adopt as my son, adamantly refusing to give him up when I was so sure you would be only too eager to hand over responsibility and get on with your own life.' He brushed his lips across her cheek, then pressed each eyelid closed in turn before trailing a slow evocative path down to the edge of her mouth. 'There was no woman of my acquaintance that I could envisage assuming a motherly role to an orphan child, and faced with your blatant animosity it seemed almost poetic justice to take you as my wife and tame your splendid pride. What I didn't bargain for was the involvement of my emotions.' His smile held such incredible warmth, she felt treacherously weak. 'You were a pocket spitfire, opposing me at every turn. Yet you were so angelic with Rachel and my father, charming to my friends, and I found myself deliberately using every ploy I could engineer in an attempt to break down your defences.'

He paused, taking time to bestow a long, lingering kiss that melted her very bones. His arms held her close, yet she stood strangely still, waiting, wanting so desperately for him to say the words she longed to hear.

'There were times when I was tempted to kill you for being so blind. I love you. *Love*,' he reassured her with a gentle shake.

Joy unfurled itself and spread with tumultuous speed through her veins, and she reached up to lock her hands behind his neck, pulling his head down to hers as she initiated a kiss so incredibly sweet it took only seconds before he deepened it with passionate intensity.

When at last he lifted his head, she could only press her cheek into the curve of his shoulder as he slid an arm beneath her knees and lifted her high against his chest.

'Where are you taking me?' she whispered.

'Indoors.' Aleksi's eyes were warm. 'To bed.'

A soft laugh bubbled from her throat as he carried her into the bedroom, and her eyes sparkled with witching promise as he let her slide down to stand on her feet.

Unable to resist teasing him a little, she protested softly, 'I'm not in the least tired.' Linking her hands together at his nape, she reached up and touched her lips against the corner of his mouth.

He lifted a hand and brushed a stray tendril of hair back behind her ear with incredible gentleness. His smile was warm and infinitely seductive, and she stood looking at him, seeing the strength of purpose etched on those dark arresting features, the passion evident in the depth of his eyes.

A slight tremor shook her slender frame as she

reached out and slowly removed his briefs, then her own before unfastening the clip of her bikini bra. Collecting a towel, she carefully blotted every trace of seawater from his body, then she stood still as he took the towel from her hand and gently returned the favour before letting the towel fall to the floor.

Without a word she reached up and pulled his head down to hers, and her lips brushed across his own, trembling a little as she instigated a hesitant exploration, then she drew him towards the bed and pulled him down beside her.

'Please make love to me.' The plea left her lips as scarcely more than a whisper, and her mouth parted in welcome to his as he wrought a devastating assault on her senses, plundering until she clung to him unashamedly.

It seemed an age before he broke the kiss, and she almost died at the wealth of deep slumbrous passion evident.

'I intend to,' he told her gently. 'For the rest of my life.'

* * * * *

A PASSIONATE SURRENDER
HELEN BIANCHIN

CHAPTER ONE

'CRISTOS.'

The husky imprecation held an angry silkiness as Luc Dimitriades tossed the faxed report down onto his desk.

Detailed surveillance of his wife's movements during the past nine days revealed few surprises, although one caused his eyes to narrow with contemplative suspicion.

Reflex action had him reaching for his cellphone and keying in a series of digits.

'Put me through to Marc Andreas,' he instructed curtly as soon as the receptionist picked up.

'Doctor has a patient with him.'

'It's urgent,' he said without compunction, and identified himself. 'He'll take the call.'

Minutes later he had official confirmation, and his expression hardened as he reached for the inter-office phone.

Clear, concise instructions set his plan in motion, and after replacing the receiver he stood to his feet and crossed to the large plate-glass window.

The city and harbour spread out before him in splendid panorama. Sparkling blue sea, tall office buildings in varying height and design of concrete,

5

steel and glass. Expensive two- and three-level mansions nestled between trees and shrubbery on a carved-out rock-face overlooking the inner harbour.

Small craft moored in safe anchorage dotting inlets and coves. The bustling water-cats and ferries vying with a huge tanker being guided by tugboats into berth. The familiar arch of Sydney's bridge, the distinctive architecture of the opera house.

It was a familiar sight. Yet today he didn't register the view. Nor the expensive furnishings, the genuine art gracing the walls of his luxurious office.

There was no pleasure of the scene evident in his broad, chiselled features, little emotion in his dark brooding gaze as he lapsed into reflective thought.

A brief marriage in his early twenties to his childhood sweetheart had ended tragically with Emma's accidental death mere months after their wedding. Grief-stricken, he'd thrown himself into work, putting in long hours and achieving untold success in the business arena.

Remarriage wasn't on his agenda. He'd loved and lost, and didn't want to lose his heart again. For the past ten years he'd enjoyed a few selective relationships...no commitments, no empty words promising permanence.

Until Ana.

The daughter of one of his executives, she'd often partnered her widowed father to various functions. She was attractive, in her mid-twenties, intelligent and she possessed a delightful sense of humour.

What was more, she wasn't in awe of him, his status or his wealth.

They'd dated a few months, enjoyed each other in bed, and for the first time since Emma's death there was an awareness of his own mortality, his accumulated wealth…the need to share his life with one woman, have children with her, forge a future together.

Who better than Ana in the role of his wife? He cared for her, she was eminently suitable, and he could provide her with an enviable lifestyle.

The wedding had been a low-key affair attended by immediate family, followed by a few weeks in Hawaii, after which they settled easily into day-to-day life.

A year on, the only blight on the horizon was Celine Moore, an ex-mistress, very recently divorced and hell-bent on causing mischief.

Luc's mouth tightened into a grim line as he recalled the few occasions when Celine had deliberately orchestrated a compromising situation. Incidents he'd dealt with with skilled diplomacy and the warning to desist. Something Celine refused to heed, and her persistence became an issue Ana found difficult to condone.

Less than two weeks ago an argument over breakfast had ended badly, and he'd arrived home that evening to discover Ana had packed a bag and taken a flight to the Gold Coast.

The note she'd left him declared a need for a few days away to *think things through*.

Except *a few days* had become nine, and the latter thirty-six hours of which had resulted in unreturned calls from voice-mail and text messages left on her cellphone.

Her father, upon confrontation, swore she wasn't answering *his* messages either, and he had every reason not to lie.

Rebekah, her younger sister and business partner, also disavowed any knowledge of Ana's whereabouts, other than to cite a holiday resort on the Gold Coast, from which enquiries revealed Ana had checked out within a few days of registering.

Hence Luc had no hesitation in engaging the services of a private detective, whose verbal updates were now detailed in a faxed report.

Ana's actions merely confirmed Luc's suspicions. A newly leased apartment and employment weren't conducive to a temporary break.

However, he could deal with that, and numerous scenarios of just *how* he'd deal with it occupied his mind. Foremost of which was the intention to haul her over his shoulder and bring her home.

Something, he decided grimly, he should have done within a day or two of her leaving, instead of allowing her the distance, time and space she'd vowed so desperately to need. Yet she'd done the unexpected by attempting to cover her tracks... without success.

Surely she couldn't believe he'd let her separation bid drag on for long?

The inter-office phone rang, and he crossed to the desk to take the call.

'The pilot is on standby, and your car is out front.'

Smooth efficiency came with a high-priced salary.

'Petros will have a bag packed by the time you reach the house.'

'Thanks.'

An hour later Luc boarded the private jet, sank into one of four plush armchairs, and prepared for take-off.

'Go take a lunch break.'

Ana attached the ribbon, tied a deft bow, utilised the slim edge of the scissors to curl the ribbon ends, then set the bouquet of roses to one side.

It was her third day as an assistant at a florist shop in the trendy suburb of Main Beach. She'd entered the shop on a whim, bought flowers to brighten her newly acquired apartment, and, noticing the owner's harassed expression, she'd jokingly asked if the owner required help, citing her experience as a florist. What she didn't impart was that she co-owned her own business in an upmarket Sydney suburb.

Incredible as it seemed, acquiring a job had been as simple as being in the right place at the right time.

Fate, it seemed, had taken a hand, although eventually she'd have to address her sojourn from Sydney, her marriage.

A hollow laugh escaped her throat as she caught up her shoulder bag and walked out onto the pavement.

It was a beautiful early summer day, the sun was warm, and there was a slight breeze drifting in from the ocean.

The usual lunch crowd filled the many cafés lining Tedder Avenue, and she crossed the street, selected an empty table and sank into a seat.

Efficient service ensured almost immediate attention, and she gave her order, then sipped chilled bottled water as she flipped through the pages of a magazine.

An article caught her eye, and she read the print with genuine interest, only to put it to one side as the waitress delivered a steaming bowl of vegetable risotto. There was also a fresh bread roll, and she picked up a fork and began eating the delectable food.

The chatter from patrons seated at adjoining tables provided a pleasant background, combining with the faint purr of vehicles slowly cruising the main street in search of an elusive parking space.

Expensive cars, wealthy owners who strolled the trendy street to one of several outdoor cafés where *lunch with friends* was more about being *seen* than satisfying a need for food.

Ana liked the ambience, enjoyed being a part of it, and the similarity to equally trendy areas in Sydney didn't escape her.

It was relatively easy to tamp down any longing for the city where she'd been born and raised. Not so easy to dismiss the man she'd married a little more than a year ago.

Luc Dimitriades possessed the height, breadth of shoulder and attractive good looks to turn any woman's head. Add sophisticated charm, an aura of power, and the result was devastating.

Australian-born of Greek parents, he'd chosen academia and entered the field of merchant banking, rising rapidly through the ranks to assume a position that involved directorial decision-making.

Inherited wealth combined with astute business acumen ensured he numbered high among the country's rich and famous.

For Ana, all it had taken was one look at him and the attraction was instant, cataclysmic. Sheer sexual chemistry, potent and electric. Yet it was more than that…much more. He affected her as no man ever had, and she fell deeply, irretrievably in love with him.

It was the reason she accepted his marriage proposal, and she convinced herself it was enough he vowed his fidelity and promised to honour and care for her.

THE CATCH OF THE DECADE one national newspaper had captioned when Luc Dimitriades had taken Ana Stanford as his bride.

Maybe, given time, his affection for her would become love, and a year into the marriage she was content. She had an attentive husband, the sex was to die for, and life had assumed a pleasant routine.

Until Celine, always the temptress, re-entered the scene, newly divorced, and *hunting*...with Luc as her prey.

Subtle destruction, carefully orchestrated to diminish Ana's confidence. The divorcee was very clever in aiming her verbal barbs out of Luc's hearing. Implying an affair, citing dates and times when Luc was absent on business or when he'd extended a business meeting to include dinner with colleagues. Merely excuses given in order to be with Celine.

Doubt and suspicion, coupled with anger and jealousy built over a period of weeks.

Even now, the thought of Celine's recent contretemps made Ana grit her teeth. Despite Luc's denial, where there was smoke, there were embers just waiting to be fanned into flame. And infidelity was something she refused to condone.

Angry words had led to a full-scale argument, and afterwards Ana had simply made a few phone calls, packed a bag and taken the midday flight to the Gold Coast.

Apart from the note she'd left him, her only attempt at contact was a recorded message she'd left on Luc's answer-machine, and she doubted it would appease him for long.

'Ana.'

The voice was all too familiar, its inflexion deep and tinged with a degree of mocking cynicism.

There had been no instinctive sixth sense that might have alerted her to his presence. Nothing to warn of the unexpected.

Ana slowly raised her head and met her husband's steady gaze. Unwanted reaction kicked in, and she banked it down, aware on a base level of the damning effect he had on her senses.

She felt vulnerable, exposed, and way too needy. It wasn't a feeling she coveted, at least not now, not here, when she'd vowed to think with her head, not her heart.

Fat chance. All it took was one look, a few seconds in his presence, and her emotions went every which way but loose!

How was it possible to love, yet hate someone with equal measure?

She could think of any number of reasons to justify the way she felt... Ambivalence, out-of-whack hormones. The desire to hurt, as she hurt.

Why, then, did she possess this crazy urge to feel the sanctuary of his arms and the brush of his mouth on her own? The heat of his body ...

A silent screeching cry rose from somewhere deep inside. *Don't go there.*

Instead, she forced herself to subject him to an analytical appraisal, deliberately noting the broad facial bone structure which lent his features a chiselled look that was enhanced by piercing dark eyes, a firm muscled jaw, and a mouth to die for.

Well-groomed hair as dark as sin grew thick on

his head, and he wore it slightly longer than was currently in vogue.

Attired in a three-piece business suit, deep blue shirt and impeccably knotted silk tie, he exuded an aura of invincible power.

Tall, dark and dangerous was an apt descriptive phrase, she perceived, sensing the ruthlessness hovering just beneath the surface of his control.

'Mind if I join you?'

'What if I say no?'

He offered a faint smile, and wondered if she knew how well he could read her. 'It wasn't a rhetorical question.'

Ana held his gaze. 'Then why ask?'

Luc took the seat opposite, ordered black coffee from a hovering waitress, then focused his attention on his wife.

She looked pale, and she'd lost a few essential kilos from her petite frame. There were faint shadows evident, as if she hadn't been sleeping well, and her eyes were dark with fatigue. Instead of its usual attractive style, her honey-blonde hair was pulled back into a pony-tail.

His silent appraisal irked her unbearably. 'Are you done?' Her voice sounded tense even to her own ears.

He resembled a sleekly powerful predator deceptively at ease. Except his seemingly relaxed façade didn't fool her in the slightest. There wasn't any doubt he'd pounce...merely a matter of *when*.

'No,' Luc intimated as she pushed the bowl of partly eaten food to one side.

'Eat,' Luc bade quietly, and she threw him a baleful glare.

'I've lost my appetite.'

'Order something else.'

She barely resisted the temptation to throw something at him. 'Should I ask how you discovered my whereabouts?'

His gaze didn't waver, and his eyes were cool, fathomless. 'I would have thought the answer self-explanatory.'

'You hired a private detective.' Her voice rose a fraction. 'And had me followed?'

'Did you think I wouldn't?'

Hadn't this scenario haunted her for the past few days? Invading her sleep, unsettling her nerves?

The waitress delivered his coffee, and he requested the bill.

'I'll pay for my own meal.'

He shot her a hard glance. 'Don't be ridiculous.'

She checked her watch. 'What do you want, Luc? I suggest you cut to the chase. I'm due back at work in ten minutes.'

Luc selected a paper tube of sugar and emptied it into his cup. 'No, you're not,' he declared silkily.

Her gaze locked with his. 'What do you mean... *no*?'

'You no longer have a job, and your apartment lease has been terminated.'

She felt as if all the breath had suddenly left her body. Angry consternation darkened her eyes, and faint pink coloured her cheeks. 'You have no right—'

'Yes.' His voice was deadly quiet. 'I do.'

She badly wanted to hit him, and almost did. 'No, you don't,' she reiterated fiercely.

'We can argue this back and forth, but the end result will be the same.'

'If you think I'll calmly go back to Sydney with you,' she began heatedly, 'you can think again!'

His gaze seared hers. 'This afternoon, tonight, tomorrow. It hardly matters when.'

Ana rose to her feet, only to have his hand close over her arm, halting her intention to leave.

Without pausing for thought she picked up the sugar container and hurled it at him, watching with a sense of horrified fascination as he fielded it neatly and replaced it on the table, then calmly gathered up the scattered tubes.

'I intend to file for divorce.' Dear heaven, where had that come from? Until now it had been a hazy choice she'd considered and discounted a hundred times during the sleepless night hours since fleeing Sydney.

His gaze seared hers. 'Divorce isn't an option.'

She stood trapped as the silence stretched between them, a haunting entity that became more significant with every passing second, and there was little she could do but comply as he exerted sufficient pressure to ensure she sank down onto the chair.

'Don't you have something to tell me?' Luc prompted with deceptive mildness, and glimpsed her apprehension before she successfully masked it.

'Go away and leave me alone?' Ana taunted in return.

'Try again.'

A muscle twisted painfully in her stomach, and she barely suppressed the instinct to soothe it with her hand.

He couldn't possibly know. *Could he?* She went suddenly cold at the thought. For the past few weeks she'd alternated between joy and despair.

'I'll make it easy for you,' Luc ventured with deadly softness. 'You're carrying my child.'

'A child that is also *mine*,' Ana said fiercely.

'*Ours.*' His silky tone sent shivers down her spine. 'I refuse to be relegated to a weekend father, restricted to sharing my son or daughter on a part-time basis.'

'Is that why you came after me? Because I suddenly have something you want?' Her eyes darkened to the deepest sapphire, her anger very real at that precise moment. Yet inside she wanted to weep. For the child she'd conceived. For herself, for wanting the love of a man who she doubted would ever love her.

'I'd rather be a single parent than attempt to raise a child in a household where its father divides his time between its mother and his mistress. How could the child begin to understand values, morals, and integrity?'

'Mistress?' His voice was quiet.

Too quiet, she perceived, and suppressed a faint shiver.

'You accuse me of having an affair?'

'Celine—'

'Was someone with whom I shared a brief relationship three, four years ago.'

'According to her, the affair is ongoing.'

'Why would I need a mistress when I have you?'

Remembering their active sex life, the sheer delight they shared in bed, brought a tinge of colour to her cheeks. 'For the hell of it?' she ventured carelessly, adding, 'Because you're insatiable and one woman isn't enough?'

His features hardened and assumed an implacable mask. 'Don't tempt me to say something I might regret.'

'Go back to Sydney, Luc.' She was like a runaway train that couldn't stop. 'There's nothing you can say or do that'll persuade me to return with you.'

'No?'

She sensed the steel beneath the dangerously silky tone, and suppressed an illusory premonition.

'The last time I heard, coercion carries no weight in a court of law.'

He held a trump card, and he had no hesitation in playing it. 'However, embezzlement does.' He paused, watching her expressive features in a bid to assess whether she had any prior knowledge William Stanford had indulged in creative accounting over a six-month time span.

'Excuse me?'

Luc chose his words with care, weighing each for its impact. 'The bank's auditors have discovered a series of discrepancies.'

'How can that involve me?' she queried, genuinely puzzled.

'Indirectly, it does.'

Even a naïve fool could do simple arithmetic, and she considered herself to be neither. 'You're implying my *father* is responsible?' she demanded in disbelief. 'I don't believe you.'

He reached inside his jacket, withdrew a folded document and placed it in front of her. 'A copy of the auditors' report.'

Ana touched the paper hesitantly, then she opened the document and read the report.

It was conclusive and damning, the attached spreadsheet listing each transaction lengthy and detailed.

She felt herself go cold. Embezzlement, theft... they were one and the same, and a punishable crime.

Luc studied her expressive features, witnessed the fleeting emotions, and anticipated her loyalty.

'It was very cleverly done,' he revealed with a degree of cynicism. So much so, it had been missed twice. He wasn't sure which angered him more...the loss of trust in one of his valued executives, or the fact William Stanford had relied on his daughter's connection by marriage to avoid prosecution.

'How long have you known?' Ana queried with a sense of dread, unwilling to examine where this was going, yet desperately afraid her wildest suspicion would be proven true.

'Nine days.'

Coincidentally the time she wrote him a note and took a flight north. Did he think that was the reason she left?

Men of Luc's calibre always had a back-up plan. And this was personal. Very personal.

'What do you want, Luc?'

'No divorce. Our child.' He waited a beat. 'My wife in my home, my bed.'

'Go to hell.'

One eyebrow rose in mockery. 'Not today, *agape mou*.'

Pink coloured her cheekbones and lent her eyes a fiery sparkle. 'You think you can make conditions and have me meekly comply?'

'*Meek* wasn't a descriptive I considered.'

Dear heaven, he was amused. She stood to her feet, gathered her bag and slung the strap over her shoulder, then she turned in the direction of the florist shop, aware that Luc fell into step at her side.

'I intend explaining to the letting agent and my

employer that you're a presumptuous, arrogant bastard with no right to dictate my life.'

'And your father will go to jail.'

Her step faltered as she threw him a look that would have felled a lesser man. 'How come you get to make the rules?'

'Because I can.'

'And I get to choose whether to resume my marriage to you, in return for no charges laid against my father.' There was no doubt Luc viewed this as just another business proposition. Well, damn him. She'd do the same. 'What of restitution?'

'It will be taken care of.'

'And his job?'

'Already terminated.'

She was dying inside, inch by inch. 'His references?' she pursued tightly.

'I have a duty of disclosure.'

Something that would make it almost impossible for her father to gain a similar position anywhere in Sydney…possibly even the country.

'I'll think about it,' Ana conceded, endeavouring to ignore the prickle of apprehension steadily creating havoc with her nervous system.

His eyes were hard, their expression implacable. 'You have an hour.'

She closed her eyes, then opened them again, and released the breath she'd unconsciously held for several seconds.

'Are you this diabolically relentless in the business

arena?' Stupid question, she mentally castigated. His steel-willed determination and ruthless decision-making had earned him a reputation as one of the city's most feared negotiators.

His silence sent an icy chill feathering the length of her spine, and she cursed him afresh.

They reached the florist shop, and she turned towards him, her eyes gleaming with hidden anger as she met and held his dark gaze.

'There are a few conditions.'

His gaze hardened, and he resisted the urge to shake her within an inch of her life. 'You're hardly in a position to stipulate conditions.'

Did he know how much she hurt? Just looking at him caused her physical pain, remembering the hopes and dreams she'd held, only to have them shatter one by one.

She began counting off the fingers of one hand. 'I want your word you won't attempt to deny me my child once it's born.'

Something moved in his eyes, an emotion she didn't care to define. 'Granted.'

'Your fidelity.'

'You've had that since day one.'

She looked at him long and hard, then lifted an eyebrow in silent query. 'Not according to Celine.'

'Naturally, you choose to believe her over me.' His dry tones held a damning cynicism she chose to ignore.

'There's just one more thing,' she pursued.

It was impossible to tell much from his expression, and she didn't even try.

'And that is?'

'I want it all in writing and legally notarised before I give you my answer.'

As an exit line it took some beating, and she didn't look back as she stepped into the florist shop.

'I wasn't expecting you.'

Stiff formality replaced a former easy friendliness, and Ana silently cursed Luc afresh.

'I'm responsible for my own decisions,' she assured evenly. Her gaze was steady as the silence stretched into seemingly long seconds before the shop's owner offered,

'He doesn't look the type of man who'd take *no* for an answer.'

Wasn't that the truth! 'I can give you this afternoon, if that's OK?'

'I've already put in a call to the employment agency.'

What else did she expect?

'Are you going to return to Sydney with him?'

'Possibly.' Ana deposited her bag out back, and checked the order book, then she set to work.

Concentration was the key, but all too frequently it wavered as she examined one scheme after another, only to discard each of them. Where could she go that Luc wouldn't find her?

A faint shiver raised the fine hairs on the back of her neck. If he'd had a private investigator following her every move, it was feasible the man was still on duty. It gave her a creepy feeling, and made her incredibly angry.

Luc had played the game with consummate skill in presenting her with a *coup de grâce*.

But the game had only just begun, and she intended to play by the rules…her own.

CHAPTER TWO

How long would it take Luc to consult a lawyer and have the requested paperwork completed? With his influence and connections, she doubted he'd have a problem.

The shop was busy, there were several phone orders, and people walked in off the street to select purchases. Single roses, bouquets, cut flowers for a special hospital visit...the requests were numerous and varied.

She was in the middle of assembling decorative Cellophane and gathering baby's breath when the door buzzer sounded for the umpteenth time. She automatically glanced up from her task to greet the new customer, and saw Luc observing her actions.

There was an element of formidability existent, a sense of purpose that was daunting, and Ana was conscious of an elevated sense of nervous tension.

Her hands paused as her gaze locked with his, then she bent her head and focused on fashioning pink and white carnations into an elaborate spray.

Ribbon completed the bouquet, and she attached the completed card, the instruction slip, then transferred it to the delivery table.

'Are you done?' Luc queried silkily, his gaze

caught by a tendril of hair that had worked its way loose from her pony-tail, and he restrained the urge to sweep it back behind her ear.

She shot him a cool glance. 'I finish at six.'

The atmosphere in the room seemed suddenly charged, and she could almost feel the latent electricity apparent.

His eyes narrowed with a chilling bleakness. 'You can do better than that.'

'We're busy.' Hot damn, she was so polite it was almost comical. She made a thing of checking the time. 'I'm sure you can manage to fill in a few hours.'

He could, easily. However, he didn't feel inclined to pander to her deliberate manipulation. 'One hour, Ana,' he warned in a voice that was deadly soft.

'Are you mad?' the older woman queried the instant Luc left the shop.

'Certifiably,' Ana agreed imperturbably.

'Gutsy, too. I admire that in a woman.'

She was a fool to think she could best him. Except she was damned if she'd allow him to set down terms and expect her to abide by every one of them without a fight.

'I'm going to be sorry to lose you, honey. We were just beginning to get along.'

'I could be back,' Ana said with humour, and heard the other woman's laughter.

'I doubt he'll let you get away again. Now, why don't you go finish up? I can manage the rest.' Her eyes twinkled with mischief. 'Besides, I'm not averse to a woman stirring a man up a bit.'

Leave, and not be here when Luc returned? 'You're wicked.'

'Good luck, honey. If you're ever back up this way again, call in and say hello.' She withdrew an envelope from her pocket. 'Your pay.'

'Keep it in lieu of notice.'

'Some would. I won't. Now go.'

It took five minutes to walk to her apartment, and once inside she headed straight for the kitchen, extracted bottled water from the refrigerator, uncapped the lid and drank until her thirst was quenched, then she made for the bedroom, stripped off her clothes and hit the shower.

She washed her hair, then dressed in jeans and a singlet top, opted to forgo make-up and piled her damp hair into a loose knot atop her head.

Packing would probably be a good move, but somehow achieving it indicated her imminent return to Sydney, and sheer stubbornness ensured she put off such a task for as long as possible. Besides, how long did it take to empty a few clothes and possessions into a travel-bag?

It was five when the intercom buzzed, and Ana's stomach did a quick somersault at the sound. It had to be Luc. No one else knew her address.

She cleared him through security into the main lobby, and then waited for the lift to reach her designated floor.

Her doorbell rang all too soon, and she took a calming breath as she crossed the lounge.

He stood looming large in the aperture, dark and vaguely threatening. He'd removed his jacket and hooked it over one shoulder, his tie was missing, he'd loosened the top few buttons of his shirt and folded the cuffs back from each wrist. It lent him a casual air that was belied by his deliberately enigmatic expression.

Ana met his gaze with fearless disregard, and ignored the increased thud of her heartbeat. 'I refuse to be treated like a runaway child on the verge of being dragged home by its parent.'

He didn't move so much as a muscle. 'Whatever happened to *hello*?'

She drew in a deep breath, then released it slowly. 'You want *polite*?'

One eyebrow assumed a mocking slant. 'Shall we start over?' Luc countered coolly.

'Not in this lifetime.'

He let his gaze rove slowly over her slim form, then pinned her blue eyes with his own. 'For the record, my relationship with you is hardly paternal.'

His drawling tone caused her resentment to resurface. 'You're setting down rules, taking away my freedom of choice,' she retaliated, watching as he remained in the doorway.

'I've given you an option,' Luc corrected silkily.

'Sure, you have.' She speared him with an icy blue glare. 'With only one possible answer!'

He stepped into the lounge and shut the door. 'Did you imagine I'd have it any other way?'

Ana closed her eyes, then quickly opened them again. 'You've made it quite clear the child I carry is the main issue.'

She watched as he withdrew an envelope from the inside pocket of his jacket and extended it towards her. 'The legalities you requested.'

Stark legalese held an awful clarity she was loath to accept. Yet what other course did she have?

She lifted her head and met his steady gaze. There was a glimpse of something faintly dangerous in those dark depths she didn't care to define, and she returned her attention to the printed pages.

There were further clauses outlining conditions that covered every eventuality…and then some.

'You expect me to sign this?'

'A legal agreement was your idea.' Luc's tone was silk-smooth.

He was right. But that didn't make it any easier to attach her signature beneath his.

Luc took the document from her outstretched hand and tucked it into his jacket pocket. 'Do you want to eat out, or order in?'

Food? 'I thought you'd want to head back—' She paused, unable for the life of her to say *home*. 'To Sydney.'

'*We,*' Luc corrected, adding quietly, 'And you need to eat.'

'Such solicitousness is touching.'

'Don't be facetious.'

She spared him a long, thoughtful look, assessing the latent power, his innate sensual chemistry and its degree of sexual energy.

For the past nine days he'd filled her mind, invading it in a manner that was tortuous as she reflected on his long strong body, the feel of sinew and muscle, skin on skin, as his lovemaking transcended the physicality of mere sexual coupling.

It was there in his arms where she lost herself to any rational thought, and became a witching wanton eager to gift and receive each sensual delight.

For then she could qualify a one-sided love, content that it was *enough* not to have love returned in kind. She could even accept his heart remained locked in the memory of Emma, his first wife, hopeful that with time affection might become something deeper, more meaningful.

At no stage had she envisaged the existence or presence of a mistress.

And now there was to be a child...

She desperately wanted the marriage to survive. But there had to be trust, and honesty.

Was Luc's word, verbally and noted in legalese, sufficient?

After all, words were only an expression of intention, and easily disregarded or broken without honour.

'Are you done?'

The silkily voiced query held a slight edge which

snapped her back to the present, and her chin tilted in silent defiance. 'No.'

As long as she lived, she'd never be *done* with him. The trick was never to allow him that edge of knowledge.

His eyes narrowed slightly. 'How long will it take you to pack?'

She'd brought few clothes with her, bought less, and the little personal touches she'd added to the apartment would have no place in Luc's elegant Vaucluse mansion.

'I can be ready in fifteen minutes.' She could do *cool.* At least for now.

Without a further word she crossed into the bedroom, placed the empty bag onto a chair, and began the task of transferring her belongings.

Luc moved to the kitchen, opened the refrigerator and extracted bottled water, filled a glass and swallowed the chilled liquid.

Then he retrieved his cellphone, keyed in a series of digits and instructed his pilot to be on standby for the return flight.

There was, he decided grimly, no point in delaying the inevitable.

Don't look back, Ana bade silently as she walked at Luc's side to the car. He stowed her bag in the boot as she slid into the passenger seat, then within minutes he fired the engine and eased the car out from its parking bay.

Luc chose a restaurant at one of the upmarket hotels, and confirmation of their reservation indicated he'd phoned in ahead.

Her appetite seemed to have fled, and she picked at the starter, nibbled a few morsels from the artistically presented main, and chose fresh fruit in lieu of dessert.

'Not hungry?'

Ana spared him a level glance. 'No.' If he suggested she should eat more, she'd be hard pressed not to tip the contents of her plate into his lap.

Luc deferred to her preference for tea and ordered coffee for himself from the hovering waitress.

She watched as he spooned sugar into the dark brew, noting the shape of his hand, the skin texture and the tensile strength evident.

He had the touch, the skill, to drive her mindless with a tactile slide of his fingers, and she hated herself for the sudden increase in the beat of her heart.

Sexual chemistry. It had a power of its own. Damning, lethal.

It took considerable resolve to sip her tea with a semblance of calm, and she felt a sense of relief when he signalled the waitress for their bill.

Three quarters of an hour later they crossed the Tarmac and stepped aboard the luxurious Gulfstream jet, whose gently whining engines increased in pitch the instant the outer door closed.

Smooth, very smooth, Ana conceded minutes later as the jet wheeled its way out onto the runway, then cleared for take-off, gathered speed and rose like a silver bird into the sky.

The light was fading as dusk approached, and there was an opalescent glow as the sun slipped beneath the horizon in a brilliant flare of orange tinged with pink.

Darkness descended quickly, and all too soon there was nothing to see except an inky blackness and the occasional pinprick of lights as the jet followed the coastline south.

Ana made no attempt at conversation and simply leaned back against the headrest and closed her eyes, successfully shutting out the sight of the man seated at her side.

It didn't, however, shut out her chaotic thoughts.

A return to Sydney meant the re-emergence of the lifestyle she'd sought to briefly escape. There was her father, Rebekah, the florist shop.

Worst of all, there was Celine Moore. Her nemesis and her enemy.

Absenting herself for more than a week hadn't solved a thing. The problems remained. A hollow laugh rose and died in her throat. All that had been achieved was a metaphorical stay of execution.

Who would win? The wife or the mistress?

CHAPTER THREE

'Good evening, Ms Dimitriades.'

Ana returned the greeting and offered Petros a faint smile as she slid into the rear passenger seat, aware that Luc crossed behind the vehicle and slipped in beside her.

Within minutes Petros eased the car forward, cleared the private sector and joined the flow of traffic vacating the airport.

At this time of night they'd make good time to Vaucluse, and she sank back against the soft leather upholstery, intent on viewing the passing surroundings.

Bright lights, coloured flashing neon…the muted noise of a big, cosmopolitan city.

To her it was *home*, where she'd been born and raised, with an endearing sense of the familiar.

A blustery shower sprang up, splattering the windscreen with fine rain-spray and diminishing visibility.

It seemed to close in, heightening the close confines of the car and her proximity to the man seated at her side.

Silence stretched between them like a yawning chasm, and she thought of a safe topic of conversation, only to discard it. Why pretend?

Vaucluse was a prestigious suburb with magnificent views over the inner harbour, and Ana's nerves tensed as the car turned in between the electronically controlled gates leading to Luc's architecturally designed home.

Stretching over two blocks of land, the elegant double-storeyed mansion possessed imposing lines, archways, and high-domed windows. It was set in well-kept grounds, the sculptured gardens maintained by Petros, who resided in rooms above the garages, and whose duties covered numerous chores supplemented by twice-weekly household help.

The car drew to a halt beneath the wide portico, and Ana emerged before Petros could move round to open the door, thereby incurring his faintly pained expression.

She stood as Luc disabled the security system and unlocked the panelled double doors. He swung them wide and she entered at his side.

Marble floor tiles in varying shades of cream bordered by dark forest-green covered the spacious foyer, and there were expensive works of art gracing the walls. Formal lounge and dining-room were positioned to the right, informal rooms and a spacious study lay to the left. The focal point was a wide, sweeping marble staircase leading to the upper floor which held no fewer than four bedrooms, each with *ensuite*, the master suite, and a private sitting-room.

'I'll serve refreshments,' Petros indicated as he moved into the foyer after securing the doors.

'Not for me.' Ana softened her refusal with a slight smile, and made for the stairs. She felt disinclined to extend the façade any longer than necessary.

Luc followed in her footsteps, and she turned to face him as they reached the landing.

'I'd prefer to have a room of my own.'

His expression didn't change. 'No.'

Resentment flared. 'What do you mean...*no*?'

'I would have thought my answer held sufficient clarity.'

'I don't want to sleep with you.'

'Perhaps not...tonight,' he amended silkily, and caught the flicker of pain in those deep blue eyes before it was successfully hidden.

'Not *any* night!'

'Brave words, Ana.'

He moved ahead of her with indolent ease, her bag in hand, and she watched in silence as he entered the master suite only to emerge seconds later empty-handed.

She wanted to rail against him, hating the power he possessed and her inability to retaliate in kind. She was caught in a web, tied to him by the child she'd conceived, and held there by family loyalty.

'*Go to hell*, Luc,' she evinced bitterly as he drew level.

He paused, and caught hold of her chin, tilting it so she had little option but to meet his steady gaze.

'Careful, *pedhaki mou*. I might be tempted to take you there.'

Her eyes widened at the silkily voiced threat, and her lips shook slightly as his hand slid to cup her cheek. 'I don't scare easily.'

The edge of his mouth quirked. 'One of your admirable qualities.' He released her and moved towards the head of the stairs.

He would, she knew, check with Petros for any messages, make the required calls, scan his electronic mail, and deal with the urgent stuff...all of which could take half an hour, or more.

It gave her time...to do what? Settle in? The thought was laughable.

Ana entered the master bedroom and came to a halt a few steps into the large room. Nothing had changed...had she really expected it to?

The king-size bed with its dark, richly patterned duvet and numerous pillows was a focal point. Furniture comprised matching sets of multi-layered chest of drawers in varying heights, and there were dual *ensuites*, dual walk-in wardrobes. A deep-cushioned sofa and a chaise longue completed a room that was designed for comfort and pleasure.

Sensual pleasure.

A feathery sensation scudded the length of her spine, and she cursed beneath her breath as memories of what she'd shared with Luc in this room rose damnably to the surface.

Vivid, sexually electrifying, and shameless.

Dear heaven. How could she slip beneath those covers and pretend everything was the same?

It didn't bear thinking about. Yet she had to face the situation.

But not tonight, she determined as she crossed to the upholstered stool at the foot of the bed, caught up her bag and retreated to another room, where she unpacked an oversized T-shirt, toiletries, then crossed to the adjoining *en suite*.

She should phone her father, then her sister to let them know she was home. Although if either opted to call, it would be to her cellphone, and there was time enough tomorrow to apprise them both of her return.

Now all she wanted to do was undress and slip into bed. Although there were too many thoughts chasing through her brain to promote an easy slide into sleep.

She was wrong. The events of the day, the flight, each took their toll, and combined with the effects of pregnancy ensured she was asleep within minutes of her head touching the pillow.

Ana woke slowly, drifting pleasantly towards consciousness, unaware for a few disoriented seconds of her whereabouts.

Then it all came flooding back...the flight, Sydney, *Luc*.

Her eyes widened as she recognised the master

suite, the large bed…and the familiar dark-haired male head resting on the pillow beside her own.

How could she be *here* when last night…?

'You were asleep.' Luc's voice was an indolent drawl, and her gaze became trapped in his for a few heart-stopping seconds, then he shifted, moving that powerful frame into a sitting position with fluid ease.

Ana closed her eyes, then opened them again. There was too much warm olive-toned flesh moulded into enviable shape by muscle and sinew.

The smattering of chest hair made her fingers itch to tangle there, and she longed to reach up and curl her hands round his nape and drag his mouth down to hers.

Except she did none of those things. Instead anger rose to simmer beneath the surface as she sought to inch away from him.

'You have no right—'

'Yes, I do.' He lifted a hand and brushed back a swathe of hair from her cheek.

She scrambled to the side of the bed, only to have him reach out and halt her flight.

'Let me go!'

'No.'

She lashed out at him, and struggled wildly as he pulled her onto his lap. Not a good position, she discovered. She was too close, much too close. And the dictates of her brain were at variance with the demand of her senses.

The thought of succumbing was more than she

could bear, and she stilled, aware that fighting him was a futile exercise.

'Don't.' The single negative held a beseeching anguish. 'Please.'

It was the heartfelt plea that got to him, and he caught her chin between thumb and forefinger, tilting it to examine her features.

Her eyes were deep enough to drown in, their emotions stark with a vulnerability that twisted his gut, and his gaze narrowed at the fast-beating pulse drumming at the base of her throat.

Her mouth shook a little, and he watched as she sought control. But it was the shimmering moisture in her eyes, and the single escaping tear running in a slow rivulet down one cheek that tore a husky imprecation from his lips.

With incredible gentleness he smoothed the moisture with his thumb, then he lowered his head and trailed his mouth over her cheek.

He let the palm of one hand slip down her arm and settle against the curve of her waist.

Their child grew there, a tiny embryo that would succour and gain strength. Its existence touched him as nothing else could.

'Come share my shower.'

'I don't think so.' He couldn't know just how much it cost her to refuse. Yet to slip back easily into the relationship they'd shared would indicate she condoned his use of emotional blackmail... something she hated him for. And Celine...dear heaven, she didn't even want to go *there*!

She slid from his grasp, aware it was only because he let her, and she gathered fresh underwear and retreated into the *en suite*.

Her stomach felt as if it didn't belong to her, and she pressed a hand to her navel in an attempt to soothe the disturbance.

Fifteen minutes later, showered and dressed in tailored trousers, singlet top and jacket, she felt measurably better, and she caught up her shoulder bag and ran lightly down the stairs to the kitchen where Petros was preparing eggs Benedict and the smell of freshly brewed coffee was ambrosia.

'Luc is in the dining-room. You will join him there.' He spared her a warm smile. 'I have made you tea.'

'But I prefer—'

'Tea. Caffeine is not recommended during pregnancy.'

Anà wrinkled her nose at him, feeling her spirits lighten a little. 'Bossy, aren't we?' Hunger assailed her, and she took a slice of toast from the stacked rack Petros had just added to the breakfast trolley, nibbled on it, then filched a fresh strawberry and popped it into her mouth.

She curled both hands over the trolley handle. 'Want me to take this through?'

'Really, Ms Dimitriades,' the man chastised with

an aloofness that brought forth a smile. 'Most definitely not.'

'Don't you think you could call me *Ana*?' she cajoled, then added teasingly, 'I'm almost young enough to be your daughter.'

He drew himself up to his full height. 'You are the wife of my employer. I could not begin to be so familiar.'

A laugh bubbled up in her throat and escaped as a mischievous chuckle. 'You call him *Luc*,' she reminded, and met his level glance.

'We have known each other a long time.'

'So how many years do I have to wait before you accord me the honour of using my Christian name?'

'Five years,' he responded solemnly, skilfully transferring grilled bacon onto a heated platter and placing it on the trolley together with the eggs. 'At least.'

'In that case, I get to wheel the trolley.'

His mouth parted in silent protest, then he pursed his lips as he caught her cheeky grin, watching as she took care of the chore and leaving him to tidy the kitchen.

The informal dining-room was at the back of the house, overlooking the pool, and caught the morning sun.

Ana reached it in seconds and swept through the open door. 'Breakfast...at your service.'

Luc was seated at the head of the table, the day's

newspaper spread out in front of him, a half-finished cup of coffee to one side.

His jacket hung over the back of his chair, on top of which lay his tie. A briefcase and laptop rested on the floor near by.

He looked up at the sound of her voice, cast the trolley a quizzical glance, then folded the newspaper.

'How did you manage that?'

'Feminine wiles and logical rationale.' She shifted platters onto the table, added fresh coffee, tea, and toast, then she drew out a chair and sat down.

She poured herself tea, added milk, then helped herself to eggs and toast.

Heaven, she decided after the first mouthful. No one but Petros made eggs Benedict this good.

'I imagine you'll call your father and Rebekah this morning?'

'Yes.' She took a sip of tea, and felt her stomach settle. 'Dad, as soon as I finish this.' She indicated the plate with her fork. 'Then I'll go into the shop.'

'Not to work.'

There was almost an edge of command apparent, and she paused in the process of transferring a portion of food to her mouth. 'Of course, to work.'

'There's no need for you to work.'

'Are we talking *today* specifically?'

'At all.' There was no mistaking the clarification.

'Now that I'm pregnant?' Her voice was quiet, too quiet.

'I don't see the necessity for you to be on your

feet all day, put in long hours, and become over-tired.'

She replaced her cutlery with care and pushed her plate aside. 'Instead, you'd prefer me to join the social-luncheon set, shop a lot and rest each afternoon like a delicate swan?'

'You can shift your interest in the shop to that of silent partner, and have Rebekah employ an assistant.'

'No.'

'I'm not giving you an option.'

His voice was silk-smooth with an edge of anger she chose to ignore.

'Don't try to manipulate me, Luc.' Heat flared, turning her eyes into brilliant blue shards. 'I won't stand for it.'

'Finish your breakfast.'

'I've lost my appetite.' She stood to her feet and tossed the napkin onto the table. 'I have a few calls to make.'

He caught hold of her arm, halting her flight, and she had no illusions his grasp would tighten if she attempted to struggle.

'Tell Rebekah to employ your replacement.' Those who knew him well would have blanched at the silkiness in his tone, recognised the predatory stillness apparent…and quailed. 'Or I will.' He waited a beat. 'Meanwhile, ensure your time at the shop is kept to a minimum.'

'Go to hell.'

His gaze chilled. 'Don't push me too far.'

She ignored the urge to respond as he released her arm. Instead she chose dignified silence, and walked out onto the terrace and descended the few steps to the garden.

There, she extracted her cellphone and called her father, confirmed her return and suggested lunch, only to have it postponed due to a business meeting until the following day.

He sounded distracted, anxious. Regretful?

Dammit, she wanted answers, or at least a reason *why* a man known for his loyalty and integrity had done something so out of character. And she needed to hear it from *him*.

But not today, she conceded as she retraced her steps.

CHAPTER FOUR

PETROS was clearing the table when she entered the dining-room.

'Luc has left for the city.'

'I'll need the keys to my car.'

The manservant continued loading the trolley with breakfast dishes. 'I don't think that's a good idea.'

Ana spared Petros a level glance. 'Luc is aware of my plans for the day.'

'Didn't agree with them, though, did he?'

'I have things to do, places to go.'

'The shop,' Petros concluded. 'Where you'll work all day.'

'I help run a business,' she reminded firmly.

'Luc will disapprove.'

She picked up her satchel, slung the strap over one shoulder and collected her car keys. 'I'll make sure he knows you told me so.'

'I'll drive you.'

'Thanks.' She was aware just how deep the man's loyalty went to his employer. 'But, no thanks.'

The shop was situated among a group of boutique shops in trendy Double Bay, and possessed a regular clientele.

Rebekah had a talent assembling flowers into an

art form, and went the extra mile to match blooms to both the recipient and the occasion. Ana took care of business…ordering, supplies, overseeing deliveries, liaising with the customers.

Wire, scissors, ribbon…and more than a little magic had earned Blooms and Bouquets a well-deserved reputation.

Ana entered the shop just after nine, and breathed in the scent filling the air, sharp and sweet, heady.

The slim blonde arranging blooms in a decorative basket glanced up at the sound of the electronic bell.

'Ana! It's so good to see you! When did you get back?'

'Last night.'

Ana found herself caught in an affectionate hug, from which she disentangled herself to meet Rebekah's keen appraisal.

'OK, what gives?'

'As in?'

'Your cryptic phone messages didn't come close to explaining the reason you flew the coop. And I don't buy Celine was the only reason,' Rebekah warned. 'So *tell* me.'

She could prevaricate, but what was the point? 'I'm pregnant.'

There was initial surprise, then her sister's mouth curved into a warm smile and her eyes lit up with pleasure, only to narrow slightly seconds later. 'So how come you're not dancing with joy?'

'It wasn't planned.'

Rebekah appeared sceptical. 'And that's a problem?'

'Not exactly.'

'But something's bothering you. Want to share?'

She was silent a few seconds too long, and Rebekah's voice gentled a little.

'Have you told Luc the extent of Celine's interference? Or just how vicious she's been?'

What difference would it make? 'No.'

'Don't you think you should?'

'I can handle Celine.'

'Darling,' Rebekah cautioned in rebuke. 'Given half a chance she'll eat you up and spit you out.'

Ana offered her sister a wry smile. 'Thanks for the vote of confidence.'

'I care about you.' She waited a beat. 'That's it? There's nothing else?'

Ana was torn between confiding their father's problems, and keeping silent. 'Blame it on raging hormones,' she dismissed with a negligible shrug, and even managed a rueful laugh.

'At a guess, my gorgeous brother-in-law would prefer his wife to remain at home?'

It was nothing less than the truth. 'Got it in one.'

'So that's why you came into work?'

A faint smile curved the edges of her mouth. 'You know me well.'

'As I have no wish to have Luc flay me alive,' Rebekah declared judiciously, 'from this day forward I take care of any heavy stuff. OK?'

'Maybe.'

'And you take an hour for lunch.'

'A concession I don't need.'

'You do the computer stuff.'

Ana assumed a pained look. 'Who said you get to be *boss*?'

Rebekah gave her a cheeky grin. 'I do.'

'Like I'll listen?'

'You could try.'

She deposited her bag, snagged a uniform coverall and donned it, then crossed to examine the order book. 'OK, let's get to it.'

They worked together with the ease of long practice, and the deliveries went out on time, the Interflora orders were dealt with, and there was genuine pleasure in consulting with a prospective bride wanting something different for her bridal bouquet.

Ana was unpacking roses, glorious, long-stemmed, tight-budded blooms, when Rebekah handed her the cordless phone.

'The father of your child.'

Checking up on her. 'Luc,' she acknowledged, and heard his silky drawl in response.

'I thought we agreed you'd limit your hours at the shop.'

'I don't recall accepting your suggestion to do so.'

'Don't split hairs.'

'Is that what you think I'm doing?'

'Ana.' His voice held a warning threat she chose to ignore.

'Your concern is touching.'

'We'll continue this discussion later.'

'I can't wait.' She ended the call before he had a chance to utter a further word.

Not a good move, she reflected, given they were dining out that evening with friends. Correction…a few of Luc's colleagues and their partners. Wives, girlfriends, and mistress.

Ana had no doubt Celine Moore would make sure of the inclusion in a continuing effort to put the cat among the pigeons. The glamorous Celine was the queen of all felines…dangerous and deadly. While women recognised her power and were disturbed by it, men looked no further than stunning looks and her incredible sexuality.

Reneging on the evening was out of the question, and Ana felt the onset of nervous tension as the afternoon drew to a close.

'Go home,' Rebekah advised. 'I can manage things here until we close.'

'That bad, huh?'

'Nothing a leisurely shower and skilfully applied make-up won't fix.'

Ana rolled her eyes. 'Thanks.'

'You're welcome.' Rebekah offered a cheerful grin. 'Wear something gorgeous, and go knock Celine off her perch.'

'As if. She has claws of steel.'

'You have a few advantages. As well as Luc's ring on your finger, you're carrying his child.'

'The ring hasn't had any effect. What makes you think pregnancy will?'

Rebekah shot her a level look. 'We're talking *Luc*,' she reminded. 'Not someone like the rat I married and divorced in record time.'

Ana was all too aware of the impact an unsuccessful marriage had on her sister's life, the bitterness and rejection, the heartache. Three years had helped heal the wounds, but the emotional scars ran deep, leaving a wariness and distrust of men.

Support was a given, but she'd learnt to hold back on expressing verbal sympathy. Only a caring few knew Rebekah's hard exterior was merely a shell she wore to protect an inner vulnerability.

How would Rebekah react on hearing her brother-in-law had utilised emotional blackmail to bring Ana home?

'Go,' Rebekah bade. 'I'll do the markets.'

'That's unfair.' Sharing the pre-dawn run to buy fresh flowers at the markets each day was a given. 'I'm pregnant, not sick. Besides, you've had to do it while I was away.'

'I doubt Luc will hear of it.'

'Luc,' she assured, 'doesn't dictate my life.'

It wasn't something she wanted to give much thought to as she fought the late-afternoon traffic *en route* to his palatial home.

Petros greeted her as she entered the foyer. 'Luc will be delayed a half-hour, Ms Dimitriades.'

'Ana,' she corrected for the umpteenth time, aware

having Petros use her Christian name was a battle she'd probably never win.

The man's role was multi-faceted, at times his manner bore resemblance to military training. His age was indeterminable, but she pinned it between early-to-mid-fifties, and there was a sharpness about him that belied his household position.

General factotum, without doubt, but she was unable to shake the suspicion he also acted as bodyguard on occasion.

When she'd queried Luc, he merely relayed Petros had moved from his late father's employ to his own.

'It would be disrespectful for me to be so familiar with the boss's wife.'

Exasperation tinged her voice. 'Oh, put a sock in it.'

'Where precisely should I put the sock?'

She was strongly tempted to tell him. Instead, she chose silence, squared her shoulders and mounted the stairs with as much dignity as she could muster.

Selecting what to wear should have been simple, except there were too many choices. Classic black, or scarlet? Maybe the emerald sheath? One of the pastels with its floating chiffon panels?

Fifteen minutes later she threw her hands up in the air, tossed a black sheath with a lace overlay onto the bed, retrieved black stiletto-heeled pumps and caught up filmy black underwear *en route* to the *en suite* bathroom.

When she emerged Luc was in the process of discarding his clothes, and her heart faltered, then missed a beat as he shrugged out of his shirt.

Broad shoulders were accentuated by superb musculature and smooth-textured skin. A smattering of chest hair tapered down over his midriff and disappeared beneath his waistline.

She retained a vivid memory of what it was like to touch his warm flesh, to feel the flexing of muscle beneath her tactile exploration…with the pads of her fingers, her lips. The slide of her body on his, the faint hiss of his breath as he sought control. Her own barely audible groan as heat spiralled and encompassed every nerve-end until she became lost in shimmering sensation…sizzling, unprincipled, *raw*.

Slim-fitting black silk hipster briefs barely covered tight buttocks, and as he shifted she caught sight of the powerful bulge of his arousal.

Dear God, what was the matter with her that she stood here transfixed by the mere sight of him?

How *could* she be turned on, when she believed she had every reason to hate him?

With deliberate movements she sank down onto the edge of the bed and pulled on tights, smoothing them over each calf, then her thighs.

Unbidden, her gaze flicked towards him, and became trapped in his own.

For one heart-stopping minute everything remained still. There was only him, and the electric tension that fizzed between them like a broken live wire curling at random. Dangerous, deadly.

Then in seeming slow motion he stripped the silk briefs from his body, and walked with blatant unconcern into his *en suite*.

Seconds later the hiss of the shower acted as the catalyst that released her limbs from their trance-like state.

With shaky movements she caught up her dress, stepped into it, then slid home the zip.

Hair and make-up took longer than she anticipated.

Her fingers shook as she pinned up her hair into a fashionable knot, and she winced more than once when she jabbed her scalp. The application of eyeshadow and eyeliner required a skill that had suddenly gone haywire, and she had to start over twice before she achieved a desired result.

She was aware the moment Luc re-entered the bedroom, and she sensed his swift appraisal, felt the lick of heat sweep through her veins in damning recognition of his presence...and deliberately turned away to select minimum jewellery.

It didn't help that her senses were alert to the brush of silk against his body, the faint rustle of fine cotton as he added a shirt, or that her imagination ran riot at the thought of trousers by Armani being pulled up over powerful, hair-roughened thighs, followed by the almost silent snap of a waist fastener, the soft, sliding close of a zip.

Sensual warmth pooled deep within, radiating to a heavy ache that heightened her senses to quivering *need*.

Was he similarly affected? Somehow she doubted it.

And she was caught in a web of pride, anger and resentment that forbade her making the first move.

Was he game-playing? For a man with a high sex drive...

Her mind came to a screeching halt, and her body stilled. Had he seen Celine in her absence? The mere thought that he might have tore the breath from her body.

Dear heaven... *No*. The rebuttal was a silent scream. Fidelity. He'd given his assurance on that score, even put it in writing. Except they were only words. And Celine was a seductive temptress most men would find difficult to resist.

Men are from Mars, Women are from Venus. Wasn't that the catch-phrase of the new millennium? Concisely translated...women wanted love; men wanted sex.

'Problems?'

Her fingers fumbled with the clasp at her nape. 'I can manage.' Except attaching the fastener remained elusive, and she was supremely conscious of him as he crossed to her side, removed the gold chain from her nerveless fingers and smoothly tending to its closing.

Did he stand there a few seconds longer than necessary? Was the slight brush of his fingers against her nape deliberate, or merely accidental?

Get a grip! The silent chastisement held self-derision as she slid her feet into stiletto pumps and caught up an evening bag.

'Ready?'

Ana turned to face him and met the bland expression in those dark eyes. 'As ready as I'll ever be.'

Their hosts resided in a restored mansion right in the heart of Double Bay, where street parking was the only option and therefore made recognition of fellow guests' cars almost an impossibility.

Trendy cafés, narrow terrace houses converted into boutiques lent a cosmopolitan air where the wealthy lingered over lattes and watched the social élite mix and mingle.

The mesh shrieked both old and new money that reflected an eclectic style not generally seen anywhere else in the city.

Ten guests were assembled in the magnificent lounge, and Ana wasn't conscious of holding her breath until she released it in a tiny rush on discovering Celine was nowhere in sight.

She requested orange juice, and sipped it as she was drawn into conversation by a mutual acquaintance who seemed intent on lauding the expertise of the cosmetic surgeon currently in vogue.

Scintillating conversation, she accorded mentally, wondering at the priorities in some women's lives. Yet looking good was important if they wanted to keep a wealthy husband who provided the lifestyle they enjoyed, for there was always a younger version waiting in the wings, willing and eager to please.

Working out, enhancing the muscle-toned body, the regular manicures, pedicures, hair-styling, facials, body massage, the designer clothes, jewellery…all to gild what they perceived as a required image. As the years passed, the more desperate they became, and 'going abroad' was a well-touted excuse to have the latest 'nip and tuck' in America, Switzerland or France.

'What do you think, darling?'

'You'd never know,' Ana responded, dutifully endorsing the cosmetic surgeon's success.

'He's incredible. Frightfully expensive, of course. But then…'

'One must do what one has to do.'

'Absolutely.'

The guest moved on, and seconds later Luc curved an arm across the back of her waist.

'Don't you think you're taking togetherness a little too far?'

'No.'

'Forgive me. I forgot we're playing a game.'

'And that is?'

'Happily married,' she said without missing a beat.

His gaze narrowed. 'Careful, *kyria*. There's a limit to my patience.'

'As there is to mine.'

It was at that precise moment the hired help ushered in the last guest, and all heads turned as one at the sound of that husky feminine laugh.

Celine. The dark hair was beautifully coiffed, her

make-up spectacular; the woman could rival any international model. Add stunning looks, symmetrically perfect features, and she was a knock-out.

Partnering her was her handbag for the evening…a handsome man whose polished good looks and manner were almost too much for any mortal male.

A model? A gentleman escort who hired out his services?

Not nice, Ana alluded cynically, and mentally chastised herself for being uncharitable.

The air-kiss routine was a little too contrived to be genuine, Celine's gaze brittle, and there was a lack of warmth in her smile.

Like a pre-set guided missile she turned towards Luc and shot him a stunning glance that conveyed to everyone present just *who* she intended to target her attention.

Ana could almost *hear* the unspoken threat…and felt her stomach muscles clench in silent antipathy.

'The evening's entertainment has arrived,' she said quietly, and felt Luc's fingers tighten at the edge of her waist.

'Behave.'

'I wouldn't dream of doing anything else.' She hardly had time to take a breath, and Celine was before them, exuding an exotic blend of expensive perfume, and a gown that looked as if it had been sprayed on, so lovingly did it hug her slender curves.

'*Luc*, darling.'

The brush of her lips to his cheek was more than

a mere salutary greeting, and Ana gritted her teeth in vexation.

'Celine.' An acknowledgment that was polite to the extreme, and her smile a mere facsimile.

The seating at dinner was either badly mismanaged or created by adroit manipulation on Celine's part.

One could almost be amused by it, Ana decided with resignation as she sank into a chair opposite Celine's partner.

There were numerous ways she'd choose to spend an evening, but observing her husband's ex-mistress eating him alive across the table wasn't one of them.

It was a great shame she couldn't indulge in a glass of wine to dull the edges, and food didn't quite do it for her. In fact, given the way her stomach was behaving, she had to wonder whether food of any kind was advisable.

'Dieting, darling?'

Implication was the mother of invention. 'Coping with a migraine.' Not entirely untrue, for a few hours in Celine's company was guaranteed to provide Ana with a headache.

Celine effected a faint moue, and directed at Luc a warm seductive smile.

Ana speared a prawn with unnecessary vigour, and attempted to do justice to the delectable starter.

The main dish followed, and she took minuscule servings, which she subsequently picked at, only to discard her cutlery after a few morsels.

Conversation flowed, as did the wine, and she had to wonder if she was the only person who noticed Celine's increasingly seductive behaviour.

There was a moment where Celine cast Luc a particularly blatant smile and deliberately moistened her lips, causing Ana to gnash her teeth.

She was sorely tempted to pick up her glass and throw iced water in Celine's face. If nothing else, it might cool her down.

Except such an action would only cause an unforgivable scene.

It was during dessert that she felt something touch her leg.

Accidental, or contrived to draw Ana's attention to the fact Celine was grazing a sheer Lycra-clad toe against Luc's leg beneath the table…or worse?

Enough, Ana decided, was *enough*.

'Lost your shoe, Celine?'

Ana had to give her credit…the woman was a superb actress.

'No. What makes you think that?'

Give it up, Ana decided. Here, *now*, was not the time or the place for a showdown. Instead, she curled the fingers of her left hand into a fist beneath her napkin, and barely restrained herself when she felt Luc's hand close over her own.

To what purpose? Silent commiseration, or an attempt to soothe her suspicions?

With a surreptitious movement she shifted her fist

to his thigh, and dug her nails into solid muscle…hard.

To give him credit, he gave no indication there was a silent battle of wills being played out of sight. Instead he merely uncurled her fingers and lifted them to his lips in a gesture that brought a slight stain of pink colour to her cheeks.

Only Ana glimpsed steel beneath the projected warmth evident in that dark gaze…and something else she didn't care to define. Anger, annoyance?

She told herself she didn't care.

'One trusts you enjoyed your sojourn on the Coast?'

Why did she have the impression no conversation with Celine was safe? The words were politely couched, the tone innocuous. Except she knew all too well how Celine operated, and *innocence* wasn't on her agenda.

'It proved to be a pleasant break.'

A perfectly shaped eyebrow rose fractionally. 'Alone?'

Oh, my, it was like tiptoeing through a minefield!

'You find that surprising?'

'Luc appeared a little distracted by your absence.'

Ana swept his strong features with amusing warmth, lingered over-long on his generously curved mouth and endeavoured to control the shivery sensation feathering down her spine. 'How nice to be missed.'

He still retained hold of her hand, and she attempted to pull it free without success.

This close she was aware of the subtle and expensive brand of his cologne mingling with the fabric of his clothes, the warmth of his skin. Apparent was a sexual energy, giving hint to a raw primitiveness that was exciting and vaguely frightening.

It brought forth vivid memories of their lovemaking...the wildness, the hunger, and the tenderness.

She missed the closeness, his touch, the times she lay in his arms living the moment when it was almost possible to believe he cared.

Except there was always a degree of control, something he never quite lost, and she wondered what it would take to have him become totally mindless.

Did he know how she felt? Dear heaven, how could he not?

'Shall we adjourn to the lounge for coffee?'

Ana opted for tea, and sipped the mild brew slowly as she stood at Luc's side.

Celine seemed intent on bewitching her companion for the evening...an action surely designed to make Luc aware what he was missing.

Were fellow guests observing Celine's charade? Or was she being overly sensitive?

'Finished?'

She glanced at Luc as he removed the cup and saucer from her hand. 'Thank you.'

'Shall we leave?'

A faint smile curved the edges of her mouth. 'I thought you'd never ask.'

Playing *polite* for the past few hours had taxed her acting skills. *Get used to it,* a tiny voice taunted.

His gaze narrowed. 'Tired?'

'If I say *yes*, will it invite a lecture?'

'Without doubt.'

'Then *no*, I'm not tired.'

'You're pale,' he observed.

'And your beard-shadow is beginning to show.'

A humorous gleam showed momentarily in those dark eyes, then it was gone, and she tried not to stiffen as he placed an arm across the back of her waist.

It took a while to reach the car, for there were the shared reminders of upcoming events, two extended invitations to consider, and the inevitable delay before the last 'goodnight' was exchanged.

The vehicle purred through the quiet street, and Ana leant her head back against the cushioned rest and closed her eyes.

She didn't feel like rehashing the evening, or querying any one of Celine's actions.

Soft music floated out from the speakers, and she felt the breath sigh from her body as tense muscles began to relax.

There was a part of her that wanted to weep for what she couldn't have; another part needing to scream at Celine for deliberately setting out to take what little she did have.

Instead, she did neither, and when the car drew to a halt in the garage she released the seat belt, slid to her feet, and as soon as Luc deactivated the security system, she entered the house and made her way upstairs without uttering so much as a word.

He didn't follow, and she undressed, removed her make-up, then unpinned her hair and slid into bed.

It was a while before Luc entered the bedroom, and he unhooked his jacket, released his tie, toed off his shoes, then stripped down to silk briefs before crossing to stand looking down at the woman who was his wife.

Vulnerable in sleep, she appeared almost fragile. Her skin had a translucent quality, and he wanted to brush the pads of his fingers over its softness, and push back the swathe of hair that rested against her cheek.

Slender shoulders, feminine, muscle-toned arms, and delicate hands. Capable hands, which were quick and deft, slim fingers with nicely shaped polished nails.

He winced at the memory of how they'd dug into his flesh only hours before, and the edge of his mouth quirked in humour at the reason why.

There was the knowledge he could slide in beneath the covers and reach for her, aware that in sleep she wouldn't resist. The touch of his lips to the sensitive hollow at the edge of her throat, the fleeting trail of his fingers to the swell of her breast...the unerring path to the moist crevice at the apex of her thighs.

He could cajole with expertise, utilise unfair persuasion, and she would be his.

Except he wanted her awake and aware, to come to him with warmth and need in her heart. More, much more than that, he wanted all that she could gift him...with her generous willingness of spirit, from the depths of her soul.

And that, he accepted, wasn't going to happen any time soon.

CHAPTER FIVE

ANA had nominated a restaurant not far from Blooms and Bouquets for lunch with her father.

Although the occasion proved something of an anticlimax, for he arrived late, greeted her affectionately, then he apologetically declared he couldn't stay long.

Of average height, he'd always had a presence. It was in the way he held himself, the easy way he moved. Yet today he seemed... Diminished, she perceived a trifle sadly.

They ordered from the menu, and sipped chilled water as they waited for their food.

'Are you OK?'

Was it something in her tone that caused the pain reflected in his eyes?

'Luc told you.'

To pretend ignorance was a useless exercise, and she hated the guilt that momentarily haunted his features.

'Did you think he wouldn't?'

He had the grace to look embarrassed.

What would his reaction be if she confided Luc had used the knowledge as leverage to effect a reconciliation?

A waiter served their order, and they both ate, mindful of the need not to linger.

'I only have one question,' Ana began without preamble. *'Why?'*

'There was a woman...' Her father paused, then continued with obvious reluctance. 'By the time I discovered she was playing at least three men against each other, I'd run up a fortune on credit.'

The most immediate question came to mind. 'What will you do now?'

'Sell the apartment, and try to rebuild my reputation. Overseas,' he elaborated. 'I have connections in New York.'

Maybe it would be a good move, and she told him so.

'Did you enjoy the Coast?'

'It's good to be back.' A fabrication, yet the stark truth wasn't something she was prepared to confide. Although there was something she could share, and did. 'How do you feel about becoming a grandfather?'

His smile reflected pleasing warmth, and he covered her hand with his own. 'Are we talking a *fait accompli*?'

It was after two when Ana returned to the shop, and the remainder of the afternoon passed quickly as she brought computer records up to date, dealt with accounting entries, and handled the phone.

Traffic was heavy, and it took a while to reach Vaucluse. The thought of a shower, changing into casual clothes, and a long, cool drink…in that order, was uppermost in her mind as she garaged the car.

A light meal, maybe she'd view a video, then she'd catch an early night.

Petros emerged into the foyer as she entered it, and she offered him a stunning smile. 'Hi, how was your day?'

'The usual, Ms Dimitriades. And yours?'

'The same.' Her response held a musing solemnity that wasn't lost on the manservant.

'Luc asked that I inform you he'll be late. A business dinner, I understand.'

'So it's just me, and the kitchen cat. A salad will be fine.'

His lips thinned in visible disapproval. 'I have prepared something more substantial than a salad. If you'll kindly tell me where and at what time you'd like to eat, I will be on hand to serve the meal.'

'And the kitchen cat?' It was a query she couldn't resist, and brought forth the glimmer of a smile.

'Sulked the entire time you were absent.' As did the master of the house, although one didn't use *sulk* and *Luc Dimitriades* in the same sentence. A heightened temperament was more appropriate.

'Then I should make amends.'

One would imagine if Luc owned a four-legged feline, it would be an exotic breed. Except Oliver had turned up at their back door a month ago, hungry, wet, and looking pitifully pathetic. Towelled dry, given a saucer of milk, he declared the house his new abode. And stayed. Supposedly consigned to the kitchen and laundry, he enjoyed the run of the house from morning until night.

'An excellent suggestion.'

Ana found Oliver curled in his laundry basket, and he eyed her carefully as if weighing up whether to greet her or not. She had, after all, not been around for a while. Except there was something in the tone of her voice, a caring gentleness to her touch that won him over, and he allowed instinct to rule by rolling onto his back.

Unconditional affection, Ana reflected as she stroked Oliver's arched throat, then his exposed belly.

If only it were as uncomplicated with the human species, she mused as she ascended the stairs to the upper floor.

After a leisurely shower she donned jeans, a blouse with its edges tied in a careless knot at her midriff, gathered the length of her hair into a careless knot, then she retraced her steps to the kitchen, where Petros was in the process of arranging a succulent stir-fry on a bed of steaming rice.

Ana caught up a fork and dipped it into the rice, directed Petros a cheeky grin at his mock-severity, and collected a plate. 'I'll go eat on the terrace.'

The air held the balmy warmth of early summer, and she had a yen to feel the slight breeze against her face, breathe in the faint scents of growing blooms, and gain some tranquillity.

'It's my job to serve you.'

She spared him a level glance and began spooning rice and stir-fry onto her plate. 'We've had this argument before.'

'I'm sure we'll have it again.' Petros released a long-suffering sigh. 'Luc would—'

'Luc isn't here,' she reminded solemnly. 'So do me a favour and lighten up.'

He appeared to tussle with his conscience. 'Very well.'

It was a beautiful evening, and the view from the terrace out over the inner harbour spectacular. Everything appeared so still, the water glassy-smooth with small craft moored close in to the rock-faced cliffs.

Above, the sky was pale with an opalescent glow that appeared as the sun sank lower towards the horizon. Soon streaks of colour in varied shades of rose-pink would appear, brightening to orange in a final flare before the dusk preceded night.

It was easy to let her mind wander back to the first time she came into this house. The pleasure in loving the man who'd brought her here, and the promise of what could and would be, in spite of the knowledge a part of his heart would always belong to Emma, the young girl he'd married and lost much too soon.

In the eleven years between his first and second marriage there had been women. A man of Luc's wealth and calibre was an inevitable magnet for female attention. She could accept that.

She could even handle the relatively harmless flirtatious games played out by the social set.

A mistress, however, was something she refused to condone.

Celine would have Ana believe the affair was alive and well. But was it? Luc swore *no*. So who did she believe?

'If you've finished, I'll take your plate.'

She turned at the sound of Petros's voice and offered him a winsome smile. 'Thanks. It was delicious.'

'Would you like some dessert? Fresh fruit?'

She shook her head.

'Some tea, perhaps?'

'I'll come in and get it.'

'Stay there.' He looked out over the gardens. 'It really is very pleasant at this time of evening.'

The edges of her mouth tilted. 'Conversation, Petros?' Her eyes assumed a slightly wicked gleam. 'You so rarely indulge.'

'I'll fetch your tea.'

Ana moved from the table and curled onto a nearby chaise longue. Seconds later there was a soft plop as a furry bundle landed beside her on the cushion and Oliver began systematically digging in his front paws, circled twice, then settled into a ball close to her thigh.

She lifted a hand and stroked the cat's head, then fondled his ears, and was rewarded with a quiet throaty purr.

'Well,' Petros exclaimed softly as he carefully placed a cup and saucer on the side-table. 'It appears he's decided to attach himself to you.'

Oliver lifted his head, offered Petros an unblinking feline stare, then rested his chin on his paws.

'I'll go fetch you a sweater.'

Ana sipped the tea, and when darkness fell she donned the sweater Petros brought, taking care not to disturb Oliver.

Electric street-lights were visible in the distance, and seemed to merge with stars in an inky sky. 'Would you like more tea?'

She turned towards Petros, whose silent tread she'd failed to detect. 'No, thanks.'

It was there Luc found her, asleep, her head resting against the cushioned rest.

She wasn't to know Petros had remained indoors keeping her in plain sight until Luc returned home. Or that both men exchanged brief words before the manservant crossed to the foyer and took the internal stairs to his flat.

Luc stood in front of the chaise longue, looking at her features in repose, then he hunkered down and gently tucked a stray tendril of hair behind her ear.

She stirred, and he cupped a palm over her shoulder and ran it lightly down to rest at her elbow, watching as her eyelashes fluttered, then swept slowly upward.

'What are you doing out here, *pedhi mou*? Stargazing?'

Ana reached out a hand and found an empty space where the cat had slept. 'Oliver?'

'Petros has settled him into his basket for the night.' He rose to his full height in one fluid movement, then he leant forward and lifted her into his arms.

She didn't feel inclined to struggle. 'I can walk.'

His mouth brushed her temple. 'Indulge me.' He carried her easily, dousing lights, setting the security alarm as he moved through the house, then he ascended the stairs and traversed the gallery to their bedroom.

'I don't think—'

His lips touched hers, savouring with a slow provocative sweep of his tongue. And left her wanting more.

He shouldered the door shut and advanced towards the bed. 'Is it so important that you think?'

She thought sadly of hopes and dreams, of what was, and what could be. Mostly, she thought of *now*.

'Yes.'

He slowly lowered her to her feet, and let his hands slip down to cup her bottom. Then his head descended, and his lips caressed hers with a gentleness that made her want to weep.

'I don't want to do this.'

It was an ache-filled whisper that curled around his heart and tugged a little.

'Then tell me to stop.'

Dear God…she hungered for his touch.

The slow, tantalising sweep of his tongue caused heat to lick through her veins, and her body swayed into his, as if driven there by a force stronger than she.

His mouth parted, moving hers to open to accept his probing exploration, and she whimpered in part need, part protest as he deepened the kiss.

He spread one hand over her buttocks and slid the other up her spine to hold fast her nape, and wrought havoc with her senses.

It wasn't enough, not nearly enough.

She needed to feel her skin against his, without the barrier of clothes, and her fingers tore at the buttons on his shirt, loosening them, then she dragged the cotton free from his trousers.

A low, guttural sound emerged from her throat as he pulled off her sweater, and followed it with her blouse, then her bra.

A hand shaped her breast, his thumb on one roseate peak, caressing until heat pooled at the juncture of her thighs, flaring in a radiating spiral that almost drove her mad.

Buttons, fasteners, each were undone in haste and fell to the carpet, quickly followed by silk, until there was nothing between them.

Ana cried out, and the sound became lost against the invasion of his mouth as he tumbled her carefully down onto the bed.

Then his body rose over hers, large, powerful, and fully aroused. His eyes were dark with passion, hard muscle and sinew corded as he supported his weight above hers.

There was leashed control apparent as he brought his mouth down to her breast, and suckled there, taking her almost to the edge of pain before trailing a path to her navel, pressing a tracery of light kisses over her stomach as he moved low.

She should cry out for him to halt this madness before it went any further. But she was powerless to utter so much as a word.

She needed his possession, craved it. To deny him was to deny herself, and she damned her sybaritic soul as he tipped her over the edge, then held her as she fell.

He entered her slowly, inch by exquisite inch until she thought she'd go mad. He was in control, his hands cupping each hip, holding her there as he set an unhurried rhythm that made her want to weep.

When she would have quickened and deepened the pace he brought his mouth down over hers in a kiss that alternately cajoled, caressed, *soothed*.

His release when it came completed her, and his shuddering body brought feminine satisfaction for as long as it took for her emotions to settle.

He lay on his side, facing her, with one arm tucking her body in close to his.

He pressed a kiss to the edge of her shoulder. '*Pedhi mou*, I adored your reluctance.'

'I hate you.'

'Uh-huh.' His lips reached her elbow, then trailed to the inside of her wrist.

'Celine—'

'Has no part in what we share together,' he assured, and felt the rapid acceleration of her pulse.

'That isn't how she sees it.'

His lips were as light as the brush from a butterfly's wing as he retraced a path and settled in the sensitive curve of her neck.

'You want to talk of another woman, when the only woman who interests me is *you?*'

Oh, God. He had the touch to drive her wild. 'They're only words.'

'What would you have me say?'

I love you. The silent, beseeching cry came from her heart. And it broke a little with the knowledge they were words he would never declare.

He reached down and drew the bedcovers over them both, then caught hold of her chin and tilted it so she had no choice but to look at him.

'You are mine, *kyria*. You carry my child. It is enough.'

He was wrong. It wasn't nearly enough.

'You want to continue this discussion?'

It took every effort to force her voice to sound calm. 'Why?' She swallowed the betraying lump in her throat. 'There is nothing to discuss.'

CHAPTER SIX

'YOU intend going in to the shop?'

She met his gaze across the breakfast table, then deliberately sipped her tea. 'Yes.'

'Deliberate defiance, Ana?'

She took a deep breath, then slowly released it.

'Rebekah has consigned me to taking orders, managing the computer records, and handling the phone. If necessary, we'll employ someone to help out. Satisfied?'

'Not entirely.'

'Tough.'

Something moved in the depths of his eyes. 'You're playing a dangerous game, *agape mou*.'

My lover. Did he imagine all it took was one night in his arms? 'Nothing has changed, Luc.'

'You think not?'

The insistent burr of her cellphone precluded the necessity to answer, and she read the text message, then gathered up her satchel. 'I have to go.'

He slid a hand through a swathe of her hair and held it firm as his mouth closed over hers in a brief evocative kiss that stirred her senses and left her wanting more.

Then she was free.

'Enjoy your day.'

She didn't want to think about the musing gleam in those dark eyes, nor the faintly mocking tone in his voice.

Nevertheless, both haunted her as she traversed the main thoroughfare leading towards Double Bay.

If Luc imagined *sex* resolved everything, then he was mistaken, she determined as she halted behind a stream of traffic waiting for the lights to change.

In the cool light of day there were several recriminations. Mostly against herself. For succumbing to Luc's seduction, and displaying only a token resistance to shared intimacy.

Warmth flooded her veins at the mere thought of the night, and her stomach did a slow somersault as she recalled her response.

The sound of a car horn heralded a return to the present, and it was almost eight when she entered the shop.

It proved to be a busy day, with numerous phone calls with delivery orders, which necessitated the need to order more stock to fill them.

'Go take a lunch break,' Rebekah urged. 'Sit outside in the fresh air at one of the sidewalk cafés. You can bring me back a sandwich, pastrami on rye with salad, mayo, and hold the mustard.'

It was a lovely day, a slight breeze teased the leaves in the tree-lined street, and warm sunshine filtered down from an almost cloudless blue sky.

Double Bay had a style all its own with élite boutiques, numerous cafés, and close to the sea there was a hint of it in the air, a freshness that meshed with mild early-summer temperatures.

She felt the need for exercise, and crossed the street to the next block, then chose a café where there were a few empty tables beneath sun umbrellas.

A waiter materialised from inside the café, took her order, and delivered it in record time. She viewed the tastefully presented chicken and salad sandwich with anticipation.

So far she had very few pregnancy symptoms except a faint queasiness first thing in the morning. But her appetite had changed, and it amused her the foetal infant's demands ran to six small meals a day instead of the normal three. If she failed to pander to its whims, the result was nauseousness. Definitely a babe with a mind of its own!

'Ana.'

Oh, lord, please, *no*, not Celine. But it was she, looking the glamour queen in impeccably styled clothes, and perfectly applied cosmetics.

'You don't mind sharing, do you?'

Now that was a dubious statement, if ever there was one. Did she mean to convey a *double entendre*? 'The table, Celine?'

'Of course, darling. I only want coffee.' She slid into a chair. 'And we need to talk.'

'We do?' She was strongly tempted to stand to her feet and leave. Except fascination kept her seated. 'Regarding?'

'Why, *Luc*, of course.'

Of course. Who else? Ana made a point of checking her watch. 'I'm due back at the shop in a few minutes.'

'Luc and I were discussing the situation yesterday.'

'Really?' She glimpsed the triumphant gleam apparent in the other woman's gaze, and slanted one eyebrow. 'A deliberate *oops* moment, Celine?'

'Luc and I go back a long way.'

She'd had enough. '*Back* is the operative word. As in *past*.' She stood to her feet and gathered up the bill. 'Do yourself a favour. Get over it, and move on.'

'Perhaps you should ask yourself why Luc chooses not to terminate the affair.'

She felt sickened by it all, the innuendo fed by her own self-doubt. Worse, the steady barbs of verbal poison Celine had delighted in aiming at every opportunity.

'Accept you've become obsessively compulsive over a man who doesn't want you.' Strong words, but she was way past abiding by the niceties of good manners. 'The *affair* finished before your marriage, and my own. As Luc tells it, your time together was brief, and it was he who ended the relationship.'

She felt slightly light-headed, almost faint. A rush of blood to the head? she queried silently in an attempt at wacky humour. 'I'm not into human *ownership*, Celine,' she managed calmly. 'If Luc wants to discard me and lose his marriage, he's perfectly free to do so.'

On that note she entered the café, collected Rebekah's sandwich to-go, paid the bill, then she left without so much as a glance in Celine's direction.

'You look…frazzled,' Rebekah commented when Ana entered the shop.

'Put it down to an unwelcome lunch guest.'

'Celine?'

'Ah.' She offered a sweet smile as she took a seat in front of the computer. 'You didn't even need three guesses to get it right.'

'She called into the shop, intent on cornering you. That woman is a pest.'

'You're not wrong.'

'What are you going to do about her?'

'You mean, apart from getting mad?' She downloaded the afternoon's batch of orders and printed them out. 'I'm handling it.'

'Maybe you should have Luc handle it.'

'Go running to him with a sob story that's as pitiful as it's pathetic? And admit I can't deal with it?' She punched in a code, and checked data on the screen. 'No. It's my problem, my call.'

Mid-afternoon Ana logged in an order for a delivery of flowers Friday afternoon together with an additional arrangement fee. It was a service Blooms and Bouquets offered, and had proven popular with numerous social hostesses when giving a private dinner party in their home.

Floral arrangement was an art form, and a professional could assemble an artistic display in a fraction of the time it would take the inexperienced.

However her heart seemed to miss a beat and falter when she wrote down the client's name, address and contact number.

Celine.

There had been no recognition, no personal greeting. Just the requisite facts.

The obvious question had to be *why* Celine had chosen Blooms and Bouquets when there were any number of florists with whom she could have placed the order.

The woman's motive had to be suspect. Mischief and mayhem? Without doubt, Ana concluded with a grimace.

'What's up?'

Ana gathered her wits together, and relayed the order.

'I'll take care of it,' Rebekah said at once.

'No. I will.' Celine obviously had no intention of giving up. 'This is another battle in an ongoing war,' she determined grimly.

'Luc won't approve.'

'He doesn't need to know.'

'He will,' Rebekah warned. 'Celine will make sure of it.'

'Her order makes it business,' she qualified.

'It's personal,' Rebekah argued. 'And we both know it.'

'So? What's the worst she can do?'

Celine's apartment was in an exclusive Rose Bay residential tower.

Obviously the divorce settlement had been favourable, Ana deduced as she entered a sumptuous suite whose visible decorative theme featured-leopard print cushions scattered on off-white deep-cushioned sofas and single chairs, with stunning framed prints of prowling leopards in various poses adorning the walls.

Ana could almost hear their collective jungle snarl, and silently attributed Celine's choice as being strikingly pertinent to the woman's personality.

Neutral tones featured as a background, and she mentally selected the brilliant orange flash of strelitzia as the focal colour with a native mix in pale green and gold.

Celine's greeting lacked civility, but then she hadn't expected anything less. Today wasn't about floral arrangements. It was another step towards a war between two women who each wanted the same man.

However, she could at least get on with the pretence, and she went straight into professional mode. 'Shall we get started? It would help if you'll tell me the look you want to achieve.'

Maximum effect for less than minimum price, and heavily discounted at that, Ana perceived some time later as Celine threw every suggestion out the window.

'Work with me, Ana.' The haughty command held arrogance.

It was time for a reality check. 'What you want is unachievable for the price you're prepared to pay.'

'Your profit margin has to be outrageous.'

She wanted to turn on her heel and walk out. Almost did, except they were still on a business footing, albeit that it was shaky ground.

'Rebekah and I pride ourselves on the quality of the blooms we supply, and our fee is standard.'

She closed the display folder and slid it into her briefcase. 'I suggest you consult someone else.'

Celine's expression hardened. 'I really can't be bothered wasting any further time on this. Itemise your quote, and I'll sign it.'

Business was *business*. Ana set everything down in meticulous detail, checked it, acquired Celine's signature, and gave her the customer copy.

Celine flicked the paper with a lacquered nail. 'For this amount, I'll expect perfection.'

'I doubt you'll have any reason to complain.' But you'll do your best to find something to denigrate Blooms and Bouquets, and take great pleasure in doing so.

Ana should have taken notice of her initial instinct and refused the job. So why hadn't she? Sheer stubborn-mindedness in not allowing Celine to triumph in any way.

'I hope you don't think you've won.'

Ah, the real purpose for her presence here. 'I wasn't aware we were in competition.'

'Don't play me for a fool.'

'I would never do that.'

'Just think, darling.' Celine's false smile took on a spiteful quality. 'I had Luc before you. Remember that, and wonder how you could possibly be an adequate substitute.'

'Yet you married someone else.' She couldn't help herself. 'One can only imagine it was because Luc didn't ask you?'

'Bitch.'

'Go get a life, Celine. And stay out of mine.'

'Not a chance. There isn't a thing you could say or do that would influence me.'

'I'm carrying Luc's child.'

Celine arched a brow in supercilious condemnation. 'And that's supposed to send me into retreat mode?'

'Forgive me, I forgot you don't possess any scruples…moral, or otherwise.'

'Got it in one, darling.' Celine examined her perfectly manicured nails, then speared Ana with a killing glance. 'Don't for a minute think you have an advantage in spawning a Dimitriades heir.' Her laugh portrayed the antithesis of humour as she raked Ana's slender form. 'Pregnancy isn't an attractive look. Who do you think Luc will turn to when you resemble a waddling whale?'

'You've mixed metaphors,' Ana managed calmly.

Quite a feat when *calm* didn't come close to the anger burning inside. 'And some men are blown away by a woman's conception.'

'Poor Ana.' Condescension positively dripped off her tongue. 'You're delusional if you imagine Luc is one of them.'

It was time to leave before she said or did something regrettable.

'Good afternoon, Celine.' Ana moved into the foyer and let herself out the door. Her steps were measured as she crossed to the lift, and it was only when she cleared the building that she allowed herself to vent some of her pent-up anger.

There were two messages on her voice-mail. Luc, and Rebekah. She used speed-dial to connect with her sister.

'Problems?'

'Just checking to see if you weathered the Celine appointment OK.'

'It could have been worse. I'll be at the shop in fifteen minutes.'

She reached Luc on his private line, and attempted to control her spiralling emotions as he picked up.

'Dimitriades.'

'You left a message to call.'

'So I did.' His voice was a faintly inflected drawl, and she envisaged him leaning back in his chair.

'I'm about to get into the car and drive,' Ana warned.

'So keep it brief?'

She could sense the wry humour in his voice, and retaliated without thought. 'Yes.'

'Jace is flying in from the States on Sunday. Ask Rebekah to join us Monday evening for dinner.'

The Dimitriades men were from the same mould...tall, dark, ruggedly attractive, and dynamite with women. Jace Dimitriades was no exception.

'Playing matchmaker, Luc?'

'The suggestion came from Jace,' Luc responded, indolently amused, and Ana gnashed her teeth, all too aware of the tension that existed between her sister and Luc's cousin.

'Don't plan on Rebekah accepting.'

'*No,*' Rebekah refused emphatically less than twenty minutes later. 'Not in this lifetime.'

'OK.'

'Just—*OK*? You're not going to cajole, persuade, twist my arm?'

'No.'

'Jace is—'

Ana offered a cynical smile. 'Another Luc?'

'Quite capable of issuing an invitation himself,' Rebekah completed.

'Which you'll have the greatest pleasure in refusing?'

'Yes.'

It was as well the phone rang, and Rebekah took the call while Ana crossed to the computer.

'Dad,' Rebekah informed as she replaced the handset. 'He wants us to join him for dinner...

tonight. Says it's very important.' She cast Ana a pensive glance. 'Do you have any idea what it's about?'

Oh, lord. The whole truth wouldn't sit well. Perhaps she could get by with imparting only some of it?

'He mentioned having contacts in New York when we had lunch yesterday.'

Rebekah's gaze sharpened. 'You think he might consider taking a position there?'

'I guess it's possible.' Why did she feel as if she was digging a proverbial hole with every word she spoke?

'Presumably he'll tell us about it tonight.'

Which meant she should ring Luc and tell him she wouldn't be home for dinner.

He was in a meeting, and she sent him a text message, then didn't bother checking her cellphone until she arrived home.

'Luc will be delayed until six-thirty,' Petros informed when she walked through the door.

By which time she'd be on her way into the city to meet her father and Rebekah…if she was lucky. 'Thanks.'

She headed for the stairs, and on reaching the bedroom she stripped, took the quickest shower on record, then dressed with care in an elegantly tailored ultra-violet trousersuit.

Ana was putting the finishing touches to her makeup when Luc entered the room. He'd loosened his tie, undone the top few buttons on his shirt, and he held his jacket hooked over one shoulder.

He looked the powerful magnate, a sophisticate whose forceful image projected an dramatic mesh of elemental ruthlessness and latent sensuality.

His eyes were dark, almost still, and her heart jolted a little in reaction. There was a part of her that wanted to close the space between them, touch light fingers to his cheek, then pull his head down to hers in a kiss that invited as much as it promised.

She wanted to smile, and offer 'Tough day?', then share her own in musing commiseration.

Except she did none of those things. Instead, she dropped a lipstick into her evening bag and caught up her keys.

'You got my text message?'

Luc tossed his jacket down onto the bed, and pulled his tie free. 'Yes.' He began releasing the buttons on his shirt, then pulled it free from his trousers. 'Petros will drive you. Ring me when you're through, and I'll come collect you.'

'Don't be ridiculous. I'll drive myself.'

'No,' he said evenly. 'You won't.'

Anger rose with simmering heat. 'The hell—'

His eyes seared hers, dark and infinitely dangerous. 'We can do this the hard way,' he relayed silkily. 'The result will be the same.'

'Aren't you overreacting just a touch?'

'It's not open to negotiation.' He toed off his shoes, then released the zip on his trousers. 'You *want* to circle the city streets trying to find a parking space? Walk alone in the dark to the restaurant venue?' His voice held a chilling softness. 'Then repeat the process at the end of the evening?' He waited a beat. 'You really believe I'd let that happen?'

He stripped off his briefs, then walked naked into the *en suite*.

Ana felt no satisfaction in the argument, and a wicked little imp urged her to march in there after him for the last word. Except there would be only one end, and she didn't have the time.

Instead she took a deep, steadying breath, and made her way downstairs, aware that Petros was waiting in the foyer.

'You get to play chauffeur.' She even managed a faint smile as she preceded him out to Luc's Mercedes.

'Luc has your best interests at heart.'

She slid into the front passenger seat, and waited until Petros slipped in behind the wheel. 'He's a dictatorial tyrant.'

The car eased forward and covered the distance to the gates. 'You're the wife of a wealthy man who prefers to implement precautions, rather than dismiss them and take unnecessary risks.'

'So shut up, and dance to the puppeteer's tune?'

'Some would be grateful.'

'This particular *someone* doesn't like being given orders.'

He entered New South Head Road. 'Where to, in the city, Ms Dimitriades?'

The irony was they weren't meeting in the city, but at Double Bay, and she named the restaurant, thanked him when he drew to a halt immediately outside it, then stepped into the plush entrance.

Her father and Rebekah were already seated at a table, and she greeted them with affection, then she requested mineral water and perused the menu.

'I've put the sale of my apartment in the hands of an agent, and I fly out to New York tomorrow,' William Stanford revealed when the waiter had taken their orders.

Rebekah threw questions thick and fast, and it was evident their father's answers failed to satisfy.

When William settled the bill, indicating the need to leave in order to pack, Rebekah summoned the waiter for tea and coffee, querying as soon as it arrived, 'You already knew, didn't you?'

'The possibility of New York, yes,' Ana stressed carefully.

'Why this sudden move? And I don't buy the necessity to sell the apartment.' Her eyes narrowed. 'He's in some kind of trouble. At a guess, Luc's involved, which means it's something to do with the bank.' Her lips pursed, then thinned to a grim line. 'Suppose you tell me the truth. All of it. Not just what you think I should hear.'

The telling was virtually a verbatim explanation of what William Stanford had confided over lunch.

'Just assure me you played no part in Luc's decision not to prosecute,' Rebekah pleaded. 'I'd kill him if I thought he'd dragged you back into a marriage you'd decided you no longer wanted.'

She was too clever by half. 'I wanted a break from Celine's tiresome behaviour.'

'And that's it? All of it?'

It was all she could bring herself to admit, and she resisted the childish urge to cross her fingers behind her back to minimise the lie. 'Yes.'

Something jogged her memory. 'I almost forgot. Luc suggested you join us for dinner Monday night.'

'Kind of him. Persuade Petros to serve moussaka and I'll bring him flowers.'

'I've no idea whether Luc plans eating out or at home. I'll ask and let you know. There's just one more thing...Jace will be there.'

'No.' Rebekah's response was immediate and adamant.

'*No*, because it's Jace? Or no, end-of-story?' Ana queried, and saw Rebekah's mouth thin.

'I can't stand the man.'

'Because he rubs you up the wrong way?' There was more to this than she thought. Rebekah had met him during one of his previous visits to Sydney, but they hadn't dated...at least, not that she was aware.

'That's the understatement of the year,' her sister growled, and Ana felt bound to ask,

'Don't you wonder *why*?'

'Oh, yes, sister dear.' Her voice held bitterness. 'I know precisely why. I just don't care to explore it.'

Ana was silent for a few seconds as she carefully weighed her words. 'Maybe you should.'

Rebekah speared her with a killing glare. 'Don't play amateur psychologist.'

'That wasn't my intention.'

'Oh, dammit.' Rebekah appeared contrite, for she hadn't meant to overreact. 'I'll come to dinner. It'll give me the utmost satisfaction to put Jace Dimitriades in his place.'

Tiredness crept over her, which, combined with the events of the day, resulted in the need to bring the evening to an end. 'I'll call a cab.' She extracted her cellphone and keyed in the necessary digits.

'You didn't drive in?' At her sister's faint grimace she indicated, 'I'll drop you home.'

She did, and Luc was waiting at the door as Rebekah brought her car to a halt.

'Your guardian angel.' She leaned forward and brushed a light kiss to Ana's cheek. 'I'll see you in the morning. And thanks.'

'For what?'

'Being you.'

Ana slid out from the car, waved as Rebekah eased the car forward, then she entered the foyer and met Luc's dark scrutiny.

'I was waiting for your call.' There was silk threading his voice.

'Why, when Rebekah offered to drop me home?' she asked reasonably.

'It's late.'

'We stayed on to talk a while.'

He took in her pale features, the faint smudges beneath her eyes. 'You should have ended the evening before this.'

'Don't,' she warned. 'Tell me something I already know.' The events of the day, Celine, a vivid reminder of William Stanford's folly, being less than totally honest with Rebekah…all seemed to manifest itself into a blazing headache. Add tiredness, and it wasn't an enviable combination.

'Go on up to bed. Can I bring you anything?'

She wanted to say 'Just *you*'. As it used to be, before Celine reappeared on the scene. But the words never left her lips, and she shook her head, feeling almost undone by the underlying care apparent.

She would have given anything to believe it was for her alone, and not because of the child she nurtured in her womb.

He set the security system, and doused the lights, then he followed her upstairs to their room, slipping out of the jeans and polo shirt he'd donned after his shower.

They both slid into bed at the same time, and he snapped off the bedside light, then gathered her close.

He dealt with her faint protest by closing his mouth over her own, sweeping his tongue in an evocative tasting that made him want more, much more, and he shaped her lissom body with his hands, aware of the slight tenderness of her breasts, the quivering response as he trailed an exploratory path over her stomach to the sensitive apex at the top of her thighs.

He pleasured her with such acute sensitivity it was all she could do not to cry out as sensuality reached fever pitch, and she clung to him, urging his possession until he joined his body to her own.

His mouth covered her own as they scaled the heights of passion in a rhythm only lovers shared.

Afterwards she fell asleep in his arms, and she had no knowledge that the man who held her lay awake in the darkness, lost in reflective thought.

CHAPTER SEVEN

ANA followed the delivery van into the bowels of Celine's apartment building, and secured the lift while Harry, the delivery guy, transported the buckets of cut flowers.

'That's everything, Harry?'

'The lot.'

'OK, let's go.'

Harry did the heavy work, then left, and Ana utilised the laundry as her work-station.

'I trust you won't make a mess.'

Ana glanced up from separating various stands of natives, and aimed for a pleasant smile. 'It'll be minimal, Celine, and contained here.'

A half-hour should have been sufficient, but it took twice that as Celine changed her mind on previously agreed displays.

If Ana had been mean-spirited, she would have said it was a deliberate attempt to minimise her ability and expertise.

She silently repeated 'the customer is always right' mantra, and maintained a professionally polite demeanour. But it was difficult, very difficult!

At last all three displays finally earned Celine's

grudging approval, and Ana began restoring the laundry to its former tidiness.

It didn't take long, and she emerged into the hallway, empty buckets in hand, her equipment neatly stacked in a holdall.

'Watch your back, darling,' Celine advised coolly as she led the way to the door. 'I play to win.'

'And you don't care who you hurt in the process?'

The woman plucked an imaginary speck from the sleeve of her blouse. 'Not at all.'

'Naturally, Luc is the prize.'

'Of course.'

'You've neglected one aspect in your campaign,' Ana said carefully.

'And what's that?'

'Luc's willingness to play.'

'You don't get it, do you?' Celine queried. 'Men of Luc's calibre think nothing of maintaining a mistress.'

'While the wife turns a blind eye, accepting the lifestyle, social prestige, and unlimited spending money in lieu of fidelity?'

'You could do much worse.'

'Sorry, Celine. That's not what I want for myself or my child.'

A concerted smile tilted Celine's carefully painted mouth. 'Can I take that as a given?'

'Absolutely.'

It wasn't the best exit line she'd ever offered, but she derived a sense of dignity as she walked from the apartment and took the lift down to the basement carpark.

It was late when she arrived home. Luc's Mercedes wasn't in the garage, and when she checked her cellphone there was a text message relaying a business meeting had run over time and they intended winding it up over dinner.

A message Petros confirmed as she made her way through the foyer to the kitchen.

'I've made vegetable soup, with a steak salad.'

Oliver appeared through the doorway and stalked across the tiles to brush himself against her leg. She bent down and scratched behind his ear, then stroked his tummy when he rolled over onto his back.

'I'll go shower and change, then be down in about fifteen minutes.'

Tonight she chose to eat indoors, and afterwards she settled down in front of the television set, channel-hopped, then riffled through the collection of DVDs, found one that appealed, and slotted it into the player.

At nine Petros brought her freshly made tea, then he retired to his flat.

The movie ran its course, and she wavered between slotting in another or going to bed.

Bed won, and she settled Oliver in the laundry, then made her way upstairs.

She reflected on the day's events as she discarded her clothes, lingering on Celine's pernickety fussing with the floral displays. A dinner party. She wondered how it was going, and who were the guests.

Then her hands froze.

No. Surely not. Luc's *business meeting* was a legitimate meeting…wasn't it? He wouldn't, couldn't be one of Celine's dinner guests. *Could he?*

However, the seed of doubt was planted, and steadily over the next hour it took root.

Imagination was a terrible thing, Ana accepted as she plumped her pillow for the umpteenth time and checked the bedside clock.

Eleven-o-five. So it was a leisurely meal, with Luc and his associates lingering over coffee.

She was still awake at eleven-thirty, convinced the business meeting was long over…if in fact there had been any meeting at all!

Damn Luc. If he'd dined as a guest at Celine's apartment, she'd kill him. In her mind, she conducted the argument they would have, the accusations she'd fling, and the physical fight that would follow. Then, she reasoned, she'd throw a few clothes into a suitcase and walk out of this house, his life, and never return.

Luc Dimitriades would never see his child, never again see *her*, and…

The peal of the telephone was a stark, intrusive sound that jolted her into action, and she fumbled for the bedside lamp, then picked up the receiver.

'Luc?'

'He'll be home soon, darling.' Celine's voice was

recognisable and held a distinct purr. 'Just thought I'd let you know.'

Ana heard a click as the call ended, and she slowly lowered the receiver down onto its cradle.

A few choice oaths slipped from her tongue as she stared blankly at the opposite wall. *Bastard.* How could he?

All too easily, she concluded silently.

She switched off the lamp and settled down in bed to stare emptily into the room's darkness for what seemed an age.

Images ran through her mind. Luc sharing Celine's table, conversing with fellow guests. A cynical laugh rose in her throat. Or maybe there were no guests at all, and it was strictly dinner *à deux*.

And afterwards… Dear heaven, she didn't want to think about *afterwards*.

He'd promised fidelity. Would he, *had* he broken that promise?

Get real, a tiny voice taunted. As if he's going to admit to it.

A slight sound made the breath catch in her throat, and she tensed as the bedroom door opened, then closed with an almost silent click.

He didn't turn on a light, and seconds later she heard the faint rustle of clothes being discarded. He'd probably shrugged out of his jacket and loosened his tie as he ascended the stairs, and it wasn't difficult to picture him unbuttoning his shirt, pulling it free from his trousers and tossing it onto the bedroom chair.

Shoes and socks would follow, and she detected the slide of a zip fastener as he prepared to remove his trousers.

All that remained were his briefs, and they too would be discarded to suit his preference to sleep naked.

For a moment she had a mental image of his tall, tightly muscled frame. The breadth of shoulder, the tapered waist, lean hips, powerful thighs. The fluid way he moved.

The mere thought he might have been at Celine's apartment incensed her, and her body tensed as she felt the faint depression of the mattress.

If he came close… Her mind seethed with a number of possible scenarios, each featuring various forms of retribution.

For the space of a few seemingly long seconds it seemed as if he was settling to sleep, and she slowly released the breath she'd unconsciously held from the moment he'd slid into bed.

The brush of his thigh and the touch of his arm as he curled his large body into the curve of her own brought an instant reaction.

Ana jabbed her elbow into his ribcage in a stark movement that took him completely by surprise, and the breath hissed from his throat as she kicked both heels into his shins.

'Don't you *dare* touch me!' The words scarcely

left her mouth when she followed them with a scandalised yelp as he used both arms to hold her close. 'Let me go, damn you!'

He was too big, too strong, for her to escape, and any attempt she made to kick his shins was prevented as he scissored both her legs between his own.

In one easy movement he rolled onto his back, carrying her with him, holding her there with galling ease as he reached out a hand and switched on the bedside light.

She looked magnificent in her fury, Luc perceived through narrowed eyes. Her hair was loose and tumbled, her cheeks flushed, her eyes brilliant sapphire shards meant to tear him to shreds.

The nightshirt she wore didn't begin to cover her and rode high over her hips.

'Now,' Luc growled huskily. 'Suppose you explain what this is all about.'

Ana struggled afresh, and managed to free one of her hands. She acted without thought, barely conscious of swinging her arm in a swift arc until her palm connected with his cheek. The sharp sound seemed loud in the silence of the room, and there was a part of her that registered horror at having lashed out at him.

Dear God. Such anger culminating in one retaliatory slap.

Her eyes widened in shock as she saw his features harden, facial muscles tightening into a visual mask of anger.

'Let me go!'

'Not in this lifetime, *pedhaki mou*.'

'You're hurting me.'

'No. I'm being extremely careful not to.' He had no trouble restraining her hands, and he was quick to take evasive action as she brought her head down and attempted to bite his arm. 'Stop it. You'll only hurt yourself.'

'Go to hell.'

'You consign me there with increasing regularity.' His voice was a hateful drawl that irked her unbearably. 'This isn't the first time I've had to attend a business dinner and arrived home late. Why such a reaction *tonight*?'

She wanted to hit him, and tried, only to find the effort futile. 'As if you don't know!'

His features bore a sculpted hardness, and his eyes were dark. Temper held in tight control, but there, none the less. 'If I knew, I wouldn't need to ask.'

Ana made a further attempt to pull free, and failed. 'I hate you.'

'For what, specifically?'

Her anger moved up a notch. 'This afternoon I spent an hour in Celine's apartment arranging flowers for a dinner party she was having tonight.' She threw him a fulminating glare. 'Twenty minutes ago she rang to tell me you were on your way home.'

Luc went still. 'You believe I was with Celine?' His voice was quiet. Way too quiet.

'You do the maths.'

'You think I'd lie to you?'

She didn't answer, couldn't. Her voice seemed to have temporarily disappeared.

'Worse,' he continued silkily. 'Come from her bed to yours?'

Icily bleak eyes riveted hers, trapping her in his gaze, and she caught the grim resolve apparent as he captured her head and held it fast.

'You expect me to accept your word unconditionally?'

'Is that so difficult?'

'Based on blind faith?' Ana lashed out with scepticism. 'My naïvety?' She was on a roll. 'Please. Don't insult my intelligence.'

He held on to his temper with difficulty. 'Why would I go out for hamburger when I have fillet steak at home?'

Oh, my. 'That's some analogy.'

'*Cristos.*' The oath held a dangerous softness that sent apprehension scudding down the length of her spine. 'This has gone far enough!'

In one fluid movement he slid from the bed and picked up the phone, then swore and crossed to the small antique desk, flicked on the lamp, then he opened a drawer and pulled out a phone book.

It took him only seconds to riffle through the pages, find the appropriate one, scan the relevant names and punch in the required digits.

Ana told herself she wasn't going to listen, but

she'd have had to put both hands over her ears to close out the sound of his voice.

Hard, inflexible words, with no hint of observing any social niceties, they carried an unmistakable warning to cease and desist from verbal stalking, or he'd take legal action.

His controlled anger held a menacing quality as he replaced the receiver and turned to face her.

'Give me all of it. From the beginning.'

'Celine?'

'*All*, Ana. Every hint, each accusation…don't leave anything out.'

It took a while, but at last she was done, and her face paled at his expression.

'That's it?'

Most of it…unless you counted the tone of voice, the malicious intent.

He wanted to pull on some clothes, collect his keys, drive to Celine's apartment and issue her with a writ. And while he had the power to get his lawyer out of bed, there was the due process of the law to observe, and no judge was going to comply at this hour of the night.

'You should have told me all this before.'

'I thought I had. Some of it,' she amended, and incurred his dark look.

'She won't bother you again.'

Want to bet? Somehow she doubted Celine would fade gracefully into the woodwork. Ana had blown her out of the water, and revenge would surely follow.

Luc slid into bed and gathered her close. 'Don't ever keep anything from me again.'

His mouth sought hers, and a hollow protest rose and died in her throat as he forced her jaw wide and plundered at will.

It became a ravaging assault on her senses, flagrant, primitive, and demanding, until he conquered each and every one of her defences.

Then, and only then, his mouth gentled fractionally and took on an eroticism she fought hard to resist.

Hungry, sensual, he caressed with devastating expertise, coaxing her capitulation until he sensed the moment she stopped fighting him.

One hand moved, catching the hem of her nightshirt before tugging it over her head, then he reached forward and began tracing the outline of her breast, watching her eyes dilate as sensation arched through her body.

Not content, he teased and tantalised the delicate peak before shifting to its twin, and she gasped as he spread his fingers and trailed a path to her waist.

Sensation spiralled through her body, and she made no protest as he brought his head down to hers in a kiss that drove her mindless.

With care he gathered her close and rolled over so their positions were reversed, then he eased into her, taking it slow as he controlled each plunge until she was driven almost mad with need.

In desperation she grazed her teeth over the hard muscle and sinew at his shoulder, then trailed low to one male nipple...and rendered a love-bite that brought the breath hissing between his teeth.

'So you want to play, hmm?'

It was she who groaned out loud as he took revenge in tantalising every pulse-beat, each sensory pleasure spot until she began to beg, and she cried out as he took her high, held her there, then caught her as she fell.

For a while she didn't want to move, didn't feel she could, and she rested in his arms, luxuriating in the slow drift of his fingers along the edge of her spine, soothing as his lips brushed her temple, then slipped to taste the delicate hollows at the base of her neck.

Minutes later he shifted her to one side, then slid to his feet and walked naked to the valet frame, collected his wallet, removed a credit slip from a leather sleeve, and handed it to her.

'The restaurant at the Ritz-Carlton Hotel. I picked up the tab for four.' He moved to the phone. 'You want I should ring Henri, the *maître d'*, and have him confirm what time we left?'

The date, the amount, both tallied. Irrefutable proof.

'I owe you an apology.' It wasn't easy to say the

words. It was even harder to look at him. But she did, and didn't let her gaze waver.

For someone as delusional and determined as Celine, it wouldn't have proven too difficult to discover Luc's plans and slip a waiter money to phone her when Luc left the restaurant.

'Accepted.'

CHAPTER EIGHT

ANA knew as soon as she hit the traffic snarl that she should have taken Rebekah's advice and left the shop earlier. Now she'd be impossibly late.

Dammit. Why *me*? she silently demanded of the Deity. Except no one was listening. The traffic remained stalled, and the only certainty was the knowledge she wouldn't be going anywhere in a hurry.

Luc *would not* be pleased. The evening's event was a prestigious fund-raiser, and the guest speaker a prominent American ex-president.

Everyone who was *anyone* would be there. Including Celine. But not, she prayed God, seated at the same table.

She checked the time, and hesitated between two options. Ring Luc from her cellphone, or wait for him to contact her.

Better make the call. He answered on the second peal, and the sound of his voice did strange things to her equilibrium.

It was damnable the effect he had on her, even from a distance. Elevated heartbeat, a faint breathlessness, and heat…the acute sexual awareness of shared intimacy. Past, present, future. She only had to think of him to have numerous erotic images flood her mind.

Get over it, she remonstrated silently.

'I won't say you should have left the shop before now.'

'Please don't. I'll be there whenever this line of traffic begins to move.'

It did, eventually, and she reached home with the sure knowledge it would take more than a miracle to shower, change, dress and *shine* in less than ten minutes.

She managed it in thirty, the scarlet bias-cut silk organza gown with its knee-high ruffled split a masterpiece of fabric and style. The simply cut bodice and shoestring straps completed a stunning design, complemented by her upswept hair, expertly applied make-up, and minimum jewellery.

Luc had been dressed when she first entered the bedroom, and now she bore his analytical scrutiny with a degree of uncertainty.

Was the gown too over-the-top? She'd fallen in love with it when she'd seen it displayed on a model. On impulse she'd extracted her credit card, added matching stiletto-heeled evening sandals and evening bag. Only to have reservations as to her sanity in expending so much on a single outfit.

'If you're aiming for the *wow* factor, you've achieved it.'

Success! She sent him a dazzling smile. 'Ah, a compliment.'

He looked stunning in anything he wore, for he exuded a certain intrinsic *something* that isolated him from other men. Difficult to pin down to any one thing, it was a combination of height and stature, the way he held himself and the way he moved. It was also the compelling quality that hinted at a raw primitiveness beneath the surface. The self-assurance of dynamic power, latent and devoid of arrogance…but there, none the less.

He would command attention in jeans and a sweat-shirt. Attired in evening clothes, snowy-white shirt and black bow-tie, he was something else.

Her eyes held a wicked gleam. 'If I return it, you might get a swelled head.' She collected her evening bag, and gathered up a matching wrap. 'Shall we leave?'

'Yes.' He crossed to her side. 'But first—' He lowered his head, wanting, needing the taste of her, and his mouth captured hers in a kiss that tore the foundations of her composure…as he meant it to.

Reassurance…his, or hers? He told himself it was for her. And knew he lied.

The city hotel venue was crowded, the entrance brightly lit, a cavalcade of cars lined up waiting for valet parking, and there was security everywhere.

It took a while to get through the cordoned area, and by the time they reached the grand ballroom most everyone had passed through the doors and was seated.

Photographers were busy capturing the *crème de*

la crème of the rich and famous for the society pages of leading newspapers and national magazines.

It was, Ana perceived, *smile* time. Glitz and glamour, expensive jewellery, the drift of exotic perfumes meshed with the buzz of conversation as Luc caught hold of her hand and led the way to their reserved table.

They slipped into their seats just as centre lights dimmed and the MC began his opening speech outlining the charity's achievements, their projections for the coming year, and the specific purpose for this evening's gala event.

Waiters moved unobtrusively, weaving with precision through the many tables as they delivered starters, and wine stewards hovered attentively.

From where they were seated it was possible to see the VIP table, and she caught a glimpse of the ex-president, the silver, almost white, well-groomed hair, the lightly tanned complexion, the easy smile.

Conversation at their own table was interesting and varied, and she was supremely conscious of Luc seated at her side.

Last night… *Don't go there*, an inner voice cautioned. It was difficult not to recall her anger, the rage, and her reaction. She'd never physically hit anyone in her life. The thought she'd attempted to strike him appalled her.

All day she'd managed to put it to one side as she became caught up with a rush of orders and customers.

Now, she found her attention being drawn back to the accusations she'd flung at him…and the result.

How was it possible to *hate* someone one moment, be filled with contrition the next, then participate in lovemaking as if nothing mattered except the moment?

It was like riding a crazy emotional roller coaster.

'Amazing man, isn't he? No one would imagine from looking at him that he once held the fate of a nation in his hands.' The guest leaned in close. 'Apart from our state premier, everyone else at his table is security.'

'I imagine security men and women are evenly spread throughout the room,' Ana inclined politely.

She was spared from further comment as the state premier was introduced and the waiter began removing plates.

At the conclusion of the main course, Ana quietly slipped from her seat and went in search of the powder room. She was one of several women in need of the facilities, and afterwards she took a minute in front of the mirror to freshen her lipstick.

'Don't go crying to Luc again, darling.'

Celine, and on a mission. With no doubt as to the target.

'What makes you think I did?'

'Oh, *please*. Luc and I have no secrets from each other.'

Did her hand shake? She hoped not. 'Don't you have anything better to do?'

'Than *what*, precisely?'

'Meddle in other people's lives. Mine, in particular.'

'I can't believe I'm not getting through to you.'

'Oh, you are, Celine,' she assured. 'Loud and clear.' She paused a beat. 'Pity it's such a waste of your time and energy.'

'Luc is—'

'Free to choose, Celine.' The emphasis was deliberate. 'It would appear he's chosen me.'

The other woman's expression was scathing. 'Simply because you wear his ring and carry his child? Darling, how naïve are you?'

She slid the capped lipstick tube into her evening bag and turned away from the mirrored wall. 'I have nothing further to say to you.' She moved back a step, only to pause as the other woman caught hold of her wrist. 'Take your hand off me.'

'I could point out a number of successful businessmen whose wives turn a blind eye to their husbands' indiscretions.'

'I'm not one of them.' Calm, she had to remain calm. If she lost her temper, this debacle would digress into a physical cat fight.

Celine's lacquered nails bit into Ana's arm. 'Luc rang today and warned he wouldn't be able to see me for a while because you were making things difficult.' Her smile held a vindictiveness that was vaguely frightening. 'Not a wise move, darling.'

She'd had enough. 'Keep this up, Celine, and you'll have charges laid against you.'

Celine rendered a vicious pinch, then flung Ana's arm wide. 'Luc would never allow it.'

Ana moved towards the door, then paused. 'Perhaps now would be a good time to tell you I was in the room when Luc rang you last night.' She walked into the carpeted foyer and re-entered the ballroom.

The ex-president had already begun his speech, and Luc shot her a studied glance as she slipped into her seat, then returned his attention to the man at the podium.

The speech concluded amid enthusiastic applause, then the lights brightened and the waiters busied themselves serving the dessert and coffee.

'Are you OK?'

Now, there was a question. 'Solicitous attention, Luc?'

'Let me guess,' he drawled. 'Celine bailed you up in the powder room?'

'Got it in one.'

'Whereupon you told her to get lost, and she retaliated?'

'Ah, you possess psychic powers.'

'Damage control is—'

'Something at which you excel.' She hadn't meant to sound bitter, and she saw his gaze sharpen.

He caught hold of her hand and linked her fingers through his own, holding them firmly when she endeavoured to pull free.

'We dealt with this last night.'

'Did we? I thought we just had sex.'

'That, too.'

The waiter placed cups and saucers onto the table, and she indicated tea in preference to coffee.

'I'll take you home.'

'I don't want to leave yet.' Her gaze was remarkably clear. 'And escape isn't the answer.'

'Nor is a heated argument in public,' he accorded drily, and she arched one delicate brow.

'Is that what we're about to have?'

'Count on it.'

Ana picked up an extra tube of sugar, broke it and stirred the contents into her tea. 'Energy for the fight.'

'Don't push me too far.'

She proffered a deliberately sweet smile. 'I'm shaking.'

'So brave.'

His faint mockery brought a surge of anger. 'What can you do to me that you haven't done already?'

Something shifted in his eyes, and she felt a trickle of apprehension slither down her spine. 'Careful, *pedhi mou*.'

It seemed pointless to further the civility façade, and she sipped her tea, indulged in animated conversation with a fellow guest, then became the epitome of politeness when Luc indicated they should leave.

Her face ached from the smile she kept in place

as they paused at one table and another to talk with friends and acquaintances, and she stood silently at the hotel entrance as the valet called up their car.

Ana didn't offer a word during the drive to Vaucluse, and once inside the house she made straight for the stairs.

Luc re-set the security alarm and entered their suite as she tried unsuccessfully to release the clasp fastening the slender gold chain circling her throat.

He shrugged out of his jacket, undid his tie, loosened his shirt buttons, then crossed to her side.

'Let me try.'

His fingers were warm against her nape, and she wanted to sweep away from him. Except what good would it do except exacerbate an already volatile situation?

He freed the clasp in seconds, then turned her round to face him.

'You want to fight, or do we call a truce?'

Vengeance tinged her voice. 'Fight.'

'Then throw the first punch.'

She made a fist and aimed for his chest, felt it connect against hard muscle and sinew...and bruised her knuckles.

'Your knees are supposed to buckle as you sink to the floor.'

'Want to try again?'

He was amused, damn him. She gave him a baleful glare as she nursed her hand. 'Not particularly.'

He smoothed his palms over her shoulders, slipping the straps free, then he tended to the zip fastening her gown.

The red silk organza slid to the carpet in a heap. All she wore were thong briefs and stiletto heels, and his breath caught in his throat at the beautiful symmetry of her slender curves.

Pale, satin-smooth skin, firm breasts, a slim waist, toned thighs.

He had an unrelenting urge to touch her, shape those curves with his hands, taste her. And when he was done, bury himself inside her, absorb her shuddering climax, then climb the heights with her and share a mutual shattering of the senses.

Luc reached out and cupped her face, then he lowered his mouth down over hers…and gave a grunt as her fist executed a stunning hook just beneath his ribcage.

'I think that's known as the element of surprise?'

His retribution was swift, and she gasped as he lifted her up against him and hooked her legs around his waist.

She felt him toe off one shoe, then the other, and he shifted her higher as he dealt with his belt, his trousers. His shirt was wrenched off and tossed to the floor, then he stood looking at her, his features raw with something intensely primitive.

The heat and hardness of his arousal pushed against the scrap of silk covering the apex of her thighs, and in one smooth movement he slid his fingers beneath the thin strap and disposed of it.

Dear heaven. There was nothing measured or controlled about him. Only electrifying passion and a fierce need for consummation.

Ana waited for the moment he would plunge deep inside, and felt her eyes begin to glaze over as he rocked her slowly against him, exposing her clitoris to the satin-smooth hardness of his shaft.

'Luc—' She could barely speak as sensation exploded in an upward spiral that had her moaning out loud.

Just as she thought she could bear it no longer he walked to the bed and tumbled them both down onto the mattress.

Now. Did she cry it out? She couldn't be sure, and she groaned when he covered her mouth with his own in a kiss that duplicated the sexual act itself.

She reached for him, and he evaded her touch, choosing instead to trail a path to her breast where he savoured one tender peak before rendering attention to its twin, suckling there until she cried out with a mixture of pleasure and pain.

Not content, he moved low over her navel, then traced a tortuously slow path to render the most intimate kiss of all.

He wanted to have her beg for his possession, to feel the hunger, the want, and *need* him as much as he needed her.

The passion was mesmeric, *magical.* Too much. Way too much and beyond her control. Slow, silent tears trickled down over her temple and became lost in her hair as she tossed her head from one side to the other as she craved a release only he could give.

Her body shuddered in reaction, and he raised his head, saw the devastation etched on her features, then he shifted to close his mouth over hers in an evocative kiss that made her want to weep afresh.

It was then he slid into her, taking care with long, slow strokes that culminated in an explosive crescendo.

Afterwards he pulled up the covers and held her close, trailing a light, feathery path along her spine in a soothing gesture until her breathing steadied to an even beat.

'Rise and shine.'

Ana registered Luc's voice, the words, and opened her eyes a fraction.

It was Sunday morning, she didn't need to go into the shop, and she had no particular inclination to get out of bed at…she took a moment to check the time…eight o'clock.

She spared him a glance, and saw he'd already showered and was dressed in casual jeans and a polo shirt. He looked vital, and far too lethally male for any woman's peace of mind. Especially at this early hour.

'You'd better have a good reason for suggesting I *rise* and *shine*.'

Luc indicated the tray resting on the bedside pedestal. 'Tea and toast. Fruit.'

She slid into a sitting position, realised she wasn't wearing a thing and pulled the sheet high. '*You* made this?'

He sat down on the edge of the bed. 'Don't sound so surprised.'

'Thank you.' Her lips curved into a slight smile. 'Presumably you want to get me out of bed, rather than keep me in it…so what gives?'

'I plan to take the boat out onto the harbour for the day.'

Given the *boat* was a luxury cruiser moored at a marina, he'd obviously planned ahead. She had to ask. 'Are you inviting anyone else along?'

'No.'

Better and better. 'What time do you want to leave?'

'As soon as you're ready.'

She looked beautifully tousled, her skin flushed from sleep, her eyes deep and lustrous. He reached forward and pushed a wayward lock of hair behind her ear.

There was a need to spend time with her, in order to help repair some of the damage caused by Celine's interference.

'Are you going to sit there and watch me eat?'

He looked completely relaxed, although even at ease there was a leashed quality evident. A sensual element that never failed to stir her emotions.

'I've already had breakfast.'

She finished the tea and toast, then peeled the banana and ate it. 'I need to shower.'

He caught up her silk wrap and handed it to her. 'I'll see you downstairs. Twenty minutes?'

She made it in fifteen, choosing jeans and a knit top over a bikini, and she'd snagged a sweater in case of a cool breeze.

The skies were an azure blue with hardly a cloud in sight, and there was warmth in the early-summer sun as they gained the large marina.

After a hectic week, the prospect of cruising the harbour seemed an idyllic way to spend the day. Luc's cruiser was a sleek-looking craft with gleaming white paint, expensive fittings, and contained a roomy cabin, master suite and bathroom.

Within minutes of boarding Luc started the engines, then eased the craft out into open waters. Ana stood at his side, admiring the rocky promontories where beautiful harbour-side mansions dotted the landscape, the numerous coves and bays.

Craft in varying shapes and sizes were out on the harbour, some with definite destinations in mind, others just idly exploring the waterways or putting down anchor to try their luck at fishing.

The muted sound of the powerful engines was a pleasant background noise. 'Are you meeting Jace at the airport?'

Luc spared her a quick glance. 'His flight gets in late. He'll take a cab to the hotel and call me in the morning.'

There were questions she wanted to ask, and she struggled with them, not willing to spoil the day or upset the delicately balanced truce they shared.

The sun rose higher in the sky, dappling the waters with reflected light, and around midday Luc cut the engines and dropped anchor.

'Lunch. Do you want to eat in the cabin, or outside?'

'Outside,' Ana said without hesitation, and took bottled drinks from the cabin refrigerator while Luc unpacked the large chilled cooler.

Petros had been busy, she perceived as she checked out roast chicken, succulent ham, various salads, fresh bread rolls and fruit. It was a feast, and she set it out on plates, added cutlery, then sank onto one of the cushioned squabs.

Luc settled down opposite and layered a roll with chicken and salad, then bit into it with evident enjoyment.

Ana followed suit, reflecting a week ago she'd been in a different place, endeavouring to sort out a wealth of ambivalent emotions.

Would Luc have come after her if he hadn't discovered she was pregnant? And if she'd demanded a divorce, would he have insisted on a reconciliation, or merely called his lawyer?

She wanted to know the answers, but she didn't have the courage to ask the questions. What if the answers Luc gave weren't what she wanted to hear?

Did he care for her, *really* care for her? Or was she merely a convenient wife who suited his needs?

In bed, they were in perfect accord. Out of it, she spent time trying to convince herself she should be content with the status quo.

A week ago, she'd thought she had choices and options. Now they'd been taken away from her.

'I value what is mine. That's a given.'

Value wasn't *love*, she added silently. Would he have followed her to the Coast if she hadn't been pregnant?

'Yes.'

Her eyes widened beneath the tinted lens of her sunglasses. 'You read minds?'

'You have expressive features. *Yes*…I would have hauled you back to Sydney.' He paused fractionally. 'And no,' he continued with chilling softness. 'Not solely because I discovered you carry our child. Or as some form of misguided revenge for your father's misappropriation of bank funds.'

Dared she believe him? She wanted to, desperately. The repetitive beep of a cellphone was an intrusion, and it took a few seconds to realise it was her own. The caller ID wasn't one she recognised, and there was surprised relief as she read a text message from her father confirming his safe arrival in New York together with the name of his hotel.

Ana put a call through to Rebekah and relayed the news, then she cleared away the remains of their lunch while Luc fired up the engines and headed south towards Botany Bay.

It was so warm, she stripped down to her bikini, took time to cover every exposed inch of skin with sun-screen lotion, then she spread out a towel and let the sun and fresh salt air work their soporific magic.

She must have dozed, for when she woke the sun had moved lower in the sky. It was still warm, but she sat up and pulled on the knit top, then rose to her feet.

The engines were silent, and she saw Luc sprawled comfortably at ease near by, reading a novel.

At that moment he glanced up and discarded the book. 'Ready to go home?'

'Yes. Thank you,' she added with sincerity.

Humour tugged the edges of his mouth. 'For what, specifically?'

'Organising the day.'

'My pleasure. We'll go out somewhere later for dinner.'

The thought of dressing up didn't appeal. 'Why not collect take-out and eat at home?'

'Anything in particular?'

Crispy noodles, heaps of vegetables, prawns and rice. 'Chinese?'

'Done.'

She looked at him in surprise. 'You're not going to override me?'

'Why would I do that?' he queried, and caught the gleam in her eyes as she laughed.

'You're being indulgent.'

'Is that such a terrible thing?' His light, teasing drawl brought an answering smile to her lips.

She could almost imagine they had taken a step back in time to the early days of their marriage, only to dismiss the thought as being fanciful. Yet there was a part of her that wanted what they once shared…the affection, fun, the spontaneity. The uninhibited loving, when there had been no doubts and she retained few insecurities.

It was almost six when they left the marina. Luc stopped *en route* to Vaucluse and picked up Chinese take-out, which they ate with chopsticks directly out of containers seated at a table on the terrace. Oliver sat close by, eager with expectancy for the occasional morsel of food.

Afterwards they watched the sunset, the brilliant flaring of orange streaked with pink and purple, followed by the gradual fading of colour with the onset of dusk.

It had been a near-perfect day, and she was reluctant to have it end. Tomorrow would see a return to work, and in the evening they were due to dine out with Jace and Rebekah.

Let's not forget Celine, Ana accorded silently on the edge of sleep. The woman was bound to wreak more havoc, given half a chance.

CHAPTER NINE

MONDAY was busy, orders flowed in, and what breaks Ana and Rebekah were able to take were minimal.

Consequently, it was almost six before they were able to get away from the shop, and traffic seemed even slower than usual as Ana headed for Vaucluse.

Luc pulled into the driveway seconds ahead of her, and she followed the Mercedes into the garage, parked, then slid from the car.

'You're late.'

There was disapproval in his tone, and Ana flashed him a stunning smile. 'Well, *hell*, so are you.'

She thought she caught a glimpse of humour in those dark eyes as she drew level, and her lips parted in surprise as he slid a hand beneath her nape and pulled her close.

'You have a sassy mouth.'

His head descended, and she was powerless to prevent the firm pressure of his mouth on hers as he bestowed an evocative kiss that left her wanting more.

'What was that for?'

He traced the fullness of her lower lip with an idle finger. 'Because I felt like it.'

Dear heaven, did he have any idea what he did to her? In bed, without a doubt. But out of it? Just the thought of him sent the blood coursing through her veins. Sexual chemistry, she perceived, was a powerful entity.

And *love*? To find a soul mate and gift one's heart unconditionally…to have the gift returned… Was it unattainable in life's reality? Or did that kind of love only exist in romantic fantasy?

There were times in the depths of passion, she thought it was possible. Except in the dark of night it was all too easy to believe the touch of a man's hands, the feel of his mouth, meant much more than it did. And without the words…

Although better no words, than a meaningless avowal that would only leave emptiness.

Get a grip, Ana berated silently. You knew when you married him that love wasn't part of the deal. Why should anything have changed? Except in the deepest recess of her heart she'd hoped that it might.

'What's going on in that head of yours, hmm?'

She blinked at the sound of his voice, and switched from passive reflection to the present in an instant.

'Contemplating how Jace and Rebekah will react to each other,' she declared with a blandness that didn't deceive him in the slightest.

Luc curved an arm over her shoulders as they made their way towards the foyer. 'I have no doubt Jace will handle her without much effort.'

As you handle me? Aloud, she retaliated, 'Rebekah wouldn't agree with you.'

Ana ascended the stairs as Luc paused to consult with Petros, and she began discarding clothes as soon as she entered the bedroom. Thirty minutes in which to shower, wash and dry her hair, dress and be ready to depart the house didn't allow for leisurely preparations.

The sound of cascading water masked the faint snick of the shower door opening, and she gave a startled gasp as Luc entered the cubicle.

'What do you think you're doing?'

He took the bottle of shampoo from her hand and poured a liberal quantity into his palm, then began massaging it into her hair.

'Indulging you.'

His drawling tone curled around her nerve-ends and tugged a little. 'I don't need you to indulge me,' she said fiercely, endeavouring to ignore the pleasure spiralling through her body. God, that felt good, so good!

His hands moved to her nape, then worked magic on her neck and shoulders. An appreciative sigh escaped her lips, and she felt the warmth within slowly build to a burning heat.

Luc rinsed the suds from her hair, smoothed back the wet length, then he lowered his mouth over hers in a soft, evocative kiss that had her leaning in to him, wanting, needing so much more.

His arousal was a potent, virile force, and she

whimpered a little as he eased back a little, gentling the kiss until his lips were just brushing hers. Then he held her at arm's length, and let his gaze roam over her slender form.

The thought of their child swelling her body almost brought him undone. The beauty of it, the miracle...

Already he could see the slight difference in the shape of her breasts, the aureoles, and he traced each contour and lightly cupped their weight, exalting in her faint intake of breath as he brushed each tender nub with his thumb.

He let one hand slip down to cover her waist, and wondered how long it would be before it began to thicken. A few more weeks...longer?

'Luc—'

'I want to look at you,' he said gently.

'Don't...' It was a token protest, for there was something magical happening here. Surely she could be forgiven for wanting to capture and hold the moment.

'Don't *what*?'

She made a last-ditch attempt at sensibility. 'We'll be late.'

His smile held musing humour. 'So, we'll be late.'

'Rebekah will never forgive me.' She gave a husky groan as his hand slid low over her abdomen and sought the sensitive clitoris. All it took was the glide of his fingers, and she became lost...*his*.

He lifted her easily, and she wrapped her legs

around his waist, then sank into him, loving the slow slick slide as she accepted his length.

Her mouth angled in to his, and she felt she was drowning, awash in libidinous sensation as his tongue tangled with hers in an oral simulation of the sexual act itself.

It was he who controlled the rhythmic pacing, its depth of penetration, and he cradled her as she climbed the heights, then caught her as she fell.

Like this, nothing else mattered. Only the man, the moment. It was possible to believe everything in her world was OK. No intrusions, no designing ex-mistress, and no nebulous ghost of his first wife to cloud the perfection of what they'd just shared.

Later there would be a reality check. But for now he was hers...in body, and affection. Was it so wrong to want it all? His heart, his soul?

Ana told herself she should be content with the positives...she was his wife, she was carrying their child.

The negative was Celine, who'd stop at nothing to cause trouble.

And then there was Emma, who'd occupied a brief part of his life before leaving it. In all honesty, she could hardly begrudge him the memory, and didn't.

It was almost eight when they entered the restaurant, and Ana sensed the tension apparent before she even reached their table.

'Ana.' Jace rose to his feet and greeted her with an affectionate hug, brushed his lips to each cheek in turn, then held her at arm's length. 'You are beautiful, *pedhaki mou*. I swear, if you were not already married to my cousin, I'd have no compunction in stealing you away.' His dark eyes held a devilish twinkle. 'If he dares to mistreat you, I promise to kill him.'

'Flatterer.' She offered him a winsome smile, then slid into the chair the waiter held out for her.

The resemblance between the two cousins was notable in that they shared the height, the breadth of shoulder, the dark, attractive good looks of their heritage. Add power, a dangerous alchemy, and it became a combustible combination.

How many years separated them? One, two? It could only be a few.

'You knew I didn't want to be with Jace one-on-one,' Rebekah remonstrated quietly as Luc and Jace perused the selection of wines.

'I'm sure you managed OK.' Given the thoughtful and rather musing expression Jace wore, it wasn't difficult to imagine he'd succeeded in getting beneath Rebekah's skin.

The waiter presented the menu, and they ordered a starter followed by a main, waived dessert in favour of the cheeseboard.

'So tell me how it is with the florist industry,' Jace drawled, and his eyes were watchful, sharp, beneath an indolent demeanour.

'I've been away for a few weeks,' Ana said lightly. 'Rebekah can expound on it.'

'To what purpose? I doubt Jace's interest is genuine.'

'On the contrary. I'm very interested in everything you do.'

Oh, my, this was assuming all the portents of a verbal clash.

'Really?' Rebekah didn't appear to care, but Ana knew her sister too well. The question had to be whether Jace saw beneath the practised and protective façade.

'You want to hear a florist's day begins at four in the morning when she leaves for the city flower markets? If she arrives there later than five, all the quality blooms have already been bought.'

She held out her hands. 'These are the major tools of our trade.' She gave them a rueful glance. 'They're in water, they get cut, scratched, blistered, and retain permanent callouses. Gloves don't work, they're too unwieldy, and creams don't begin to repair the damage. Forget manicures and nail polish.' Her faint grimace held fleeting cynicism. 'You want more?'

'You've left out standing on your feet all day, and dealing with difficult customers. Deliveries that go to incorrect addresses?' Jace drawled quizzically.

Rebekah chose silence, although Ana knew it cost her.

The food was delectable, and they ate with enjoyment.

'How long are you staying in Sydney?' Ana queried, directing her attention to Jace, whose home base was a private residence in New York's fashionable Upper East Side.

'As long as it takes to wrap up a few property deals. Has Luc told you I intend dragging him down to Melbourne day after tomorrow?'

'Not yet.'

Jace's smile held devilish humour. 'Can you manage without him for a few nights?'

'Easily.'

Luc caught hold of her hand and brought it to his lips. 'You're supposed to say *no*.'

His dark eyes held a lazy warmth that was wholly sensual, and she felt the answering kick of her pulse as it quickened in pace.

'Really?'

Jace chuckled, and touched the rim of his wine glass to Ana's water goblet. 'Salute. I know of no other woman who would dare take Luc to task.'

'My wife delights in deflating my ego.'

'Count yourself fortunate, cousin.'

Ana caught Rebekah's expressive eye-roll, and steered the conversation onto safer ground. 'Let's do dinner and the movies while Luc is away.'

'Wednesday night?'

'Done.'

'Do I get to have a say?' Luc queried mildly.

'None whatsoever.'

'Have Petros drive you.'

'Don't be ridiculous.'

'I could invite myself to stay over,' Rebekah suggested.

'Better,' Luc acquiesced. 'Petros still gets to be chauffeur.'

'Remind me to hit you when we get home.' She made the threat sound amusing, but there was no humour in the glance she cast him.

'I'll look forward to it.'

She couldn't win, so why try? Except the banter kept things light, and Jace and Rebekah's presence made for a pleasant evening.

It was after ten when they left the restaurant and drove home. Traffic was minimal, ensuring there were no delays at controlled intersections, and the lull provided a pleasant reminder the day was almost done.

'What time are you leaving for Melbourne?'

'Eager to be rid of me, *pedhi mou*?'

'Must I answer that?'

Together they entered the house, and Ana climbed the stairs to the upper floor while Luc set the security alarm.

She was in bed and on the verge of sleep when he joined her, and she made no protest as he gathered her close.

His lips nuzzled the warm scented skin at the edge of her neck, then trailed a path up the sensitive cord to savour the lobe of her ear before tracing the line of her jaw.

She adored the feel of him, the hard muscle and

sinew, the shape and contours of a body that was wholly male.

He made her come alive, as no man ever had, and the blood sang in her veins, heating her skin and activating every nerve cell until all her senses meshed and she became one throbbing entity.

Great sex. The best. For a while she lost herself in sensual euphoria, totally enraptured by the man who held her heart and captured her soul.

Ana glanced up at the sound of the electronic door buzzer, and her lips parted to form a warm smile. 'Jace.' Her greeting held genuine affection as he crossed to the counter. 'How nice to see you.'

He leant forward and brushed his lips to her cheek. 'And you, Ana.'

'Is your visit business or pleasure?'

His dark eyes held humour. 'One could say both.'

'Rebekah has stepped out for a few minutes.'

'Then I shall wait.'

Her grin was unrepentant. 'Thought you might.'

'Am I that transparent?'

She tilted her head a little, pretending to consider his mocking query. 'You're a Dimitriades,' she answered lightly. 'Transparency isn't one of your traits. Playing the game *is*.' Her expression sobered. 'Take care with my sister.'

The amusement disappeared. 'Or else you'll come out fighting?'

'Count on it.'

'I consider myself duly warned.'

'I don't suppose you're going to give me any hint of your intentions?'

'No.'

'Damn.'

He lifted a hand and tucked a stray tendril of hair back behind her ear. 'I can see why my cousin put a ring on your finger.'

'And that would be?'

'To put you off-limits to other men.'

'He might care to remember I put a ring on *his* finger.'

His gaze sharpened. 'Problems, Ana?'

The telephone provided a welcome interruption, and she wrote down the verbal order, took credit-card details, then tended to a customer who walked in off the street.

Rebekah's return coincided with another telephone call, and Ana dealt with it, aware that Luc's cousin was intent on buying roses. At least two dozen, she determined as Rebekah gathered them together, then spread Cellophane paper on the work table and carefully positioned the blooms.

Just as Ana replaced the receiver, a man entered the shop, chose a prepared bouquet, then bought and paid for it.

Busy didn't begin to describe it, and Ana checked the orders that should be ready for the delivery guy to collect on the late-morning run, glanced at the wall clock, and continued with preparations.

Whatever was happening between Rebekah and Jace reached a conclusion, and she acknowledged his 'goodbye' with a smile and watched as he exited the shop.

'That man,' Rebekah vented quietly as she joined Ana at the work table.

'What about him?'

Rebekah consulted the order book, then retrieved tissue, Cellophane wrap, and skilfully selected carnations, baby's breath. Nimble fingers spread them into an artistic display, and she caught ribbon from a stand of varied ribbon rolls, cut off a length and tied it within seconds.

'He doesn't understand the word *no*.'

'Really?'

'Do you know what he just did?' Rebekah didn't wait for an answer. 'He bought three dozen roses, paid for them, wrote on a card, then handed them to me.'

'Such an unforgivable sin,' Ana declared, tongue-in-cheek, and incurred her sister's glare. 'What did the card say?'

'*"Dinner tonight. Seven."*'

'Naturally you're not going to go.'

'Of course not.'

'And you'll be out when he calls.'

'Got it in one.'

Ana put the completed bouquet to one side, perused the next order, and began assembling it. 'Maybe you should share dinner with him—'

'Are you insane?'

'And tell him exactly what you think of him,' she continued, ignoring Rebekah's interruption.

'If I didn't know you cared,' her sister declared with mocking cynicism, 'I could almost imagine you *want* me to go out with him.'

'Not all men are like Brad.'

'Yeah, sure. Well, excuse me, but I don't feel inclined to go through the bullshit just to find out.'

'Jace is—'

'Nice? Come on, sweetheart. Most men present a civil façade. At first,' she qualified. 'Then if you don't *deliver* you get called every name under the sun. Mr *nice guy* becomes the octopus from hell.' She drew in a deep breath and released it slowly. 'And I've never been one for indiscriminate sex just for the sake of scratching an itch.'

'So cocoon yourself in cotton wool and play it safe?'

'Yes.'

It was an adamant reply, expected, and one she chose not to pursue. 'OK.'

Rebekah slanted her sister a sharp glance. 'Just *OK*? No verbal lecture?'

'No.'

'Now you're pissing me off.'

'You want to fight...go fight with someone else.'

'Such as Jace? Over dinner?'

Ana hid a faint grimace as she observed the way

her sister plucked blooms from numerous tubs. 'The blooms don't deserve to suffer.'

'No, they don't.' Rebekah crossed to the counter and collected the bouquet of roses sitting there. 'These can go back into stock.'

'Jace has paid for them in good faith.'

'So? I should just leave them there?'

'Take them home.'

'The hell,' Rebekah declared inelegantly. '*You* take them home.'

'They were a gift to you.'

'They're going back into stock.'

Ana paused, then quietly offered, 'Don't allow a mistake in the past cloud your chance of happiness in the future.'

'With Jace Dimitriades? Are you nuts?'

'Jace, *personally*,' she pursued, 'or *any* man?'

Rebekah opened her mouth, then closed it again. 'Knowing what I went through with Brad, during and after the marriage, you're suggesting I dive into shark-infested waters again?'

'Sharks *bite*.'

'And you don't think Jace will?'

'If he does, I know you'll bite back.'

Rebekah threw up her hands, rolled her eyes in expressive disbelief, then burst into laughter. 'I give up!'

'Besides,' Ana ventured with a hint of devilry. 'If you bite, you might acquire a taste for him.'

'*Hah*. And the cow jumped over the moon.'

They were saved from further cynicism by the simultaneous peal of the telephone and the door buzzer.

Business, Ana conceded, took priority. But it didn't prevent the silent thought that Jace Dimitriades might be just who Rebekah needed to restore her faith in the male of the species.

It was mid-afternoon when Ana picked up her cellphone on the second ring, identified Luc's private number on-screen and activated the call.

'How do you feel about attending a movie première tonight?'

'We're talking gala event, or slipping quietly into a city theatre?'

'Fox Studios.'

Definitely *gala*.

'It slipped my mind until Caroline reminded me this morning.'

The ultra-efficient secretary who kept track of Luc's business and social diary.

'What time do we need to leave?'

'Seven. Petros will have dinner ready at six. Try not to be late.'

For once she managed to get away from the shop ahead of time. Largely due to Rebekah's prompting, and the help of their new assistant.

Choosing what to wear didn't present a dilemma, and she plucked a delightful multi-layered gown from its hanger, spread it on the bed, and paused to admire the brilliant mix of deep blue and peacock-green. A luminous thread made the colours shimmer beneath the light. Exquisite for evening wear, it highlighted her blonde hair and matched her eyes.

'What is the movie, and who are the lead actors?' Ana queried *en route* to the studios.

'The lead actress is an American-based Australian, so is the producer.'

Of course. She'd read about its upcoming release in numerous publicity slots on television. It promised to be colourful and amusing, as well as entertaining.

Parking wasn't a problem, and they joined fellow guests entering the auditorium. *Invitation only,* it was a glamorous event with several city socialites and notables attending.

Celine's presence was guaranteed. The only thing Ana could hope for was they were seated far apart.

Social mingling was a refined art, she mused as a fellow guest called Luc's name. There were pleasantries to exchange, the occasional opinion that touched on business…and the need to have instant recall of a host of names.

She had to hand it to Luc…he didn't appear to falter.

'You possess an awesome memory,' she murmured as they moved forward, and he cast her a musing look.

'It's an acquired skill.'

'Very much part of *business*.' She hadn't meant an edge of cynicism to creep in.

'An essential courtesy,' he elaborated, his gaze

sharpening as he caught the nervous slide of her fingers over the elegant beading of her evening bag.

'I can promise she won't get near you.' His voice was calm, unruffled, and Ana cast him a startled glance.

'You intend sticking to my side all night?'

A tinge of amusement momentarily softened his features. 'Like glue.'

'This could get interesting.'

His fingers threaded through her own. 'I'm counting on it.'

'United we stand?'

His expression sobered, and she caught a brief glimpse of the steely determination exigent. 'Yes.'

So his aim was to present *togetherness*. Just *how* together did he intend them to portray?

Very, Ana conceded, half an hour later. The light brush of his fingers down her arm; the arm loosely circling her waist; the way his fingers sought her nape and effected a brief, soothing massage there; the way his palm rested between her shoulder blades and moved fractionally.

It represented a tactile reassurance as they stood conversing with fellow guests, and there was a part of her that wished it was for real.

Her body felt alive with evocative sensation, and she was almost willing to swear she could feel the blood course through her veins, activating all her nerve-ends.

Was it possible to tune in to someone to such a

degree you felt you were meant to be like two halves of a whole? That only *this* person was your soul mate, never to be replaced by anyone else?

Love. Unconditional, abiding love. A gift without equal...beyond price. Reciprocal, it represented heaven on earth.

A light, fleeting touch to her lips caused her to start in surprise, and she was powerless to still the surge of emotion that rose from deep inside as she met Luc's unfathomable gaze.

For a moment she was acutely vulnerable, and she caught her lower lip with the edge of her teeth to prevent their faint tremor.

Had he glimpsed what she tried so desperately to hide?

His finger traced the curve, lingered at its edge, then he lowered his mouth to hers in a sweet evocative kiss that was all too brief.

She felt her eyes widen, and her voice emerged as a shaky whisper. 'What was that for?'

His smile completely disarmed her. 'Because I wanted to.'

Oh, my. For a few heightened seconds she wasn't conscious of anyone else. There was only Luc, and the moment.

Ana saw the inherent strength apparent, the integrity...and something else. Then it was gone, and she wondered if she'd imagined a quality beneath the slumbering passion evident.

Get a grip, she cautioned silently as she blinked

rapidly to dispel the image. He's merely playing a part.

There was a need to re-focus her attention, and she glanced idly round the auditorium, catching sight of a familiar face here and there…and found herself trapped in Celine's gaze.

Venom was reflected there. Sheer, unadulterated hatred.

It was as if time hung suspended, and Ana unconsciously held her breath. She lifted a hand to her throat in protective self-defence, then sought to cover the gesture by touching the diamond pendant resting there.

Dear heaven. How could anyone be filled with such malevolence? Or be so possessed by an obsessive emotion that it led towards destruction?

A shiver of apprehension slithered down Ana's spine. Premonition? But what? And where and when?

This was a civilised society, and Celine moved among the echelon of Sydney's wealthy élite. Realistically, what damage could she cause?

It was one thing to be prone to envy and jealousy, but quite another to act on it.

'Ana. Luc. How nice to see you here.'

Ana recognised the feminine voice and entered into conversation with one of the city's society matrons whose untiring support to charity organisations was legendary.

It produced, as it was meant to, an invitation to an upcoming event during the following month.

'You're keeping well, Ana?'

A polite query, or had the woman heard news of her pregnancy? Word flew with the speed of lightning in the social set.

'Fine, thank you.'

She was spared anything further by an announcement over the speaker system advising the guest stars had arrived and would soon be entering the auditorium.

Red carpet, security...light background music. It was all part of the hype and glamour of the evening.

As one, the invited guests turned towards the red carpet waiting for the first VIP to enter, and Ana felt Luc's arms circle her waist as he drew her back against him.

His breath was warm as it fanned her cheek, and she gave in to temptation and leaned in to him, exulting in the way his arms tightened a little.

Held like this, she could almost imagine everything was right in their marriage. That he adored her, and nothing, *no one* could come between them.

To know, irrevocably, the night and every night for the rest of their lives would end with a shared intimacy that was uniquely theirs...

A reverent hush was heard through the auditorium as the first star guest appeared at the head of the red carpet, followed soon after by another.

The female lead was exquisitely dressed, her long

hair beautifully styled, make-up expertly applied, and a figure to die for.

Recent emotional tragedy had marred her life, but it was undetectable in her smile, her soft laughter, the way she crossed from one side of the red carpet to the other as she paused to greet guests who'd come to see her.

As an actress, she was superb, and Ana silently applauded her in admiration for her ability to put her personal life aside in public.

The lead actor followed, and he was charm personified as he worked the room, doing his job for the publicity machine.

The usual entourage appeared, together with the director and producer, then they were through and the invited guests were encouraged to take their seats.

Celine, Ana was relieved to see, was seated three rows to their left, and she felt herself relax as the lights dimmed and the curtain swept open.

Throughout the film she was conscious of Luc's close proximity. The warmth of his hand as he held her own, the shared glance and quiet laughter when a pertinent clip stirred the audience.

The film ran a little over two hours, and there was a collective sigh when the credits began to roll, followed by applause.

It had, Ana admitted, been an entertaining experience, and one she'd enjoyed. She said so as the lights came on, and they joined guests in a slow-moving queue departing the cinema.

Tea, coffee, champagne were being offered in the auditorium, encouraging guests to linger and discuss the film.

Would Celine elect to join them there? It seemed impossible to imagine she wouldn't, and Ana sipped tea as she waited for the moment her nemesis would intrude.

Except the minutes slipped by to become several, and there was no sign of her. Unusual. Definitely unusual. Celine was not one to miss an opportunity!

'Ready to leave?'

Ana caught Luc's quiet drawl, and inclined her head. 'Whenever you are.'

It took a while to slip free and leave the auditorium, for there were acquaintances, friends whom they paused to speak to…but no Celine. Had she already left?

The Mercedes whispered through the city streets, and Ana let her thoughts drift to speculate on Rebekah's date with Jace Dimitriades.

Had it been successful? She fervently hoped so. Tomorrow she'd discover the details…

Luc traversed the New South Head road to suburban Vaucluse, then he turned the car into the sweeping drive leading to their home.

Minutes later they entered the foyer and took the stairs to their suite.

Luc closed the door behind them, then crossed the

room to her side. With infinite care he unclasped the pendant at her nape and placed it on a nearby pedestal, then his hands closed over her shoulders as he turned her round to face him.

Ana was powerless against the softness of his mouth as it caressed her own, his touch an evocative supplication as it teased and tasted in a manner that melted her bones.

His tongue took a low, sweet sweep, tantalising with the promise of what would follow, and she angled her mouth to his, seeking deeper exploration in the prelude to passion.

With evident reluctance he lifted his head and sought the zip fastening of her gown, sliding it free so the soft fabric fell at her feet in a silken heap.

The absence of a bra had proven a provocation all evening, and the thought of freeing her smooth breasts, weighing them in his hands, caressing them with his mouth, the edge of his teeth, had almost driven him wild.

Did she have any idea how heart-stoppingly beautiful she was? Not just in body, but of heart and soul?

So generous and giving, she was part of him, and he sought to show her with his hands, his mouth, exulting in her sultry moan as he took her high, only to emit a husky groan as he helped her tear his clothes free to allow her the same privilege.

Ana loved the taste of his skin, the faint male muskiness, and the light sheen of sensual heat that rose as she trailed her mouth to his shaft and savoured there.

Too soon he dragged her up against him, kissing her deeply as he carefully pulled her onto the bed, and his loving became the sweetest she'd ever known. Power and gentleness. Acute sensuality and hunger. Together they meshed as one in an intoxicating ravishment that was all-consuming. *Mesmeric*.

After-play was inevitably the sweetest, the slow drift of hands, the soft touch of lips...the languor of complete satiation.

Tomorrow he would leave for Melbourne. Three days, two nights. She'd miss him...dreadfully.

CHAPTER TEN

ANA woke late, discovered within minutes that Luc had already left, and tried to stem her feeling of disappointment as she showered, dressed, and prepared for the day ahead.

As always the morning part of the day was the busiest, with processing orders, tying preparation time in with the four scheduled delivery pick-ups.

There were the usual delays and interruptions, and a prospective assistant won their hearts and the job when she offered an immediate start.

'OK, last night, dinner, Jace,' Ana queried during a lull around midday. 'Tell me.' They'd sent the new girl out for a lunch break and an order for sandwiches.

Rebekah seemed strangely hesitant. 'Not what I expected.'

Her eyes narrowed. 'What do you mean...not what you expected?'

'The restaurant was great, the food better than great...' She trailed to a halt, and effected a slight shrug. 'It was just...different.'

'As in?'

'We talked.'

Ana's mouth curved into a musing smile. 'You didn't expect to talk?'

'I mean, discussions, opinions, views.'

'Anything in particular, or just generally?'

'A day in the life of a florist. Anecdotes.'

'And…nothing?'

'No teasing, flirting, or attempt at seduction.'

Jace seemed intent on playing it cool, Ana perceived, and wondered if he would see through her sister's façade, past the hurt and the betrayal to the heart of a woman who had so much love to gift to the right man.

'Are you seeing him again?'

Rebekah chewed the edge of her lip in a gesture of pensive distraction. 'I don't think so.'

I don't think so was an improvement on the definitive *no* her sister would have uttered a few days ago.

Ana chose not to pursue it further, and she turned her attention back to the computer screen.

The phone rang, and she picked up the receiver. 'Blooms and Bouquets, Ana speaking.' The greeting was automatic, her voice warm, friendly and professional.

'I want to place an order if you can guarantee delivery before this afternoon.'

It would be tight, but do-able, and Ana wrote down the relevant details, double-checked the address and keyed it into the computer, took credit-card details, and concluded, 'May I have your name, please?'

'Celine Moore.'

Oh, hell. Celine had never placed a phone order with them before. The question popped into Ana's head...*why now?*

'Problems?'

'Hopefully not.' She bit the edge of her lip, then ran another check on written and computer details to ensure they matched. 'That was Celine.'

Rebekah's eyebrows rose. 'She's ordered flowers?'

'A rushed delivery before noon,' she confirmed. 'Now, why am I suspicious?'

'You think it's a deliberate set-up?'

'I think there's a definite purpose.'

Rebekah crossed to the counter, checked the details, then moved back to the work table. 'I'll do it now.'

Lunch was something Ana ate during a brief break from the computer, and she ignored her sister's admonition with a mischievous grin as she screwed up the paper from her take-away sandwich and tossed it successfully into the wastebin.

'Think you've won, huh?' Rebekah demanded with a teasing laugh. 'Mid-afternoon you get to sip tea at the café and browse through a magazine. *Capisce?*'

Ana wrinkled her nose. 'Since when did you speak Italian?'

'Heard it on television.'

There was a lull around two, then the pace picked

up as Rebekah readied orders for the afternoon delivery.

The door buzzer sounded, followed by Rebekah's softly voiced curse, and Ana glanced up from the computer screen to check the cause, then immediately wished she hadn't, for there was Celine in a whirl of indignant volubility bearing down on her.

Rebekah stepped forward to intercept the woman's progress, only for Celine to bypass her and continue to where Ana sat behind the counter.

'Is there a problem, Celine?'

'Would I be here, if there wasn't?'

'Perhaps you could be specific?'

The divorcee drew herself up to her full height and assumed an expression of hauteur. 'I ordered a delivery of flowers this morning. They haven't reached the person for whom they were intended. I specified same-day delivery and paid the extra cost to have them there prior to midday.'

Ana called up the order on computer, then she checked the order book...a double system to minimise an error in recording apartment and private house numbers.

She scrolled through the day's listing...there it was. 'Apartment 7, 5 Wilson Place.' She named the suburb.

'No, no. It was apartment 5, 7 Wilson Place.'

Aware how easy it was to transpose numbers, Ana took particular care ensuring she got them right, repeating the numbers and writing them down, then requesting the customer to repeat them again as she keyed them into the computer. It wasn't a totally infallible system, but it came close.

'I don't believe I made a mistake,' she said quietly, and saw the angry glitter in Celine's eyes intensify.

'*You* made the error, you're liable. What's more, I've cancelled my credit-card purchase details.'

'I'll check with the delivery firm, and have him double-check his delivery details.'

Celine began tapping the tips of her elegantly polished nails against the counter top. 'Get on to it, Ana. I'm not moving from here until this mess is sorted out.'

Ana used speed-dial, accessed the courier, explained the problem, and held while he checked his records. Minutes later she had the address confirmed, and she ended the call.

'The order was delivered to the address you gave me. Apartment 7, 5 Wilson Place.'

'I refuse to place any further orders with you.' Celine's voice rose, deliberately, Ana suspected, to ensure the two customers who had just entered the shop could hear. 'This is the second time in a week you managed to stuff something up.'

As an actress, she was superb, Ana conceded. Total melodrama, right down to the hand gestures, the tone, the body language. She had to still the desire to applaud her performance.

'That's your choice, Celine.' On her way home,

she'd do a little investigation of her own and visit both apartments. If only to satisfy herself Celine was bent on creating deliberate mischief.

'You haven't heard the last of this,' Celine declared haughtily, and she swept from the shop in a blaze of triumph as the two customers hastily replaced two prepared bouquets and followed suit.

Rebekah released a pent-up sigh. 'Charming.'

'Surely you jest?' The query held uncustomary cynicism.

'With friends like Celine, who needs enemies? More pertinent, what are we going to do about her?'

'I have an idea in mind.' She relayed it, and Rebekah grinned in response.

'We'll both reconnoitre the scene, then go on somewhere for dinner and catch a movie.'

'Done.'

It was after six when they managed to lock up, and a short while later they entered Wilson Place, parked, then entered the apartment building.

They called the manager, explained the situation, and proceeded through to the bank of lifts.

The occupant of Apartment 7 *had* received an unexpected delivery of flowers and figured to keep them.

Alerting the florist listed on the accompanying card of the error wasn't an option the occupant considered.

It was a case of exiting the building and crossing to the adjoining building where they repeated the process, and discovered apartment 5 was owned by a Celine Moore.

'Bingo.'

'Are you thinking what I'm thinking?' Rebekah asked quizzically as they retraced their steps to the car.

'Subterfuge and sabotage?'

'Oh, I'd say there's a very good chance...like one hundred per cent.'

Ana slid in behind the wheel and slid the key into the ignition. 'So...what do you think we should do about it?'

'Confrontation, definitely.'

'You, or me?'

Rebekah's gaze held a purposeful gleam. 'Oh, allow me.'

'You will employ subtlety.'

'Like hell. No one plays a game like this one and gets away with it.'

'OK, let's go home, hit the shower, then go eat.'

They did, and incurred Petros's long-suffering expression. 'I prepared dinner, Ms Dimitriades.'

'Ana,' she corrected from habit. 'And I told you at breakfast we'd probably eat out.'

'You didn't ring and confirm.'

She'd meant to, she really had. 'I'm sorry. I hope you didn't go to a lot of trouble?'

'Apricot chicken with rice, steamed vegetables, and a lemon soufflé.'

It made pizza eaten alfresco sound positively peasant-style in comparison.

Ana turned to her sister and arched an eyebrow. 'Want to eat in, or out? Your choice.'

'Have you had your dinner, Petros?' Rebekah asked, and the manservant shook his head.

'Not yet. I intended to serve you both first.'

'Then you must eat ours instead. We're going up to the Cross to get pizza.'

Petros gave a good imitation of being totally scandalised. 'King's Cross?'

'The same.'

'I must urge you very strongly against going there. Luc would not approve.'

Ana wrinkled her nose at him. 'Luc isn't here.'

'He'll find out.'

'Only if you tell him.'

'It's really most inadvisable.'

'There are two of us, we're only going to eat pizza, then drive on to the cinema complex. What can happen?'

'At least let me drive you.'

'We promise not to park in a side-street, and we both have cellphones,' Ana relayed. 'Trust me, at the first hint of trouble you'll be the first person we call.'

'There are any number of places in which to eat pizza. Why the Cross?'

'Because,' Rebekah said carefully. 'I have a friend who works there, and he makes the best pizza I've ever tasted.'

Petros was clearly torn, and Ana almost felt sorry for him. 'We'll be fine. I'll ring when we're done and on our way to the cinema.'

'Thank you.'

'Anyone,' Rebekah declared with a touch of exasperation as they cleared the driveway, 'would think he had adopted a paternal role.'

'He's answerable to Luc,' Ana said simply.

'Who is an exceedingly wealthy man.' She cast her sister a rueful glance. 'Protective, possessive…or just plain cautious?'

Possessive? 'He's involved in huge money deals.'

'And protective of his pregnant wife.'

'Who is responsible for a Dimitriades heir.'

'That was way too cynical. Why?'

They reached Rose Bay, and took the circuitous route towards Double Bay. 'Blame it on hormones and a preoccupation with Celine's latest contretemps.'

'You think it's aimed at gaining Luc's attention?'

'Without doubt.'

Rebekah pulled up at a set of traffic lights. 'Luc is a hunk.'

'Thanks.'

Rebekah laughed, shifted gears, then eased the car forward as the lights went to green. 'Like, you're worried?'

Ana didn't answer, and Rebekah swore briefly. 'Dammit, you *are* worried. Has he given you a reason to be?'

She hesitated a second too long. 'Not really.'

'Don't you trust him?'

Oh, God. Did she? *Completely?* 'I don't trust Celine.' Wasn't that the truth!

'You didn't answer my question.'

Rushcutter's Bay was in the foreground, and any time soon they'd reach the Cross.

'They once shared a relationship.'

'So?' Rebekah released a sound that was akin to a snort. 'I was once married to a man, whom if I never see him again, it would be too soon!'

'That doesn't add up.'

'The hell it doesn't.'

The El Alamein fountain came into sight, and Rebekah's attention became focused on finding a space to park the car. Not easy at the Cross, and Ana was relieved at the distraction.

At this time of evening with daylight beginning to fade, the main street held a mix of people of various cultures whose mode of attire ranged from the norm to the bizarre.

Men in fashionable suits, flashing an over-indulgence of jewellery, looked a little too slick and polished to be ordinary businessmen. Professionals, certainly, but *ordinary*…not.

Then there were the flamboyant types, whose mode of dress bordered on the outrageous, sporting a range of body piercing that almost defied description.

The pizzeria was situated on the main street, and

Rebekah led Ana indoors, greeted the head pizza-maker, then found a table close to the window.

Oven-fired, delectable, mouth-watering aromas filled the small room, and Ana consulted the menu, Rebekah, then placed an order for a large combination pizza to share.

Declining wine or coffee, she settled for tea while Rebekah chose strong espresso.

It was interesting to watch the street scene, to see the people who came to observe and those who came to work. Touts stood in front of doorways outlined in flashing lights, bright neon, cajoling the passers-by to come inside and be entertained by strip-shows, nude showgirls.

As the evening crept on, there would be the pimps, the prostitutes, and a steady parade of vehicles dropping off the girls, picking them up. There was more use per square mile of cellphones at the Cross than anywhere else in the city.

That was the visible. The invisible was the existence of a darker world, backstreets where drug deals and less than salubrious activities were done.

Their pizza was served, and after one bite Ana had to agree the taste was out of this world. Ambrosia.

'Has Luc given you reason to distrust him?'

Rebekah had the tenacity of a terrier unwilling to give up a bone, and Ana closed her eyes in exasperation, then quickly opened them again.

She shrugged her shoulders in a gesture of eloquent indecision. 'He flies interstate regularly on business, overseas...New York, London, Paris, Athens. How would I know if anyone joined him there?'

Rebekah's expression became thoughtful. 'Luc cares for you.'

Ana took another slice of pizza and bit into it.

'If it weren't for the child—'

'Oh, *rubbish*. Think about it! He gave you space on the Coast before hauling you home. He could easily have had Dad charged...but he didn't. He's given Celine the flick in no uncertain terms.' She paused for breath. 'Get real. The man adores you!' She leaned forward and covered her sister's hand with her own. 'Besides, he's not the type to play around.'

'Easy to say.'

Rebekah eased back in her chair. 'I think I'm going to hit you. In fact, I'm darned sure of it!'

Sisterhood was a wonderful thing. Ana summoned a smile. 'I'll return the favour if ever our positions are reversed, and Jace Dimitriades gets the better of you!'

'That's a favour going wanting,' Rebekah assured with alacrity.

It was after eight when they entered the cinema complex, and the movie had a feel-good plot, with light-hearted humour and great acting. They emerged at the end of the session, walked to the car, then drove home to sit sipping hot chocolate as they recounted amusing aspects of the film.

There was a text message from Luc on Ana's cellphone, which she chose to ignore. Received while she was in the cinema, it was brief to the point of abruptness.

If he wanted to speak to her, he could ring again.

He did, just as she slipped into bed.

'You didn't return my call.'

'Well, hello to you, too,' she responded with pseudo-politeness.

'I didn't wake you?'

She almost made a facetious reply, then thought better of it. 'No.'

'I rang earlier. Petros said you were out.'

'Eating pizza at the Cross, then taking in a movie.'

She could almost feel the silence weighing in from the other end of the line. 'If that's a joke, it's a bad one.'

'Rebekah has a friend who makes the most divine pizza.'

'At the Cross,' he chided with chilling softness.

She was beginning to enjoy this. 'Uh-huh.'

'I trust you won't be going there again?'

'We might.'

'You're having fun with this, aren't you?'

Her smile was deliciously wicked. 'Oh, yes.'

'Just remember I'll be home day after tomorrow,' Luc declared silkily. 'Will you be so brave then?'

'Of course. You don't frighten me in the least.'

'Careful, *pedhaki mou*.'

'Always. Goodnight.' She ended the call and switched off the phone.

CHAPTER ELEVEN

'DANGER at twenty paces,' Rebekah warned, *sotto voce*.

Ana glanced up and saw Celine bearing down on her. Here we go again, she accorded silently. The witch from Rose Bay.

'I suppose you think you're clever.'

'Another problem, Celine?'

The woman's eyes glittered with anger. 'What right do you have to check up on your customers?'

'Any complaint regarding delivery is always investigated,' Ana said smoothly. 'You accused Blooms and Bouquets of making an error and rescinded payment of your account.'

'That allows you to badger people?'

There was no doubt this was going to get nasty. 'Badger, Celine? My sister and I checked both apartment addresses personally. The lady at apartment 7, 5 Wilson Place confirmed she'd received a delivery not meant for her. We were able to ascertain apartment 5, 7 Wilson Place is owned by you.'

'What nonsense. Why would I send flowers to a vacant apartment?'

'Why, indeed?'

Celine's features became a study in white fury. 'Are you accusing me of foul play?'

Ana had had enough. 'Your words, Celine. Not mine.'

She didn't see it coming, and it happened so unexpectedly, so quickly, there was no time for evasive action.

In one swift movement Celine swept a large glass vase off the counter.

It knocked against Ana's arm, sending a shower of water over her thighs, and shattered on impact with the concrete floor, sending shards of glass in all directions.

What came next was unbelievable, and she gasped out loud as Celine shoved her so hard she lost her balance, skidded on the wet floor, and went down in seemingly slow motion.

'You *bitch*,' Rebekah hissed angrily, and Ana registered the sound of a palm connecting with flesh.

The next instant Rebekah hunkered down, her face pale as she checked for injuries.

Ana raised stunned eyes, then followed her sister's gaze. There was glass everywhere, blood streamed from a gash on her arm, another on her leg, her hand where she'd attempted to soften her fall.

'Stay there,' Rebekah instructed. 'Don't move. I'm ringing the ambulance.'

Oh, dear God…the fall…could she miscarry? No, surely not. It hadn't been a hard fall. 'An ambulance is definite overkill. It's only a few cuts. Get some paper towels, and I'll clean myself up.' Initial surprise had begun to wane, and in its place was shocked disbelief.

'Petros, then.' Rebekah was already dialling, and seconds later she spoke rapidly, then replaced the receiver. 'He's leaving immediately. Now, let's get you into a chair, then I'll attempt to clean up this mess. But first,' she said with angry determination, 'I get to take a photo to use as evidence.'

'You're kidding me, right?'

'No.'

It took only brief seconds, then she caught hold of Rebekah's outstretched hands and stepped gingerly over to the chair. Broken glass crunched beneath her shoes, and she stood still as her sister brushed glass from her clothes.

'Are you OK?'

It hadn't been a heavy fall, and she said so. 'Apart from a few cuts, yes.'

'Sit down, and stay there while I get rid of all this.' She plucked disposable towelling into sheets and carefully stemmed the flow of blood.

Minutes later the glass was swept into a dustpan, and the vacuum cleaner sucked up any remaining splinters. A few swirls with the mop to remove the water puddles and everything was restored to normal.

Petros appeared soon after, and Ana registered he must have broken the speed limit to arrive so quickly. He took one look, and his eyes went black with anger.

'I'll take you to the hospital.'

'Home, Petros. It's only a few scratches.'

'The hospital, Ana,' he reiterated firmly. Without pausing, he scooped her into his arms, ignored her protest, and spoke to Rebekah over his shoulder as he walked towards the door. 'I'll ring as soon as the doctor has attended to her.'

It was, she registered with amusement, the first time he'd used her Christian name. Later, she'd tease him about it. But for now she was content to have him take charge.

The Mercedes was double-parked at the kerb, the passenger door open, and he lowered her into the seat.

'Petros, I didn't know you cared.' Flippancy was the only way to go, and she glimpsed a muscle clench at the edge of his jaw before he straightened and moved round the car to take the wheel.

The hospital staff were efficient. Excruciatingly so. Petros hovered, then retreated, only to reappear minutes later.

Two gashes required sutures. They examined her from top to toe, did an ultrasound, admitted her for observation, and the obstetrician conducted an examination.

Petros stood guard in the room, and only left it on instruction from the sister-in-charge.

'You're fine, my dear.' The obstetrician reassured, 'The baby is fine. No sign of foetal distress.'

'I can go home?'

'Tomorrow.' He offered a faint smile. 'We'll keep you in overnight as a precaution.'

Why did she get the feeling this was a conspiracy?

As soon as he left she rang the shop, spoke to Rebekah, then she settled back against the cushions and reflected on Celine's actions, retracing to the moment the woman entered the shop.

Had Celine meant to cause deliberate harm? Or was it merely a heat-of-the-moment thing? It was difficult to judge.

A nurse brought in tea and a few courtesy magazines, followed soon after by the sister-in-charge, who queried her level of comfort.

Lunch came and went, and reaction must have taken its toll, for she woke from a light doze to find Luc seated in the chair beside her bed.

'What are you doing here?'

He rose to his feet and moved to her side. His faint smile held warmth, but there was something evident in his eyes she didn't care to define.

'Is that any way to greet your husband?' He lowered his head and closed his mouth over hers in a light, evocative kiss, lingered, then he took it deeper in a desperate need to feel her response.

Did she have any idea what he'd gone through in the last few hours? Petros's call had shattered him, totally, then cold, hard anger set in as he swiftly organised his return to Sydney. Something that was achieved within minutes, then he'd simply walked out of a meeting, taken the car one of his colleagues immediately made available, and headed to the airport.

He made a few calls from his cellphone, called in favours, enlisted the services of the city's top obstetrician, checked with the hospital, then he rang Celine.

His eyes hardened as he recalled her sickening coquetry, the shocked surprise, followed by consternation over the accusations he levelled at her. Then, when he left her in no doubt as to his intended action, there was anger and vitriol.

The hour's flight had seemed like an eternity, and he'd instructed Petros to sit on the speed limit between the airport and hospital.

He already had the obstetrician's report, but he desperately needed visual reassurance.

No one had halted his passage through Reception, nor did anyone query his presence as he bypassed the lift and took the stairs. At the first-floor nursing station the sister-in-charge opened her mouth in protest, then quickly closed it again as she witnessed the grim determination evident.

He didn't pause when he reached Ana's suite, and simply pushed open the door with clear disregard for a courtesy knock. And came to a halt at the sight of her propped against a bank of pillows.

Her head was turned slightly to one side, and her eyes were closed in sleep.

For a long moment he just stood there, drinking in her features in repose. It took tremendous will-power to restrain himself from crossing to the bed and lifting her into his arms.

He almost did, and would have if he thought the movement wouldn't hurt her.

Instead, he'd settled himself in the chair and waited for her to wake.

'Hmm,' Ana murmured as his mouth left hers and trailed up to brush against her temple. 'Nice.'

She could almost sense his smile, and a slow warmth heated her skin. This close she could breathe in the scent of him, the subtle cologne meshing with a male muskiness that was his alone.

He brushed his lips across her forehead, lingered, then pressed one eyelid closed before slipping down to the edge of her mouth.

She angled her head a little and parted her lips against his own in a kiss that promised, but didn't take as it became frankly sensual, tasting, probing, then easing back to graze a little.

When at last he lifted his head she could only look at him in bemusement. 'Maybe I should become a hospital patient more often.'

'Not if I can help it.'

He looked gorgeous, so intensely male, so much a part of her. It seemed important to endorse the obstetrician's reassurance. 'The baby's fine.'

Luc lifted a hand and brushed light fingers across her cheek. 'What about *you, agape mou*?' His hand moved to cup her chin, tilting it a little. 'Want to tell me what happened this morning?'

Her gaze held his, clear and unblinking. 'It's over.'

'Yes. It is.' He traced the pad of one finger over her lower lip.

'I have no doubt Petros has relayed his version.'

'Indeed.' He felt her mouth tremble, and his eyes darkened. 'Rebekah, also.' His hand slid round to cup her nape, gently massaging the back of her neck and into the base of her skull. 'I can promise Celine will never get close to you again.'

It must be reaction, but there was something happening here...something deep and meaningful. Except it was just out of reach, and she couldn't quite grasp hold of it.

He cared, without doubt. But was it merely fondness for someone he held in affectionate regard?

'You're the one she wants,' Ana said simply. 'And I'm in the way.'

'The only one in the way is Celine.' His voice held a dangerous quality.

The door swished open and a nurse collected the chart, then crossed to the bed to take Ana's vital signs. Minutes later they were punctiliously recorded, and she left the suite to continue her round.

'Is there anything you need?'

Oh, my, how did she answer that? She lifted a hand, then dropped it again, and shook her head. 'Petros packed a few things and brought them in.' She offered him a winsome smile. 'He called me *Ana* for the first time ever.'

'Quite an achievement.' He skimmed a hand over her shoulder. 'Are you in any pain?'

Not the physical kind. No matter how she attempted to understand Celine's driven action, a lingering shock remained. She wasn't concerned for herself, but her unborn child was something else.

She closed her eyes in the hope she could also close her mind to the woman's vicious jealousy-motivated action.

'Go home, Luc,' she bade quietly.

'Not a chance.' He crossed to the chair and folded his length into it.

When next Ana looked he was still there, and she shook her head in silent remonstrance. Nursing staff came and went with monotonous regularity, and the arrival of the dinner trolley with an extra meal for Luc brought a further protest.

'There's no need for you to stay.'

'Indulge me.'

This was too much. He was too much. 'I haven't heard your cellphone ring once.'

'It's turned off.'

The in-room television provided visual entertainment, and Luc finally conceded to leave long after visiting hours were over.

Ana was unaware of the private security guard posted in the corridor out of her sight, or that Luc had the nursing station on alert.

It was undoubtedly over the top, but he didn't give

a damn. No one toyed with him or one of his own without paying the price.

He reached his car, slid in behind the wheel, and eased it out from the hospital car park. There were other issues that were long overdue. Way overdue, he amended grimly.

First, he'd reorganise his business interests and take Ana to the beach house on the Central Coast.

Petros was hovering inside the door when Luc entered the house. 'Ms Ana is well?'

'Yes, thank God. She'll be home tomorrow.'

'Nasty business.'

Luc shot the older man a level glance. 'It's been taken care of.'

'One would hope so.'

There was no need for further words. Luc's influence was a known entity. As an enemy, he was deadly.

A slight smile tugged the edges of Luc's mouth. 'She told me you called her *Ana*.' One eyebrow slanted. 'Quite a departure from your usual formality.'

'I shall see it doesn't happen again.'

'I imagine she'll never let you forget it.'

Petros allowed himself a warm smile. 'No, I don't suppose she will.'

CHAPTER TWELVE

THE new day's dawn brought a sense of new beginnings, and Ana rose early, showered and dressed, then participated in the morning's hospital routine. The obstetrician called in, she ate a healthy breakfast, then she dealt with the discharge process prior to Luc's arrival at nine to take her home.

Petros emerged from the front door as Luc's Mercedes drew to a halt beneath the wide portico, and he opened the passenger door as Luc slid out from behind the wheel.

'It's good to have you home, Ms—'

'*Ana,*' she interrupted firmly, the glint in her eyes fearsome. 'If you dare call me anything else, I'll *hit* you.'

'Very well.'

She looked at him in silent askance.

'Ms—'

'Just...Ana,' she said gently.

'You've lost that particular skirmish,' Luc declared as he preceded Petros indoors, and the older man hid a faint smile.

'So it would appear.'

'Everything is in order?'

Petros inclined his head. 'All that remains is for Ana to pack a bag.'

She paused mid-stride at the foot of the stairs. 'What do you mean, *pack*?'

Luc curved an arm along the back of her waist and urged her towards the upper floor. 'We're spending a few days at the beach house.'

'Don't you have to go into the office?'

'The world won't stop if I'm not there.'

No, it wouldn't. But Luc was a man who kept a constant eye on the business ball.

They reached the bedroom, and she surveyed the large suite, appreciating its familiarity. Two bags reposed on the long stand at the foot of the bed. One closed, the other empty. His laptop rested on the floor.

Luc turned her into his arms and lowered his head down to hers. His mouth was incredibly gentle as it brushed her own, and she linked both hands at his nape to hold him there as she deepened the kiss.

His hands shifted, one slipping down to cup her bottom while the other slid up to fist her hair.

Dear heaven, she needed this. The feel of him, his touch, his male scent, and the warmth and heat of his embrace.

A faint groan rose and died in her throat as he trailed a path along the edge of her jaw to linger close to the sensitive hollow beneath her earlobe, then he followed the cord at the edge of her neck and nuzzled there before slipping down to savour the delicate arch of her throat.

With obvious reluctance he eased back and pressed a light kiss to the edge of her mouth. His heart beat in tune with her own, heavy and fast.

'Go pack, *pedhi mou*. Otherwise we won't be heading anywhere soon.'

It didn't help that he was right, although she conceded they had time ahead of them. Consequently she slipped out of his arms and collected a few clothes together, then she followed Luc down to the car.

In less than an hour they reached the beach house. Although *beach house* was hardly an adequate description for the delightful double-storeyed home built only metres from the sandy foreshore. The external walls comprised tempered tinted glass, and palm trees and shrubbery lent privacy whilst providing tranquil views out over the ocean.

Petros had rung ahead, for there were provisions in the pantry, fresh milk and juice in the refrigerator, and the house was spotlessly clean.

Ana crossed the lounge and stood close to the huge expanse of glass, drinking in the deep blue waters of the Pacific Ocean, clear today of any craft. She could almost smell the salt-spray and feel the crunch of sand beneath her feet.

'Feel like a walk along the beach?'

She turned and took hold of Luc's outstretched hand, then together they left the house and took the

short path through the palm trees and planted shrubbery to the bank of white sand leading down to the
water.

It was a beautiful day, warm with brilliant sunshine and hardly a cloud in the sky.

The gently curved cove appeared isolated, and
Ana had the uncanny feeling they could have been
alone in the world.

They strolled down to where the sand was packed
and damp from an outgoing tide, then they followed
the tide-line towards an outcrop of rocks in the distance.

There were questions she wanted to ask, but she
was hesitant to begin, and unsure if his answers
would be what she wanted to hear.

So much had happened in the past few months. So
many misunderstandings and misconceptions. Un-
truths and false accusations.

One could never go back, she reflected sadly, or
undo the things said and done. There was only one
direction, and that was forward. Yet some things in
the past could affect the future if they weren't confronted and resolved. For only then was it possible
to move on.

And one of those things in the immediate past was
Celine.

Perhaps she could begin there.

'Did Celine mean anything to you?' Nothing like
taking the bull by the horns!

Luc stopped walking and turned towards her. His

eyes were dark, and she could almost sense the latent anger that simmered beneath the surface of his control.

'No. We shared a brief relationship several years ago,' he reiterated quietly. 'She wanted marriage, I didn't. I moved on, and she married someone else.'

'Yet you continued to see each other,' Ana pursued, and glimpsed a muscle tense at the edge of his jaw.

'We lived in the same city, moved in the same social circle.' His expression assumed wry cynicism. 'We observed a state of polite civility.'

'Until her divorce.'

He slid his hands up her arms to cradle her shoulders. 'After her divorce,' he corrected. 'Why would I want to have anything to do with another woman, when I have *you*?'

Something stirred deep inside and began to unfurl. Hope. Dared she begin to *hope*?

'She embarked on a relentless campaign,' Ana ventured, holding his gaze.

'I've initiated legal action against her.' His hands slid up to cup her face. 'She'll pay, and pay dearly. If she has any sense, she'll relocate to another city. Preferably another country.'

As an enemy, he was ruthless. 'I see.'

'Do you, Ana?' His eyes searched hers, dark with passion and another emotion she couldn't define.

'Emma—'

He placed a finger to her lips, closing them.

'Emma was my youth,' he said gently. 'I mourned her loss. Not so much for myself, but for the too short a time she spent on this earth.' His mouth curved into a warm smile. 'She was sunshine, laughter, and she was my best friend.' He traced the outline of her lower lip. 'But she could never be *you*.'

She felt her bones begin to melt, and her eyes seemed to ache with suppressed emotion.

'You stole my heart, and captured my soul.'

She almost swayed on her feet. Was he saying he *loved* her?

'Luc—'

He didn't let her finish. 'You're my life, my love. Everything.'

Her eyes shimmered with unshed tears, and she blinked rapidly to stem their flow. Except one spilled over and trickled slowly down her cheek.

He followed the trail with the pad of his thumb, and his smile was almost her undoing.

'How could you not know, *agape mou*? Each time I held you in my arms, whenever we made love? Didn't you feel it in the beat of my heart, my touch?'

Oh, God, she was going to cry. 'You never said the words.'

'I'm going to have to teach you Greek.'

'I thought—'

He gave her a gentle shake. 'I married you for the convenience of having a woman in my bed, a social hostess?' His eyes became dark. 'If that's all I wanted, I would have remarried years ago.'

She opened her mouth, then closed it again.

'I love you, Ana. *Love*. The *till death us do part* kind. Without you, I wouldn't want to live.'

She wasn't capable of saying a word. All this time she'd thought affection was the foundation of their marriage. Now she was filled with a wondrous disbelief.

'Celine worked her poison with diabolical success,' Luc continued. 'Worse, you chose to believe her, and nothing I said seemed to convince you otherwise.'

Diabolical success? Yes, it had been that. Celine had known which buttons to push and how to screw each one of them down.

'When you left for the Coast, I thought a few days might help you reflect and gain some perspective. Instead, it merely worked against me.'

He shaped her cheek, and let his thumb slip down to linger at the edge of her mouth. 'Do you have any idea how terrified I was of losing you?'

Her lips parted, but anything she might have said remained locked in her throat.

'Or how I felt when I discovered you were pregnant with our child?'

'You used emotional blackmail.'

'It was the only weapon I had.'

'You wanted the child—'

'I wanted *you*.' He brought her close and tilted her chin. 'Sweet Ana. Our child is a wonderful bonus, a joy I rejoice in because it represents *life*. Yours, mine, *ours*. But make no mistake. *You* are my reason for living. My heart. My soul.'

She reached up and pulled his head down to hers.

'I love you. I always have. Always will. For the rest of my life.'

Then she kissed him, deeply, emotively with great passion, and it was a while before they broke apart to draw breath.

'How dedicated are you to walking along the beach?'

Her eyes held an impish twinkle that matched the laughter in her voice, and he chose to humour her.

'Do you have a better idea?'

She held up her hand and began counting options off on her fingers. 'We could walk, and talk some more. Move up onto dry sand, sit down, admire the ocean view and reflect on the spirituality of *being*. We could engage in a discussion about how much longer I'm going to work.'

'You know how I feel about you working.'

Her eyes were large pools of brilliant sapphire, and deep enough for a man to drown in. And he was beginning to sink…

'Please.' She threaded her fingers through his own, and brought them to her lips. 'Mornings.'

'Three days a week.'

'Four,' Ana amended.

'For another two months,' he conceded.

'Three.'

He slid his hands up to cup her face. 'What in hell am I going to do with you, woman?'

'Love me,' she said solemnly. 'You do it very well.'

'What hope will I have if we produce a blonde-haired, blue-eyed little imp...your image in miniature?' he groaned, bringing his mouth down to hers.

'She'll twist you round her little finger at the first blink of an eye.' She offered him a delighted smile. 'And you'll become her devoted slave for life.'

'Without doubt.' The thought of holding their child for the first time almost brought him undone.

'Of course, it could be a boy...' A dark-haired babe who'd grow tall and strong like his father. She felt quite misty-eyed at the image.

'Are we all talked out yet?' Luc teased as he curved an arm over her shoulders.

'We could go back to the house...'

'I guess that's an option,' he acceded indolently, loving the soft chuckle that escaped her lips.

'And indulge each other?' Ana pretended to consider. 'Now, there's the thing. It's not even lunch-time.'

He took pleasure in watching her play the game. 'Do you have a specific time in mind?'

'Well,' she began carefully, 'given that I'm slightly incapacitated,' she indicated the dressing on one forearm, and her bandaged hand, 'it would mean you'll have to do most of the work. Perhaps you might like to rest first?'

'Minx.'

'Of course, the foreplay needn't be too...' she trailed to a delicate pause '...energetic.'

His deep, throaty laughter startled a resting gull, and it flew into the air uttering a shrill squawk before circling towards the rocky outcrop.

'Let's just see whose energy is depleted first, hmm?' He swept an arm beneath her knees and lifted her high against his chest.

'Put me down.' A delicious chuckle found voice. 'What if someone is watching? Whatever will they think?'

'That we're two people very much in love.'

And they'd be right. Thank God. 'Then it's OK.' She pressed a kiss to his temple. 'But please put me down.' Her eyes were level with his own, and for a moment it seemed as if they each caught a glimpse into each other's soul. 'I want you to conserve your energy.'

Her smile melted his heart. 'And you're doubtful I will, if I carry you back to the house?'

'Well, I wouldn't want you to be diminished in any way.'

Luc let her slip carefully onto her feet, then he looped an arm around her shoulders. 'Home, *agape mou*. I need to hold you, touch, make love to you.'

She turned her head to look at him as they began retracing their steps. 'Ditto.'

It had been, Ana reflected much later as the sun sank down below the horizon, the most perfect day.

Luc stood behind her, his arms curved round her waist, and she leaned back against him, exulting in the feel of his lips as he sought the sensitive hollow at the edge of her neck.

'Beautiful.'

He wasn't referring to the view beyond the wall of glass, but the woman he held so close to his heart.

His wife, the love of his life.

THE GREEK
BRIDEGROOM
HELEN BIANCHIN

CHAPTER ONE

THERE were some days when it just didn't pay to get out of bed, Rebekah groaned as she lifted her head from the pillow and caught sight of the digital clock.

It was blinking, indicating a power failure through the night had disrupted the alarm mechanism.

She fumbled for her watch, checked the time and uttered a muffled oath as she slid from the bed, then cursed out loud as she stubbed her toe on her way to the *en suite*.

The icy blast of water ensured the quickest shower on record, and, dressed, she raced into the kitchen, dished out fresh food for the cat, snatched a container of orange juice from the refrigerator, gulped a mouthful, then she collected her bag and took the lift down to the underground car park.

Seconds later she slid in behind the wheel of the Blooms and Bouquets van, inserted the key into the ignition…and nothing.

Don't do this to me, she begged as the engine refused to kick over. *Please* don't do this to me! During the ensuing minutes she coaxed, cajoled, promised, and still it remained as dead as a doornail.

She restrained the urge to scream in frustration. Talk about having Friday the thirteenth on a Tuesday!

Raising her head heavenward and praying to the deity didn't work either.

What else could go wrong?

It was better she didn't ask, for it might tempt fate to fling another disaster in her path.

There was nothing else to do but get behind the wheel of her MG and send the sleek red sports car purring through Sydney's suburban streets.

Not exactly a suitable vehicle in which to transport flowers to the Double Bay florist shop she co-owned with her sister, Ana.

In the early pre-dawn hours there wasn't much traffic, and already the city was stirring to life. Pie-carts were closing up after the long night, the council street-sweeping trucks whined along, clearing debris from the gutters, and fruit and vegetable vendors transported their supplies from the city markets. Taxis carrying businessmen to catch the early flights interstate, petrol tankers beginning deliveries.

It was a time of day Rebekah enjoyed, and she activated a popular radio station on the console and felt her spirits lift with the upbeat music.

Soon the sun would lift above the horizon, and the grey shadows would disperse, bestowing everything with light and colour.

A sweeping glance was all it took at the markets to determine the best of the blooms were gone, and she figured her order, placed it, then turned the car towards Double Bay.

The shop was situated in a trendy élite area, and

thanks to a bequest from her late mother the business was free from any loan encumbrances.

It was six-thirty when she unlocked the outer door and she tripped the lights, filled the coffee percolator, then set to work.

While the percolator took its time, she booted up the computer and downloaded email orders, then she checked the fax machine.

They were in for a busy day, and there was a need to adjust her order. She crossed to the phone, made the call, then she rang a mechanic to go check the van.

Hot, sweet black coffee boosted her energy levels, and she was on her third and last cup for the day when Ana arrived.

Looking at her sister was akin to seeing a mirror image of herself...almost. They shared the same petite height, fine-boned features, slender curves and naturally blonde hair. Two years separated them in age, with Ana the eldest and twenty-seven. Their natural personalities were similar, although Rebekah felt she held an edge when it came to determined resolve.

The necessity for self-survival in an abusive relationship had provided a strength of will she hadn't been aware she possessed. It had also implanted an ingrained distrust of men.

A year's engagement to Brad Somerville, a beautiful wedding, embarking on a dream honeymoon...nothing prepared her for the sudden change in the man she'd vowed to love and honour less than ten hours before.

At first she'd thought it was something she'd done or said. Verbal abuse was bad enough; physical abuse was something else. Jealous, possessive to the point of obsessiveness, he soon killed any feelings she had for him, and after three months of living in a hellish marriage she'd simply packed a bag and walked out of his life.

Following the divorce she'd legally reverted to her maiden name, bought an apartment, adopted a beautiful Burmilla kitten whom she'd named Millie, and lived to work.

'Hi.' Rebekah summoned a sympathetic smile as she glimpsed the slight air of fatigue evident in Ana's expression. 'Late night? Morning sickness?'

'That bad, huh?' her sister queried as she crossed to the computer and began cross-checking the day's orders.

'Maybe you should listen to Luc and cut down your hours.'

Ana shot her a telling glance. 'You're supposed to be on my side.'

Rebekah wrinkled her nose in humour. 'I am, believe me.'

'What would I do in that great house all day? Petros is the ultimate manservant.'

The phone rang, and Ana picked up, listened, then handed over the cordless receiver. 'For you.'

It was the mechanic with word all the van needed was a new battery, which he'd install, and mail her the account.

'Problems?'

'The van wouldn't start.' She relayed the repercussions, then took the next phone call.

It didn't get better as the morning wore on. A difficult customer took most of her patience, and another complained bitterly about the cost of florists' delivery charges.

Food, she needed food. It was almost midday, and the energy boost from juice, coffee and a cereal bar had clearly dissipated.

'I'll go pick up a salad sandwich. Then you can take a lunch break.'

Ana glanced up from the computer. 'I can eat lunch on the run just as well as you.'

'But you won't,' Rebekah said firmly. 'You'll buy a magazine, seat yourself at any one of the nearby café's, and take your time over a latte and something sensible to eat.'

Ana rolled her eyes. 'Tea,' she amended with a grimace. 'And if you begin treating me like a precious pregnant princess, I'll hit you!'

She laughed, a low, throaty chuckle, and her eyes held a mischievous gleam. 'Petros?' she hazarded. The middle-aged manservant had been part of Luc's household for years, well before she'd first met Ana's inimitable husband. 'Does he still refer to you as Ms Dimitriades?'

Ana's laughter was infectious. 'He considers anything less would be regarded as undignified.'

She adored her sister, and they'd been the best of friends since she could remember, sharing, caring, *close*. Ana's marriage to Luc Dimitriades a year ago had been one of the happiest moments of her life.

'Luc has made a booking for dinner this evening.'

Ana named the restaurant, and Rebekah's eyebrows rose a fraction. It numbered as one of the ritziest places in town. 'We'd like you to join us. Please,' she added. '*Two* Dimitriades men are too much for one woman to handle.'

Rebekah felt an icy shiver slither the length of her spine, and the nerves in her stomach tightened into a painful ball. Please let her voice give no hint to her inner turmoil. 'One of Luc's cousins is in town?' Amazing she could sound so calm, when her defence mechanism had already moved to *alert*, and her mind issued the silent scream *Please don't let it be Jace*.

'Yes. Jace arrived yesterday from the States.'

No. The silent scream rose and died in her throat as Jace Dimitriades' image rose to the fore to taunt her.

Tall, broad shoulders, chiselled features, piercing dark grey eyes, and a mouth to die for.

She had reason to know how it felt to have that mouth possess her own. Even now, a year later, she still retained a vivid memory of Luc and Ana's wedding, partnered as her sister's maid of honour with Jace as Luc's best man. How for several hours she'd been aware of Jace's close proximity, the touch of his hand at her waist, the brush of his body against her own as they assembled for bridal group photos.

Dancing with him had been a nightmare. Sensual

heat spiked her blood and sent it racing through her veins. Sexual chemistry at its most base level.

Hadn't that been the real reason for her momentary escape onto the terrace within minutes of Luc and Ana taking their leave?

Yet Jace was there, standing close, almost caging her against the terrace railing as she turned to move away.

That had been her mistake, for it brought her much too close to him. The next instant his lips brushed her cheek, then slid to savour her mouth, and in a moment of sheer madness she angled her mouth to his own.

His instant response was devastating.

Shocked didn't cover it. No one had kissed her quite like that. As if somehow he'd reached down into the depths of her soul, tasted, savoured, with intent to conquer. It left her feeling as if she'd leapt off a high cliff and was in dangerous free fall. Exhilarated by the instinctive knowledge he would catch her...before she hit the ground.

Who was the first to break contact? To this day she couldn't be sure. All she remembered was something inexplicable in those dark grey eyes, a stillness that held a waiting, *watching* quality as she went from shock to dismay in a few seconds flat.

Anger kicked in, and she slapped him...hard. Then she walked away, aware that he made no effort to stop her. She rejoined the wedding guests, and smiled until her facial muscles ached.

Afterwards had come the rage...with herself for initiating something so foolish, and with him for indulging it.

Now Jace Dimitriades was back in town, and Ana and Luc expected her to make up a foursome for dinner?

'*No,*' she reiterated aloud.

'No…you don't want to.' Ana's gaze narrowed as she attempted to analyse her sister's expression. 'Or no, you can't?'

'Choose whichever one you like.'

Ana appeared to take a deep breath. 'OK. Are you going to tell me about it, or do I have to drag it out of you?'

'Neither. Simply accept I decline your invitation.'

'That won't wash, and you know it. You haven't seen Jace since the wedding.' Her sister's eyes assumed a speculative gleam. 'What did he do? Kiss you?'

Oh, my. 'On what do you base that assumption?' she managed calmly, and saw Ana's gaze narrow.

There was a telling silence. 'It's not like you to wimp out,' her sister said at last.

Wimp? 'Forgive me, but I'm not in the mood to embark on a verbal fencing match with a man who'd enjoy every thrust and parry!'

'Think of the fun you'll have in besting him,' Ana offered persuasively.

Rebekah glimpsed the mischievous challenge in those guileless blue eyes, and her lips curved into a slow smile. 'You're wicked.'

Ana grinned. 'The black Versace halter-neck will be fine.'

A backless creation which didn't allow for wearing a bra? 'I haven't said *yes*.'

'We'll come by and collect you. And drop you home again.'

She could imagine how easily, *smoothly* Jace could intercede and insist he escort her home in a taxi.

'*If* I agree,' she qualified, shooting Ana a warning glance. 'I'll drive my own car.'

'*Brava.*' Ana's eyes gleamed with humour, and Rebekah shook her head in mock-despair as her sister executed the *victory* sign.

It was almost seven when Rebekah slid from behind the wheel of her MG and allowed the uniformed attendant tend to valet parking.

For the umpteenth time she silently questioned her sanity. Except *retreat* at this late stage wasn't part of her agenda.

How had the past year affected Jace Dimitriades?

Did he have a lover? Was he between relationships?

Fool, she mentally derided as she entered the restaurant foyer. Men of Jace Dimitriades' calibre were never without a woman for long. She recollected Ana relaying Jace regularly commuted between London, Paris and Athens. He probably had a mistress in each major city.

The *maître d'* greeted her with polite regard, elicited her name, the booking, and directed her to the lounge bar, where patrons lingered over drinks.

The ambience spelt *money*…serious money. The floral displays were real, not silk imitation. The carpet thick-piled and luxurious, the furniture expensive.

A pianist was seated at a baby grand, effortlessly providing muted background music, and the drinks stewards were groomed to the nth degree.

Refined class, Rebekah conceded as a steward enquired if he could assist locating her friends.

He succeeded with smooth efficiency, and she followed in his wake.

'Mr Dimitriades.' His acknowledgement held deferential respect, and she had a ready smile in place, polite words of gratitude on her lips as she tilted her head.

Only to have the smile freeze as she saw it was Jace, not Luc, who had moved forward to greet her.

'Rebekah.'

In one fluid movement he came close, lowered his head and brushed his lips to her cheek. The contact was stunningly brief, but it robbed the breath from her throat for all of five seconds before anger hit.

'How dare you?' The words escaped as little more than a vehement whisper.

One dark eyebrow slanted, although his eyes held a watchful expression. 'You expected formality?'

She didn't trust herself to respond. Her attention was held, *trapped,* by the man standing within touching distance.

Tall, so tall her eyes were on a level with the loop of his impeccably knotted silk tie, and his breadth of

shoulder was impressive sheathed in exclusive tailoring.

In his mid-thirties, his broad, chiselled facial bone
structure gave hint to his Grecian ancestry, and there
was an inherent quality in those dark grey, almost
black eyes that took hold of her equilibrium and tore
it to shreds.

No one man deserved to exude quite this degree of
power...nor possess such riveting physical magnetism.

Sexual alchemy at its zenith, she acknowledged
shakily as she attempted to gain a measure of control
over her rioting emotions.

One look at him was all it took for her to remember
how it felt to have that mouth close over her own
with diabolical finesse. Exploring, coaxing...and
staking a claim.

She was suddenly aware of every breath she took,
every heightened pulse-beat, and the way her heart
seemed to thud against her ribcage.

It was crazy, *insane* to feel like this. In the name
of heaven, *get a grip*. To allow him to see just how
deeply he affected her was impossible.

Why, suddenly, did she feel as if she'd walked into
a danger zone? And that it was *he*, and not she, in
command of the situation?

Dammit, she'd accepted Ana's invitation, and she
owed it to her sister and Luc to be a pleasant guest.
Hadn't she dressed accordingly, and given a promise
to sparkle?

CHAPTER TWO

PROJECTING *joie de vivre* required effort, and there was a very real danger she'd verge towards overkill.

A glass of wine would help dull the edges, but she'd had nothing to eat since lunch. Consequently iced water seemed a wise choice, especially as she'd need all her wits to parry words with Luc's inimitable cousin.

The restaurant's chef was reputed to be one of the city's best, and numbered among the country's finest. Hence, the selection offered was meant to tempt a gourmand's palate.

Rebekah ordered soup as a starter, requested an entrée-size meal as a main, and deferred a decision on dessert.

She settled back in her chair and glanced towards Jace. 'You're in Sydney on business, I believe?'

There was nothing like taking control and initiating conversation.

'Yes.' He met her level gaze, held it, and wondered if she had any idea how well he could read her. 'Also Melbourne, Cairns, Brisbane and the Gold Coast.'

'Interesting. Presumably matters which require your personal attention?'

How would she react if he revealed *she* was one

of them? He inclined his head. 'I'm unable to delegate in this instance.'

Property he wanted to sight? Yet in a high-tech age, it was possible to scan digital images at the speed of light, and as he shared some investment interests with Luc, why couldn't Luc act on his cousin's behalf?

The waiter delivered their starters, and Rebekah toyed with the soup, spooning the contents automatically without affording it the appreciation it truly deserved.

'Tell me something about floristry.' Jace's voice was pure New York, and she waited a beat before countering,

'An idle query, or genuine interest?'

His eyes held a humorous gleam. 'The latter.'

'The art, or a day in the life of…?'

'Both.'

'Floral artistry comprises a good eye for colour and design, shapes appealing to the customer's wants and needs, the specific occasion.' If he wanted facts, she'd supply them. 'Which blooms suit, room temperature, the effect the customer wants to achieve.'

She lifted her shoulders and effected a light shrug. 'Knowledge where exotic out-of-season stock can be bought and how long it takes to air-freight it in. And the expense involved. Unfortunately there are always those who want the best at minimum cost.'

'I'm sure you manage to apprise them that quality comes with a price?'

'Don't be fooled by Ana and Rebekah's petite stature,' Luc drawled. His mouth curved into a warm smile. 'I can assure both sisters pack a powerful verbal punch.' He turned towards Ana and brushed light fingers down her cheek. 'My wife, especially.'

'It's a defence mechanism,' Ana responded sweetly. The waiter removed their plates, and Rebekah's gaze shifted to Jace in a deliberate attempt at dispassionate appraisal.

Superb tailoring emphasised an impressive breadth of shoulder, and the deep blue shirt with its impeccably knotted silk tie accented his olive textured skin.

All she had to do was look at him, and warmth flared to uncomfortable heat as her mind spun into overdrive, remembering how it felt to have his mouth on hers. From there it was just a step away for her mind to spiral out of control, imagining what lay beneath the trappings of his conventional attire.

Don't go there. Dear heaven, what was *wrong* with her? No one, not even her ex-husband in the heightened throes of pre-marital passion, had been able to arouse such an intense reaction.

She was conscious of every breath she took, and co-ordinating cutlery with morsels of food and the actual eating process was fraught with nervous tension.

Was Jace aware of her inner turmoil? Dear God, she hoped not.

Oh, for heaven's sake, she mentally chastised. You're only sharing dinner with him, and acute vulnerability could be conquered…couldn't it? Or at least successfully masked. Besides, Jace Dimitriades was only a man like any other man, and hadn't Brad been charm personified in the beginning? Only to turn into a wolf in sheep's clothing.

Except instinct warned comparing her ex-husband to Jace Dimitriades was akin to associating an ill-bred canine with a powerful panther.

There was a part of her that wanted to replace her cutlery, stand to her feet, and leave. Retreat to the safety of her car, return to her apartment with her sanity intact.

Except such an action was a cop-out, and besides, what excuse could she present? *Act,* she commanded silently. You deal with people every day in the shop and utilise psychological skill to handle difficult customers. How difficult could it be to deal with Jace Dimitriades for a few hours? There was the added advantage of Ana and Luc's presence to provide a buffer. It should be a breeze.

Fat chance! She felt about as relaxed as a cat on hot bricks!

Why hadn't she listened to her initial instinct and remained adamant at not doing this? Because she cared for her sister. At least, that was the simple answer. The more complex one didn't bear contemplating.

Maybe some wine would loosen her nerves a little, and she indicated the wine steward could fill her glass. Seconds later she took an appreciative sip, and felt the grape's delicate bouquet slip into her bloodstream.

It was a relief when the waiter presented the next course. Her appetite was non-existent, and although her meal was a decorative vision in cuisine artistry, her tastebuds appeared to be on strike.

Travelled south for the duration, she accorded with silent wry humour, aware to an alarming degree just where they'd chosen to settle.

Eat, she commanded silently. Focus on the food. The evening would eventually come to a close, and she'd never have to place herself in this position again.

She may as well have told herself to go jump over the moon for all the good it did, for she was supremely conscious of every movement he made. The economical use of his hands as he apportioned each morsel of food. The way the muscles at the edge of his jaw bunched as he ate. His hands were broad, tanned with a sprinkling of hair, the fingers tapered with neatly shaped nails.

How would those hands caress a woman's skin? Lightly skim the silken surface, discover each pleasure pulse and linger there?

Her mind came to a screeching halt. What was the matter with her? She couldn't blame the wine, for she'd only consumed a few sips, and alternated it with chilled water.

'You have an early start in the morning?' Luc queried solicitously.

Could she conceivably use that as an excuse to slip away soon? 'I have to be at the flower market around four-thirty.'

Jace's gaze narrowed. 'Every day?'

'Six out of seven.' It didn't bother her. Never had,

for she was a morning person. However, after a four-teen-hour day on her feet anything less than six hours' sleep and she was wrecked.

'I'll order coffee.' Luc signalled the waiter, and she joined Ana in choosing tea, all too aware coffee would keep her awake. How long had they been here? Two hours? Three?

They were almost done, and within half an hour she'd be free to slip behind the wheel of her car and drive home.

Wonderful, she determined as Luc fixed the bill, and she stood to her feet, collected her evening purse, and followed Ana to the foyer.

Her skin prickled in awareness of Jace's close proximity, and it took considerable effort to move at a leisurely pace. She could almost feel the warmth of his body, and her own stiffened at the light touch of his hand at the back of her waist as they gained the pavement.

'I'll see you to your car.'

'I had a valet attendant park it for me.'

Ana tilted her face as Jace leant down to brush his lips to her cheek. 'Luc and I can give you a lift back to the hotel.'

'I'm sure Rebekah won't mind.' Jace straightened and shot his cousin a measured look. 'I'll be in touch tomorrow.'

Rebekah uttered a silent prayer that Luc would in-tercede, only the deity wasn't listening. Ana leant for-ward and brushed her lips to her sister's cheek, accepted Jace's affectionate 'Goodnight', then she moved with Luc towards their car.

It was so smoothly effected, she could hardly believe she'd been cleverly manipulated. His hotel *was en route* to her apartment. Given she had to pass right by the main entrance, it would be churlish to refuse.

However, her mind screamed in silent denial as she waited for the attendant to fetch her car. She didn't want to be alone with him, ever, and especially not in the close confines of her MG sports car.

What had prompted him to suggest it when she'd been so painstakingly polite all evening? She hadn't flirted, or given him any reason to think she coveted his attention.

Dammit, just get in the car, drop him off at the hotel, then that'll be the end of it. Ten, fifteen minutes was all it would take.

There wasn't a lot of leg-room, and it gave her a degree of satisfaction as he folded his lengthy frame into the front passenger seat.

Rebekah didn't waste a second, and she gained the street, then headed towards Double Bay. Idle conversation, simply for the sake of it, wasn't on her agenda, and she didn't offer a word as she took liberties with the speed limit.

Ten minutes and counting.

It was a beautiful late-spring evening, the dark sky a clear indigo sprinkled with stars. Cool, sharp temperatures promised another fine day, and she directed her mind to the shop's orders and the stock she'd need to purchase from the markets.

It didn't work, for she was supremely conscious of the man seated beside her. In the close confines of the car she was aware of the subtle tones of his cologne, the clean smell of his clothes...and the faint male muskiness that was his alone.

Rebekah felt the tell-tale prickle of her skin as her body began an unbidden response. There was warmth, and heat pooled deep inside, intensifying with damning speed as her pulse accelerated to a crazy beat.

His hand rested on one knee, which was close, much too close to the gear-shift, making it impossible not to touch him whenever she changed gears. Avoiding contact without appearing to do so required care, and she wondered if he sensed her disquiet.

What if he did, and he was silently amused? Oh, dammit, just *drive*. In another five minutes she'd be free of his disturbing presence.

One more set of traffic lights and she'd enter the outer fringes of suburban Double Bay. A sense of intense relief began to descend as she turned into the street housing the main entrance to his hotel, and she drew to a halt in the impressive forecourt.

A uniformed bellboy moved towards the car, and Rebekah turned towards Jace. 'Goodnight.'

In one fluid movement he captured her face with his hands, then lowered his mouth to hers in an evocative kiss that invaded and seduced. All too brief, it held the promise of *more*.

Shocked surprise encompassed her features as he lifted his head, and her mouth parted, only to close again as he offered a huskily voiced *au revoir* before sliding out from the low-slung seat.

She caught the faint gleam in those dark eyes before he turned and walked towards the main entrance.

Damn him. What did he think he was playing at?

She moved the gear-stick with unnecessary force, then sent the car into the street. Her apartment was situated two blocks distant, and she reached it in record time, easing the MG down into the underground car park.

In the lift she castigated herself for not predicting Jace's move. He'd bargained on the element of surprise, and had won.

So what did it matter? She was unlikely to see him again. But it irked unbearably he'd caught her unawares, and provided a not so subtle reminder that he was aware of her vulnerability, and, even more galling, susceptible to him.

She should have slapped his face. Would have, if his action hadn't rendered her momentarily speechless.

Ten o'clock wasn't *late*, and with only six hours' sleep ahead of her she should go straight to bed. Instead, she slid off her stilettos and roamed the apartment, too emotionally wound up to settle to an easy sleep.

Nothing on television held her interest for long, and after utilising the remote to flick through every channel she simply switched off the set, collected a magazine and flipped through the pages with equal uninterest before discarding it in disgust.

A derisive sound emerged from her throat as she doused the lights and made for her bedroom.

She could still *feel* Jace Dimitriades' touch when she began removing her clothes. As she cleansed her face of make-up she was positive she could still *taste* him, and she took up her toothbrush and cleaned her teeth, twice.

So vivid was his powerful image, she was prepared to swear he was there with her as she lay in bed staring into the room's darkness.

Over and over the evening replayed itself, and the memory of his kiss taunted her, awakening her imagination to such a level it became impossible to sleep.

Jace Dimitriades drained the last of his coffee, reached for his suit jacket and shrugged it on, collected his wallet and cellphone, then he exited his hotel suite, took the lift down to ground level and walked out into the sunshine.

He had an hour before he was due to join Luc at a business meeting in the city. Time enough to achieve his objective, he determined as he crossed the street and walked the block and a half to his intended destination.

Blooms and Bouquets was ideally sited, the window display colourful with expertly arranged blooms in numerous vases on stands of varying heights. A background wall held a similar display, and the overall look from outside was a mass of floor-to-ceiling flowers.

The result was visually stunning, and a testament to the two sisters who owned the boutique.

He pushed open the door, registered the electronic buzzer, and offered a greeting to Ana, swivelled his head to include Rebekah, who was deftly assembling a bouquet of orchids at the work table.

'Jace, how wonderful to see you.' Ana slid off her chair behind the computer and joined him. 'Is this a social call?'

He leant down and brushed his lips to her temple. 'How are you?' His smile held affectionate warmth. 'In answer to your question...social and business.'

'Then let's get business out of the way first.'

The phone rang, providing a convenient interruption. Not that he really needed one, but it helped. 'Answer that. Rebekah can organise the order.'

Could she, indeed? From the moment he stepped into the boutique all her senses had snapped into full alert. It was crazy the way her body reacted to the sight of him. Amend that to just *thinking* about him, she admitted wryly. Hadn't that very thing kept her awake last night?

Any hope of having Ana deal with him was shot, leaving her with little option but to place the bouquet taking shape onto the work table and move forward to assist him.

He looked...incredible, the dark grey business suit fashioned by a master tailor, fine cotton shirt, impeccably knotted silk tie. But it was the man himself who took hold of her composure and tore it to shreds.

She didn't like the feeling at all. It had taken two

years to repair the damage Brad had wrought and re-store a measure of confidence. To have it undermined in any way was something she'd defend to the death.

Rebekah slipped into the polite, professional role with practised ease. 'Do you have anything particular in mind?'

Good, his presence rattled her. He'd caught the faint tremble in those capable hands, sighted a glimpse of her inner struggle as she geared herself to deal with him. Signs she wasn't anywhere near as calm as she'd have him believe.

'A journey is but a series of many steps.' The quote teased his brain, although he couldn't be sure of its accuracy or its origin, only that the words were per-tinent.

Rebekah Stanford intrigued him. He admired the look of her, the strength of character apparent. The exigent sexual chemistry. But it was more than mere physical attraction. There was mystery surrounding her, something he couldn't quite pin down.

During the past year he hadn't been able to dismiss her from his mind. Her features teased his subcon-scious, the scent and feel of her. The way she'd re-sponded to his touch haunted him…and destroyed anything he thought he could feel for another woman. Plural, he amended ruefully, aware of the few women he'd sought to fill a void.

Now he was back, intent on combining business with pleasure…or was it the other way round? Intent on determining if memory of an emotion still existed, and if it did, just what he intended to do about it.

'Roses.' Their velvety texture, exotic perfume, the exquisite petals so tightly budded just waiting to unfold.

'What colour do you have in mind?'

Rebekah moved towards the temperature-controlled cabinet and indicated several vases holding a variety of colours.

There was the perfection of white, glorious pinks and corals in their various shadings, and deep, dark red.

He didn't hesitate. 'The red.'

She opened the glass door, removed the vase and carried it to the work table. 'How many would you like? The cost—'

'Is immaterial,' Jace concluded. 'Three dozen.'

'Would you like them delivered? An extra charge applies.'

'I'll handle delivery.'

A woman undoubtedly. Hostess, friend, or lover?

If it was a lover, he must possess all the right moves. He'd only been in the country two days.

Rebekah gestured towards a stand containing cards for every occasion. 'Perhaps you'd like to choose a card and write on it while I fix these.' She was already reaching for Cellophane, and mentally selecting ribbon.

Within minutes the bouquet was ready, and she attached the card, accepted payment, then handed him the roses.

Jace took time to admire their assembled artistry, then he presented her with them. 'For you.' He observed a gamut of emotions chase across her expressive features, and saw her struggle with each and every one of them.

'Excuse me?'

'The roses are for you. I suggest you read the card.'

Rebekah read the words with a sense of mounting disbelief. *'Dinner tonight. Seven.'*

'I'll collect you.'

'You don't know where I live.' *What was she saying?* She had no intention of sharing dinner with him.

'Ana will give me the address.'

'No.'

One eyebrow slanted in mocking humour. 'No, Ana won't give me the address?'

'No, I won't accept your invitation.' The thought of spending time with him wasn't a good idea.

'I promise not to bite.'

'Thanks, but no, thanks.' She held out the magnificent sheaf of roses. 'Please take these. I can't accept them.'

'Can't, or won't?' His New York-accented drawl held humour, and something else she couldn't define.

Ana? Where was her sister when she needed her?

It took only a glance to determine Ana was still on the phone. 'I don't date.'

The stark admission appeared to have no effect at all. 'Seven, Rebekah.' He turned and walked from the shop, and her reiterated *no* fell on deaf ears.

She swore, and followed it with a husky litany that damned the male species in general and one of them in particular.

'Oh, my,' Ana declared as she replaced the receiver. 'What did he do? Issue an indecent proposal?'

'He asked me out.' Rebekah's voice came out as an impassioned hiss.

'And that's the extent of his crime?'

Rebekah tossed the bouquet of roses onto the work table. 'I'm not going.'

'Of course not.'

'How dare he come in here and order roses...?' She could hardly contain her anger. '*Three dozen* of them.' Her eyes flashed blue fire. 'Then give them to *me*?'

Ana clicked her tongue and shook her head. 'Very bad taste.'

Rebekah's mouth tightened. 'I'm not accepting them.' She pushed the bouquet into her sister's hands. 'You take them home.'

'Why not you?' Ana queried reasonably.

'I'll return them to stock.' She spared them a glance, and her artist's eye admired the blooms' beauty. Just for a moment she felt a twinge of remorse.

No man had gifted her anything in a while. And never flowers.

'Who does Jace Dimitriades think he is?' It was a question that required no answer, and she banked down a further tirade as a customer entered the boutique.

Rebekah was glad of the interruption, although she seethed in silence for the rest of the day. A number of scenarios as to how she'd deal with him crossed her mind. Some of which, should she put them into effect, would be sure to get her arrested for causing grievous bodily harm.

'Do you have a number where I can contact him?'

It was late afternoon, and Ana was about to leave.

'Jace?'

'Of course, *Jace*.'

Ana's features assumed a thoughtful expression.

'It's been two years since your divorce. Don't you think it's time you emerged into the real world again?'

'You're advocating I have an affair?'

'Who are you afraid of?' Ana queried gently. 'Jace or yourself?' She walked to the door, paused and turned to give her sister a warm smile. 'Think about it.'

Rebekah opened her mouth, then closed it again.

As an exit line, it was without equal.

CHAPTER THREE

IT WAS after six when Rebekah eased the MG into the underground car park and rode the lift to the seventh floor.

Indecisiveness was not one of her traits, yet for the past hour she'd changed her mind at least a dozen times.

On entering her apartment she crossed to the phone, looked up the number for Jace's hotel, punched in the digits, only to replace the receiver minutes later. Jace Dimitriades didn't appear to be in his room, and a request for his cellphone number was politely declined.

Damn. Failure to contact him meant she had little option but to shower and dress in record time. Or stand him up.

Oh, for heaven's sake, she chided silently. A few hours, good food, pleasant conversation... What did she have to lose?

Her sanity, she conceded half an hour later as she replaced the in-house phone, gathered up her evening purse, car keys, then rode the lift down to the lobby.

He stood tall, the image of masculine strength, emanating a sense of power only those totally at ease with themselves were able to exude.

Rebekah met his probing gaze, caught his warm smile, and felt her stomach execute a slow somersault.

Any mental assurance she could survive the evening began to dissipate. Was it too late to change her mind? *Way too late,* an inner voice mocked with derision.

Jace watched the fleeting emotions evident, defined each and every one of them, and felt a sense of male satisfaction in knowing he affected her.

'Rebekah.' He moved forward, appreciating the cut and style of her clothes. The slim black skirt and matching jacket highlighted the creamy texture of her skin, and her make-up was minimal. A touch of gold at her ears and her throat added a pleasing addition. Her hair was drawn into a smooth twist, and his fingers itched to remove the pins and let it fall free.

What would she do if he drew her into his arms and covered that pretty mouth with his own? Undoubtedly she'd react like a frightened gazelle, he decided grimly.

What damage had her ex-husband done to kill her natural spontaneity? Something hardened inside him at the array of possibilities, resulting in a surge of anger against a man he'd never met.

'We'll take my car.'

'I've hired a vehicle for the duration of my stay,' Jace said smoothly, and glimpsed her faint disconcerted glance before it was quickly masked.

She wanted to retain control. It made her feel secure, and she suppressed the momentary uneasiness at Jace's increasing ability to undermine her confidence.

Together they walked through the entrance doors, and Jace led her towards a gleaming Jaguar, unlocked the passenger door and saw her seated, then he crossed in front of the car and slid in behind the wheel.

Rebekah's awareness of him became more pronounced within the close confines of the car, and she banked down the onset of nervous tension. Difficult, when her pulse had already increased its beat and she could feel the thud of her heart.

This was madness. She should have said an emphatic *no*, and, failing that, not left it until the last minute to rescind his invitation.

Except on reflection, his inaccessibility hadn't really given her much choice.

In the restaurant, Jace deferred to her preference in wine, ordered, then requested the menu.

Rebekah wasn't sure she could eat a thing, for her digestive system seemed to be in a mildly chaotic state. And it wasn't just her digestive system!

Oh, *move along,* an inner voice prompted. You're here with him. At least try to enjoy the evening. *Pretend.* Surely it can't be too difficult. You managed OK last night.

Yes, but then Luc and Ana had been present. Now she was on her own, and she'd been out of the social scene for too long. It was two years since she'd exercised her social skills to any great degree. One date soon after her divorce had proven to be disastrous, and at the time she'd vowed not to repeat it.

'Tell me what made you choose to be a florist.'

She took a sip of superb chardonnay, and replaced the goblet onto the table. Blooms and Bouquets…she could do shop-talk. 'The perfection of professionally grown blooms, their textures, colours and scents. The skill in assembling them together so the image conveys something special to the person to whom they're gifted.'

Jace watched her features become animated, her blue eyes deepen and gleam like blue topaz as she elaborated on her craft. Did she know how attractive she was? Or how deeply she appealed to him?

On every level, not just the physical.

'The pleasure, comfort and solace they provide for every occasion,' she continued, smiling in reflection of the many memories she'd shared where warmth and the sheer joy of making someone's day a little brighter became paramount.

'One imagines there's a downside?' he probed, and watched as she wrinkled her nose.

'Early starts, long days on your feet, dish-pan hands from having them constantly in and out of water.' She offered him a wry smile. 'Difficult customers who are impossible to please. The rush to get orders out on time. Incorrect addresses, mistakes made with deliveries by the courier.' She effected a negligible shrug. 'Like any business, there are the accompanying problems.'

The waiter delivered their starters, and they each

began eating. The prawn cocktail was succulent with a delicate sauce on a bed of shredded lettuce, and Jace forked his with evident enjoyment.

Did he enjoy women as much as he enjoyed food? She almost choked at the thought. *Where had that come from?*

She lifted her goblet and took a sip of wine. 'Your turn, I think.'

He set his empty dish aside and regarded her with a thoughtful gaze. 'New York-born to Greek immigrant parents. Graduated from university with a degree in business management.'

Rebekah held his gaze and attempted to define what lay beneath his composed exterior. 'The condensed version,' she acknowledged. '*Business management* covers a broad spectrum.'

'I specialise in takeovers and buy-outs.'

'Large companies with their backs against the wall?'

'Something like that.'

'It fits,' she said simply.

'On what do you base that assumption?'

'You have a ruthless streak,' she inclined with thoughtful contemplation, aware it was more than that. Leashed strength meshed with an animalistic sense of power, a combination which boded ill for any adversary.

'I imagine you wheel and deal with cut-throat determination.' She paused a beat. 'Mostly you win.' She doubted he ever lost…unless it was a deliberate tactical manoeuvre.

'An interesting character analysis,' Jace accorded with musing cynicism.

The waiter removed dishes, and the wine steward refilled their goblets.

Soft piano music provided a pleasant background for the muted buzz of conversation.

'You have family in New York?'

'Parents, one brother, two sisters, and several nieces and nephews.'

Was he removed from them, too caught up being a high-flying entrepreneur and too involved in his own life?

'My mother insists we all get together once a fortnight for a family dinner,' Jace drawled. 'Madness and mayhem would be an accurate description.'

'But fun?' She had a mental image of adults laughing, chiding children, noisy chatter and a table groaning with food and wine.

'Very much so.'

Did he take his women...it had to be plural, although presumably he was discriminative...to visit?

'Not often, no.'

Rebekah endeavoured to still her surprise, and failed. 'You read minds?'

'It's an acquired skill.'

'One in which you excel.'

Jace inclined his head, but there was no arrogance apparent, just the assurance of a man well-versed in the vagaries of human nature and possessed of the ability to deal with them.

It was during dessert that Rebekah happened to

glance towards the restaurant entrance. Afterwards she couldn't say what drew her attention there. Instinct, perhaps? Some deep, inner, protective element alerting her to danger?

For a few heart-stopping seconds she prayed she was mistaken, but she'd have known that profile anywhere, the angle of his head...

'What is it?'

She registered Jace's voice, and tried to tamp down the sick feeling that filled her stomach.

'Rebekah?'

Oh, God. *Think,* she bade silently. There's a good chance he won't see you, and if he does, what can he do?

Plenty.

Jace witnessed her pale features as the colour leeched from her cheeks, and her eyes had dulled an instant before she veiled them with her lashes. What, more relevantly *who* was responsible for rendering her as still as stone?

'Do you want to leave?' His voice was quiet, but serious in its intent.

She wanted to say *yes.* Now, quickly, quietly.

Except that was a coward's way out, and she'd vowed the day she legally severed all ties with him she'd never allow Brad Somerville to intimidate her again. Ever.

'My ex-husband has just walked in the door.'

Was she aware that with so few words she'd conveyed so much? Somehow he doubted it.

'Is it a problem?'

If she stuck with the truth, how would Jace Dimitriades deal with it? A hollow laugh rose and died in her throat. Why in hell would he *want* to?

'No,' she denied, and knew she lied.

Jace's eyes narrowed as he observed her monitor her ex-husband's progress towards a reserved table, and witnessed her fleeting expression the moment the man recognised her presence. It was neither embarrassment nor awkwardness…but fear.

'Well, *hello.*'

Rebekah kept her head erect, her eyes wide and steady. The action was a well-practised one, for she could never be sure what Brad's next move might be.

'Brad.' The acknowledgement was stilted, remote.

'Introduce me to your…companion.'

'Jace Dimitriades.' Jace's voice held a faintly inflected drawl and was dangerously quiet, almost lethal. He made no effort to rise to his feet or take Brad's extended hand.

Rebekah saw something move in Brad's gleaming gaze, recognised the early-warning sign of his temper, and felt her apprehension accelerate.

Brad focused his attention on Rebekah. 'Keeping it all in the family, darling?'

'The *maître d'* is waiting to show you to your table,' Jace intimated with deceptive mildness. Although anyone with any nous would see it as a dismissal. Those who knew him would have quailed at the leashed savagery lurking just beneath the surface.

Brad inclined his head. 'Of course.' His voice softened with silky threat. 'Take care, Rebekah.'

She hadn't realised she'd been holding her breath until she released it, and she forced herself to pick up her spoon and scoop a small serving of fruit, then eat it.

Calm? She felt the antithesis of *calm*. Yet she'd learned her lessons well, and it was far better to attempt normality. In the beginning, after the shock of discovering Brad's dual personality, she'd gone through an entire gamut of emotions...from heartbreaking tears, to anger, remorse, dislike, only to discover it made things worse.

'We can go somewhere else for coffee.'

Rebekah picked up her water glass with a steady hand. 'It's OK.'

Not, Jace determined as he surveyed her features. She was far too pale, and her actions were too rigidly controlled for his liking.

Almost as if she guessed his intention to summon the waiter and request the bill, she voiced quietly, 'Please, don't.'

'His presence here is making you feel uncomfortable.'

Now, that had to be the understatement of the year.

'You don't understand.'

His eyes narrowed, and she sensed a watchful quality evident. 'You think if we leave, he'll have won?'

He was too astute for her peace of mind. 'Yes.'

'Meanwhile you eat food you no longer taste, sip water or wine while we wait for coffee,' he pursued in a silky voice. 'And tie your stomach in knots during the process.'

She knew Brad's *modus operandi* only too well. Interpretation of her ex-husband's wild mood swings, anticipating his reactions had become an integral part of her survival.

'It's better this way,' she said coolly.

'Not for you,' Jace declared with certainty, and saw the slight lift of her chin as she met his gaze.

His own didn't waver from hers as he ordered coffee from a hovering waiter, and he settled the bill, waited patiently for her to finish, then he led her from the restaurant.

'I'll take a taxi,' Rebekah said stiffly, and incurred his swift dark glance.

'The hell you will.'

She didn't say a word, couldn't, for her throat was tight with nerves, and she walked at his side in silence, then slid into the passenger seat the instant he unlocked the car.

It didn't take long to reach her apartment building, and during the short drive she stared sightlessly out the window, unaware of the familiar scenery, the traffic.

Her mind was filled with the scene in the restaurant, Brad, and the electric presence of the man seated within touching distance.

'Thanks for dinner.' Politeness had been ingrained from a young age. She reached for the door-clasp, and froze as his hand captured her wrist.

'Is your ex-husband likely to confront you?'

She paused a few seconds too long. 'Why would he do that? He has no control over my life.'

Jace had questions he wanted to ask, but now was not the right time to get answers…even if she'd be willing to give them to him. 'I'll be in Melbourne for a few days with Luc. I'll ring you.'

'There's no need.'

He leaned closer and slid a hand to capture her nape, tilting her head so she had to look at him. 'Yes,' he said quietly. 'There is.'

For a heart-stopping second she thought he was going to kiss her, and she unconsciously held her breath, aware that a part of her craved the feel of his mouth on her own.

There was a hunger she couldn't quite control, and she trembled with it, wanting in that moment to be absorbed by this man. To have him take her to a place where she could temporarily forget the vindictiveness that lived inside Brad Somerville, and begin to repair the damage caused to her emotional heart.

She heard a faint sound emerge from his throat, and she swallowed painfully as he brushed his thumb over the curve of her lower lip, tracing its fullness.

His eyes were dark, too dark to determine his intent, and she felt the tension in him, the restraint, and knew instinctively the next move was hers.

All she had to do was use the edge of her teeth, the tip of her tongue on the tip of this finger to offer an unspoken invitation.

Dear God, she wanted to, she wanted *him*. Except she hesitated too long, and she thought she glimpsed the gleam of a faint smile, sensed the slight edge of his regret as she pulled back.

Then he did smile, and the hand holding her nape gentled and soothed the tension there for a few seconds, then he released her and eased back in his seat.

She felt as if her limbs were fused together, restricting mobility, and she was intensely aware of the sensual electricity apparent. Explosive and primitive, it shimmered as an elusive force, poised to shatter the shell she'd painstakingly erected around her fragile heart.

'Goodnight.' The word emerged as little more than a strangled sound, and she fumbled for the door-clasp, almost breathless in the need to escape.

Except the constraint of the seat belt stopped her, and she uttered a silent cry as his fingers sought the safety clip and unfastened it.

Within seconds she slid from the car and she almost ran the few steps to the haven offered by the entrance to her apartment building. The keys were plucked free from her purse and she selected the appropriate one as she punched the security code freeing the external door into the lobby.

From there it took only a moment to use her key to gain the area leading to the triple bank of lifts.

She was trembling by the time she reached her apartment, and inside she made for the kitchen, extracted bottled water from the refrigerator and gulped several mouthfuls before seeking a chair.

The evening was over. Although instinct warned whatever she shared with Jace was far from done.

It was as if something deep and primal was being resurrected from her soul, *his*. The sane, sensible part of her brain questioned any metaphysical connection, but the illogical part queried if they hadn't been joined together in a previous life, and their souls were forcing recognition.

Then there was Brad. She tamped down the memories and the pain. A few years was but a small window in the picture of her life. Hadn't that been the professional advice given at the time?

The sudden peal of the phone startled her, and she stood to her feet to take the call, except she was unable to reach the handset and pick up before the answering machine cut in.

Her automated greeting was brief, and she hesitated, wary as to who would be calling at this time of night.

'Having fun with your new man, sweetheart?'

It was followed by a click as the caller replaced the receiver.

Rebekah felt the blood drain from her face.

Brad. There was no mistaking his voice.

Shock jolted her senses and was quickly replaced by a sickening fear.

Her telephone number was unlisted. What ruse had he used to gain it? Had he also gained access to her cell-net number?

She crossed her arms and hugged them together across her midriff as her mind whirled with facts and possibilities.

The restraining order she'd had to take out against

him was still in place. If he chose to violate it he'd face the legal consequences.

Her body began to rock a little until she stilled the movements and crossed to sink down into a chair.

Please, *please,* she begged silently. Don't let the nuisance calls begin again.

Once, only *once* following her divorce had she dated another man. Immediately afterwards Brad had begun a series of phone calls. It had taken complaints to the police, written reports, warnings, and finally the filing of a restraining order to get him to stop.

Now, tonight, a chance meeting had started it all over again.

Thank God she was safe in her apartment. She'd chosen it deliberately for its high-tech security measures, and had installed double locks on her door as well as a safety chain.

She wrapped her arms around her knees and hugged hard. It was *coincidence*…wasn't it? Brad couldn't be having her followed? Even more frightening, monitoring her every move away from Blooms and Bouquets?

CHAPTER FOUR

THE day began much as any other, with the usual pre-dawn visit to the flower market, followed by setting all the blooms into troughs of water at the boutique.

Rebekah booted up the computer, downloaded orders, printed out hard copies, then checked whether she needed to order more stock.

Ana arrived around nine, and together they dealt with orders, customers, and the many phone calls that made up a typical day.

'Are you going to tell me how dinner with Jace went last night, or must I prise it out of you?' Ana queried during a momentary lull.

Rebekah added another spray of baby's breath to the bouquet she was assembling, made a deft adjustment, then gathered in the sheet of Cellophane. 'It was OK.'

'Just...*OK*?' her sister teased.

'If you're asking whether it became deep and meaningful... No.'

Jace was far too astute to move too fast too soon, Ana approved, silently applauding his style as Rebekah anticipated the next query.

'He said he'll phone. Am I seeing him again? I don't think so.'

'Why not?'

Because it'll cause problems for which there's no solution. The very reason she'd scaled her life down to a simplistic level. 'Why?' she countered. 'He's only here for a brief stay, then he'll return to New York. What's the point of starting something that has nowhere to go?'

She desperately wanted to confide about Brad's appearance in the restaurant, his phone call, and the disturbing fact he'd somehow gained access to her private line.

Except something held her back. There was concern for Ana's pregnancy, and besides it was too soon to determine whether Brad was bent on a single nuisance call or if he intended to resort to a repeat of his former behaviour.

She could only pray it wasn't the latter.

At that moment a customer entered the shop, and within minutes everything went to hell in a handbasket.

Luc's former mistress, the glamorous, unpredictable Celine, confronted Ana verbally, then launched into a physical attack that happened so quickly Rebekah wasn't swift enough to prevent it.

It was akin to a horror scene in a movie as Celine swept a glass vase to the floor, where it shattered, and a hard shove sent Ana down among scattered countless shards.

Rebekah gave an involuntary cry and flew to her sister's side, at the same time castigating Celine with pithy, unladylike language. 'You *bitch*,' just didn't begin to cut it.

48 THE GREEK BRIDEGROOM

Everything after that became a blur as Rebekah phoned Petros, Luc's manservant, contacted Luc on his cellphone, then she closed the shop and drove to the hospital, where she paced the visiting-room floor with all the pent-up anger of the demented as she waited for a medical professional to appear and provide a lucid report on Ana's condition.

'Your sister is fine. The ultrasound shows no sign of foetal distress. She's being transferred to a room, and one of the nursing staff will take you to see her soon.'

Rebekah's relief was a palpable thing, and she uttered a silent prayer in thanks.

It took only seconds to punch in Luc's number, relay the update and learn he was about to board a flight back to Sydney.

There was time to call the owner of the boutique adjacent Blooms and Bouquets, explain and request she tape a notice detailing a family emergency to the door.

With that taken care of, she began to relax, and she crossed to the coffee machine, inserted coins and sugared the black brew.

Hot and sweet was the best compliment she could offer, but it served to soothe in the aftermath of the past traumatic hour.

With smooth efficiency she made a series of calls, arranged replacement staff during Ana's enforced absence and notified a few regular customers their orders would be delayed.

Tears filled her eyes the instant she saw her sister

sitting upright in bed with bandages covering her hand and forearm.

'Don't you *dare* cry,' Ana warned, tempering the threat with a warm smile. 'I'm OK.'

'You might very well not have been.' The hug was a very careful one, then she stood back and brought the shaky feeling under control. Just thinking about Celine's crazy attack made her impossibly angry.

'The shop—'

'Is shut, and Jana has taped an explanation to the door.' She met Ana's clear gaze. 'Don't even think of suggesting I go back and leave you here on your own.' A determined smile lightened her features. 'I'm here until they throw me out.' Or at least until Luc arrives, she added silently.

'Promise me you won't work late tonight.'

Rebekah crossed fingers behind her back. 'You've got it.' Did it matter her interpretation of *late* wouldn't match that of her sister? A small transgression from the truth shouldn't count.

She deliberately made no mention of Celine. If Ana wanted to talk about it, so be it. Otherwise the subject was best left alone…for now. Luc, no doubt, would take appropriate action.

Various members of the nursing staff moved in and out of the suite as they conducted routine checks, and a proffered tray of tea and biscuits proved welcome.

Not long afterwards Ana drifted into a light doze, and Rebekah slipped into the corridor to use her cell-phone.

A tall, dark-suited figure strode towards her, and

for a split-second her heart stopped. The two Dimitriades men were alike in height and breadth of shoulder, with similar features. Except this was Ana's husband, not Jace.

'Rebekah.' Luc clasped a hand over her shoulder. 'How is she?'

The words were almost cursory in his urgency to see his wife, and she offered him an understanding smile. 'OK,' she assured, and her eyes hardened. 'You're going to deal with Celine?'

His expression became harsh, almost lethal. 'It's done.'

She didn't want to contemplate what action he'd taken, and didn't ask. Whatever it was, she could only be glad she wasn't the one on the receiving end of Luc's wrath. He had the look of a predator who'd staked the kill, and by the time he finished with his quarry all that would remain would be skeletal bones.

'Ana is asleep.' She touched a light hand to his. 'I'll check in later.'

'Thanks.' Momentary warmth lightened his eyes, then he turned and entered the suite.

Rebekah drove to Blooms and Bouquets, popped in quickly to thank Jana for her help, then she unlocked the shop and set to work. A few regular customers were understanding of the circumstances and took up her offer for free delivery. The rest would have to wait until morning.

She took time to ring the hospital, spoke to Ana, then Luc, and learnt her sister would be discharged the next morning.

It must have been after seven when she realised she'd hardly eaten all day, and she rummaged in the small refrigerator beneath the counter, discovered a pot of yoghurt and an apple, demolished both, then continued working.

At nine she locked up the shop and began deliveries. Fortunately they were contained within a fifteen-kilometre radius. Consequently it was almost ten-thirty when she entered her apartment, and she fed Millie before heading for the *en suite*, where she shed her clothes, then she took a leisurely shower and let the heated spray of water ease the kinks from a long, hard day.

Afterwards she donned a silk robe, then padded out to the kitchen. It was way too late to eat a meal, but something light with a cup of tea would take the edge off her hunger.

The message light on her answering machine was blinking, and she filled the electric kettle, popped bread into the toaster, then depressed the message-button in order for it to rewind.

Five, she determined as the first began to play.

A friend, suggesting they go to a foreign art film on Sunday; her doctor's receptionist with a reminder to make an appointment for her annual check-up; Luc, with an update and quietly chiding her for working late.

The fourth message sent her heart slamming against her ribs. 'Two nights in a row, darling? Unusual for you, isn't it?' A click as the message concluded. Then the fifth call ran... 'Taken him to bed yet?'

Brad.

She clenched her hands until the knuckles showed white.

Just then the phone rang, and she stood locked into immobility for a few seconds, then, mindful it could be Luc, she snatched up the receiver, muttered a strangled greeting, then sank down onto the floor as Brad's voice filtered through the receiver.

'Nice of you to pick up, darling.'

Rebekah replaced the receiver, disconnected the handset, then retrieved her cellphone and rang the telephone company's twenty-four-hour number, reported the nuisance calls, cited the restraining order, waited while her details underwent a computer check, and carefully wrote down the digits of her newly assigned private number.

Then she made a cup of tea, carried it into the lounge and switched on the television set in the hope of finding something light and humorous to view.

At midnight she crawled into bed and slept until the alarm woke her four hours later.

Habit was responsible for her mechanical movements as she dressed, drank strong, sweet coffee, dished fresh food for Millie, then she rode the lift down to the car park.

Dark streets with minimal traffic ensured a smooth drive to the flower markets, and with the day's stock stored in the van she did the return journey to Double Bay.

Rebekah worked with efficient speed, paused at seven-thirty to call Luc and give him her newly assigned number.

'Brad?' Luc queried sharply, and she cut in before he could continue.

'I've taken care of it. Don't tell Ana, OK?'

'Want me to intervene on your behalf?'

He was a force to be reckoned with, but she doubted even he could achieve any more than she already had.

'Thanks, but it's done. Give Ana my love. I'll call in to see her after I close the shop.'

'I'm taking her straight from the hospital to the beach house for a few days.'

'Good idea. Tell her I'll phone later this morning.'

'Rebekah.' His voice became clipped, serious. 'Don't be a hero. Brad calls you again, I want to know.'

'You've got it.' She replaced the receiver, dialled the hospital and was put through to her sister, whose reassurance was cheering.

'I'll be back at the shop on Monday.'

'We'll see.'

'Oh, lord, don't you start,' Ana groaned in response. 'If Luc had his way, he'd wrap me in cotton wool and confine me to the house.'

She managed a chuckle. 'That's not such a bad idea.'

'Got to go. The medics have arrived to prod, intrude and note down personal questions.'

Rebekah laughed out loud. 'Sounds like fun.'

'Oh, yeah? Wait until it's your turn, sister, dear.'

For a moment she caught a glimpse of the future, a family gathering on the lawn at Luc and Ana's home, two small children scampering in the sunshine; herself holding a baby...her own, and beside her a man whose face was obscured as he looked down at her.

The image faded, then disappeared, and she shivered.

As if! It was fanciful thinking, stimulated by Ana's pregnancy. And a desire for a child of her own? a tiny voice taunted.

Fool, she chastised as she turned back to the work table and ran a check of the day's orders.

Ana's replacement arrived at eight, a slim, dark-haired girl in her twenties named Suzie, and Rebekah breathed a sigh of relief as the girl proved to be quick and competent.

Together they coped with customers, readied orders for delivery, and Rebekah manned the phone.

When it rang for the umpteenth time she picked up and intoned her customary greeting.

'Rebekah?'

The New York accent gave him away, and the timbre of his voice sent her pulse racing to a faster beat as she managed a cool acknowledgement. 'Jace.'

'I'll be back in Sydney by late afternoon. Share dinner and a movie with me tonight.'

She tightened her grip on the receiver. 'I don't think that's a good idea.'

'Dinner, or the movie?'

'Both. Neither.' Oh, lord, she was losing it! 'No.'

She closed her eyes, then opened them again. 'I have to go,' she said with a hint of desperation, and hung up.

Ana rang mid-afternoon, her voice light, warm, *alive*. It was wonderful to hear her sound so happy, and Rebekah said as much.

'I am,' her sister assured. 'How are things at the shop? No problems? Is the temporary girl panning out OK?'

'So many questions,' Rebekah teased. 'Fine, no, very well. Does that cover it?'

'And you? Are *you* OK?'

Sisterly intuition? 'Of course.'

'Uh-huh.'

'I can take care of myself.'

'I know. With one hand tied behind your back.'

Rebekah choked back a laugh. 'Go give your husband the attention he deserves.'

'I intend to. I'll call you Sunday.'

The afternoon deliveries went out, they tidied up the shop, and Suzie left at five-thirty with a cheery wave and a promise to report early next morning.

Rebekah began moving in some of the outdoor displays, varied coloured cyclamen in decorative pots, Australian natives, ferns, and placed them inside, watered and tended to them.

It was almost time to lock up and go home, and she admitted to a feeling of relief the day was almost over.

The peal of the phone sounded above the muted

background music emitting from the CD player, and she crossed to the counter to pick up.

'I suppose you think you're smart, changing your number,' Brad intoned without preamble.

A sickened feeling invaded her stomach, and she drew a calming breath. Logic, not anger, she'd been advised. State facts clearly, then hang up.

'What you're doing is harassment, and there are legal measures in place to prevent you from bothering me. Why buck the law and invite trouble for yourself?'

She returned the receiver to its cradle, then moved towards the door, only to pause as the phone rang again.

At that moment the door swung inwards and she glanced up to see Jace framed in the aperture for an instant before he entered the shop.

No, Rebekah groaned silently, wishing him anywhere else but here, *now*.

'Aren't you going to answer that?'

The sound of his voice raised all her fine body hairs, and she suppressed the shiver of nerves threatening to visibly shake her slim frame.

Brad *and* Jace? It was too much. Without a word she retraced her steps and snatched up the phone.

'You sound agitated, darling. Am I finally getting to you?'

'You're wasting your time, and mine,' Rebekah added, and cut the connection.

'Problems?'

He couldn't begin to understand the hornets' nest

he'd disturbed, and she took a second to square her shoulders before turning slowly to face him.

Jace didn't like the tension creasing her forehead, the darkness in her eyes, or the edge of pain evident.

'What are you doing here?'

'No *hello*?' he drawled, staying exactly where he was. Crowding her right now would be the height of foolishness.

'I'm about to shut up shop and go home.'

He took a moment to scan the interior before bringing his attention back to her.

'Is there anything I can do to help?'

'Go away and leave me alone?' Rebekah posed, and saw his faint smile.

'I don't consider that as an option.'

The phone rang again, and she chose to ignore it.

'Want me to take it?' Jace queried smoothly, and saw her face pale. 'Brad?' He didn't need her confirmation, the shadows dulling her eyes were sufficient.

'It'll only make things worse if he hears your voice.'

His gaze hardened and his features assumed a grim implacability. 'How bad is it likely to get?'

You can't begin to know. Except the words never left her lips.

'Go collect your purse and we'll get out of here,' Jace commanded quietly.

'You should leave.' Please, she added silently. Can't you see I can't deal with you right now?

'I will, when you do.'

The insistent ring of the telephone proved the deciding factor, and she retrieved her purse, removed the afternoon's takings from the cash register, picked up her keys, then followed him out the door.

Locking up took a few seconds, and she turned towards him. 'Goodnight.' She stepped around him and began walking to her car, only to have him fall into step beside her.

'I thought we'd pick up a pizza somewhere.'

'You do that…solo. I've had a long day.' She unconsciously flexed her shoulders. 'Yesterday was even longer.' And tomorrow she had two weddings scheduled.

'You need to eat.'

'I plan to.' She reached her car, slid in the key and unlocked it. 'Alone.'

'In that case, perhaps you wouldn't mind dropping me off at the hotel on your way home. I caught a cab here.'

She retrieved her cellphone and punched in a series of digits, miscalculated one of them, and reached a wrong number.

Jace watched her expressive features, caught the fleeting emotions, and reached forward to open the car door.

'Who are you afraid of, Rebekah? I can promise not to harm a hair on your head.'

Why did she suddenly feel as if she couldn't breathe? 'Maybe it's not my head I'm worried about.'

A husky chuckle sounded low in his throat, and he spread his hands in silent surrender. 'Pizza, Rebekah. That's all. We both need to eat. Why not together?'

She looked at him. 'That's it? Pizza?'

'Pizza,' he drawled in acquiescence.

She made a split-second decision she had a feeling she might later regret. 'I know a place. Get in.'

King's Cross wasn't too far distant, and at this early hour it would be incredibly ordinary. It wasn't until post-midnight the Cross began to show its true colours, with the pimps, prostitutes, touts displaying their talents. In the back streets lay the dives and dens where the less salubrious deals were made. A place where a wrong move could mean a knife in the ribs, or worse.

Already the surroundings were beginning to change.

Graceful old residences were left behind, with small brick cottages appearing, terrace houses, and the element of care began to diminish.

'I get the feeling you're intent on showing me another side of this beautiful city,' Jace drawled as they neared the Cross.

'A landmark,' Rebekah corrected. 'Ana and I ate pizza here a few nights ago.'

'With Luc's knowledge?'

She began searching for a vacant space to park the car. 'I imagine she told him.'

Jace checked the flashing neon, the floodlit doorways. 'Afterwards, rather than before.'

'You're a snob.'

'No.' New York contained areas where you put your life on the line in daylight. After dark merely trebled the danger. 'I wouldn't want any woman of mine wandering around here after dark.'

'As long as you're moving,' Rebekah assured with a wicked grin. 'Standing still for more than a few minutes isn't recommended, unless you want someone to approach and ask your going rate for sex.'

She spotted an empty space and swung into it, then cut the engine.

'Pizza, you said?'

She led the way to a small shop on the opposite side of the street where the owner's oven-fired pizzas rated as the best she'd ever sampled anywhere. Bright red-and-white-checked tablecloths covered small square tables, empty Chianti bottles held lit candles in various stages of meltdown.

However, the aromas were redolent with spices and garlic, the service warm and friendly, and if you were fortunate enough to gain a window-seat it was a great vantage point to watch the people walk by.

'Rebekah! *Comè sta?*'

A tall Italian Adonis moved from behind the counter and enveloped her in an affectionate hug. '*Bella,* twice in one week?' the man teased. 'If I didn't know you visit only for the pizza, I might begin to think you fancy me.'

She laughed, a glorious, husky, free sound that caught Jace unawares. The frown that had been evident from the moment he walked into Blooms and Bouquets disappeared, and gone was the tension from her eyes.

'Angelo.' The mild admonishment held affection, and he shook his head with mock-regret.

'But I see this is not so,' he said as he moved her to arm's length. 'For you have brought someone with you.' There was a pause as he examined Jace, and something silent passed between them, then it was gone as he returned his attention to her. 'If you seek my approval, you have it.'

Jace saw the soft pink that coloured her cheeks as she smiled and shook her head in silent remonstrance.

'Jace Dimitriades, Angelo Benedetti.'

Angelo extended his hand and Jace shook it. 'Rebekah and I are friends from way back. *Friends,*' he emphasised quietly. 'The window table is yours.' His smile broadened as he held Rebekah's gaze. 'Go take a seat. I have pizza to make.' He moved ahead of them to the table, removed the *reserved* sign, pulled out a chair for Rebekah, indicated the one opposite to Jace, then he crossed behind the counter.

'I gather acquiring the window table is something of an honour?' Jace inclined.

'No one sits here without Angelo's personal invitation to do so.'

He picked up the menu and scanned the varieties listed. 'What do you recommend?'

'The works,' she said without hesitation. 'It's something else.'

It was, and when Angelo personally presented the aromatic masterpiece she watched as Jace savoured it with delighted satisfaction.

He fitted right into the atmosphere, spurning cutlery as he demolished the initial piece. 'Sheer ambrosia.'

'*La dolce vita,*' Rebekah accorded, and went on to reveal, 'Angelo refuses to get into the pizza-delivery game. If you want to sample his pizza, you have to come here to eat it. You get to drink Chianti or coffee, and watch the world go by.' She offered a warm smile. 'The total experience.'

Jace picked up another slice and bit into it. 'Worth it.'

The smile became a husky chuckle. 'I'm glad you think so.'

He stilled, and his gaze was dark, serious. 'Are you?'

The query was quietly voiced, but there was something in his underlying tone that brought all her defences to the fore.

He saw the shutters come down on her expression, and the smile faded from her lips. Such a soft mouth, so many fragile emotions. There was a brief moment when he wanted to smash a fist into her ex-husband's face for the damage he'd done. The little information he'd managed to prise from Luc had made him incredibly angry.

The silence stretched between them, and he ate steadily, aware that she pushed her plate to one side.

He could almost see the conscious effort she summoned to move the conversation on to a safe plane.

'Your trip to Melbourne proved successful?'

'Yes. I have meetings here early next week, then

it's Brisbane, Cairns, Port Douglas, Brisbane and the Gold Coast.'

Idle conversation. The need for it beat silence and eased the tension steadily building inside her.

'Whereupon you return to New York.'

'Yes.'

Nothing explained the sudden pain that pierced her heart, or the sensation of impending loss. What was the matter with her? Jace Dimitriades had no place in her life, any more than she had a place in his. They resided continents apart. Besides, sexual awareness was no basis on which to build...*what*? A relationship?

Dear heaven. Even the thought of sharing sensual intimacy with such a man fired the blood in her veins and sent her nervous system into cataclysmic overload.

Imagining that strong, muscled body naked, his arousal large, hard and pulsing with need. The touch of his mouth on hers, his hands shaping her breasts...

Would he hurt her as Brad had? Take his own satisfaction without any thought for hers? Cruelly taunt her to compensate for his inadequacies?

Somehow she doubted Jace was anything but an experienced and skilled lover. He exuded the confident sensual intensity of a man at ease with himself, and possessed of an intuitive awareness of what it took to please a woman.

How could she explain the yearning deep inside to discover if it was true? To give herself unconditionally to his seduction, exult in the pleasure of it as they soared towards the heights of passion together, shared a mutual shattering climax, followed by the infinitely languorous warmth of drifting fingers, the gentle touch of lips to skin...the exquisite liquid feeling that accompanied lovemaking. Very good lovemaking.

'The pizza is good?'

The sound of Angelo's voice was a stark intrusion and brought her tumbling back to reality. It took a second to marshal her thoughts together and summon a smile.

'Superb, as always,' she reassured, not quite meeting his steady gaze. She needed several more seconds before she could look at Jace.

'Can I bring you coffee? Tea?'

'Tea,' Rebekah ordered. She needed to sleep tonight.

'Make it two,' Jace added, reaching for his wallet.

'Mine,' she insisted, and extracted a note from her purse to cover the bill. 'Don't take his money,' she insisted to Angelo, who laughed with delight and pushed the note towards her.

'What if I refuse altogether?' He inclined his head towards Rebekah. 'Tonight is on the house, my friend. For old times' sake.' He turned to Jace and offered a hard glance. 'Take care of her.'

'Count on it.' Jace's voice was a silky drawl laced with intent, and drew Angelo's silent approval.

The tea arrived, a fine Ceylon blend Angelo kept

for special customers, and she savoured it with genuine enjoyment.

'Do you come here often?'

'Occasionally.'

She liked his hands, the shape and texture of them, their strength. A shiver feathered its way over her skin as she remembered how they felt threading through her hair, capturing her nape the instant before his mouth lowered to hers. Magic. He had the touch, the degree of *tendresse* to melt a woman's heart.

But not hers, she determined with quiet resolve.

'I'll drop you back to your hotel,' Rebekah offered as they farewelled Angelo before emerging outdoors onto the street pavement.

It was still light, but the sky had acquired the dull patina of approaching dusk. Soon the streetlights would spring on, and the regular patrons of the Cross would begin to appear.

Together they crossed the street to her van, and she ignited the engine then eased into the steady flow of traffic.

'How will you manage at the shop until Ana returns?' Jace queried, watching her competent handling of the vehicle, the traffic.

'I was able to get another florist to fill in today, and she's agreeable to work tomorrow.' She drew to a halt at a set of lights. 'I'm seriously considering asking if she'll work part-time. I'll need to discuss it with Ana.'

'And Brad?' He slipped that in, because he felt the need to know.

'I can handle it,' Rebekah assured tightly.

'And if you can't?' Jace pursued.

She spared him a hard glance as the lights changed up ahead. 'The legal authorities will do it for me.'

It didn't make him breathe any easier. There was something primitively evil beneath the layers of Brad Somerville's projected sophistication. Obviously well-hidden to have fooled the woman seated beside him.

The cars up front began to move, and she shifted gears, then followed the main arterial road leading to Double Bay.

It was with a sense of relief she pulled into the entrance immediately out front of the Ritz-Carlton, and she looked in silent askance as Jace removed his wallet, extracted a business card, and penned a series of digits before handing it to her.

'My cellphone number. It'll reach me any time, anywhere.' He cast her a look that was serious in the extreme. 'Call if you need me.'

He reached for the door-clasp, then turned back and fastened his mouth on hers, conducting a slow sweep of the sweet inner moistness with his tongue before deepening the kiss into something frankly sensual.

How long did it last? Scant minutes, but it left him wanting more, much more than the taste of her mouth.

He stifled a sound deep in his throat that was pure regret as he gentled her lips with his own, then he broke the contact and stepped out from the van to stand watching as she sent the vehicle moving out onto the street.

Then he turned and entered the hotel lobby, acknowledged the concierge with a curt nod, and took the lift up to his suite.

CHAPTER FIVE

REBEKAH locked her apartment door and re-set the security alarm before crossing to the kitchen to feed the cat.

A sense of trepidation tied her stomach in knots as she forced herself to check the answering machine, and she expelled some pent-up breath at the sight of its unblinking message light.

Thank God. She closed her eyes, then opened them again in a gesture of innate relief.

Although how long would it take Brad to bypass the telephone company's security and determine her new unlisted number? Technically, it wasn't supposed to happen…which didn't necessarily mean that it couldn't be done.

She lifted her arms high and stretched her body in an effort to dispel kinks from sore muscles, then she moved through to the *en suite* adjoining her bedroom and began filling the spa-bath. Half an hour relaxing there with a glossy magazine and a cup of tea was just what she needed to help her unwind from the day.

It worked just fine, and she crawled into bed, snapped off the bedside light…and lay staring into the darkness as Jace's image filled her mind.

She fell asleep with the vivid memory of how it felt to have his mouth invade hers, and sheer exhaustion was responsible for uninterrupted somnolence until the alarm rang early next morning.

Saturday numbered one of the busiest days of the week, and today didn't prove any different. Suzie was a jewel, and they worked together getting the orders organised, completed, and boxed the two wedding orders ready for the courier, dealt with customers who came in off the street, and even managed to snatch something to eat at reasonable intervals.

There was no lull, little time to think, just the need for smooth efficiency.

Ana checked in around midday, and Rebekah was delighted to hear the happiness emanate from her voice.

There was the opportunity to mention Suzie's suitability to assist part-time, and Ana's *'hire her'* clinched the decision.

'Mornings and all day Fridays and Saturdays,' Rebekah offered, named the rate of pay, and gave a relieved sigh at Suzie's enthusiastic acceptance.

There was a sense of satisfaction and achievement in that Ana was fine with her life back on track; Blooms and Bouquets would continue to operate efficiently.

Two down and two to go, Rebekah rationalised, hoping, praying that her ex-husband's nuisance calls would cease and he'd fade back into the woodwork.

That left Jace Dimitriades, and she had no idea how she was going to deal with *Jace*. If she had any sense and an iota of self-preservation she'd refuse to see him and put him out of her mind.

Fat chance. He was already there, firmly embedded in the recesses of her brain. He made her want something she couldn't have. His image teased her with endless possibilities of what it would be like to *be* with him.

Take that step, and she'd be irretrievably lost. Caught up in a sensual madness that could very well lead to her destruction.

But what a way to go.

'See you Monday.'

Rebekah glanced up from the computer and smiled as Suzie caught up her bag. 'Goodnight. Enjoy the rest of the weekend.'

'Shall do. You, too.'

The glass door swung shut, and Rebekah returned her attention to the computer. She'd save the data onto disk and take it home, where she'd load it into the laptop tomorrow and key in the appropriate accounting entries.

Three customers entered the shop to secure last-minute purchases, and she tended to the last one, then just as she was about to secure the lock Jace appeared at the door.

Just the sight of him sent her pulse racing, and set the butterflies fluttering madly in her stomach. Heat suffused her body, and she deliberately regulated her breathing in a bid to control her wayward emotions. 'I'm just about to close,' she managed evenly. 'Is there something you want?'

His answering smile did strange things to her equilibrium. 'You, to join me for dinner tonight.'

Forget control. His *you* sent her imagination into a tailspin, and she banked down riotous images of tangled sheets, naked bodies…his, *hers,* coupled together in the throes of passion.

What was *wrong* with her? The silent castigation was heartfelt. Had she been locked too long in denial? Was that it? And if so, why *this* man?

Don't answer that.

Her only weapon was humour. She lifted a hand to her chin and tilted her head.

'Ah, you're all alone in the city with no one to call, and I'll do?' What was she doing, for heaven's sake? One didn't tease men of Jace Dimitriades' calibre. 'What if I've made other plans?'

'Have you?'

Honesty came to the fore. 'No.'

'Good.'

'Don't count your chickens too soon,' she warned. 'I haven't said *yes.*'

He lifted a hand and pushed a stray tendril of hair back behind her ear. 'But you will.'

What did she have to lose? Stupid question. Maybe Ana was right, and it was time to loosen a few strings.

'Can we negotiate on a movie?'

'Done.'

'OK.'

Jace gave a deep, husky chuckle. 'You want to be chauffeur, or shall I?'

She pretended to consider both options. 'Oh, let's go for role reversal. Besides, I have a better knowledge of the city than you do.' She checked her watch. 'Pick you up at seven?'

'I'll be waiting.' He glanced around the shop's interior. 'Now, let's get you out of here.'

'I've done it a thousand times on my own.' More, if anyone was counting.

'Then indulge me and let's do it together.'

Five minutes later Rebekah walked to her van as Jace slid behind the wheel of his car.

Neither of them noticed the man seated in a vehicle thirty metres distant. If they had, it would have taken more than a casual glance to determine his identity. A cap worn backwards and wrap-around sunglasses provided a very good disguise.

There were no messages recorded on the answering machine, and Rebekah hit the shower, stepped into clean underwear, tended to her make-up, swept her hair into a smooth knot, then dressed in black evening trousers, a red camisole and matching evening jacket. She added stiletto heels, caught up an evening purse and her keys, then she took the lift down to the underground car park.

The MG was parked in its customary space, and she fired the engine and sent the sleek little sports car onto street level, then drove the few blocks to Jace's hotel.

He emerged from the lobby as soon as she drew into the entrance bay, and within minutes she rejoined the traffic.

'Where to?'

'Darling Harbour.'

'Yessir.'

Jace wondered if she had any idea how her features

lightened? Or how the darkness that was a lurking constant in her eyes disappeared when she smiled?

'Don't be sassy.'

She shot him a grin. 'Just acting out the *chauffeur* part.'

It was a beautiful evening, cool, but not uncomfortably so, and they ate seafood at an elegant restaurant overlooking the inner harbour, drank a little chilled white wine, then took in a top-rated movie guaranteed to earn the lead actors, the producer and director major award honours.

'That was great,' Rebekah accorded as they emerged from the cinema complex and began walking to where she'd parked the MG.

Fine food, beautiful ambience, fantastic movie... great date, *great man,* she reflected, aware this was her first date in a long while. Too long.

She'd played her private life so carefully since her divorce. Brad's erratic behaviour had diminished her self-image, damaged her trust in men, and left her with a heightened sense of the need for self-preservation.

Rebekah reached the MG, unlocked both doors, and slid in behind the wheel as Jace folded his lengthy frame into the passenger seat.

It wasn't a car for a tall, well-built male frame, and it brought him far too close for comfort. She was supremely conscious of his thigh close to the gear-shift, making it difficult for the edges of her fingers not to brush against him each time she changed gears.

There was an acute awareness of his clean male scent combined with the hint of his exclusive brand of cologne. Above all was the intense sensual chemistry apparent...a latent entity that threatened her libido, not to mention her peace of mind.

'Shall we stop off somewhere for coffee?'

Rebekah brought her jangling thoughts together and focused on his words, faltered for a few telling seconds, and offered hesitantly, 'It's late. I—'

'Just...coffee,' Jace reiterated quietly, aware of her escalating nervous tension. 'There are a number of cafés close to the Ritz-Carlton. We'll choose one, and when we're done I'll walk back to the hotel.'

It sounded reasonable, no strings, just the sharing of coffee as a pleasant conclusion to a very enjoyable evening.

Double Bay was known for its trendy cafés, where the day-time clientele lunched and the social élite met and lingered over coffee during the evening. Whatever the time, it was an opportunity to be *seen*.

Finding a parking space took a while, and they strolled along the street-front, chose a café and selected a table.

Coffee at its finest, Rebekah acknowledged silently as she savoured the sweet, aromatic brew. Discussing the merits of the film they'd just seen seemed a safe topic of conversation, and they engaged in an interesting exchange of views.

'You have tomorrow off?'

She stilled, and for a second her eyes assumed a wary expression. 'Yes.'

'I've booked a harbour cruise. It takes approximately six hours and leaves at ten.'

Such cruises were very popular among the tourists, and crew served lunch on board as well as morning and afternoon tea. 'You'll enjoy it.' It was a great way to see the many coves and bays around the inner harbour, view prime real estate, and relax in pleasant surroundings.

Jace held her gaze. 'Join me.'

She was willing to swear her heart stopped for a few seconds before racing into a thudding beat. 'There'll be a running commentary informing passengers of various vantage points throughout the day. You won't need me along.'

His smile held warmth and something she was reluctant to define. 'I want you along.'

'Jace…' She paused, then stumbled over the words, 'I can't keep seeing you.'

'Can't, or won't?'

Oh, lord, this was getting out of hand. *'Why?'*

There was despair in the query, and it angered him to think her ex-husband had done such a number on her.

'The truth?' His gaze speared hers. 'I want to spend time with you.'

To what end? The obvious one wasn't an option. 'I won't have sex with you.' Stark words that matched his in honesty.

'If I just wanted sex, there are several numbers I could call.'

So he could. Numbers listed in the trade papers, the telephone yellow pages...and failing that, all he had to do was ask a discreet question of the hotel staff to have the relevant information supplied.

'So,' he drawled silkily. 'Shall we start over?'

She took a deep breath and slowly released it. 'I usually do domestic chores on a Sunday.' Go to the gym, meet a friend for coffee, take in a foreign film, read, relax. It was a token excuse, and they both knew it.

Oh, *dammit*. She spread her hands in a gesture of surrender. 'All right, OK.' She was angry, with herself, *him*, for being manoeuvred into a position where it would seem churlish to refuse. 'I'll go.'

Rebekah glimpsed the gleam of humour in that dark gaze, and she could have sworn the edge of his mouth twitched. 'Such a gracious acceptance.'

She drained the last of her coffee. 'I think it's time I went home.' She stood to her feet. 'Thanks for an enjoyable evening.'

He duplicated her movements, extracted a note and anchored it on the table. 'I'll walk you to your car.'

'I'll be fine,' she stated firmly. 'Goodnight.' She turned away from him and quickened her steps, aware that he fell in beside her.

'Has anyone told you you're impossible?' she flung tersely, and missed the fleeting amusement apparent.

'Rarely to my face.'

'Obviously it's high time someone did.'

There were people seated outdoors beneath large shaded umbrellas, and she was conscious of background chatter, music emitting from speakers, and cars cruising the street searching for a parking space.

Within minutes they reached the MG, and she unlocked the door, then slid in behind the wheel, slipping the key into the ignition without pause.

Jace leaned down towards her. 'Join me for breakfast at the hotel. Eight. Then we'll head for the pier.'

Rebekah looked at him steadily. 'I'll eat at home, and meet you in the hotel lobby after nine.'

She fired the engine as he stood upright and closed the door. With consummate skill she eased the car out from its parking space and resisted the temptation to check the rear-vision mirror as she entered the flow of traffic.

Rebekah slept well and woke feeling refreshed and ready to meet the day. Choosing to wear dress-jeans and a T-shirt, she tied a sweater over her shoulders, applied sun-screen beneath her minimum make-up, and swept her hair into a careless knot atop her head.

Shortly after nine she slid her feet into joggers, caught up her shoulder bag, her keys, then took the lift down to the underground car park.

Jace had also chosen casual attire, and her heart jolted at the sight of him in jeans and a polo shirt. He held a jacket hooked over one shoulder, and he was something else.

He walked towards her, and she admired the way the jeans moulded his thighs, hugged his hips, while the polo shirt clung to his hard-muscled torso, emphasising an enviable breadth of shoulder.

'Hi.' As a greeting, it fell short by a mile, but it was the best she could do with her breath caught in her throat as he slid into the passenger seat.

'Morning.' His appraisal was swift, encompassing. 'You slept well?'

Oh, my, how did she answer that? Admit his image had filled her imagination and her last waking thought had been of him?

'Yes, thank you.' Why was she sounding so excruciatingly polite? 'And you?'

'Fine.'

His smile broadened, and her stomach curled as the grooves slashing each cheek became more defined, and tiny lines fanned out from the corners of his eyes.

Rebekah moved the gear-shift and sent the MG out onto the street, driving with practised ease as she headed towards the city pier.

He exuded latent strength...not only of the body, but of the mind. A man who went after what he wanted with steel-willed resolve, she perceived, and wondered at his strategy with regard to *her*.

A convenient but brief affair while he tended to business? Why go for emotional entanglement when he could pay for sex, then walk away?

It didn't make sense. None of his actions made sense.

Unless... No, she dismissed instantly. He wasn't attracted to her. *Intrigued,* possibly. Was he aware of the sexual chemistry that shimmered between them? Or was it one-sided and all *hers*?

Oh, for heaven's sake, get a grip, she mentally chastised. He's Luc's cousin, he's in Sydney on business, you're the sister of his cousin's wife. He's simply being kind.

So why didn't it feel like *kind* when he touched her? *Kissed* her?

So how *did* it feel? a tiny imp taunted.

Like she'd caught a glimpse of heaven on earth. Something she dared not hope for, in a place she was afraid to occupy.

Fear of rejection? Afraid it wouldn't, *couldn't* last?

She'd experienced one particular taste of hell. She wasn't keen to sample another.

But what if you're wrong? What if you're choosing to deny something incredibly wonderful simply because one man fooled you with a Jekyll-and-Hyde personality?

Just enjoy the day, why don't you? she admonished silently as they walked out onto the pier and boarded the large cruise boat equipped to carry up to fifty passengers and crew.

The sun shone brightly with the warmth of an early summer, and the sky was a clear azure. A breeze became evident as the boat moved out into the harbour, and Rebekah pointed out prime real estate built on the rocky cliff-face that bordered the many coves and inlets.

There were numerous craft moored, some small, others large and luxurious, and she indicated various landmarks, homes of the rich and famous as the boat cruised the inner harbour.

For a while they moved out on deck, and she was conscious of Jace's presence, the light touch of his hand on her arm, the way her body reacted to his as he leaned in close to follow her line of vision as she indicated certain focal points of interest.

Way out in the distance a huge tanker was slowly making its way in, and as they returned city-side there were two tugboats steaming out to meet a luxury liner, a solid, oft-used ferry boat chugging towards the North Shore, and a sleek hydrofoil bringing passengers in from Manly.

Where better to view the wide, distinctive arch of the Harbour Bridge, the graceful architectural curves of the Opera House?

Sydney was a beautiful city with one of the finest harbours in the world. Today, looking at it from a visitor's viewpoint, there was a sense of pride in the familiar, an innate feeling of patriotism.

The sun had moved overhead and was now shifting towards the west, washing the buildings, some old, some new in towers of concrete, steel and glass.

Glorious by day, stunning at night when electric light shaped the many buildings against an indigo sky, and multicoloured flashing neon added colour and interest to an intriguing night-scape.

'Beautiful.' Jace's voice was quiet, almost husky, and Rebekah turned towards him, words of agreement escaping her lips.

Except he wasn't admiring the view, he was looking at her.

For one brief minute it seemed as if the world shifted slightly, and she barely refrained from reaching out a hand to steady herself.

Crazy. Perhaps she imagined it, and it was the boat?

But no, it was moving steadily, there was no backwash, and the harbour waters were as smooth as glass.

This was bad. Really bad.

She leaned forward against the railing and concentrated on a small liner as it lay moored, then she shifted her attention to the row of city buildings.

Most all of the passengers had emerged onto the deck, and she gave a surprised start as Jace moved to position himself behind her.

It was, she realised, a polite gesture to allow others room to share the view, and his arms caged her body as he fastened his hands on the railing.

His body wasn't touching hers, but she was supremely aware just how easy it would be to lean back against him. Have him link his arms at her waist, and rest his chin against her head.

For a moment she felt as if she couldn't breathe, and panic that he might sense her discomfort forced her to regulate every breath in an effort to slow her rapidly beating pulse.

The cruise boat docked at four, and the passengers lined up ready to disembark. Jace stood behind her, and he put a hand to her waist to steady her as they stepped down the gangplank.

She felt the heat of his touch, and her stomach executed a backward flip.

Nerves, she decided, were hell and damnation. Her body seemed to be in a permanent state of flux whenever Jace Dimitriades was within touching distance.

'We're not far from the aquarium,' Jace declared. 'I checked out its location this morning. We've time for a quick tour before it closes.'

'*We?*' She shot him a startled glance. 'I don't think—'

'You have an aversion to sea creatures?'

'No.'

'You visited last week, and can't bear to do it again so soon?'

Dammit, he was teasing her. Well, two could play at that game. 'Fish?' she queried sweetly. 'You want to go see *fish*?'

His warm smile tore the breath from her throat. 'With my favourite tour guide for company.'

Rebekah gave a small mock-bow. 'Australian residents have a duty to please their overseas visitors.' She indicated a flight of steps. 'Shall we proceed?'

The staff member manning the aquarium ticket box shook her head doubtfully and reminded there was less than an hour before closing time.

'We'll walk very quickly,' Rebekah assured as Jace picked up the tickets.

Some exhibits were exotic specimens, others fearsome, especially in the large aquarium housing various predators. The enclosed areas held a damp salty smell, and Rebekah breathed in fresh air as they emerged out into the sunshine and began walking to where she'd parked the car.

'How dedicated are you to playing tour guide?' Jace queried as he slid into the passenger seat.

She turned towards him. 'You don't want to go back to the hotel?'

'I'd like to explore the Rocks,' Jace declared, and saw her eyes widen.

The area was in an old part of the city bordering on the harbour and held a variety of shops, stalls and numerous cafés and restaurants.

'You're kidding me, right?'

'We could grab something to eat there.'

This was going a bit too far. 'We've spent all day together,' she managed evenly.

'So, what's a few more hours?'

Common sense urged her to refuse. 'I have things to do at home.' It was a token protest.

'Want for me to help out?'

There was a part of her that was tempted to call his bluff just to see him undertake domestic chores.

'Somehow I can't summon an image of you handling a vacuum cleaner or wielding an iron.'

'I managed both during my years at university.'

Caution rose to the fore at the thought of him visiting at her apartment. Mutual ground, *public* ground was infinitely safer.

Rebekah ignited the engine. 'OK, the Rocks it is.' Two hours, she qualified.

They stayed twice as long, wandering at ease, pausing here and there, then Jace chose a restaurant where the food was superb, and they lingered over coffee, enjoying the ambience, the background music.

A sense of latent intimacy seemed to manifest itself, something she put down to the glass of wine she consumed during the course of the meal. She was acutely conscious of the man seated opposite, aware to a finite degree of the inherent vitality beneath his sophisticated façade. Primitive sexuality meshed with elemental sensuality...a dangerous combination, and more than most women could handle.

Yet it awakened something deep within her, an entity she was almost afraid to explore for fear of being burnt.

Safe meant not seeing him again. And, dear heaven, she had every reason to covet safety.

'Shall we leave?'

Jace's voice intruded, and she pushed her empty cup to one side. 'Yes. I have an early start tomorrow.'

He took care of the bill, and they exited the restaurant, choosing to walk the esplanade path to where she'd parked the MG.

Rebekah felt the touch of his hand at her waist, and she experienced a feeling of surprise, almost shock when it slid to capture her own.

For a moment she froze, her first instinct being to pull free, except she hesitated too long and his fingers shifted to thread themselves through hers in a loose linking that was warm, intimate.

It made her want to shift closer, feel the strength, the heat, of his body. More than anything, she longed for his arms close around her, to sink in against him, have his mouth capture her own and wreak sensual devastation.

Yet she hesitated, aware any move on her part would invite more than she was prepared to give.

At that moment his thumb slid against the sensitive veins at her wrist, then began an evocative caress as her pulse jumped and skidded to a heavy beat.

Could he tell? How could he not? she groaned inaudibly. She couldn't disguise the response of her body, and almost as if he knew he lifted her hand to his lips, lightly brushed them to her fingers, then let their joined hands fall.

Oh, my. She felt as if rockets were being launched inside her head, with the aftershocks reverberating through her entire body.

It was a fine kind of madness, fed by desire and fuelled by too vivid an imagination.

Rebekah was grateful when they reached the car, for it enabled her to break contact and slide in behind the wheel.

She wasn't capable of uttering so much as a word, and she didn't even try. Instead she focused on negotiating the traffic, and there was a sense of relief as she drew into the hotel entrance.

Short-lived, she discovered as Jace slid the gearshift into neutral, then he leaned towards her and captured her head, angling it as he fastened his mouth over hers in a kiss that tore her vulnerable emotions to shreds.

Seconds or minutes? She had no idea how long it

lasted, only that she felt cast adrift like a rudderless boat in the open sea.

Did she kiss him back? Perhaps she had. All she knew was that when he released her she felt totally lost.

She couldn't speak, and her eyes felt impossibly large as she simply looked at him, and she gave a start of surprise as he touched a finger to her lips.

His smile held incredible warmth, and she felt herself begin to melt...which was crazy.

'I'll phone you tomorrow.' He reached for the door-clasp and slid out from the car.

For a heart-stopping second she couldn't move, then she became conscious of the concierge standing at the entrance, valet parking staff, and she shifted gears then put the MG in motion.

Rebekah entered her apartment a short while later and crossed to the kitchen for a cool drink. It was then she saw the message light blinking on her answering machine.

Ana? Unlikely, given her sister preferred direct contact to her cellphone.

She crossed to the machine and depressed the 're-play' button, waiting as the tape automatically re-wound.

'How was your day with lover-boy?' Brad's voice was low and ugly. 'Don't bother changing your silent number again.' There was a click as he ended the call.

Rebekah stood still for what seemed an age, then she located the number she'd been advised to call, day or night, and filed a report.

It did little to ease her mind. Nothing to stem the sense of frustrated anger that rose to the fore as she re-set the answering machine.

She took a shower, then slid into bed to lie staring at the darkened ceiling for what seemed *hours* before she succumbed to sleep, where nightmarish dreams invaded her subconscious, and when she woke to the sound of the alarm it was as if she hadn't slept at all.

CHAPTER SIX

'BITCH. You'll pay for this.'

Rebekah clutched the receiver as the male voice vented in a sibilant tone that held more threat than if Brad had screamed the words in her ear.

The shop held two customers, Suzie was dealing with one, and the other was examining a glorious stand of gladioli.

Rationalising with him was a waste of time, but she tried. 'You're in violation—' a click indicated he'd ended the call '—of the restraining order,' she finished to an empty line.

The electronic door buzzer sounded, and she replaced the receiver, summoned a smile and turned to see Jace standing inside the door.

Her senses stirred at the sight of him. The dark three-piece suit, deep blue shirt and silk tie indicated he'd come straight from a business meeting, and he removed the lightly tinted sunglasses, silently indicated she serve the waiting customer, then browsed the various bouquets on display.

It took a while for the customer to make a choice, and Rebekah completed the purchase, then crossed to Jace's side.

She looked pale, and her eyes bore the lacklustre appearance of someone battling tiredness and, unless he was mistaken, a headache. He doubted she'd slept any better than he had.

He lifted a hand and tucked back a stray lock of hair that had escaped the knot atop her head. And watched her eyes dilate at his touch.

'Feel up to sharing one of Angelo's pizzas?'

All she wanted to do was go home, soak in a hot tub, then grab a salad, veg out in front of the television for an hour, and make up on lost sleep.

'I'd planned on an early night.'

'You've got it. I've at least an hour's work on the laptop, and I'm due to take the early-morning flight to Cairns.' He didn't add that he'd originally intended flying out tonight, but had shifted the booking to tomorrow. 'I'll be here when you close.'

His smile made her toes curl. She should refuse, but she didn't. 'OK.'

'Wow,' Suzie said with genuine awe when Jace had left the shop. 'Who *is* that man?'

Rebekah explained the connection, and Suzie rolled her eyes.

'Is your sister's husband equally attractive?'

'Equally,' she assured solemnly.

'I don't suppose there are any more male cousins here or abroad?'

'A few.'

Suzie gave an impish grin. 'I *know* I'm going to enjoy working here.'

Jace reappeared just as Rebekah was about to lock up, and gone was the formal business suit. In its place were jeans and a casual chambray shirt left unbut-

toned at the neck. He'd rolled the cuffs back and discarded shoes for joggers.

'All done?'

Luck saw them park close to Angelo's pizzeria, and
they ordered, choosing take-out rather than electing
to eat in, and strolled along the main street while they
waited on the pizza.

'Tough day?'

Jace caught hold of her hand, and she didn't object.
'Not really. Ana insisted on putting in a few hours,
against Luc's and my wishes. Fortunately Suzie is
good at taking up the slack.' She spared him a direct
glance. 'Yours?'

'Bearable.' He didn't add he'd spent most of it
wanting the day done so he could spend time with
her.

A tout called out to them from an open doorway,
only to halt his outrageous spiel as Jace directed him
a chilling look.

Angelo had the pizza boxed and ready to go when
they returned to the shop.

'Where do you suggest we eat this?' Rebekah
asked as she eased the van into the flow of traffic.

'Your apartment?'

It was her own private domain, and only family
visited her there. When it came to joining friends, she
chose a restaurant, café, cinema or shopping complex
as a meeting place.

'I don't think that's a good idea.'

'My hotel?'

A park bench? Drive out to one of the beaches? By then the pizza would be cold.

'We'll go to my place.' She shot him a direct look. 'Just be warned I intend chucking you out at nine.'

'So noted.' His drawl held an element of husky humour.

Minutes later she used her key to unlock the sliding steel grille guarding entrance to the underground car park, eased in beside the MG, then they rode the lift to the seventh floor.

As soon as she opened the apartment door Millie was there, rubbing her head against Rebekah's leg, only to back up and regard Jace with feline curiosity.

'The kitchen's through the lounge to the right.' She led the way. 'I'll show you where the plates are kept, and you can apportion the pizza while I feed Millie.'

The message light on the answering machine was blinking, and her stomach tightened.

'You want to get that?' Jace asked, indicating the machine, and she shook her head.

'It won't be anything that can't wait.' If it was Brad, she'd prefer to run it when she was alone.

They ate pizza seated at the dining-room table, and she unearthed a bottle of red Lambrusco, extracted two wine glasses, filled both, and handed him one.

There was an easy familiarity in the gesture, although nothing discounted the electric tension fizzing along her nerve threads.

'How long will you be away?' It was the only thing she could think to offer, and he finished the mouthful he was eating before responding,

'Four days. I fly direct to Cairns tomorrow, visit Port Douglas Tuesday morning, take the late-afternoon flight Wednesday to Brisbane, visit the Gold Coast Friday morning, and return to Sydney late afternoon.'

'Real estate?'

'Shopping complexes, warehouses,' Jace added as he reached for another slice of pizza.

'You assess, buy at a low price, move in a team to upgrade, promote, then sell when they're showing a handsome profit.' It was just a guess, but she imagined it to be a fairly accurate one.

Rebekah demolished two slices, then slowly sipped her wine.

'Something like that,' he declared indolently. He didn't add that he headed a family consortium with global business interests, and he kept a personal check on all of them. The Sydney arm had initiated some major staff changes at its top level, and he'd chosen to cast a personal eye over the new MD's purchase proposals. And check out if his attraction for Ana's sister was as tantalising now as it had been a year ago.

The answer was easy. The solution, however, was anything but.

The women in his life had been eager, willing, and practised in the art of seduction. Relationships clear-cut, boundaries established and recognised, and while affection formed a base, *love*, the everlasting kind, had never rated a mention.

Until the event of Luc and Ana's marriage he'd

been content with the status quo. There were any number of women he'd be satisfied to have as his wife. But none he'd covet as the mother of his children. Which had to tell him something.

For the past year he'd immersed himself in work, dated few women more than a token once or twice, indulged in selective sex, and become very aware that while it might satisfy his libido, any emotional pleasure was sadly lacking.

'Would you like some coffee?'

'Thanks. Black, one sugar.'

Rebekah stood to her feet, gathered up the plates and cutlery and carried them through to the kitchen.

The headache she'd fought against most of the afternoon intensified, and she opened a cupboard, retrieved painkillers, popped two from the pack and swallowed them down with water.

'Headache?'

She hadn't heard him leave the dining room, and her hand shook a little. 'It's nothing a good night's sleep won't fix.'

His mouth curved into a faint smile. 'Is that a hint I've outstayed my welcome?'

'No,' she managed quietly. 'No, of course not.'

The smile reached his eyes. 'Good.' He moved round the servery, took the glass from her hand and put it down, then he captured her face in his hands and began gently massaging her temples.

She opened her mouth to protest, only to have him press his thumb against her lips.

'Shh. Just relax.'

It felt like heaven as his fingers moved to massage her scalp, and she instinctively lowered her lashes so her gaze fastened on the hollow at the base of his throat where a pulse beat so strongly there.

His touch held a mesmeric quality, almost as if a part of him was invading her senses, and she swayed slightly, caught in the sensual magic he was able to evoke.

A slight sound brought her lashes sweeping wide, and she almost died at the magnetising warmth evident in his slumberous gaze.

Her lips parted involuntarily, and she glimpsed the warmth turn to heat, then his mouth slanted over hers, gently at first as his tongue took an exploratory sweep before tangling with her own in an evocative dance that demanded more, much more.

One hand fisted her hair while the other slid down past her waist to hold her fast against him, and she lifted her arms and linked her hands together at his nape as she leaned into him, exulting in the feel, the taste, the sensual heat of him.

It was like nothing else she'd experienced before as he wrapped her close, so close, his hands shaping her waist, her hips, buttocks.

His mouth left hers and nuzzled the sensitive curve at the edge of her neck, then trailed a path to nibble her earlobe before seeking her mouth as he took her deep in a sensual imitation of the sex act itself.

Almost as if he sensed he was going too far too fast he eased up a little, locking her hips close to his own so she couldn't help but be aware of his arousal.

Its potent force took her breath away, and she wondered what it would feel like to have him inside her, moving in an ever-increasing rhythm until he reached his peak.

There was a part of her that wanted to be swept away by the tide of passion. To have no thought, no scruples, no reservations. Just follow wherever he chose to lead.

Would the reality exceed the limits of her experience, and prove to be as mesmeric as she imagined it could be?

Somehow the answer had to be *yes*. This man possessed the touch, the sexual expertise to indulge a woman in a feast of the senses. From acutely sensitive to the raw and primitive.

A shiver feathered its way over the surface of her skin, raising all her fine body hairs in anticipation as treacherous desire pulsed from deep within.

She wanted the tactile touch of skin on skin, and the need for it drove her to seek the opening of his shirt. There was a primal urge to fist the material and tug it free from his jeans then drag it off so she could rain his torso with the heated pressure of her mouth. To gently nip the hard muscle tissue close to a male nipple, then caress each one with her tongue, teasing mercilessly until he groaned at her touch.

More than anything, she wanted him to bestow her the same favour, to drive her sensually wild until there could be only one end.

Her audio-visual senses were so caught up in the mindless fantasy she was only dimly aware of a ringing in her ears, and she gave a despairing groan as Jace gently broke contact.

'Should you get that?'

The phone. Dear heaven, it was the *phone*.

The answering machine picked up, and she froze. Please, *please* don't let it be Brad.

Jace held her loosely, his gaze intent as he witnessed her disquiet.

'Inviting him into your apartment isn't a good move, darling.' Brad's voice was unmistakable. 'Has he discovered you're a frigid little bitch?' There was a click as he cut the connection, the faint whirr of the answering machine as it rewound the tape.

Rebekah wanted to curl up and die. She closed her eyes in an involuntary gesture of self-defence, then opened them again to focus on the third button of Jace's shirt.

A hand cupped her chin, tilting it so she had to look at him, and she fought to hold back the moisture shimmering in her eyes.

'Don't.' Jace framed her face between his hands, and smoothed a thumb over lips made slightly swollen from his kiss.

She wasn't capable of uttering a word, and her eyes ached with unshed tears.

He saw her lashes lower to form a protective veil, and pain stabbed his gut as a single tear escaped and rolled slowly down one cheek.

'Please,' she said huskily. 'Just go.'

She felt his thumb erase the trail of moisture, and

his hands were incredibly gentle as he cradled her face.

'No.'

'Please,' she reiterated as he tilted her face.

'Look at me.'

The command was softly voiced, and she felt his fingers trail the slope of her neck, linger at its edge, then return.

The peal of the phone was an intrusive, strident sound in the stillness of the room, and he felt the tremor that ran through her body.

With one economical movement Jace reached forward, lifted the receiver, listened, then ventured in a deadly soft voice, 'Don't ring again if you value your skin.' He cut the connection and didn't return the receiver to the handset.

'I suggest you change your number.'

'I've already done that twice in the past two days.' He may as well hear the rest of it. 'The police have been notified, and my lawyer.'

He understood too clearly. 'Who each advise keeping your answering machine on to record each of his calls.'

'Yes.'

'Which have only accelerated since he saw us together at the restaurant last week.'

Rebekah didn't concur, she had no need to. Brad's reaction was self-explanatory.

'Is there a possibility he might attempt to physically hurt you?'

She paused a second too long. 'I don't think so.'

'He doesn't have a key to your apartment?'

She shook her head. 'I bought it following the divorce.' And lived with Ana between leaving Brad and obtaining her legal freedom. It had been a fraught time, laced with various incidents involving her ex-husband's harassment. She'd neither sighted nor heard from him in ages. Until Wednesday of last week. Now the torment seemed set to begin all over again.

'Would you like me to stay over tonight?'

Shocked surprise widened her eyes. 'No, of course not.'

A gleam of humour lit his gaze. 'I imagine you have a spare bedroom.'

She did, but she didn't intend for him to occupy it tonight or any other night. 'I'll be fine.'

Would she? Somehow he doubted she'd sleep easily.

'Only a fool blames another for his own inadequacies.' The words slipped quietly from his lips, and when she didn't answer, he smoothed his palm along the edge of her cheek. 'And it would take an incompetent fool to allude to a woman's frigidity.' He waited a beat. 'Especially when the woman is *you*.'

He wanted to show her how it could be between a man and a woman, watch as she came alive beneath his touch. To kiss and caress every inch of her, awaken each nerve-end, and be aware only of him. Malleable, mindless, *his*.

Except he wanted her *with* him, mind, body and

soul. Not on edge with nervous tension, or emotionally shaken.

'I think you should leave.' She just wanted to be alone, secure within these four walls, where she could sink into the hot tub, then pull on a robe, view television for an hour before slipping into bed.

'Not yet,' Jace said quietly. Not until she'd regained some colour and her eyes didn't resemble huge pools mirroring a mixture of hurt and shame.

'We were going to have coffee.' A return to the prosaic was the wisest course, and he moved round her, collected the carafe from the coffee-maker and filled it with water.

Rebekah collected her shattered thoughts together and crossed to extract coffee mugs from a cupboard, coffee beans, a fresh filter, and set it all in place.

The automatic movements helped, and within minutes they faced each other across the table as they sipped aromatic coffee.

'Tell me what it was like for you as a child.'

She recognised his diversionary tactic, and cast him a level glance. 'The usual things that shape most children's lives. Love and laughter, a few tears, happy family, school. My mother died a few years ago. Dad has very recently taken a new job in New York.'

'You and Ana are very close.' It was a statement based on his own observation, and her gaze softened.

'We're best friends as well as business partners.'

It was difficult to look at him and not be startlingly aware of the way it had felt to be in his arms, his touch, the intensity of his kiss, and the way he'd been able to transport her to a place where sheer sensation ruled.

There was a part of her that wanted to be taken there again. By him, only him. Just thinking of Jace as a lover brought a flood of heat to her body, and yet instinct warned if she allowed him into her life she'd never be the same again.

Was it worth the risk? Not if she wanted to survive emotionally. This man would invade her senses, her heart, and forever leave his mark.

'You haven't mentioned your marriage.'

The sound of his accented drawl brought her back to the present with a sudden jolt, and she tightened her grip on the coffee mug.

'What do you want to hear? That I was courted by a man for several months, engaged to him for a year, and in all that time I had no inkling a few hours after the wedding he'd turn into an abusive monster?'

He was silent for several long seconds as he held her gaze. 'It must have been hell to deal with.'

And then some. 'And you, Jace? No skeletons in your cupboard?'

'A few regrets.' Everyone had some. 'None of any consequence.'

He wanted to ease the pain he glimpsed in her eyes, but knew she'd deny him if he did. Instead, he drained his coffee, then stood to his feet.

'Time for me to call it a night.' He took his mug into the kitchen and put it in the sink, then he preceded her to the door.

Rebekah caught up her keys and followed him. 'I'll drive you back to the hotel.'

'I'll call a cab from the downstairs lobby.'

'Don't be ridiculous.'

He turned towards her and pressed a finger to her lips, then he lowered his head and brushed his mouth to her temple. 'I'll phone tomorrow.'

She opened her mouth to protest, but he was already walking towards the bank of lifts, and she waited there until the lift doors opened. Then she retreated into the apartment, locked up, set the alarm, and headed for the hot tub.

CHAPTER SEVEN

'HAS Brad been bothering you again?'

Rebekah caught the fierce sisterly concern in Ana's voice, and tried to diffuse a potentially sensitive subject. 'Why do you ask?'

'This is *me*, remember? And I don't fool easily. So spill it.'

Suzie was on a lunch break, and they were alone in the shop.

Rebekah refrained from prevaricating, but she kept it simple. 'You know the score. Every now and again Brad decides to ride the nuisance wagon. So I changed my silent number to minimise the hassle.'

'Uh-huh. This wouldn't have anything to do with the fact you've been seeing Jace?'

It was a rhetorical question, and they both knew it.

'I'm not *seeing* Jace,' she refuted, paying far more attention than necessary to the bouquet she was assembling.

'OK, we won't go there just now.' Ana's gaze held a degree of anxiety. 'Watch your back, Rebekah,' she warned gently. 'Brad is a loose cannon just waiting to explode.'

She controlled the shaky sensation that threatened to visibly exert itself, and met her sister's gaze.

'I'm doing everything I've been legally advised to

do,' she assured quietly. 'It's been two years since the divorce. I'm entitled to a life of my own.'

Ana's expression softened. '*Brava*. You, more than most.' There were assurances she wanted to reiterate, but she wisely held her counsel. 'Promise you'll phone me at the slightest hint of a problem. OK?'

Rebekah offered a wry smile. 'Want me to write it in blood?'

The phone rang, and Ana picked up, intoned the customary greeting, conversed for a few minutes, then held out the cordless receiver. 'For you. Jace.'

'Hi. How are you?'

'Do you really want to know?' His voice was low and husky, almost intimate, and she barely controlled the spiralling sensation deep within.

'How was the flight? Cairns?'

'Fine. Better if you were with me.'

The breath stopped in her throat. 'I have to go, we're really busy.'

She thought she heard his faint chuckle. 'Take care, Rebekah. I'll call you on your cellphone tonight.'

Rebekah handed the cordless receiver to Ana with a lift of her eyebrows. 'Nothing to say?'

'And risk having you jump down my throat?' There was humour in her voice, and her eyes danced with silent mischief. 'No way.'

The afternoon was busy, so much so it was almost seven when Rebekah locked up shop and slid into the van. She planned a shower, then she'd fix a steak salad and eat it with a fresh, crunchy bread roll she'd picked up from the bakery, maybe watch a video she'd rented out.

Summer was definitely on its way, for the days were becoming warmer, she perceived as she swung the van into the driveway leading down to the apartment underground car park.

It took only seconds to insert her key and have the security grille lift to allow her entry, and she eased into her allotted parking bay, cut the engine and gathered her shoulder bag, the leather briefcase with the day's computer print-outs, then she slid from the van and began walking towards the lift.

'Think you're pretty smart, dating another man, don't you?'

Rebekah froze, caught in the grip of fear as Brad stepped out from behind a concrete pillar. Calm, she had to remain calm. Try logic, a silent voice screamed.

'How did you get in here?'

'Use your imagination.'

He was taller, bigger than her, and she recognised the hard glitter in those pale grey eyes, the cruel tilt of his mouth.

Instinct had her gauging the distance to the lift well.

'Forget it,' Brad advised harshly. 'You'll never make it.'

The van...if only she could lock herself in there, she'd be safe. Except she'd locked the door, and by the time she reached it, inserted the key, he'd have caught her.

OK, if she couldn't escape, she had two options. Talk first; if that failed, *fight.*

'I can't think of anything we have to discuss.'

'Wrong, baby.'

She hated his smile, it hid pure venom. 'If I don't ring my sister within five minutes, she'll call the police.'

He recognised her bluff. 'So—call her.'

Rebekah slid open the zip fastening her bag, felt for and found the small canister, then she palmed it as she withdrew her hand, aimed and pressed the spray button.

The mace hit him in the face, and his howl of pain was animal-like in its rage.

Rebekah didn't hesitate, she ran to the lift, hit and held down the button…and prayed. If only she could get inside, she'd be safe.

Oh, come *on*, she begged, agonising if she'd have been wiser to have sought the van and locked herself in. At least she could have used her cellphone to call for help.

There was a faint electronic whine heralding the lift's descent, and she felt her heart thud in her chest as she counted off the seconds to its arrival.

She could hear Brad swearing, his voice rising to a raging crescendo, and then she didn't care any more as the lift doors swung open and she raced inside the cubicle, pushed the seventh-floor button, only to see Brad put his arm between the closing doors.

A scream left her throat, and she stabbed the *close doors* button. To little avail. His strength was accelerated by rage, and she batted his hands with the briefcase, drawing blood.

Fear drove her, and for a few seconds she thought she'd won. Except one herculean burst of strength on Brad's part pushed the doors open sufficiently for him to squeeze through.

She still had the can of mace in her hand, and she used it mercilessly before he had a chance to bring the lift to a stop mid-floor.

The cubicle wasn't large, and even blinded by the stinging mace Brad roared with rage as he lurched, arms spread wide, circling as she strove to evade him in the confined space.

Her only hope was to escape as soon as the lift stopped at the seventh floor, and she quickly identified her apartment key on its keyring, and held it poised in readiness.

There was nowhere to hide, and the timing proved lousy as Brad's hand groped her shoulder, then closed over it with steel-like strength.

A random punch slammed into her ribs, quickly followed by another to her upper arm.

At that moment the lift drew to a halt, and he dragged her out into the foyer.

'Where's your damned key?'

She'd die before she willingly gave it to him, and she wrestled with him, taking a cracking slap to the side of her face.

'Give it to me, bitch!'

Rebekah swung the briefcase at him and he

wrenched it from her grasp, then tackled and knocked her to the floor.

In one desperate move she tossed the keys as hard as she could, uncaring where they landed as long as he couldn't find them.

She heard them hit something with a resounding clunk, felt the bruising grip of Brad's fingers on her flesh, then a loud voice demanding,

'What the hell is going on here?' Followed by, '*Rebekah?* George, get out here!'

There was noise, voices, the sound of scuffling, then mercifully she was free, and hands were soothing her, Maisie, her neighbour, was issuing instructions like a nursing sister-in-charge, her chosen vocation. And her partner, George, an ex-wrestler with a body that was all muscle, held Brad in a bone-crunching grip.

Maisie called the police, helped Rebekah into her apartment, called a doctor, then she collected her camera and took photos for evidence.

Rebekah didn't argue, although she was sufficiently familiar with police procedure to know they'd do the same.

When they came, she gave a statement, which had to be typed up and signed at the police station within the next twenty-four hours. The doctor arrived and examined her, dressed a few abrasions, suggested ice-packs for the bruising, and gave her a sedative to take to help her sleep.

Maisie fussed over her, plying her with water and painkillers.

'Is there someone I should call? Your sister, brother-in-law?'

'I'll do it later.'

Maisie looked doubtful. 'You really should have someone stay with you tonight. Or you should go to your sister's place.'

'I'll be fine.'

'Sure you will. You're as pale as a ghost, and as cold as charity.' She gave a derisive snort. 'If I had anything to do with it, you'd be in hospital overnight.'

Rebekah tried for a smile and didn't quite make it. 'I promise I'll ring Ana the moment you leave.'

'Hmm. Why don't you go take a shower, and I'll rustle up something light for you to eat?' She held up her hand. 'I'll be offended if you refuse.'

It was easier to capitulate. 'Thanks.'

She stayed beneath the hot spray for a while, then, towelled dry, she donned jeans, added a cotton top, and emerged into the kitchen to discover her neighbour removing a plate of delicious-smelling goulash with rice.

'Your sister rang while you were in the shower.'

Rebekah knew the answer even before she posed the question. 'You told her?'

'She had to know. She's on her way over.' Maisie indicated the plate which she set down on the dining-room table. 'Sit and eat.'

'Yes, Mother.'

'I could be, if I'd been a child bride.' She tried to look fierce. 'You need someone to look after you.'

'I have you and George just across the hall.' She

took a mouthful of food and closed her eyes at the taste. 'I know why George married you.'

'Don't change the subject. You need a man in your life.'

'I had one, and look at the way that turned out.'

'A real man, one who'll take care of you.'

'Perhaps I'm content taking care of myself?'

Maisie gave another snort, and filled the kettle to make tea.

In no time at all the intercom buzzed, and Rebekah threw her neighbour a wry glance. 'The cavalry have arrived.'

Ana *and* Luc? There were hugs, expressions of concern, reassurances given, and decisions made.

'You're coming back with us,' Ana said firmly. 'And if you argue, I'll hit you.'

'I rather think she's had more than her fair share of that, *agape mou*,' Luc chided gently, and watched his wife's face crease with remorse.

'I didn't mean— Oh, God, Rebekah,' Ana groaned out loud.

'I know, you just love me to death, is all.'

Rebekah's cellphone pealed, and Luc moved to retrieve it from the coffee-table, where Maisie had placed everything that had spilled from her bag.

'I'll take it, shall I?' He picked up, and moved to one side of the room. His conversation was muted and spanned several minutes, then he retraced his steps and handed her the unit. 'Jace.'

She closed her eyes, then she opened them again and voiced a restrained greeting into the mouthpiece.

'Rebekah—'

Even from a distance she could sense the quiet anger beneath the surface of his control. 'I'm fine.'

'And daisies grow upside-down in the ground.' His voice held an edge she couldn't define. 'Give me your word you'll stay with Luc and Ana for a few days.'

She almost said she'd suffered worse than this. 'Tonight,' she conceded, and heard him mutter something unintelligible. Suddenly she'd had enough, and there wasn't another thing she wanted to hear…much less from a man who'd caused her more emotional highs and lows in one short week than anyone she'd ever known. 'Goodnight.'

Maisie took care of her plate, Ana fed Millie and put down fresh water, while Rebekah gathered up a change of clothes, a few essentials and pushed them into an overnight bag.

Luc crossed to her side as she re-entered the kitchen. 'Ready?'

She inclined her head, thanked Maisie, gave Millie a gentle pat, then she followed everyone out into the lobby while Luc locked up.

Ana sat in the back seat of the Mercedes and caught hold of Rebekah's hand as Luc drove to their palatial home in suburban Vaucluse.

'Do you want to talk about it?'

'Not particularly.' There was little point in rehashing it.

Ana's fingers tightened, and her voice held an uncustomary hardness. 'This isn't going to happen again.'

It was nice, Rebekah had to admit, to be taken care of. Luc and Ana's home was an architectural masterpiece set in beautiful grounds high on a hill with splendid views out over the harbour.

Petros, their politically correct manservant, fussed over her as if she were a precious piece of china. Within minutes of arrival he prepared tea and exquisite bite-size sandwiches.

Luc joined them for a while, then at a telling glance from his wife he excused himself on the pretext of dealing with business email. He brushed a light kiss to Ana's cheek, then crossed to gift Rebekah a similar salutation and departed the room.

Rebekah allowed Petros to refill her cup, and declined anything further to eat.

Ana waited only long enough for the manservant to wheel the tea-trolley from the room before leaning forward in her chair.

'Tell me exactly what happened,' she insisted sternly. 'And don't leave anything out.'

Reliving the episode was emotionally draining, although it helped her deal with it.

'The *bastard*,' Ana derided huskily when Rebekah finished. 'Luc and Jace will ensure he never comes near you again.'

Hang on a minute… '*Jace?* What does Jace have to do with it?' She drew in a deep breath in the hope of assembling a sense of calm. 'While I appreciate Luc's help, I'm quite able to take care of everything myself.'

'It's done,' Ana said simply. 'And you can stop with the fierce expression.'

'Ana—'

'It's time to bring out the big guns,' her sister remonstrated gently. 'Luc and Jace have them...in spades.'

This was getting out of hand. 'Look—'

'No,' Ana declared emphatically. '*You* look. I don't want to wake up one morning and hear Brad has somehow got to you and you're just another statistic in the assault and battery records.' She leaned forward and caught hold of Rebekah's hands. 'I was *there*, remember? When you walked out on him, and afterwards.' Tears filled her eyes. 'Jace is the first man you've dated in a long time. Only to have Brad emerge out of the woodwork and stalk you.' A tear escaped and rolled down her cheek. 'No one, *no one* is ever going to hurt you again. Ever.'

Rebekah felt her stomach curl into a tight ball at her sister's distress. 'Ana, don't. I'm OK. The police have arrested him.'

'Sure, you're OK. Bruised ribs, multiple contusions. Not to mention shock and trauma.' Her voice rose. 'I hate to think what would have happened if he'd dragged you inside the apartment. Or if Maisie and George hadn't been home.'

She caught the fierce determination apparent, and stayed any further protest...for now. *She* might be the victim, but Ana was hurting too. 'You haven't shown me the latest print-out of the babe's ultrasound. Or the radiographer's video clip.'

Ana offered a shaky smile. 'Changing the subject won't change my mind.' She stood to her feet and extended her hand. 'Come on. Let's go see pictures of your foetal niece or nephew.'

It helped to take both their minds off the earlier part of the evening, and it was there Luc found them rewinding the video tape for the third or fourth time.

'Time to call it a night for both of you, hmm?'

Rebekah caught the way his features softened as he took Ana's hands in his and gently pulled her to her feet. He would, she knew, ease his wife's apprehension and be there for her when she stirred through the night.

An ache began deep inside at the thought of being able to sink into the comfort of a man's arms, have his lips brush her forehead, trail over her cheek and settle on her mouth.

'You're to rest tomorrow,' Ana insisted as they ascended the stairs. 'Suzie is competent, and we'll manage. Coming into the shop is a no-no. OK?'

'I'll see how I feel in the morning.' It was a compromise at best, and Ana shot her a dark glance as if divining her thoughts.

'I mean it.'

Rebekah caught her sister's hand and gently squeezed it. 'I know you do.'

'Petros has made up the front guest suite for you, and you're to sleep in. Just come downstairs whenever you feel like breakfast.' Ana's features sharpened a little. 'Are you sure you're OK?'

'Yes,' she reassured. In truth every bone in her

body ached. 'I'm going to have that sedative, hop into bed, and sleep like a baby.'

She did take the sedative, and she did sleep for a few hours, only to wake in the early dawn hours feeling as if her body had been pummelled like a punching bag.

Which it pretty much had, she conceded as she slipped gingerly out of bed and made for the *en suite*.

She snapped on the light and examined her face in the mirror. A bit of concealer would cover the emerging bruise. As to the rest of her…she lifted the nightshirt and grimaced at the swelling on her ribs, the blueish-purplish colour, and knew she was fortunate none of the ribs was broken. Shallow breathing was the order of the day for a while.

There were scratches on her arm, a large, reddish welt on one forearm.

Not nice, not nice at all. But the swelling would subside, the bruises yellow and disappear. Give it a few weeks and all that would remain was the memory.

Rebekah checked her watch and saw it was much too early to dress and go downstairs. Returning to bed and trying to sleep wasn't an option, so she switched on the bedside lamp and leafed through a few glossy magazines Petros had thoughtfully provided.

Rebekah waited until Luc left the house at eight, saw Ana follow him minutes later, then she quickly gathered up her bag and moved quickly downstairs.

Petros was in the midst of clearing the dining-room table, and he turned as she entered the room.

'Good morning,' he greeted warmly. 'I trust you slept well? Ana insisted I shouldn't disturb you.' His gaze took in the bag. 'What can I get you for breakfast?'

It would be useless to say she wasn't hungry. 'Orange juice, toast and coffee will be great.'

One eyebrow arched. 'Might I suggest some fruit and cereal? Eggs with a little ham or bacon? A croissant, perhaps?'

'You're bent on spoiling me.' She took a seat and poured herself a glass of juice. There was fruit on the table, and she selected a banana, peeled and ate it.

'But toast and coffee is fine.'

There was a folded newspaper near by, and she flicked through the pages, read the headlines, her horoscope for the day, and scanned the comic strips. By which time she'd eaten two pieces of toast and had almost finished her second cup of coffee.

Rebekah retrieved her cellphone and punched in the relevant digits to summon a taxi, and she was relaying the address when Petros re-entered the room.

'You intend going somewhere this morning?' the manservant asked as he began clearing dishes.

'I need to go back to my apartment and feed my cat.'

'Luc would be most upset if I allowed you to take a taxi. I'll drive you, whenever you're ready to leave.'

'Nonsense.'

'Please, in this instance I must insist. If you'll tell me which company you called, I'll ring and cancel.'

It seemed easier to capitulate, and twenty minutes

later she slid out of the four-wheel-drive Petros used for transport.

'I'll wait until you're ready to return.'

He wasn't going to like the next part at all. 'I intend remaining at the apartment, Petros.'

His lips pursed in visible disapproval. 'Luc and Ana will be most displeased.'

'I promise I'll ring and explain.' Ana she could handle, and Ana would handle Luc. *Fait accompli.* Besides, in less than half an hour she'd be at the shop.

'Ms Rebekah, I don't think this is a good idea.'

She offered him a sweet smile. 'Thanks for the lift.' Then she turned and used her key to enter the main lobby.

Home, she breathed as she entered her apartment. There was no place quite like your own, and Millie bounded towards her, curling back and forth around her ankles, purring in delighted welcome.

The apartment looked achingly familiar, and she moved through it, straightening a vase on the chiffonier as she made her way to the kitchen.

Fifteen minutes later she'd fed Millie, changed into work clothes, and was on her way to the shop.

'You aren't supposed to be here,' Ana remonstrated the instant Rebekah walked through the door.

'I know everything you're going to say,' she responded firmly as she crossed to the work table and stowed her bag. 'But I'd rather be doing something constructive than swanning on the chaise lounge, idly flipping through the pages of a magazine.'

Take control. Hadn't that been the essence of any

professional advice she'd ever received? 'OK, where are we at?' she queried briskly.

'You've got the morning,' Ana conceded, trying for a fierce look that didn't quite come off. 'Then you're going home.'

'I've got the day,' Rebekah corrected gently. 'And I'll go home when I'm ready.'

'You're impossibly stubborn.'

'And I love you, too.'

Suzie looked from one to the other. 'Are you two going to fight, then make up? Or is this serious stuff and I should take five to let you sort it out alone?'

'Stay,' Rebekah and Ana ordered in unison.

'If you insist. Shall I mediate, or referee?'

'Neither.'

The phone rang, and Ana declared *sotto voce*, 'Saved by the bell.'

The morning was busier than usual with a number of customers coming in from the street. It was late morning when Rebekah took a quick check of their stock and reached for the phone to place an order, then arrange for the courier for delivery.

The electronic buzzer heralded the arrival of another customer, and she glanced towards the door, then stilled as Jace entered the shop.

Shock, surprise were just two of the emotions she experienced. Not the least was speculation as to why he was here when he was supposed to be in Cairns. Had his meetings concluded earlier than he'd anticipated? Yet if so, why wasn't he in Brisbane?

For a moment her gaze locked with his as he stood exuding a silent power that was vaguely frightening.

She watched as he moved towards Ana and offered an affectionate greeting, then he turned and moved towards the table where Rebekah was in the midst of gathering sprays of orchids into a large bouquet.

The nerves inside her stomach gave every impression of performing a series of complicated somersaults, and her fingers faltered as he paused within touching distance.

What could she say? Anything would be superfluous, so she didn't even try as she bore his raking appraisal.

A muscle bunched at the edge of his jaw, and she saw his eyes harden briefly, then he lifted a hand and trailed light fingers over her cheek.

'Get your bag,' he commanded gently. 'I'm taking you home.' He pressed his thumb over her lips as they parted to voice a refusal. 'No argument.' He increased the pressure slightly. 'I'll carry you out of here if I have to.'

Rebekah removed his hand, only, she suspected, because he let her. 'You don't have the right to give me orders.'

'It's a self-appointed role.' His voice was a silky drawl that feathered sensation down the length of her spine.

Everything faded from her peripheral vision. There were just the two of them, fused by an electric awareness that had everything to do with heightened sensuality. Right now she didn't need or want it.

'Go away.'

'Not a chance.'

'Jace—'

'Do you really want to do this the hard way?'

He was capable of implementing his threat despite any resistance on her part, and, given the choice, she'd opt for dignity over embarrassment.

'How did you—?'

'Find out where you were?' he completed. 'It was a process of elimination. First Luc, then Petros, and Ana.'

Rebekah moved slightly, shot her sister a dark glance and was met with a blithe smile. It was nothing less than a conspiracy, and one where the odds were stacked against her.

'There's a lot of work to get through.'

'Nothing Suzie and I can't handle,' Ana assured.

'There you go,' Jace drawled with hateful ease. 'Now collect your bag and we'll get on our way.'

'I have the van. And there is no *we*.'

'Arguing this back and forth isn't going to change a thing.'

'So concede defeat and follow you like a little lamb?' She refrained from adding *to the slaughter*... To no one, least of all this Greek-born American, would she admit she ached all over, her head thumped with pain, and she was fast approaching the need for serious time out.

'I have the car double-parked outside,' Jace informed as she reached for her bag.

'I hope the traffic officer has issued you with a

ticket.' She offered Suzie a wry smile, brushed her lips to Ana's cheek, then preceded Jace from the shop.

'None of this is *your* business,' Rebekah declared as he eased the car out from the busy thoroughfare. She was unsure whether to be relieved or disappointed there hadn't been a parking-violation ticket attached to his windscreen.

'Wrong. My involvement with you started all this.'

'What *involvement*?'

'Don't split hairs, *pedhaki mou.*'

The affectionate 'little one' got to her as she turned towards him. 'You mean you postponed business meetings and flew back to Sydney because you felt *responsible*? That's ridiculous.'

He met her gaze and held it for a few seemingly long seconds. 'Is it?' He returned his attention to negotiating traffic. 'I don't think so.'

'I fail to see the reasons for everyone's concern. I'm OK.' She was tempted to tell him there had been more damaging attacks in the past, only to refrain from the admission.

'Sure you are,' Jace discounted in a dry, mocking tone. 'You were barely standing up in there, pale as a ghost, your eyes dark with pain.' There was underlying anger apparent. 'What were you trying to prove?'

Should she tell him the truth? 'I didn't want to sit and brood.' And I didn't want to be alone, she added silently.

Jace swept the car into the entrance adjacent her apartment.

'Here's fine.' She already had her hand on the door-clasp.

'The hell it is.' He eased the car down the incline leading to the underground car park, and indicated the security lock. 'Give me your key.'

'There's no need for you to personally see me to my apartment door.'

She was a prickly young woman, and one he wanted to kiss senseless one minute and shake sense into the next. 'Just...do it, Rebekah.'

'I don't—'

'Your ex-husband has been released on bail.'

Rebekah stilled at his words, then drew in a slight breath...anything other than *slight* hurt like hell. 'Why am I not surprised?'

Brad's mother was a rich society matron who engaged high-ranking lawyers to protect her only son. On the past two occasions Wilma Somerville had rushed to his defence, blamed Rebekah for instigating the attacks, and threatened dire consequences if an official complaint was filed.

The next time Ana took matters into her own hands and persuaded Rebekah to press charges, only to have Wilma's lawyer release him hours later on bail and later persuade judge and jury Brad was a well-educated, caring man who simply needed a course in anger management. A hefty fine, and he was free.

'You're determined to personally check out my

apartment to see Brad hasn't slipped past security un-detected and may be lurking in wait for me?'

'Something like that.'

Rebekah handed him her key in silence, then when the security grille lifted he drove into the parking bay alongside her MG.

'I very much doubt he'd be so foolish,' she offered as they walked towards the lift.

Jace spared her a direct look. 'I'm not prepared to let you take the risk,' he assured with chilling soft-ness.

She'd decorated her apartment in soft green, cream with a touch of apricot in muted tones. Complemented by modern furniture and same-tone drapes. Her own individual touch, rather than the ascetic perfection of an interior decorator. The ambience was calming and peaceful…her personal sanctuary.

Her small, pale grey-tipped cat sat up on the sofa, surveying him with unblinking solemnity.

'Millie,' Rebekah indicated. 'She's very spoilt, and not used to you yet.' Whereupon Millie proved her mistress wrong by jumping down onto the carpet, padding over to Jace and began winding herself around his legs.

He bent down and fondled Millie's ears. An action which sent the cat into feline ecstasy.

'Must be your natural masculine charm,' Rebekah accorded with wry humour.

Jace straightened and one eyebrow slanted in mock-ing cynicism. 'Why don't you sit down and relax?'

Relax, with you here? she demanded silently. Fat chance. 'Thanks for bringing me home.'

'But please leave?'

'Yes.'

'Think again.'

Her eyes flew wide. 'Excuse me?'

'Independence is a fine thing,' he opined quietly. 'In this instance, there's no way you're staying anywhere alone.'

Anger flared, and it showed in her eyes, the tightening of her mouth. 'Now, look—'

'We've done that,' Jace said in a deceptively mild voice. 'We're not going to do it again.'

'Just who gave you permission to take charge of my life?'

'The decision is mine.'

'Well, you can absolve yourself from any misguided responsibility and go leave me alone.'

'No.'

She was angry before, now she was steaming. 'Brad is unlikely to do anything while he's out on bail. Even his mother's lawyer would have a hard job extricating him from jail if he did.'

His gaze focused on her features, noting the tilt of her chin and the proud determination in those deep sapphire-blue eyes. 'I'm not prepared to risk a repeat of last night.'

She wanted to lash out at him, *hurt* as she'd been hurt. Yet this was the wrong man, and her mind was spiralling in a way that made no sense at all. 'Next you'll tell me you intend staying here all day.'

He was silent for a few long seconds, then he ventured silkily, 'That's the plan.'

It was then she noticed the laptop in his hand. 'You've brought work with you?' Her voice seemed to have acquired a higher pitch, and she met his steady gaze with something akin to disbelief.

'I can work anywhere. Why not here?'

The anger bubbled over. 'You've appointed yourself *babysitter*? I don't believe this...any of it!'

His eyes hardened fractionally. 'Believe it's not open to negotiation.'

CHAPTER EIGHT

REBEKAH reacted without thought and the palm of her hand connected with his cheekbone in a stinging slap.

An entire gamut of emotions chased fleetingly across her expressive features, and Jace divined each and every one of them.

Dear lord in heaven, she'd actually *hit* him! In her eyes it made her no better than Brad. 'I'm sorry.'

The words were huskily voiced so as to be barely audible.

The air seemed filled with electric tension, and she was hardly conscious of breathing.

'Feel better?' he drawled with deceptive mildness.

Innate honesty came to the fore. 'No.'

She missed the faint gleam of humour lurking in the depths of his eyes.

'I picked up some filled bagels on my way to the shop. Why don't we have lunch?' he suggested quietly. 'Afterwards you can rest while I put in a few hours on the laptop.'

'I'm not an invalid,' she protested at once, wanting the afternoon done with so she could be alone. His presence in the apartment unsettled her. *He* unsettled her.

He shot her a level look, then he moved through

to the kitchen, set the bagels on plates and placed them on the dining-room table.

They ate in relative silence, and washed the food down with hot, sweet tea, then Rebekah curled up on the sofa with a magazine while Jace settled himself at the escritoire on the far side of the room.

She must have slipped into a fitful doze, for she woke feeling refreshed, albeit stiff and sore. A quick glance at her watch revealed it was almost five, and she experienced shock to think she'd slept for so long.

Jace glanced up from the computer screen at her first sign of movement, his appraisal swift and encompassing as she straightened and stood to her feet.

He caught the careful way she moved, and contained a renewed surge of anger against the man who'd caused her such pain.

'Feeling rested?'

She looked better, her pale features had acquired a healthy colour, although her eyes were still too dark.

'Yes.'

'Good.' He turned back to the screen and re-immersed himself in scrolling through data.

Rebekah felt the need to freshen up, and she took her time, declining the use of lipstick as she changed into jeans and a cotton-knit top.

As soon as Jace left she'd fill the hot tub, then after a long, leisurely soak she'd grab a bite to eat and crawl into bed with a book.

Millie followed her out into the lounge, then padded towards the kitchen and waited to be fed. Jace barely glanced up from the screen as she passed through.

A slight frown creased her brow as she crossed into the laundry and extracted clothes from the drier, folded and put them away.

'I've ordered in,' Jace informed minutes later. 'I hope you like Chinese.'

She turned towards him slowly. 'I thought you'd return to the hotel.'

'You thought wrong.'

A sudden suspicion occurred. 'I'm fine, if you'd prefer to leave.'

He made two more keystrokes, then closed down the program. 'No.'

'Excuse me?'

'I have no intention of leaving you here alone.'

She felt her stomach execute a few painful somersaults. 'We already had this argument.'

'Then we'll have it again.'

'I don't need to go out from the apartment before tomorrow.' She gestured in the direction of the apartment entrance. 'There's no way anyone can get in unless I open that door.'

'It doesn't change a thing.'

'You can't stay here!'

'Why not? You have a spare bedroom.'

And she could sleep easily in her bed knowing he occupied the room directly across the hall?

'Unless, of course, you invite me to share your bed?'

The element of mockery evident brought her to flashpoint. 'As if that's going to happen!'

The apartment intercom buzzer was an insistent, intrusive sound, and after a moment's hesitation she crossed to pick up the receiver, only to have Jace lift it from her hand.

Minutes later he collected their Chinese take-out, paid the delivery boy, then he unpacked the bag onto the table.

Not long after they'd eaten she gathered clean sheets from the linen cupboard and handed them to him.

'The spare room is down the hallway on the left. Feel free to watch television. I'm going to bed. Goodnight.'

She turned and walked towards her room, closed the door, then she took a shower, slid into bed and snapped off the light.

She was running, but she didn't seem to be gaining distance in her attempt to reach a safe place. And it was dark, very dark, with only brief prisms of light.

Where was she? Nothing was familiar. Only an awareness of being outdoors, damp grass, tall trees, then there was dense undergrowth that caught on her clothes, gnarled tree roots, and the dank smell associated with the cyclic rebirth, growth and decay of plant life.

Thunder rolled across the sky, followed by forked lightning, and behind her she could hear the echo of her own frantic passage towards safety.

Except it was foe, not friend, and a mental image of Brad in the role of her attacker flooded her brain.

She tripped over an exposed tree root, and she cried out as she went down. There was an imperviousness to pain as she scrambled to her feet and staggered into a running gait, fleeing as he gained on her.

Then, miraculously, the undergrowth cleared, the trees disappeared, and there was smooth lawn, a house with all its lights blazing. A beacon offering her sanctuary.

She picked up speed and ran towards it, but no matter how hard she tried she couldn't close the distance and the house remained out of her reach.

Just as she began to despair she drew close, and she was at the front door, her hand on the knob, praying it would open and not be locked.

Her relief was palpable as it swung open to her touch, and as she turned to close it Brad was there, wrenching the door from her grasp.

She screamed, pushing all her weight against it in an attempt to prevent his entry. Except it was hopeless, her strength no match for his as he forced it open.

Then she turned and ran, blindly seeking the stairs in the hope of reaching a bedroom where she could close and lock herself in.

Only to have him catch her just as she reached the landing, and she cried out as his hands closed over her arms. Screamed as they moved to her shoulders.

She heard him swear, then his voice calling her name…

The scene began to change and fade, and she was no longer on the floor, she was in her bed in the apartment, the voice repeating her name bore an American accent, and the man grasping her shoulders wasn't Brad.

This man's features portrayed concern, his facial muscles reassembling over broad-sculptured bone as concern was replaced with relief. Chillingly bleak eyes riveted hers, trapping her in his gaze for seemingly long seconds before the bleakness faded.

'Jace?' What was he doing here? It was late, she was in bed, the bedside lamp was switched on…and then she remembered.

He caught each fleeting emotion and gauged every one. 'You were having a nightmare.'

Rebekah shivered, still partly caught up in it. All she'd need to do was close her eyes and she'd become immersed in the darkness again.

'Would you like a drink?'

She became aware of the man sitting on the edge of her bed, his jeans, the unbuttoned shirt, the slightly tousled hair.

This close she was suddenly conscious of her own attire, the thin cotton nightshirt, the rumpled bedcovers.

There was a sense of intimacy apparent, something exigent beneath the surface that would ignite and flare at the slightest touch, the faintest move.

Rebekah unconsciously held her breath, unable to tear her eyes away from his. She swallowed the lump that had risen in her throat. 'Please.' Anything to have him shift away.

Yet when he did she felt a strange sense of loss, which was crazy. There was a compulsive need to straighten the bedcovers, and she finger-combed her hair, then winced as bruised muscles made themselves felt.

Jace returned with a glass part-filled with chilled water, and she took it from him, had several sips before placing the glass onto the bedside pedestal.

'Thanks.' *Please,* just go, she begged silently. She felt acutely vulnerable, and way too disturbed by his presence.

'Want to talk about it?' His dark eyes seared hers, lingered, then trailed to her mouth.

'Not particularly.'

He lifted a hand and brushed the tips of his fingers to a large bruise on her arm, and she quivered beneath his touch.

'How often did he do this to you?'

She wanted to protest it was none of his business, except the words never left her lips. An admission would raise the query as to why she'd stayed after the first attack. Brad's tears, his apparent horror and remorse at his actions, together with his fervent promise it would never happen again had influenced her to forgive him. Until the next time.

'Does it matter?'

'Yes.' There was steel beneath the silkiness, an expression she couldn't define in those dark eyes.

His hand moved to cup her jaw, and his thumb

caressed the tender flesh Brad had slapped with a hard palm, then he threaded his fingers through her hair.

Rebekah felt as if they were enmeshed in some elusive sensual spell. 'I think you'd better leave,' she voiced shakily.

Yet the words were at variance with her emotions.

There was a part of her that ached to invite this man's touch, to reach out and seek the comfort he could provide.

Oh, dear lord, just to be held close and feel the press of his lips against her temple, the beat of his heart against her own. To feel safe and protected.

Except it was more than that, much more.

She wanted, *needed* the touch of his hands, his lips on her body. She wanted *him*.

She didn't want to analyse the *why* of it. To agonise whether she should or shouldn't, or what might come after.

There was no room for wisdom, just innate need.

Her eyes ached with it, and tears rose to the surface to shimmer in the lamp-light.

He leant forward and brushed his lips to hers in a kiss that was gently evocative, and her mouth trembled slightly as she sought control over her wayward emotions.

Her lashes fluttered down in a desperate bid to close out the sight of him. It didn't work, nothing worked, for she still did battle with her sensory perception of him...his clean male scent, the warmth and the passion. Especially the passion, *there* but held in tight control.

She felt his mouth shift to the bruise on her shoulder, then slip to caress another, and something deep inside slowly unfurled and began to melt.

Were some of the carefully erected barriers coming down? Her skin was silk, and scented with a delicate perfume he failed to recognise. He wanted to obliterate the taint of Brad's touch, replace it with his own and show her how the loving could be. The intense pleasure, the acute ecstasy experienced by two people in complete accord.

The words could come later. For now there was only the tactile sensation of touch, the silent communication of want and need in the slight tremor of her body, the fast-beating pulse at the edge of her throat, and heat…hers, his, as he trailed his lips up to fasten on her own in a kiss that dispensed with any inhibitions and encouraged her response.

It was everything she craved for, evocative, erotic, with an edge of hunger that tugged at her soul. A sigh rose and died in her throat as she angled her mouth to his and deepened the kiss.

The only part of him touching her was his mouth, and he used it to devastating effect, sweeping her to a place where there was only the moment and the electrifying sensual chemistry they shared.

Rebekah cupped his face and kept his mouth on hers until he gently removed her hands as he trailed kisses down her throat and edged to the soft swell of her breast.

He eased the edges of her nightshirt aside and savoured the rounded contours before laving a tender peak.

Sensation arrowed through her body and she arched against him, only to groan out loud as he shamelessly suckled there.

With care he freed the remaining buttons on her nightshirt and the breath hissed between his teeth as he caught sight of the bruised swelling on her ribcage.

Rebekah closed her eyes against the dark anger evident, only to have them open in stunned surprise as he pressed his lips to each and every bruise in turn.

Jace trailed a hand to the curve of her waist, then rested over her hip before slipping low to tangle in the soft hair at the apex of her thighs.

It was almost too much as his lips traced a similar path, and she cried out loud as he bestowed the most intimate kiss of all.

He sensed her shocked disbelief, the sudden stillness, and felt something twist in his gut at the instinctive knowledge her ex-husband had never gifted her this form of oral pleasure. A man who was selfishly insensitive to consider his own satisfaction without thought for his partner?

Her climax when it came took her unawares, for she hadn't imagined there could be more, much more than she'd already experienced, and she gasped as he took her high again and again until she reached for him.

His skin was smooth as thick-textured satin, and she exulted in the feel of hard sinew and muscle as she freed him of his shirt.

Dear heaven, he was built with well-developed musculature, a taut waist, and washboard midriff.

It was easy to unsnap his jeans and slide the zip down, then pull them off with his help. His briefs followed, and she had a bad moment wondering if she could accommodate him.

There was an elemental quality apparent, a base, primitive need she was unable to ignore as she became caught up in the sexual thrall of him.

His hands skimmed the surface of her skin, shaping her body as he explored all the pleasure spots with the sureness of a man who knew where and how to touch to drive a woman wild.

He took her to the brink of sexual anticipation, and held her there until she begged for release, then he entered her with exquisite care, moving slowly as she stretched to fit him.

It was like nothing she'd experienced before as she absorbed his length, and she cried out as he began to withdraw, only to ease forward in a slow rhythm as old as time, lengthening each stroke and increasing its pace until she accepted and matched it.

Together they moved in unison towards a climactic explosion that shattered all of her preconceived beliefs.

Her whole body was like a finely tuned instrument beneath a master's touch, responding as it never had before. As she'd never imagined it could, she decided hazily as every nerve sang with elated pleasure.

This...*this* was how it was supposed to be. Two

people together, sharing a sensual feast that culminated in the ultimate pleasure.

Not the quick slaking of lust that Brad had subjected her to in the name of love before he rolled off her and fell asleep.

Jace was still joined with her, his lips intent on trailing a lingering path to her breasts, where they caressed and teased, then suckled there.

Tiny darts of sensation arrowed through her body, and she traced the length of his spine with her fingertips, exploring each indentation until she reached his buttocks.

She felt them clench beneath her touch, and her lips parted in a secret smile, only to gasp out loud as he began to move, slowly stroking deep within until she caught the rhythm and joined him in the ride.

Afterwards he kissed her, taking her mouth in a gentle imitation of the sexual act itself, then he gathered her in close against him and held her until she slipped into an exhausted sleep.

It was in the early dawn hours that she stirred, and, half-asleep, began to move a little, unconsciously changing position…hazily aware something was preventing her. *Someone,* she determined seconds later.

Instant recall followed, and with it came the inevitable *ohmygod* moment. *What had she done?*

Like a giant jigsaw puzzle the pieces fell into place. The nightmare, crying out, Jace, and sex. Hell, she had a vivid recollection of the sex!

'Don't,' a husky male voice adjured close to her ear.

Rebekah stilled at the sound of that deep, slightly accented drawl, and her breath seemed to lock in her throat as one hand slid to her hip while the other took possession of her breast.

'Please. Let me go.'

His lips brushed her temple and trailed to settle at the sensitive curve at her neck. 'Stay, *agape mou*.'

'My lover'. This was all wrong. It was he who should go, not her.

'Last night was—'

'A mistake?'

Oh, God. She closed her eyes, then opened them again. It had been the most beautiful experience of her life. And she could hardly blame him for the seduction. She'd wanted him as much as he appeared to want her.

'No.'

She felt his lips move to form a smile. 'Your honesty is charming.'

'It—can't happen again,' she managed, feeling wretched. She'd never been promiscuous in her life. Brad had been her first and only lover.

'Why not, *pedhaki mou*?'

He sounded vaguely amused, and she shifted, then froze as she became aware of his arousal. 'Because it can't.' It didn't help that his mouth was intent on completing a treacherous path along the slope of her shoulder.

'Uh-huh. *Because,* hmm?'

Warmth was stealing through her veins. 'Stop that.' It was a weak admonition, and they both knew it.

'You don't want me to do this?' He shifted, drawing her to lay on her back as he leaned over her and let his lips drift over her breast. 'Or this?' He caught one tender peak between his teeth and took her to the edge between pleasure and pain.

One hand splayed over her stomach, then moved low to tangle in the soft curls, and pleasure arrowed through her body as he effortlessly located the sensitive clitoris.

It took only seconds for her to scale the heights, and he held her there, enjoying her delectation, then he took possession of her mouth as she began to fall.

It wasn't enough, Rebekah decided hazily. It would never be enough. And she reached for him, welcoming the sure, hard length of him as he slid inside her.

Afterwards Rebekah lay entwined in post-coital languor, enjoying the gentle drift of fingers in a lazy, exploratory path over his warm skin.

It felt so *right*, being here like this.

They were both adults, they weren't in a relationship with someone else... At least, she wasn't. But what about Jace?

She wasn't prepared for the way apprehension feathered along the edge of her spine. What if he was just amusing himself—?

'No.' Jace slid a hand beneath her chin and tilted it so she had to look at him. 'No,' he reiterated quietly, and her eyes widened.

'No—what?'

'I number several women among my friends, but none to whom I owe my fidelity.'

'You read minds?'

'Yours isn't difficult to interpret.' With a slow smile Jace slid to his feet and strolled naked into the *en suite*.

Rebekah took pleasure in the look of him, the breadth of shoulder, the splendid musculature of his back, the tapered waist and lean, tight butt.

Just thinking about the intimacy they'd shared brought a renewed surge of heat, and a repeated longing to experience once again the incandescent sensation he was able to arouse.

Soon she'd go take a shower, dress, make breakfast, then head into the shop. And Jace? Would he take a flight back to Cairns or Brisbane and complete his reorganised business meetings?

Then what would happen? She'd return to her day-to-day life while he tied up his Australian connection, after which he'd return to New York.

Rebekah was unprepared for the devastation that hit at the thought of him leaving. Even more unconscionable was the possibility of not seeing him again.

Maybe she could have survived with her emotions intact if it hadn't been for last night. Now she didn't have a hope in hell.

Fool, she castigated in silence. She should never have allowed him to stay, and should have banished him from her bedroom the moment he entered it.

Except she hadn't. Now she had to live with it.

Jace re-entered the room and his gaze narrowed as he interpreted her expressive features. Doubts and reflective thought he could deal with. Regret was something else.

He watched her eyes widen as he closed the distance between them, and he resisted the temptation to join her in bed. Instead he tugged the sheet free and scooped her into his arms and returned to the *en suite*.

'What are you doing?'

Another woman would have offered a feline purr, wound her arms round his neck and pressed her mouth to his.

Rebekah sounded apprehensive, and totally devoid of any musing coquetry.

A muscle clenched at the edge of his jaw in recognition of what she'd become beneath her ex-husband's hand.

'Sharing the hot tub with you.' His drawl held an element of humour, and he successfully prevented any protest by the simple expediency of closing her mouth with his own.

It was sheer magic. The pulsing water, the touch of his hands as he gently massaged scented bath oil into her skin. She wanted to close her eyes and have him administer to her forever.

How long did she have? Three, four days…a week at the most.

Rebekah knew she should stop it now. Climb out of the hot tub, catch up a towel, advise him to do the same, then say…*what? Thanks, that was great. Maybe we can do it again some time?*

There could be no doubt this was just a brief interlude. To think it could be anything else was ridiculous.

Besides, her life was all mapped out. Blooms and Bouquets was her focal priority. She had a flourishing business, a nice apartment, a late-model car. What else could she want?

A man she could trust. Someone to be there for her, as she would be for him. To share the love and the laughter, the few tears and sorrow fate might provide in their lifetime. Children. The whole package.

Was it too much to hope for?

Not just any man. *This* man.

The revelation poleaxed her. For a shock-filled second she thought she might actually have blacked out.

'Rebekah?'

Oh, God. Get a grip on reality. 'It must be getting late. I need to get to the flower market, organise the day's orders.' She was babbling, her hands already reaching for the marbled surround as she rose to her feet.

A startled yelp emerged from her throat as Jace's hands closed over her waist, and she struggled as he pulled her down in front of him, then caged her within his arms.

'I have to go.'

'No,' he refuted. 'You don't.'

'Jace…' She broke off with a groan of despair as his mouth savoured the sensitive curve of her neck.

'An hour, hmm? Just an hour.'

It was closer to two before she slid behind the

wheel, fired the engine and sent the MG up onto street level.

Jace occupied the passenger seat, and minutes later she eased the car to a smooth halt outside his hotel entrance.

'Have a good day.' It was an automatic phrase, and when he leaned forward she offered her cheek, only to have him take her face in his hands and bestow an evocatively deep open-mouthed kiss.

When he released her there was delicate pink colouring her cheeks, a soft, tremulous smile parted her lips, and her eyes held slumberous warmth.

It was a look he'd deliberately sought, and one he could easily become accustomed to without any trouble at all.

CHAPTER NINE

THE rising sun coloured the landscape, promising warmth as the day progressed, and Rebekah covered the relatively short distance to the shop in record time.

The Blooms and Bouquets van was already parked out back, which meant Ana had completed an early run to the flower markets. Something she'd intended to take care of, except something...*someone*, she corrected, had caused a delay.

The scent of flowers filled her nostrils as soon as she opened the shop door, and she breathed it in, loving the delicate fragrances.

'You shouldn't be here,' Ana protested. 'At least not this early.' Her gaze sharpened, then narrowed fractionally. 'There's something different about you.'

Rebekah crossed to the work table and stowed her bag. 'I'm fine.'

'Very much *fine*. You're almost glowing.'

Her sister was a kindred soul and far too perceptive for Rebekah's peace of mind. 'A good night's sleep works wonders.'

'Or not much sleep and a long night's loving,' Ana teased. 'Ah, you're blushing.' Her smile held a witching mischievousness. 'It has to be Jace.' The man was incredibly resourceful if he'd managed to infiltrate the emotional barriers Rebekah had erected. If he toyed with her and broke her heart, she'd kill him.

'Are you going to tell me?'

Rebekah shot her sister a steady look. 'Yes, it's Jace. And no, I'm not going to tell you.'

'Spoilsport.' Her expression sobered. 'How are the bruises?'

'It'll take a few days.'

'More like a week or two,' Ana corrected. 'Luc has employed private security to keep a watchful eye on the premises.'

It was understandable Luc wouldn't risk anything happening to his wife or unborn child.

'Shall we get to work?' Rebekah suggested.

The day proved to be busier than usual, and the phone calls many. Mostly business-oriented, but Rebekah took a call from the police relating to a required clarification in her statement, and her lawyer.

Jace rang mid-morning, and again mid-afternoon.

Just the sound of his voice was enough to send her pulse racing to a faster beat.

All day she'd been caught up with the memory of what they'd shared through the night and early this morning. After almost three years of celibacy she was conscious of highly sensitised tissues and nerve-endings as a result of his possession. Each shattering climax had been more intense than the last, and even now just the thought brought heat pooling deep inside.

There was no contact from Brad, but then she hadn't expected there to be. His mother, his lawyer, the police…each would have warned him of the consequences involved if he dared risk another personal confrontation.

Looking back, she damned herself for not realising Brad had an obsessive-possessive personality. He'd been a consummate actor, fooling everyone. Except his mother and the medical and legal advisors hired to protect him.

Jace walked into the shop just as she was about to close up for the evening, and she felt the familiar jolt of her heart at his presence as he stood waiting while she shut down the computer, checked the locks, then set the alarm prior to vacating the premises.

He brushed his lips to her temple. 'Busy day?'

'Yes.' Her stomach turned a somersault or two, then settled down. 'We filled more than the usual orders.'

Jace pressed a finger to the generous curve of her mouth. 'How are you?'

So intensely aware of you, I feel as if every nerve-end is fizzing with active life. 'Fine.'

His slow smile held a degree of sensual warmth. 'Feel like driving to Watson's Bay and eating seafood while the sun goes down over the ocean?'

'You don't need to do this,' Rebekah said quietly as they walked to her car.

'Take you out to dinner?' he queried as he slid into the passenger seat beside her.

'Act the part of bodyguard,' she qualified, and sensed a sudden stillness apparent.

'You want to run that by me again?'

There was silk in that accented drawl, and it raised all her fine body hairs in self-protective defence.

'I don't want you to feel obligated in any way just because—'

'We had sex?'

It hadn't been just *sex*. She'd had sex with Brad for the few brief months she'd lived with him as his wife. Last night she'd been made love to for the first time in her life. There was, she had to admit, a world of difference between sex and lovemaking.

'Want to start over?' Jace offered with dangerous softness.

She waited a beat as she released her breath. 'I think so.'

Jace caught the slight quiver at the edge of her mouth, and wasn't sure at that precise moment whether he wanted to shake her or kiss her senseless.

'Good.' He indicated the key she held poised in her hand ready to insert into the ignition. 'Suppose you drive, and we'll discuss this further over dinner.'

The restaurant Jace suggested was a converted bath-house erected in the days long gone by to service the day trippers who visited the bay to swim and picnic.

Now it was a fashionably trendy place to eat, with an excellent menu and superb food.

It was a pretty beach, and the ocean waters were dappled with reflected sunlight. Soon the natural light would fade, and the moon would rise to provide a silver pathway from the horizon.

Jace managed to secure a table by the window, and

he ordered wine while Rebekah checked out the menu.

A prawn risotto and side salad appealed, and Jace selected something more substantial containing a variety of seafood.

'Let's dispense with the obligation issue,' he began as soon as the waiter retreated in the direction of the kitchen. He leaned back in his chair and subjected her to a thoughtful appraisal. 'My interest in you is entirely personal. Not a misguided sense of responsibility or duty due to an extended family loyalty. Or merely a means of protecting you from your ex-husband,' he revealed with dispassionate imperturbability, then added with deadly softness,

'What we shared last night. What was that? Just great sex, no emotional involvement?'

There was knowledge apparent in his dark gaze she couldn't deny. 'No.'

The waiter brought their starters and presented them with practised flair, while the drinks steward topped their glasses.

'I want to be with you. My hotel suite,' Jace elaborated. 'Your apartment. It hardly matters which, as long as we're together.'

She swallowed the lump that had suddenly risen in her throat. 'You're taking a lot for granted.'

His gaze seared hers. 'You think I'm playing a game? Using you for sex? *Amusing* myself with you?'

Oh, my, he didn't hesitate to spell it out. In a boardroom he'd be a ruthless aggressor, a feared adversary.

'Which one, Rebekah?' he pursued relentlessly. 'Or do you imagine it's all three?'

Dear heaven. 'I don't know.' She could be equally fearless. 'Only that whatever it is, it has a very limited time-span.'

'Does it?'

She was breaking up inside. 'Your life is in New York. Mine is here.'

His gaze narrowed, and when he spoke his voice was a silk drawl. 'With no possibility of a compromise?'

She met his gaze and held it. 'Your definition of *compromise* is what? You fly into Sydney when you can spare the time between cementing corporate deals? I take a week's break here and there throughout the year and visit New York?' She was on a roll, and couldn't stop. 'We meet halfway? Enjoy full-on sex for as long as it takes, then bid each other a fond farewell at the airport, smile and say *that was great, we'll consult our schedules and work out another date*, then take separate flights to different destinations on opposite sides of the world?'

He was silent for so long she became increasingly nervous. 'Are you done?' he queried with deceptive mildness.

'Yes.'

Rebekah picked up her cutlery and began eating, although her tastebuds appeared to have gone on strike, and she had to consciously control her hands to prevent them from shaking.

She had only to look at Jace to vividly recall his

kiss, the touch of his hands, his mouth on her body. It was almost indecent to feel the heat sing through her veins, tripping her pulse and causing her heart to thud in her chest.

The degree of intimacy they'd shared brought a tinge of soft pink to her cheeks.

After last night her life would never be the same. And that was an admission she had no intention of verbalising.

Rebekah finished her starter, picked at her main, declined dessert, and ordered coffee.

'I didn't thank you,' she ventured quietly as she spooned sugar into the dark brew.

'For what, specifically?'

Coming to my rescue? Dropping everything and flying to Sydney? Putting me first above important business meetings? 'Ensuring my safety.' It didn't seem adequate. 'It was kind of you.'

He considered the word, reflected on it a little. 'I think we've gone way past *kind*.'

'I hope it hasn't interrupted your business meetings.'

'So polite,' Jace gently mocked. 'I have an early-morning flight to Brisbane, followed by an afternoon meeting on the Gold Coast. I'll be back early evening.'

She needed to ask. 'When do you return to New York?'

'Sunday.'

That left only a few days. She felt as if her whole world had suddenly shifted on its axis. Soon he'd be gone, and the thought of him not being a constant in her life affected her more than she was prepared to admit.

How could she be so contrary? Fighting against allowing him into her life for days, and now she didn't want him to leave. It hardly made any sense.

A hollow feeling settled in her stomach, and she pushed her coffee to one side, unable to swallow another mouthful.

Jace watched the fleeting emotions chase each other across her expressive features. She was a piece of work, so incredibly beautiful with a sweetness that went right to the depths of her soul. Was she aware how easily he could read her? It was the one thing that had kept him sane during the past ten days.

'Finished?' He didn't wait for her answer as he signalled the *maître d'* for the bill, paid it on presentation, then he caught hold of her hand and led her out to the car.

'I'll drop you at the hotel,' Rebekah indicated as they entered the outskirts of Double Bay.

'A token resistance?'

Her stomach executed a backwards flip at his drawled query. 'I have to be at the flower markets before five in the morning, and I need some sleep.'

'So, we sleep,' Jace said imperturbably.

'I really think—'

'We've done this already.'

'*You* might have. The jury's still out with me.'

She was aware he shifted slightly in his seat. 'All

you have to say is you don't want to share the same bed with me.'

Rebekah opened her mouth to say the words, then bit them off before the first one could escape her lips. She couldn't do it, for to deny him was to deny herself.

Millie greeted them as soon as they entered the apartment, miaowing in protest because she hadn't been fed. Something Rebekah attended to at once, and was rewarded with a brief purr and a swishing tail as the cat tucked into her food.

The message-light on the answering machine was blinking, and showed three recorded messages. The first was her father in New York, then Ana with a reminder for the morning. Brad followed with sibilant invective damning Luc and Jace Dimitriades, and promising Rebekah would pay, big-time.

'Don't erase it,' Jace commanded quietly. 'Let it run in case he rings again.'

'He will.' She was certain of it.

'Each call will become another strike against him in court.'

Not too much of a strike, she accorded silently. His mother and her lawyers were a formidable team.

'I'm going to hit the shower.' Rebekah turned and moved down the hall to her bedroom.

Minutes later she stood beneath the warm spray of water, soap in hand as she lathered her skin. The subtle rose-scent misted with the steam, and she gave a startled yelp as the door slid open and Jace stepped behind her.

She didn't have a chance to say a word as he turned her round to face him, then his mouth captured hers in a gentle, evocative kiss that tugged at her heart-strings.

'You shouldn't be here,' Rebekah managed the instant he lifted his head a little, and she glimpsed his musing smile as he shaped her face with his hands.

'Uh-huh.'

He angled his mouth over hers, and this time he went deep, sweeping her emotions to unbelievable heights where there was no sense of time or place, just the heat of intense eroticism.

How long had they remained like this? she wondered with bemused bewilderment when he slowly broke the kiss. Long seconds, or several minutes?

He had the most beautiful face, she decided, taking her fill of him. Dark eyes merging from the deepest grey to black, a facial bone structure to die for, and a mouth that was heaven on earth.

She possessed the strongest inclination to lean in against him, press her head to the curve of his shoulder, and just rest there. To have him close his arms around her, and know nothing, no one, could touch her.

Jace put his hands on her shoulders and turned her away from him, then he began massaging her nape, the tense muscles at the edge of her neck, her shoulders.

There were kinks, and he eased them out, working at each one until she sighed in gratitude.

It felt so darned good, she simply closed her eyes

and went with it, exulting in his touch, the magic he seemed able to generate without any effort at all.

'Better?'

Rebekah lifted her head and breathed an almost inaudible, 'Yes,' as he gently turned her round to face him. 'Thanks.'

He caught up the soap and placed it in her hand.

'Return the favour, *pedhaki mou.*'

Her eyes widened as she registered a delightful mix of surprise and reservation.

'Too big an ask?'

To soap that masculine frame...all over? Maybe she could skip certain parts of his anatomy... Although it seemed ludicrous to feel reticent after last night.

She didn't trust herself to speak, and began lathering his chest, completing the upper part of his body, his arms, shoulders, then she stepped behind him and rubbed the soap over the muscular curve of his back, his buttocks, the backs of his thighs. Then she moved in front of him and handed him the soap.

'You can do the rest.'

His arousal was a potent force, and a soft pink coloured her cheeks.

'Too shy?'

The pink deepened, and she reached for the shower door, only to have him halt her escape.

'Stay, *agape mou.*' The husky plea undid her, and she looked at him blindly as he drew her round to face him. 'I want to pleasure you a little, then I'll take you to bed...to sleep, I promise.'

She stood mesmerised as his hands shaped her breasts, and brushed the tender peaks with the pad of his thumbs.

Liquid fire coursed through her veins, and a husky groan sighed from her throat as his lips sought the vulnerable hollow at the base of her neck, savoured there, then gently bit the soft flesh, soothed it, then trailed to the slope of her breast, where he suckled until she dragged his head away and pulled his mouth down to hers.

Her mouth was firm, her tongue an exploratory tease, and he let her run free with it, enjoying her touch as his hand trailed low over her hip, then slipped low to caress the sensitive moist folds, felt the clitoris swell and harden...and absorbed her cries as she went up and over. Again, and again.

She *ached* to feel him deep inside her, and in one fluid movement she linked her hands together at his nape, then lifted herself to straddle his hips, where she created a sensual friction that had him groaning out loud.

'Witch,' he accorded in a husky voice an instant before she sank down onto him, absorbing his length to the hilt in one slow slide. His hands cupped her buttocks as they began to rock, long, leisurely movements that increased in pace as they scaled the heights, poised at the brink, then tumbled together into a glorious free fall.

Afterwards they stepped from the shower stall, and Jace caught up a towel, fastened it at his hips, then he caught up another and dried the moisture from her body.

The bruises had become more colourful, and looked vivid against the paleness of her skin.

Jace swore low in his throat and would have said more in castigation, except Rebekah pressed a finger to his lips.

'Don't. It's done.'

He swept an arm beneath her knees and carried her into the bedroom, then he pulled back the covers, settled her down onto the mattress and slid in to curl her close in against him.

Exhaustion brought an easy sleep, and contentment kept her there until the alarm buzzed loud in the early pre-dawn hours.

'Stay there,' Rebekah bade as Jace slid from the bed and pulled on his trousers.

'I'll make coffee while you dress.' He snapped the waist fastening closed, and she gathered up fresh underwear and headed towards the *en suite*.

There was coffee perking in the coffee-maker when she entered the kitchen, and she tried not to be caught up by the look of him as she collected a cup and filled it with the aromatic brew.

Lean-hipped, bare-chested, olive-textured skin covering splendid musculature, his hair tousled, and a night's beard shadowing his features, he was something else.

'Problem?'

He was the problem. A very big problem. And it was getting worse with every day, and *night*, that passed.

Sunday. The word seemed to reverberate inside her head. On Sunday he leaves. Two nights he'd stayed over, and already she couldn't bear the thought of him not being here.

How could she become so attached to someone so soon? It didn't make sense. None of it made any sense.

Rebekah finished her coffee, then she crossed to the sink, rinsed the cup, then caught up her shoulder bag.

'I have to go.'

'You didn't answer the question.'

How could she say she'd miss him dreadfully? Or that her heart would break a little when he left?

His gaze was steady, his eyes dark with an expression she couldn't define as she stumbled to find the words.

'I appreciate you being here.' It was as close as she could get, and his mouth curved at the edges.

'I'll come down to see you safely into your car.'

He glimpsed her slight confusion. 'Have you got a spare key I can use to get back in here?'

She did, and she fetched it, gave it to him, then walked to the door.

The basement car park was well-lit, and as silent as a concrete tomb. This morning it seemed eerie, and she suppressed a faint shiver as she slid in behind the wheel.

Jace shut the door, and watched as she reversed out, then drove towards the ramp leading up to street level.

CHAPTER TEN

FRIDAY was always a busy day at the shop, with numerous orders to fill, deliveries to be ready on time for the courier, and they had two weddings booked for Saturday.

'We'd like to have you and Jace join us for dinner tonight,'

Ana issued soon after she arrived. 'Luc spoke to Jace before I left and he's deferred the decision to you.'

It sounded a lovely idea. 'Thanks, that'll be great. What time?'

'Seven?' Ana's eyes sparkled with humour. 'Petros said to tell you he'll make moussaka.'

'And dolmades?' Rebekah said hopefully.

'I'll ring and tell him.'

With Ana manning the telephone and the computer, Rebekah and Suzie worked with efficient speed, taking minimum breaks for lunch. By day's end everything was done, preparations were in place for Saturday, the market requirements tabled.

'All done,' Suzie said with satisfaction. 'Will you be OK if I leave now?'

'Sure. See you tomorrow.'

Jace was waiting as Rebekah locked up, and she

handed him the keys to the MG while she slid into the van.

Ten minutes later they rode the lift up to her apartment, and after a quick shower she selected a simple bias-cut dress in topaz-blue, added stiletto-heeled pumps, applied minimum make-up, then she caught up an evening purse and emerged into the lounge.

Jace was intent on televised news coverage, and he turned towards her as she entered the room. His smile was warm and her pulse tripped then raced to a faster beat.

'Ready?'

It was a few minutes before seven as Jace brought the MG to a smooth halt immediately adjacent the main entrance to Luc and Ana's home.

Petros opened the front door before they had a chance to ring the bell, then Ana was there with Luc to greet and usher them indoors.

'We'll have time for a drink before Petros serves dinner,' Ana informed as she moved into the lounge.

True to Ana's promise, Petros served dolmades as a starter, followed it with moussaka and delicate slices of lamb, and presented a magnificent fruit flan for dessert.

Rebekah chose to join her sister and accepted mineral water, leaving the men to drink superb red wine with their meal.

Petros was in the midst of clearing the table prior to serving coffee when the house cellphone rang, and he moved to one side, extracted the unit, spoke briefly, then handed it to Luc.

The conversation was brief, and Luc's tone sufficiently serious to warrant concern as he ended the call.

'That was the police reporting a break-in at Blooms and Bouquets. Someone was seen hurling a brick through the front window.' Luc spared Rebekah a level look. 'The culprit's been caught and identified.'

'Brad.' It was more of a statement than a question, and Luc inclined his head in acquiescence.

'We need to organise for someone to board up the window,' Ana said at once. 'Is there any other damage?'

'I'll go down with Rebekah,' Jace indicated as Luc put through a call to an emergency repair service.

Please God, don't let it be too bad, Rebekah pleaded silently as Jace drove down to the shop. It wasn't any great distance, and he pulled the car to a halt on the opposite side of the road.

A police car was parked adjacent the shop doorway, and Rebekah presented documentation as proof of ownership, then she unlocked the front door and entered the shop.

It was a mess. Vases were overturned, flowers strewn on the floor, and there was water pooling everywhere.

She felt sick, sickened at the degree of vengeance that had caused Brad to go to this extreme. The risk of being seen and caught was high, for the area bordered on the trendy café district, and was consequently well-lit and frequented by several passers-by.

Had he wanted to hurt her so much he was prepared

to go to jail? She doubted even his mother and her high-flying lawyer would be able to save Brad this time.

Maybe it would turn out to be a good thing, and he'd finally get the help he needed. But at what price?

Police procedure took a while, an emergency contractor arrived to board up the window, then Rebekah received clearance to clean up.

There was a sense of unreality, that the whole episode was merely a bad dream from which she'd awaken.

With methodical efficiency she began noting down ruined blooms, and made a list of what she'd need to re-order. Now it was a matter of physical work, clearing broken glass and floral debris.

'Where do you want me to start?' Jace asked as he discarded his jacket and began rolling up his shirt-sleeves.

She fetched a broom and handed it to him. 'You sweep, I'll dispose of the glass.'

They worked together, and it didn't take as long to clean up as she'd first thought. When it was done, she rang Ana and gave her sister a personal report, then she checked the locks and preceded Jace to the car.

'Thanks for your help,' she said quietly as she slid into the passenger seat.

'You imagine I'd have let you come down here and tackle this alone?'

His voice held a quality she didn't want to examine right now, and she retained silence for the short ride back to her apartment.

Inside, she moved straight through to the bedroom, stepped out of her stilettos, slipped off her clothes, and donned a silk robe.

Bed had never looked so good, and there was the temptation to slip between the sheets, snap off the light and drift into a dreamless sleep.

'I've made coffee.'

Rebekah turned at the sound of Jace's deep drawl, and tried for a faint smile, only to fail miserably.

He closed the distance between them and gathered her in against him. He'd expected reaction to set in, but hadn't bargained on it leaving her dark-eyed and white-faced.

'That bad, huh?' He felt a tremor rake her slim body and rested his cheek against the top of her head.

Just hold me, she begged silently. She needed to borrow some of his strength for a while. Even a few minutes would do while she replenished her own. Then she'd sip coffee, maybe put on a video in the hope of losing herself in a light, frivolous movie.

At that moment the phone rang, and she stiffened, wondering who could be calling at this hour. Then common sense prevailed as Jace released her.

'Want me to take that?' He didn't wait for her to answer as he crossed to pick up the bedroom extension.

His end of the conversation was incredibly brief, just a word here and there in confirmation, and she stood quietly as he replaced the handset.

There was a part of her that noticed the broad set of his shoulders, his stance, the way he exuded an animalistic sense of power. Inherent vitality meshed with blatant sensuality to compile a forceful image any sane person would prefer as friend rather than foe.

'Luc,' he revealed. 'Brad has been denied bail.'

The relief was palpable. This time he'd gone too far, and he hadn't been able to slip free of the legal net.

'It's over,' Jace assured quietly. 'Your statement and the evidence is sufficient to ensure he'll go to jail.'

'His mother—'

'Even her lawyer won't be able to swing anything. That's a given.'

'You can't be sure of that.'

'Yes,' he said with grim inflexibility. 'I can.' Brad Somerville would never have the chance to hurt her again. If he so much as tried, the law would come down on him so hard life as he knew it would never be the same again.

'Now,' Jace inclined as he pulled her close. 'Where were we?'

'I think we should go to bed.'

A husky chuckle sounded low in his throat. 'My thoughts, exactly.'

She shook her head. 'To sleep.'

'OK.' He swept an arm beneath her knees and carried her through to the bedroom, switching off lights as he went.

'I can walk,' Rebekah protested.

'Indulge me.'

Yet it was he who indulged her, and for a while she forgot the ugliness of the earlier hours, then he held her as she slept.

Saturday proved to be exceptionally hectic, and a few of the regular clientele called in to commiserate over the broken shop window, the break-in. Rebekah and Ana were circumspect in their explanation, even to Suzie, and it was business as usual as the orders were met, deliveries made.

It was late when Rebekah finished for the day, and she walked out of the shop into Jace's arms, laughing a little as he drew her close, bestowed a lingering kiss, then caught hold of her hand as he led her to the car.

Did he have something planned for his last night in Sydney?

She hoped so. She felt like dressing up, going somewhere special in order to hold the memory of the night forever in her mind.

He didn't disappoint. An hour later she sat sipping champagne in one of the finest restaurants the city had to offer.

The food was exceptional, the ambience fantastic, and the man seated opposite was the embodiment of everything she could ever hope for.

Yet there was a sad poignancy to the night. This was their last meal together, the last time they'd share the same bed.

Unless... No, she wouldn't even go there. Their lives, where they resided, they were too far apart for it to be possible to sustain a successful relationship.

Sure, they'd call each other. Email, fax, phone. For a while. Then the contact would dwindle down to practically nothing, and eventually cease.

But it had been great while it lasted. Better than great, she admitted. So much so, she wasn't sure she'd be able to exist without him.

They lingered, and returned late to her apartment.

The loving was the sweetest, the most sensual experience of her life. He made it so good, it was all she could do not to weep from the joy of it.

They slept for a while, then woke to pleasure each other again before hitting the shower.

'I'll make breakfast,' Rebekah declared, and he pressed a finger to her lips.

'We'll do it together.'

Bacon, eggs, hash browns, juice and strong black coffee. Except she could hardly eat a thing as she conducted a mental countdown to the time they'd need to leave for the airport.

They talked, although afterwards she couldn't recall a word she'd said, and she cleared the table, stacked the dishes, blindly forcing herself to focus on the mundane as he collected his wet-pack from the *en suite*.

She heard him re-enter the kitchen, followed by the soft sound of his overnight bag hitting the floor, then his hands curved over her shoulders as he turned her round to face him.

His hands slid up to cup her nape, then he covered her mouth with his own in a kiss that seared her soul.

When she lifted his head she could only look at him

in silence, too afraid to say the words bubbling up in her throat.

'Marry me.'

Rebekah's jaw dropped, and she struggled to find her voice. An impossibility with a host of random thoughts chasing each other inside her head.

'What did you say?' she managed at last.

'Marry me,' Jace reiterated quietly, and witnessed the gamut of her emotions. Shock, confusion, fear. He could accept the first two, but he wanted to wipe out the third.

'You can't be serious.'

'I am. Very serious.'

She was lost for words. There was one part of her that wanted to shout an unconditional 'yes'. Except sanity demanded a different answer.

He didn't give her the chance to utter it. 'You stole my heart when I partnered you at Luc and Ana's wedding. If I could have, I'd have swept you off to live with me in New York then. But it wasn't the right time…for you.'

'And you imagine it is now?' she queried sadly.

'I want to make it the right time. The question is…do you?'

'Jace—'

'I love you,' he vowed gently. 'The everlasting, "till death do us part" kind.' He made no attempt to touch her. He could, he knew, use unfair persuasion. But he wanted nothing she'd regret on reflection. 'I want to be in your life, and have you in mine.'

Was she brave enough to reach out with both hands

and accept what he offered? She wanted to, desperately.

The thought of never seeing him again was earth-shattering. Yet...*marriage*?

Rebekah met and held his gaze, aware of the strength, the perceptive quality apparent and the integrity. This man wasn't of Brad's ilk, and never would be.

Dared she take that step forward? She didn't think she could...at least, not right now. Maybe in a few months' time, when she'd become used to the idea.

'No conditions, Rebekah.'

He was adept at reading her mind, and to offer him anything less than total honesty wasn't an option.

'I can't do that.' She was breaking up inside. 'I love you.' She felt her mouth tremble, glimpsed sight of the sudden darkness in his eyes, and recognised the effort it cost him to retain control. 'The past week with you...' She faltered, unable to find the words. 'I couldn't bear to lose what we share.' She was dying, slowly, as surely as if the lifeblood was flowing from her body.

'*But?*'

Rebekah wasn't capable of saying a word.

A muscle tightened at the edge of his jaw. 'You must know I find ''no'' unacceptable.'

'Jace...' His name emerged from her lips as a husky entreaty.

He caught up his bag and slid the strap over one

shoulder. 'I have to collect my stuff from the hotel, check out, then get to the airport.'

'I'll take you.'

'No.' He leaned forward and kissed her, hard, briefly, then he straightened and walked to the door. He turned and cast her a long, steady look. 'If you want to make it "yes"…call me.' He opened the door, and closed it quietly behind him without so much as a backward glance.

Rebekah stood there in stunned silence, battling with herself to go running after him. Except she hesitated too long.

It seemed an age before she gathered sufficient energy to re-enter the lounge, and she curled up in a chair, buried her head in her arms and cried…for everything she'd just lost.

At least half a dozen times during the next hour she picked up the phone to call him, only to cut the connection before she'd keyed in the requisite digits.

Then it was too late, he'd already have boarded, and his cellphone would be switched off.

Millie jumped up into her lap, padded until she found a comfortable position, then settled and began to purr.

Rebekah abstractedly fondled the cat's ears, and didn't even try to stem the silent tears.

She had little idea of the passage of time. Eventually she stirred and began taking care of household chores, then, not content, she embarked on a thorough spring-clean of the apartment.

Food was something she couldn't face, and at seven she curled up in a chair and switched television channels until she found something that held her interest.

She must have slept, for she woke to the distant sound of the alarm ringing in the bedroom and she scrambled to her feet to go switch it off.

CHAPTER ELEVEN

ANOTHER day. Her first without Jace. Where was he now? On a stop-over at Los Angeles?

Oh, dear God, *what had she done*?

It was a first to display uninterest at the flower markets; at the shop she assembled blooms and bouquets automatically, devoid of her usual enthusiasm. At night she ate little, showered, then climbed into bed in the spare room after lying awake in her own for hours agonising that Jace wasn't there to share it with her.

Two, three days, four. Each one becoming more unbearable. She couldn't sleep, she didn't eat.

On the fifth day Ana took her by the shoulders, shook her a little, then demanded,

'OK, what gives?' She took a deep breath. 'And don't feed me any garbage about missing Jace. It's more than that.'

Sisterhood was a wonderful thing. Rebekah didn't know whether to laugh or cry. She did neither, and went straight to the truth.

'Jace asked me to marry him, and I said *no*,' she said starkly.

'You *what*?' Ana demanded in disbelief.

'I said no,' Rebekah reiterated, adding, 'For now.'

'Jace asked you to marry him, and you *refused*? Are you mad?'

'Wary. Scared,' she qualified wretchedly.

'Of loving him, and being loved in return?'

'All of that.' And more. 'His base is New York. It's a long way from home.'

'If you love him,' Ana began, then clicked her tongue in silent remonstrance. 'You *do* love him?'

Did she breathe? 'Yes.'

'Then what in hell are you doing here? Book the next flight out and go tell him.'

In her mind she was already winging her way there. 'The shop—'

'Suzie and I can manage.'

'Luc—'

'Leave Luc to me. Maybe we need to consider our options,' Ana suggested. 'Whether we want to sell, or have someone manage the place on our behalf.'

'But Blooms and Bouquets is—'

'Ours? It can still be ours, if that's what we both want. Just not run exclusively by us.'

'We've put so much into this place.'

'Maybe it's time to move on. I have a husband and soon there'll be a child. Both of whom are my life.' Ana drew in a deep breath, keyed in a few strokes, and brought up an internet site.

'What are you doing?'

'Booking you on a flight to New York.'

'I can't—'

'Yes, you can.' Her fingers flew over the keyboard, poised, then she added keystrokes, muttered to herself, added a keystroke or two more, then waited for confirmation. 'Done,' she said with satisfaction a short while later. 'You fly out tomorrow morning.' She named the airline, the flight number and departure time. 'Your electronic ticket will be despatched by courier within the hour.'

It was all going too fast, and she opened her mouth to say so, except Ana got in first.

'Don't,' she cautioned. 'For once in your life take hold of the day and go with it. What do you have to lose?'

What, indeed? she queried as she checked her bag, showed her passport, and moved through Customs into the departure lounge early next morning.

Her initial protest that Jace might be in another city…hell, another country, were dispensed with at once by Ana, who'd assured she'd already checked such details with Luc.

'Surprise him,' Ana had insisted. 'You have his office address, and that of his apartment. If by chance he's not at either place, you have his cellphone number. You can call him.'

So here she was, in a state of high anxiety, about to board a flight to the other side of the world.

Was she doing the right thing? Worse, would he still want her? They were questions she'd asked herself constantly during the past fifteen hours. Twice, she'd almost cancelled out.

The agony and the ecstasy, she accorded wryly as the plane soared into the air. Knowing that it was mostly of her own making didn't help at all.

If she'd listened to her heart instead of her head, she'd have shouted a joyous *yes* when Jace asked her to be his wife. Instead, she'd applied numerous reasons why she shouldn't be with him, rather than all the reasons she should.

Dammit, she was a fool.

Words that sprang to mind repeatedly during the long flight, the disembarkation process, and the cab ride to her hotel.

If you want to make it 'yes', call me. Except she hadn't called, nor had he called her.

What if he'd decided she was too much work, and had taken up with another woman?

If he could do that in so short a time, he wasn't worth having, she decided as she slid from the cab and followed the concierge's direction to Reception.

Her suite was on a high floor overlooking Central Park, but she barely glanced at the view before she unpacked a few essentials, then took a shower.

Ring him, a silent voice urged when she emerged dressed and feeling marginally refreshed.

It was crazy to be so nervous, she decided as she checked his cellphone number, then keyed in the digits.

Her hand shook a little as she waited for him to pick up.

'Dimitriades.'

Hell, he sounded different. Hard, inflexible.

Rebekah swallowed, then found her voice. 'Jace?'

There was a second's silence. 'Where are you?'

Oh lord. 'In a hotel.'

'*Where,* Rebekah?'

For a moment she couldn't think. 'It's opposite Central Park.' Memory kicked in, and she named it, then added her room number.

'Don't move. I'm on my way.'

He ended the call, and she replaced the handset, aware she had no idea where his office was situated in relation to the hotel. Or even if he was in his office.

It could take him up to an hour or longer to get here.

Time she could use to call her father, and catch up. On the other hand she could leave it until tomorrow to ring him. A call to Ana held more importance, and she checked the time difference, calculated it was the middle of the night in Sydney, then opted to send a text message instead.

As the minutes ticked by she was conscious of the onset of nervous tension. Her stomach felt as if it was tying itself in knots, and she couldn't keep her hands still for longer than a few seconds.

Rebekah examined the contents of the bar-fridge, checked out the cupboards and drawers, leafed through the complimentary magazines, and scanned the hotel directory folder, the breakfast menu.

Perhaps if she made herself a cup of coffee—

The doorbell rang, and she almost dropped the cup.

Then she was at the door, unfastening the lock with fingers that shook a little.

Jace seemed to fill the doorway, and her gaze became trapped in his. Held there by some mesmeric force.

For a moment neither of them moved, and everything faded from her peripheral vision. There was only the man, nothing else.

'Are you going to ask me in?'

His slightly accented drawl broke the spell, and she stood aside.

'Of course.'

He closed the door carefully behind him, then turned to face her, seeing her uncertainty, the nervousness, knew he could dispense with it, and would any time soon.

'Would you like coffee?' Rebekah asked in a strained voice.

Whisky would be more appropriate. Had she any idea what he'd gone through in the past week? The hour it had taken for him to get here?

'Coffee isn't a priority right now.'

Oh, to hell with it. She hadn't come all this way to play verbal games. If he was waiting for her to make the first move then, dammit, she would!

Without thought she reached out a hand, fisted it in his shirt and pulled him close. Then she drew his head down and sought his mouth. Her heart and soul went into the kiss, slaking a need that had been denied too long.

It took only seconds for his hands to settle over her shoulders, then ease down her back to cup her buttocks as he held her against him, and it was he who took control in a devastating oral supplication that tore the breath from her body.

Her lips were soft and slightly swollen when he

lifted his head, and he traced the lower curve with a gentle finger.

'What took you so long?'

'Stupidity,' Rebekah said with innate honesty, and Jace smiled as he pressed a light kiss to the tip of her nose.

She locked her arms around his waist and pressed her hips in against his, felt the power of his arousal, and exulted in his need.

'Are you going to say the words,' he drawled gently, 'or do I have to drag them out of you?'

'Yes. The answer's *yes*.'

His mouth found hers, and this time there was such an element of *tendresse*, her heart softened and began to melt.

'Good.' His hands shaped her body, lingered, then moved up to capture her face. 'When?'

'When...*what*?' she queried, definitely distracted by the way his lips were caressing her closed eyelids, a temple, before trailing down to the edge of her mouth.

'Will you make an honest man of me?'

His fingers were toying with the buttons on her blouse in seemingly slow motion. There was all the time in the world, and he was in no hurry.

'Early next year?' she posed, not really focusing on planning a wedding date right now.

'Uh-huh.' He tugged the blouse free from the waistband of her skirt, then gently pulled it free.

'The end of the week.' He began working the zip on her skirt. 'A traditional ceremony in Sydney.' The skirt slid down to the carpet. 'I initiated the requisite paperwork while I was there.'

'You're crazy,' Rebekah said huskily as he undid her bra fastening.

His mouth closed over hers fleetingly. 'Crazy in love with you.'

She was willing to swear her heart stopped for a few seconds before kicking into a faster beat. 'Thank you.'

Jace lifted his head. 'For what?'

'For having enough faith in what we share to walk away and let me realise for myself that what I feel for you is *love*.'

He brushed his lips to her cheek. 'I don't think you have any conception just how hard it was for me to do that.'

She thought of the long, lonely nights when she woke and realised he wasn't there. How she jumped at every ring of the phone. The meals she wasn't able to eat because of an aching heart. And the knowledge that life without Jace in it would be no life at all.

'Yes, I do.' She eased his jacket off, then began unbuttoning his shirt. 'You're wearing too many clothes.'

'Want some help?' he asked quizzically, and she shook her head.

'Believe me, the pleasure is all mine.'

And it was. She took it slow, savouring the removal of each item until he stood naked before her. Then she pushed him down onto the bed and straddled him, watching in delight as his eyes dilated and became heavy with passion.

Instinct ruled as she tasted him, and she savoured each moment the breath hissed between his teeth, the faint groan, the slight tremor as she embarked on a sensual feast where boundaries and inhibitions didn't exist.

Then it was Jace's turn, and he showed no mercy in his pursuit of gifting her the ultimate in primitive pleasure. It was she who cried out, she who reached for him and begged his possession.

When they came together it was with raw, primeval desire. Brazen, tumultuous. *Magic*.

The long aftermath held a dreamy quality, a gentle, tactile exploration with drifting finger-pads, soft kisses, and such an acute sensitivity it made her want to cry.

'Hungry?' Jace murmured as he nuzzled the soft hollow at the edge of her neck.

'For you, or food?'

She felt his mouth curve against her throat.

'When did you last eat, *agape mou*?

'On the plane.' How many hours ago? Eight, ten?

'I'll order Room Service.' He bestowed a brief hard kiss. 'Then we'll shower, and you get to grab some sleep.'

He chose a light meal, and he extracted a half-magnum of champagne from the bar-fridge, opened it and poured the contents into two flutes.

'To us.'

He touched the rim of his flute to hers, and her

bones melted at the wealth of passion evident in his dark gaze.

'I love you.' She wanted, needed to say the words, and Jace took hold of her hand and brought it to his lips.

'You're everything to me,' he vowed quietly. 'More than I ever dreamed it was possible to have.' He turned her hand over and buried his lips in her palm. 'My life.'

She wanted to cry, and the tears welled up and shimmered there, threatening to spill.

He lifted his head, saw them, and pressed his lips to each eyelid in turn. 'Don't.'

The long flight, the nervous excitement, the love-making had taken its toll, and she was helpless to stem the flow as they spilled over and trickled down each cheek in twin rivulets.

He smoothed them with his thumb, then fastened his mouth on hers in a gentle, evocative kiss.

Their meal was delivered a short while later, and they fed each other morsels of the light, fluffy mushroom omelette, the salad, and Rebekah alternated the champagne with bottled water.

She was almost asleep on the chair, and it was all she could do to remain awake as they showered together, then, dry, she let Jace carry her to bed, where she curled up against him and was asleep within seconds of her head touching the pillow.

It was a while before Jace gently freed himself from her embrace and slid from the bed. He extracted his cellphone and made a series of calls. Then he rejoined her in bed and gathered her close.

There was, Rebekah accepted, nothing quite like the power and prestige of serious money.

Jace used it mercilessly to ensure everything went according to plan, and she experienced a sense of stunned disbelief as he organised return flights to Sydney the next day for them both, accepted Luc and Ana's offer to have the wedding at their home, gave them carte blanche to have Petros arrange caterers and liaised with the guest list.

The phone calls were lengthy and many, with Ana relaying she'd seen a wedding gown to die for, and everything down to the finest detail would be successfully organised in time for *the* day.

The fact that it was seemed nothing short of a miracle.

Even the weather was perfect, with brilliant blue skies, sunshine, and the merest hint of a breeze to temper the day's warmth.

'Ready?'

The gown, as Ana had promised, was something else.

Ivory silk with an ivory lace overlay that had a scalloped hemline resting just below the knee. Elbow-length sleeves in ivory lace, and a high neckline. The headpiece was a pearl band with a short fingertip veil bunched at the back of her head, and she carried a single long-stemmed white rose. Her only jewellery was a diamond pendant and matching earrings.

'Yes.' Rebekah turned to her sister and gathered her close in an affectionate hug. 'Thanks for everything.'

'You're welcome,' Ana responded gently. 'OK, let's get this show on the road.'

Luc was waiting downstairs to lead her out into the grounds, where the guests were assembled on chairs either side of a red carpet facing a delicate wrought-iron gazebo.

'Beautiful,' Luc complimented quietly as he took her arm. His gaze slid to his wife, and the warmth of his smile brought a lump to Rebekah's throat.

Together they walked out onto the terrace, traversed the short flight of steps, and made their way towards the gazebo. The guests stood and those lining the red carpet threw rose petals in Rebekah's path.

She saw Jace standing at the assembled altar, and she caught his gaze and held it as she made her way towards him.

A light, husky laugh escaped her lips as he drew her close and kissed her, thoroughly.

The celebrant cleared his throat, and they broke apart.

It was a simple ceremony, the words deeply moving, and Rebekah fought back the faint shimmer of tears as Jace slid a wide diamond-encrusted ring onto her finger.

There was the flash of cameras, voiced congratulations, and a shower of rose petals as they trod the red carpet as man and wife.

Champagne and food were served in a marquee

erected close by, guests greeted and thanked, then all too soon it was time to change and leave for the airport.

Ana helped her remove the headpiece and veil, then assisted with the zip fastening of the gown.

Rebekah freshened up, then slipped into an elegant trouser suit, added comfortable heeled shoes, then turned towards her sister.

'I'm going to miss you dreadfully.'

'We'll email each other every day, and talk on the phone. Jace has promised me you'll both visit at least twice a year.'

Rebekah's expression sobered a little. 'A month ago—'

'Don't look back,' Ana cautioned gently. 'You have today, and all the tomorrows.' She brushed her lips to Rebekah's cheek. 'Embrace them and be happy.'

'How did you get to be so wise?' Rebekah asked shakily.

'If you cry, I'll hit you.'

'Sisterly love,' Luc drawled from the doorway, whilst Jace offered,

'Shall we divide and conquer?'

'I think so,' Luc said with musing indolence as he crossed to his wife's side and drew her close.

Jace extended his hand, and Rebekah's toes curled at the way he looked at her. 'Ready, *agape mou*?'

'Yes.' And she was. Ready to go anywhere he chose to lead.

Together they made their way downstairs, and as they reached the car Rebekah turned to her sister.

'OK, this is it. The last goodbye.' She gave Ana a quick hug. 'I'll ring you from Paris.' Then it was Luc's turn. 'Look after her,' she said fiercely.

'Every minute of every day,' he promised solemnly.

'Go,' Ana pleaded, on the verge of tears.

Two sisters, two destinies, Rebekah mused as Jace took the main road leading towards the airport.

'We'll visit soon. And you have my word we'll return for the birth of Ana's child.'

Rebekah felt something begin to soar deep within, and she turned to look at him. 'Have I told you how much I love you?'

She had, several times through the night. They were words he'd never tire of hearing. Words he'd say to her, over and again for the rest of his life.

'If you do, I'll pull the car to the side of the road and kiss you.'

Her eyes assumed a wicked sparkle. 'An act that would probably cause a public spectacle.'

'Count on it.'

'Then I guess we need to wait for a more appropriate moment?' She began counting off each finger. 'Let's see, there's the long flight, with a brief stop-over in Los Angeles. Thirty-six hours in total before we reach Paris.'

'Forty-eight,' Jace corrected with a musing smile. 'We have a not-so-brief stop-over in Los Angeles.'

Rebekah gave a laugh that was part delight, all mischief. 'Can't keep your hands off me, huh?'

He shot her a gleaming glance. 'Want me to try?'

Her expression sobered. 'No,' she assured quietly. 'Not in this lifetime.'

He waited until he passed the hire car in at the airport before he gathered her close and kissed her, thoroughly. So thoroughly she temporarily lost any sense of time or place.

Then he unloaded their bags from the boot, hefted the strap of one bag over his shoulder and gathered up the other, and caught her hand in his.

Together, as they would always be, for the rest of their lives.

MILLS & BOON®

Helen Bianchin v Regency Collection!

MILLS & BOON®

Let us take you back in time with our Medieval Brides...

The Novice Bride – Carol Townend

The Dumont Bride – Terri Brisbin

The Lord's Forced Bride – Anne Herries

The Warrior's Princess Bride – Meriel Fuller

The Overlord's Bride – Margaret Moore

Templar Knight, Forbidden Bride – Lynna Bannin

MILLS & BOON®
The Sheikhs Collection!

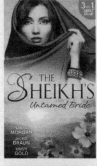

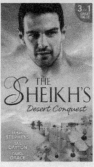

6_MB518